THE MARK OF CAIN

www.totallyrandombooks.co.uk

Also by Lindsey Barraclough:

LONG
LANKIN

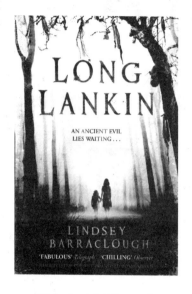

'Fabulous' *Telegraph*

'Chilling' *Observer*

'I struggled to put it down . . . I hope
everyone discovers Lindsey Barraclough'
TES

THE MARK OF CAIN

LINDSEY BARRACLOUGH

THE BODLEY HEAD

THE MARK OF CAIN
A BODLEY HEAD BOOK 978 1 782 30019 9

First published in Great Britain by The Bodley Head,
an imprint of Random House Children's Publishers UK
A Random House Group Company

This edition published 2014

1 3 5 7 9 10 8 6 4 2

The Random House Group Limited supports the Forest Stewardship
Council® (FSC®), the leading international forest certification organization.
All our titles that are printed on Greenpeace-approved FSC®-certified
paper carry the FSC® logo. Our paper procurement policy can be
found at www.randomhouse.co.uk/environment.

Set in 11/17 pt Palatino by Falcon Oast Graphic Art Ltd.

Bodley Head Books are published by Random House Children's Publishers UK,
61–63 Uxbridge Road, London W5 5SA

www.randomhousechildrens.co.uk
www.randomhouse.co.uk
www.totallyrandombooks.co.uk

Addresses for companies within The Random House Group Limited
can be found at: www.randomhouse.co.uk/offices.htm

THE RANDOM HOUSE GROUP Limited Reg. No. 954009

A CIP catalogue record for this book is available from the British Library.

Printed in Great Britain by Clays Ltd, St Ives plc

For my parents, Ron and Gre,
and my sister, Jill

Maiden in the Mor Lay –
Maiden in the Mor Lay,
in the mor lay –
Seuenyst fulle,
seuenyst fulle.
Maiden in the mor lay,
in the mor lay –
seuenystes fulle ant a day.

Welle was hire mete.
Wat was hire mete?
The primerole ant the –
the primerole ant the –
Welle was hire mete.
Wat was hire mete?
The primerole ant the violet.

Welle was hire drying.
Wat was hire drying?
The chelde water of the –
the chelde water of the –
Welle was hire drying.
Wat was hire drying?
The chelde water of the
welle-spring.

Welle was hire bowr.
What was hire bowr?
The rede rose and the –
The rede rose and the –
Welle was hire bowr.
What was hire bowr?
The rede rose and the lilye
flour.

Middle English lyric

Maiden in the Moor lay –
Maiden in the moor lay,
in the moor lay –
Seven nights full,
seven nights full.
Maiden in the moor lay,
in the moor lay –
seven nights full and a day.

Good was her food.
What was her food?
The primrose and the –
the primrose and the –
Good was her food.
What was her food?
The primrose and the violet.

Good was her drink.
What was her drink?
The chilled water of the –
the chilled water of the –
Good was her drink.
What was her drink?
The chilled water of the
well spring.

Good was her bower.
What was her bower?
The red rose and the –
The red rose and the –
Good was her bower.
What was her bower?
The red rose and the lily
flower.

We hurry through the wood along the narrow dirt path that runs by the edge of the brook. Zillah's swollen-knuckled old fingers grip my small hand as I stumble alongside her.

'Keep up, child. We have to make haste,' she urges. 'It is not good for us to be so close to the watermen. We must take care not to be seen.'

The wood begins to thin, and the stream, no longer confined by the narrow channel running between the alder roots, broadens out before winding its eager way through the water meadows and down to the river.

Zillah stops, raises herself as straight as her humped back will allow, shades her eyes and looks every way about her, from the dark line of the woods behind to the tree-clumped horizon ahead.

A harsh cra-ak, cra-ak. *Zillah's hand tightens for a moment as a few rooks rise out of the grass and fly off up to the clouds. She gently pulls me towards the sloping bank.*

'This is the best place,' she says, 'for it was here that we found you, Aphra, just here, a little babe wailing by the waterside. Scrape up some mud, the softest you can find.'

I hoist up my skirts, and with feet sinking into the moist dirt of the bank, find a patch between the buttery primroses and the bright spears of new reeds. A startled water hen, red beak bobbing, waddles off on huge starry feet then drops into the river and paddles away.

I bend down, push my fingers into the wet clay and scoop two handfuls into the earthen bowl Zillah holds out for me, while her eyes dart about this way and that.

All at once she seizes my arm and whispers urgently, 'Quickly, child, back into the trees – a waterman is coming!'

Zillah pulls me so hard I flounder up the muddy bank, and totter along behind her as she dashes across the clumps of reedy grass towards the woods. From the dark shelter of the trees, while Zillah stands gasping and kneading her wheezy chest with her knuckles, I look down towards the water. A wherry passes by the bank where I dug out the mud. The old waterman, his weather-browned head bent almost to his chest, rows two men upriver a little before ferrying them across to the southern side.

'Is that where my mother came from?' I ask. 'Did she bring me here over the water?'

Zillah is ready to move on. 'We've told you often enough, child, she was long away when we found you, who knows where. Now come, you must find a small red stone.'

I search among the roots, lift scattered leaves.

'That is too big . . . that too heavy . . . too grey.' Zillah tosses them aside.

Then, under the shaggy roof of a toadstool, a gleam of jewel red catches my eye. I stoop down. Nestled close to the stalk is a little gleaming garnet of a pebble. I hold it up to my eye and try to peep at Zillah through the tiny hole in its middle.

'Ah – you have found a bloodstone,' she says proudly, then

bends in close to whisper in my ear. 'Above us in the skies, the celestial spirits are forever in combat with the unquiet dead, and the blood drops of the fallen come down to earth as little stones like this. Keep it safe.'

Back in the house in the woods, Zillah and I sit together at the scrubbed table, heads together over the lump of mud. As she instructs me, I wet my fingers from the pitcher, take the clay and shape a manikin, a small doll I can fit into the palm of my hand.

'Rufus Goode – think Rufus Goode,' Zillah breathes as the light begins to fade behind the shutter. 'See his face, Aphra, as you work him. Remember the filthy words he uttered.'

Rufus Goode, this is your head, squashed into your shoulders, these tubes of clay are your arms and legs. I push them close in to your body, smear them with water and lavender oil from the flask.

'Now open his chest, and put in the little bloodstone for his heart, Aphra,' says Zillah. 'And this one hair from his own beard. It is all you need. Work it into the clay. Now close him up.'

Rufus Goode, here is your face: I am making it with a sharp stick, carving out your big watery eyes, your swollen nose, your thin-lipped foul-speaking mouth drooping to the left.

Zillah shows me how to make a little shirt for him, from the sweat-soiled neckerchief which came loose from Goode's throat when I snatched at it to throttle him as he pushed me down into the mud. It was on this dirty rag that we found the hair.

3

'There is now a spirit thread between you, Aphra,' says Zillah. 'You and Rufus Goode. Let him dry slowly. Not near to the fire or he will crack. You can do as you wish with him. Remember what that wicked man did. What does he deserve? Give curse for curse, Aphra.'

The door opens and Damaris ducks under the lintel, a basket under her arm, the limp claw of a dead chicken poking out from under the cloth.

'My, that is a good poppet, Aphra,' she says, drawing in to look, the thick yellow hair escaping from her kerchief and brushing my shoulders. 'What will you do to him?' She glances at Zillah before moving away to pluck the bird.

In the evening I go up to watch the manikin drying where I have laid him, on the small chair beside my pallet under the eaves of the house in the woods.

Whispers creep up the ladder from the room below.

'You should not have shown the child how to make a poppet, Zillah.'

'That Rufus Goode is a filthy man, Damaris. He caught Aphra near the black pool. If I had not heard her screams . . .' She waits for a moment, then says, 'He cursed the girl as we came away. You know as well as I, she must be the one to deal with that. We can only show her what she must do . . .'

Damaris lowers her voice still more. I hold my breath to catch the words: 'You know, there is something about the girl, Zillah. The spirits come to her.' Damaris pauses. 'I – I have heard the child whispering in the voice of another.'

I do not hear what Zillah says in answer, she speaks so softly.

'Aphra has gifts beyond even our own, Zillah,' Damaris continues. 'Maybe her mother saw it in her – was afeared of her – and cast off her own infant in the river; if she ever had a mortal mother, that is, and was not just pushed up through the foul, black mud eight years ago for us to find. She should not learn those cursed arts, Zillah.'

'But she found a bloodstone . . .'

'Anyone can find a bloodstone.'

'She was meant to come to us. We are the three-headed goddess, Damaris. I am the past, you are the present and the child is the future . . .'

Damaris says nothing.

'I have bound you to me, Rufus Goode,' I whisper, running a dirty fingernail across his face. 'I think I will rip out your heart.'

BELTANE EVE – 30th APRIL 1567

I am in such an excitement I can barely wait for evening.

'Can we go yet?' I ask Zillah as the sun is still passing across the open sky above the clearing. She gives me pots to clean in the stream.

'Is it the time?' I ask Damaris as the sun dips behind the high leaves of the oak leaning over the cottage. She gives me twigs to twist out the cobwebs in the corners.

At last the hour comes.

As the shadows lengthen on the grass, I dance ahead of Zillah and Damaris into the woods, to collect green branches for the Bringing In of the Summer.

'Can I do it? Can I ask the hawthorn mother?'

'No—' Damaris begins, but Zillah raises her hand to quieten her, and nods to me. Gleefully, I stretch my arms around the ancient trunk in the middle of the grove, rest my cheek against the gnarled bark and whisper close, 'Let us take your wood, hawthorn mother, to fill our house this Sabbat night . . .'

A gust of wind creaks the tree, moves the branches, rustles the new leaves.

I smile at Zillah, then begin to twist one of the thorny boughs to break it. But the branch will not be snapped. It snatches itself back, whipping its barbs across my cheek, leaving rows of thin, bloody lines. In stinging tears, I run to Zillah's arms. She glances at Damaris, then, without a word, moves me to the edge of the thicket. While I wipe my face on my apron, the two women quietly gather the green branches, then we return to the house together, all subdued through the twilight trees, to hang them from the beams.

Afterwards, when the great glittering beasts, the Lion and the Bear, begin their nightly prowl across the sky, we carry bundles of dry sticks into the clearing in front of the cottage and throw them carefully together on the earth to make our Balefire. Zillah takes a brand from our hearth and sets the faggots all alight. For a short while the three of us forget what happened in the hawthorn grove, lift our skirts and laugh and jig in and out of the fire, swift, and not too close to its leaping heart.

But into my head comes the little manikin under the eaves, almost dry, wrapped in his neckerchief shirt. I look up at the gable shutter and picture him there on my cane-bottomed chair.

'Aphra! Aphra!'

Damaris is shrieking.

I turn, look down at a huge spear of flame flaring up my skirts, flap at it with my hands. A razor-sharp stinging spreads over my leg. I suck in breath and smell roasting meat. Zillah pushes me to the ground, presses me down.

'Honey! Milk!' she screeches to Damaris.

With shuddering breath Zillah heaves me up in her frail arms and lurches towards the cottage. My head is pounding. I cannot be quiet. Birds clatter up out of the trees at my screaming as we stumble by.

In the cottage Zillah lays me down on the table, clamps a hand over my mouth, bends close to my ear.

'Hush that noise!' she urges. 'Use the pain! Send it into the poppet up above. Use it for your hate. Use it! Do not cry out! Never cry out!'

While I whine between clenched teeth, tossing my head from side to side, Zillah busies herself with the muslin wrappings drenched in honey and the cooling milk-soaked cloths. Damaris, to the side, tears up plantain leaves, weeping, whispering through her tears. 'It was the hawthorn mother that did this. Aphra did not please her. She should not have tried to break the boughs.'

'Nonsense,' says Zillah. 'It was no more than a mishap. Give me the leaves. They should ease her pain.'

I try to do as Zillah says: send the pain into the little manikin drying on the chair up in the eaves.

ST HELEN'S DAY, 2nd MAY 1567

I can make a fist, hold it in front of my eye and blot out the new moon. That is the size of the burned flesh on my thigh. It is so sore it keeps me from sleeping. Zillah says the skin will never be smooth as it was before, but I should be glad that remedies were close at hand and that she and Damaris are healers. She says others have died from lesser wounds than mine.

She gently lifts the covering and I make myself look at the oozing, broken blisters. I remember the jagged, sizzling flame and the pain, and begin to tingle with sweat.

'Hush your grizzling,' Zillah says, bringing clean muslin and more soothing honey. 'I told you before, do not waste your power crying out.'

Damaris comes with the news that Rufus Goode's heart has burst in his chest, and the sexton of St Michael and all the Angels is even now digging his grave. I knew the moment it happened because I felt the spirit thread snap, but I did not tell my mothers. Damaris studies me with an anxious glance. I thought Zillah would be happy with me, but even she is uneasy; she had not expected a death, merely a sickness.

Here I am, a child, and Rufus Goode has died.

I will keep the little bloodstone close to me always, so I will never forget what I can do.

Two years later
ST JOHN'S EVE – 23rd JUNE 1569

Sick, needy, miserable people come to the house in the woods
– mostly women – mostly in the dark.

Many times I sit on my pallet above, curled hands around
knees, and watch through the hole between the laths the
darting spark of a small lantern approaching through the night
trees.

I steal quietly from my bed and peep through a large crack
between the boards that allows me to see almost everything that
goes on in the room below. I watch and listen and learn
secret things that Zillah and Damaris would not wish me to know
at so tender an age. But at ten years I have already learned how
artful they must be when laying charms; how all must be done
in the proper order, all the words correct in accordance; that
sometimes there is no remedy for a fault, an incompleteness
in the charm, for then the spell can turn against the person who
is casting it. Even cunning folk have died that way.

This is how it goes: a soft, nervous knocking at the door,
murmuring, a fearful woman, low-voiced, trembling, grabbing
at Zillah's hand, whispering close in Damaris's ear. After a
while the chanting begins, the swirling of water, the fragrance
of wild plants crushed with a stone, mixing in a jug, the silver
bowl, blood-letting, binding.

The house fills with spirits – the spirits that Zillah and
Damaris call up to do their will.

I know them all: Tilly Murrell, the witch-child of Hunger-hill, Little Clim, Dorcas Oates, Matty the Boy. They do my mothers' bidding, then float up to my place in the loft. I can just see their glassy forms on the edge of my eye as they sit on my shoulders, play with my hair, laugh in my ears in their airy way, and flit in and out of the rafters above me like darting swifts.

Sometimes the spirits try to climb inside my head and peer out of my eyes. Now and then I allow them, suffer them to speak out of my mouth for their play, but only when I wish it.

Matty the Boy laughs in his little high voice, and with my hands I let him beat on a horn cup with a tin spoon until Damaris calls up for me to stop the noise.

Dorcas Oates was drowned by her own people in the sea, and I cannot abide for long the feel of the close, cold water and the briny smell of samphire and bladderweed.

Little Clim shivers. His mother thought he was a changeling and left him out in the woods alone for the fairies to take back and return to her the child they stole away, but they never came. He tastes of earth and leaf mould.

Tilly Murrell I do not let in at all, for she is a sly, deceitful little spirit, and I might not get her out again.

I have no fear of them. Indeed, I know little fear at all.

Yet it is fear, though not mine, that saves me from the flames, this first time at least.

ST JOHN'S DAY – 24th JUNE 1569

It is early evening, just at twilight. I am still below, laying down the fresh rushes on the floor, breathing in the scent of the water meadows from where Zillah has gathered them earlier in the day, when a timid knock rattles the latch. Damaris opens the door and a plain young woman, without beauty, grace, or a lantern, steps over the threshold, looking furtively behind her.

I must be studying the woman far too curiously, for Zillah, who is at the table binding herbs into bundles, glances at me.

'Up the ladder, Aphra,' she says and I obey, but no sooner have I reached my little space under the eaves than I lower myself down to my knees and put my eye to the crack in the boards.

The young woman weeps and weeps. A few meagre coins spill onto the table. The charming begins; the air grows close and heavy with spells. I feel the spirits rise, chattering, buzzing up the ladder to draw close to me. Little Clim and Matty the Boy want to play, but tonight I shoo them quickly off. They dart away, one through the shutter and the other into the spaces in the thatch above.

I climb onto my pallet, listening to the murmuring voices below, and watch the evening draw in until the sky deepens to mid-blue, then indigo. The planet Venus hovers low over the treetops.

The young woman is ailing. There is something inside her withering away and she is brimful with poison. Although tonight she has made her way to us through the woods, in seven days she will be able to walk no longer, and in three days beyond the seven, she will be dead. I know this because I can see the dying lights are already lifting off her skin; those tiny inside parts of the body that float away into the air, shimmering little points, as life begins to draw to its close.

When the dying lights are gathering, so the flesh becomes more and more like thin gauze and I can pass through it even more easily. Zillah and Damaris do not know this, and they do not know I can see the lights.

I leave my pallet and lie close to the boards to watch the woman. I breathe in deeply, then swim lightly downwards through the air and into her skin. My own body waits behind, the eye still to the floor.

I am sitting in the rush chair.

A fierce pain surges up from my stomach through my limbs into my fingers and toes, which curl rigid like claws. Zillah's hands are on my head, warm and comforting, but unable to ease the pain. Damaris rubs my arms with a paste of comfrey and rue. I drop my head so they will not see my eyes, which look out of hers, but I can bear the suffering no more than a few seconds, and am glad to return to my little space under the eaves.

Zillah calls up the ladder. 'Aphra! Aphra! Up, child! Take this woman back to the wood's edge. She has no lantern and is fearful she will be lost.'

I know my way through the woods in the darkness, but take a lantern to light the narrow way for the young woman's sake; wringing her hands and muttering to herself, she stumbles on the tree roots and gasps each time a low branch snatches her hair, thinking some demon has caught her. Having felt the pain she endures, I am surprised she can walk so far. She stops, whimpering at each owl's hoot, every brushing of the undergrowth by stoat or badger. At last I am glad to leave her under the silver birches near the earth track that leads to Beesden Parva, where she dwells, though not for much longer.

A low mist curls over the heath, but the moon is rising bright enough to light her way home.

I turn back, and immediately stop in bewilderment, gripping one of the white birch trunks to steady myself. A red glow is swelling up over the treetops, a glow spangled with showers of sparks and flaming wisps of thatch that curl and drift before twisting into flickering trails of smoke. Threading my way swiftly in and out of the trees, I hear the clamour of voices and the roar and crackle of fire, feel its heat, smell the smoke and the sweet and bitter odours of burning.

I blow out the lantern and steal up quickly, silently, along the narrow hidden path.

Peering through the tree trunks, my face and arms hot and burnished in the reflected light, I watch a handful of men whooping with glee, kicking up their legs and dancing around the house in the woods. Huge, vivid, snarling flames are eating up the blazing cottage. Tongues of fire lick the

blackening timbers, feast greedily on our stores of apples,
flitches of bacon, herbs, potions and unguents. I can hear our
vessels – our flasks, bottles and bowls – cracking, exploding
in the furnace while the house whistles, whines and groans.

Even the trees behind the cottage have taken fire, their
leaves darkening and crumpling.

Two large men cross in front of my hiding place, the backs
of their necks sweat-shiny, flecked with black flakes. I move
back slightly into the shadows.

'Are you certain the cunning women were inside?' says
the first.

'We heard them in there. We barred the door,' answers
the other.

'Did you be sure to watch the chimney? They didn't fly out
of it on their brooms?'

'We looked most careful, and we heard them screaming.
Can you not smell them? Like swine flesh.'

'What of the maid?'

'Don't know, John. We hoped she might be in there also.
We'll know when the fire dies down.'

'She's only a child.'

'Makes no difference.'

I slip away. I do not believe Zillah and Damaris are burned
in the house. They would not have screamed like the man said
they did. Zillah would have bade Damaris be quiet as she bade
me when I was burned in the Balefire.

For days afterwards I wander the woods, calling for my

mothers, seeking them in our familiar places. I sleep under bushes, wrapped close in my apron, eating mushrooms, roots, herbs, digging up chestnuts and beech nuts from the little winter stores the squirrels have forgotten, each morning hurrying back along the secret trails, the serpent's path and old Brock's track, to the house in the woods. Every day I expect to find it still, its whitewashed walls bowed under the low, curving thatch, woodsmoke trailing out of the chimney into the crown of the oak above. And every day I shudder at the sight of the heap of hot, burned timbers under a layer of whitening ash.

The men come, waiting for the embers to cool, but in the first days, the heat drives them away. Each day they return, and I am there hidden, watching as they poke among the smouldering ruins with long branches, turning over the scorched wood, searching, I know, for the remains of Zillah and Damaris. But so long as they do not find them, I seek them still, calling, waiting and calling.

One morning, weary and aching through sleeping yet one more night in a damp hollow, I smell burning pitch, wood and smoke and stumble back to the clearing. Even hidden in the trees, I feel the heat on my cheeks as another fire leaps and dances in the ruins of the burned cottage, consuming once more, and for ever, the uncovered, blackened corpses of my two mothers.

'That's it, then, John. Gone for good now,' says one of the men, who had been there on that other night. 'No trouble from *them two no more. Well burned twice – or they'll come back.'*

'That's right, you got to make sure,' says another. 'He's crafty, that devil, Old Nick. Knows all kinds of ways to bring them back to do his wickedness. Man over Medford way said a hanged witch came back in his wife's body. Made no end of mischief. They hanged her again and that was an end of it.'

Another man approaches with a long branch to poke the flames.

'I heard of that one,' he says. 'Didn't pin her down proper the first time they buried her. Rushed it 'cause it got dark. It's like with these two here. We'll have to keep going over this lot. Only takes a bit of skelton left unburned – then them Bonesmen can call up the spirit on their bone flutes.'

'Or grind 'em down for magic potions.'

'Devil take 'em, them Bonesmen. I'd like to see them strung up, I would, digging up the dead.'

'Didn't find no child here, though, John.'

'No matter. She'll die soon enough without no vittles, and even if she lasts until the winter, no Christian soul will take that one in.'

But I am not afeared of ice nor snow. I am a creature of the cold. I was found by lantern light, on the eve of Candlemas Day in the heart of the winter, and had not perished in that bitter place by the edge of the water. The frost suits my flesh. The season that brings death to others enlivens me, and I breathe in the north wind as the breath of life.

When the evening draws in and the men depart, I creep out

and stand as close as I dare. While the hot smoke curls around me, I cannot stop tears, spitting as they fall one by one onto the seared black earth around my feet.

Somewhere in that heap of burning wood and bone is my bloodstone.

Then I turn my back on the remnants of all I have known, keep my eyes and ears open, and learn how to stay alive.

Even as the summer passes and the days begin to shorten, the earth feeds me.

A turnip field, nuts, berries and roots, a stream rippling with trout, a skylark baked over a fire in its own little clay oven, split the clay open and the feathers come away. Rabbits last a week, hares even longer if you can catch them, and the fur makes warm mittens. Hedgehogs are slow-moving and cook up tender. Wrap a hedgehog in clay like the skylark, and the prickles are no trouble. Zillah showed me how to trap, Damaris to bake.

Wait for the goodwife to leave her cottage, then lift a shawl, a blanket, a piece of bread, some slippers, move on quickly. Move on. Stay in the shadows, be a shadow, round the edges, in the woods, under the thick trees when it rains, in the sheds and barns when the wind blows and the snow comes. Move on quick. Eat when you can, take when you can, sleep when you can.

I learned my craft, listening and watching.

I sought out the Bonesman, Micah, and his apprentice, Absalom, on the old pedlars' ways, but they found me first, on *the hollow path beneath the arching trees at High Missingham on the northern washes. They gave me a draught of bone ash and ale. Micah played his flute and I saw visions of the other-world. Human bones make strong magic. It is said the Bonesmen can resurrect the dead and make them dance on their own graves.*

Desperate women know where to find me; tell each other in whispers behind trembling fingers when I am about – a cake for a charm, a coin for a spell. They search for me, wait for me in the groves of ash, never rowan, elder or holly, for to be near to the wood of those hallowed trees is a torment to me – the merest brush of their bark and my skin erupts into sores.

It gives me more pleasure to settle a debt or a quarrel by taking revenge, blowing an ill wind, raising boils, rashes and consumptions, or worse, than ever it does to cure or bless. I know how to heal, but it is the dark and dirty work I am paid for, and relish.

Move on quick, behind the hedges, off the byways, through weeks, then months, then years.

Six years later

ST BARTHOLOMEW'S DAY – 24th AUGUST 1575

On a yellow-hot day, they catch me for a vagrant over Hunsham way. In an unguarded moment, drinking from a stream in the evening sunshine, I am set upon by gleaners, returning home with the spoils of their day in the fields. They take hold of me roughly, keep me close in a barn, and at daylight stand me up before the Justice.

His Lordship looks down at me. I avoid his stare, and remain steady on my worn, stolen slippers.

'We have no name for you. What is your family? Which is your parish?'

I do not wish to speak with him, and close my eyes to shut him out.

'We will keep you confined until you tell us your name.'

I cannot bear to be locked in.

'Aphra. I am Aphra.'

'And your family?'

'None.'

'Your age?'

I am not certain.

'Your age?'

'Sixteen years, I believe, give or take.'

'Your parish?'

'My parish is the reeds and the rushes.'

'Aphra of the rushes, then – the law is plain,' says the

Justice. 'You must be marked for your vagrancy, so others will not seek to follow your example.'

He turns away quickly to address the two burly men holding my arms. 'Do what has to be done.'

They drag me outside, and take me down through the village towards the smithy. A crowd is gathering. Some cross themselves as I pass by. A young woman spits at me, and many of the others began chewing their cheeks to make spittle to do the same, but as my gaze falls on each of them in turn, they swallow it down and look away.

The larger of the two men, Slater, pushes me down in the dirt beside a broad tree stump, its flat top smeared with old dried blood. The other, Deeks, catches tight hold of my hands. I struggle, but the man is stronger than he looks.

'You ready, Jaggers?' shouts Slater. He grabs my hair and winds it round his thick fingers, takes my head tight in his two chapped hands, and forces it down onto the top of the stump and holds it there. Splinters graze my cheek. Slater smells of ale and bad meat.

'Hurry, Jaggers! She's a squirmer, this one.'

Through my squashed eyes, I see a large man come out of the smithy. He wears a grimy leather apron. Huge veined muscles strain against the sleeves of his smock. In one hand he holds a foot-long iron rod, pointed sharp at one end, and in the other swings a heavy metal mallet.

I know him. I have come across him before, over Shersted way. He will not touch me.

21

'Which ear?' Slater calls.

'Don't matter which one,' shouts Jaggers. 'Stretch it out so there's enough skin to get me spike in. Hurry up! I've got a job waiting.'

I let Slater fumble for my left ear. He pinches it tight and pulls the lobe flat against the top of the stump, pushing my face in the other direction.

I feel Jaggers's bulk close to me, smell burned wood, iron, sweat, feel the point of the spike on my skin, his face leaning in.

I force my head sideways, open my eyes and look into his.

'You!' He reels back slightly, his ruddy skin draining of colour, shiny beads appearing on his forehead.

'What you doing? Get on with it, man!' Slater shouts.

'I'm not doing it,' says Jaggers.

'It's the law, man,' says Deeks. 'She's a vagrant.'

'Do it yourself,' says Jaggers, turning back to the smithy.

'Give us your spike, then!' Slater shouts after him.

'You're not doing it with my tools!' Jaggers calls back, still walking away.

'Anyone got a spike?'

Slater and Deeks loose their hold. I stagger to my feet, wipe the spit off my face, rub my tender ear and, once again, sweep my gaze slowly across the crowd.

A child begins to cry. The people study me curiously at first, then lower their eyes as mine meet theirs. One by one, they begin to move away, a few glancing back at me as they go.

Deeks looks me up and down. Then he lifts his foot and lands a mighty kick on my calf. The shock throws me off balance for a moment, but my eyes stay on his face.

'Get off!' he snarls. 'Go away! But if you so much as come this way again . . .'

I draw back my lips and smile, brush the dirt off my skirts and turn my back.

For a while I stand at the entrance to the smithy and stare at Jaggers as he hammers the red-hot strip of metal on his anvil, then picks it up with his tongs and plunges it into the fire.

'I know you're there. Leave me be,' he calls.

'How's your sister over in Shersted?' say I.

'Go your ways,' he says, without looking up. 'You know she's like to die.'

'Is dead already, I believe. Maybe they han't told you yet.'

'Go your ways.'

Six years later
THE BLIND DAYS OF MARCH 1581

Sometimes the weaknesses of the world catch up with me. It has rained for twenty days and my garments are sodden. The damp sits miserably in the plaid shawl I lifted from the charcoal burner's wife in the woods beyond Boxton Green. My worn slippers let in the muddy water.

I think of Zillah and Damaris, of the warmth of our little house, and find my way back to our old woods, thinking I will be met and welcomed there by my old life, that the dream I carry with me of the past will become real merely because I wish it so.

But there is nothing to be seen in our clearing. Not a clump of grass nor the smallest sapling has taken root in this dark, wet, barren earth, all these twelve years on.

I push a mush of dead leaves aside with my foot, disturb a piece of black wood which powders under my heel. The heavy raindrops spatter on the rotted crumbs, spreading them over the earth, uncovering and then washing clean a gleaming red pebble with a hole in its heart.

My bloodstone.

With disbelief, then delight, I bend down, take it out of the soil and hold it to me like a treasure. I lift my face to the watery air, take a last look around the clearing, then turn my back.

I wander through the trees and on to the riverbank where I once scooped out the clay for the manikin. The ground is thick with purple violets.

I stand by the water's edge, looking across to the south, still in a small flutter of childish fear that I should be seen by the watermen, still asking myself whether that is where I came from. I walk on by the alders and dipping willows until, in the last of the evening, I come to a ford, and splash through the water to the other side.

On the second of the three Blind Days, when no magic, no divination can be done, a fever takes hold of me on the road from Shersted to Mistleham.

The Bonesmen cannot be called upon to mix a potion for me. They are men of the fen country, and never stray so far south. The wise woman, Mother Winnery, who healed me once before, at a price, is far out of reach on the northern marshes. Wherever I go, word flies from one cunning woman to the next to be wary, and not to cross my path, so there is none to conjure a charm to make me well. I have power over the life and death of others, but have not the skill to cure myself.

The rain will not cease. I stumble from one dripping copse of trees to the next. There is little shelter away from the woods, and I am shunned and moved on from byre and pound, too sick and weary to force my will.

I keep walking as best I can, for the land is flat and marshy and there is nowhere to rest other than in the ditches. The early spring meadows are sodden and do not yield up their nourishing plants.

I gather my wits enough to read a palm out on Hilsey marsh for a mouthful of bread and a rest in the sheep-pen. I steal up in the night, let myself into the cot and take the goodwife's dry shawl and shoes and leave the wet behind on the floor.

I find the path through the marsh by the light of the flickering corpse candles that Zillah told me were the souls of the unbaptized flitting between heaven and hell.

When the grey watery dawn rises over the reeds, I am long on the road from Hilsey to the sea.

And at last I come to Bryers Guerdon.

I seek charity at the house of the priest, Piers Hillyard. His vixen of a housekeeper will not allow me even one night's sleep in a corner of the barn, but Hillyard comes after me with some cheese and small beer, then sends me down to the marshes to seek shelter.

A track leads down the hill from the priest's house to his little church of All Hallows, set back in its protecting circle of trees. Priests are always good for scraps to eat, but I avoid their churches, for I cannot bear the touch of consecrated ground beneath my feet.

From the shelter of the tall hedgerow on the other side of the track, I pass All Hallows, my eyes firmly ahead.

But all at once my steps falter, my head spins. I feel a flush of sweat sweep over my body.

Swaying, I turn and look about for a place to sit, but all is wet grass, straggly bushes and thick mud. If I passed into the churchyard I might find refuge among the tombstones, or in the church itself, but nothing would induce me to walk that way.

The hedgerow wants its new leaves. Through the fretwork of black twigs I see, beyond the eastern wall of the church, further than the last straggling headstones, a stretch of swampy ground and a pool overhung by an ugly, crooked tree.

The lychgate draws my gaze. As I run my eye over the wooden gates standing a little way open, and the bowed, over-hanging roof above, dripping in the endless rain, I realize that it is not the fever that has overwhelmed me, but the gate itself. It is as if I have strayed into the shaded borders of the other-world, the spirit-world beyond our own. Here in this place of enchantment, the thin curtain between the worlds shifts and changes, conceals and uncovers without mortal aid.

A tingling runs through my body.

This is a place of ancient magic, on the margin of earth and water, sacred to the men of stone, bronze and iron, long before time and memory.

I fear some terrible mischance here, think I smell smoke on the air. My burned wound aches. Confused and weakened, I trudge on, but cannot resist looking back again and again.

The marsh-dwellers, in their huts of willow, mud and reeds, have little to share and are wary of strangers. They look into my eyes and turn from me, threaten me with sticks, tell me to be gone.

I move further away from the dwellings of the sheep and

cattle herders, where scrawny, wet ewes plod away from me and thin lambs skitter sideways out of my path. I tear up clumps of grass, rip up handfuls of drooping marsh flowers, to grind with my teeth for sustenance, stumbling on through the high reeds alongside the channels of fresh water towards the wide open sea-mouth of the far river. From time to time I kneel and try to drink out of my cupped hands, but the water is becoming brackish; I am drawing ever closer to the salt creeks.

Forcing up my head, I see through a bleary haze a solitary withered tree. Almost hidden beneath it, among a tangle of scrubby bushes, is a small hut with earth walls and a roof of knotted reeds. I stagger towards it.

The crude door, of thin boughs bound together with twine, scrapes inwards against a heap of straw. The space within is damp and foul-smelling. Deep shadows linger in the corners. A rough wooden bench, no more than a plank of wood resting on two gnarled tree stumps, runs along the wall under a small square opening of window, half covered with a mat of plaited grass, through which sprays of drizzle blow in. Hanging from hooks lashed to the rafters are carcasses of hare, rabbit and weasel, dried fur clinging to bone, with all flesh and blood sucked, scratched and picked out. A dun-coloured ragged garment hangs on the back wall, on a piece of branch thrust into the wattle.

I sink down into the dirty straw and know nothing more for a long while, drifting in and out of the world, sometimes half opening my eyes and seeing the shimmer of stars against the black shape of night above the bench. In one strange dream, I think an angel comes to me where I lie. I feel his breath, see close to me the golden strands of his hair, but when the dawn inches its way across the walls of the shelter and I awake to the harsh croak of a crow on the roof above me, I am alone.

Another night, perhaps another day, passes by outside the dirt walls. The angel leans over me and I swallow water from a thick clay bowl that tastes of earth.

On the third night he bends over me once more and drips cool water between my parched lips. I open my eyes. The moon's yellow face fills the square of window and I look upon the angel at last.

I am not afraid, though angel he is none. The diseased and disfigured came to the house in the woods for solace and heal-ing. I watched them from my loft. They did not repel me, and neither does he. This hideous, deformed creature has given me water – life. The well-favoured shunned and despised me, re-fused me shelter, but this brutish thing, more beast than man, yet man he is, affords me the refuge of his dwelling place, and I draw close to him, though his strange face and long arms bear the dreaded marks of the leper.

His speech is little more than rough sounds in his throat; perhaps he has never needed to utter a word to another human soul for a long time. He barks out his name to me – 'Cain! Cain! Lan-kin! Lan-kin!' and repeats mine – 'Aff-ra! Aff-ra! Aff-ra!'

SPRING INTO SUMMER 1581

Days pass, and clumsy words come to him, never clear, but I begin to catch some meaning in them. He shares his kill – raw coney, rat, goose and crow, ripping them apart for me with his sharp teeth. When I am well again, I will make a fire to cook, but for now I need to grow strong, and have eaten bloody meat before.

When the rain eases, and my illness passes a little, Lankin carries me out into the wilderness of sea-channel and fresh-water spring, of reed mace and tussock grass.

And I see that though the long man lives in a world of which the margins are water, he will not cross it, whether it moves or is still. He will not even pass over a place if he senses water running below the ground. He drinks hesitantly from one small spring only, bubbling out a short way from the hut, and if we draw near to a pool or stray too close to a ditch, the creature flinches and turns away.

When I ask, Lankin twists his face, trying to form words to tell his story, using dumb show when the words fail him. Water seems to mean for him a blinding tangle of choking weed and filthy, frothing green bubbles; young men laughing as they whip and thrash a misshapen, ugly boy back into the creek with springing willow wands, again and again. Water is lungs bursting on the edge of drowning, and the weakness that follows, for days and days.

He roams his own hidden paths and tracks, creeping round the pools and channels, skirting unseen the dwellings of those who make their rude living on the marshlands, but in the end he always comes to the water. He can never escape this place.

YULE 1581

Months pass in his company; then, like the shiver of a cobweb in a lift of air, I feel the first tremor of flesh and spirit being crafted in the dark, secret heart of me. And for this small bud I long to be the willing, tender arms, sweet scent and soothing words I never knew myself.

Together Lankin and I gather little clouds of sheep wool from thorny boughs or hedges, to comb and spin into the softest blankets. We weave a cradle from green willow wands and silky grass, and cushion it with goose down and velvety moss.

10th JULY 1582

In the dead of the night, under a bloody rust-red moon, I give birth after long, tortured hours (Do not cry out, Aphra). It is a thin, ill-made creature that mews once, then gives up its life, not a thing that could ever have lived and grown, or found a place to exist in the world.

And in the same hour that it comes, so Lankin disappears with it, and I lie seething with burning cheeks and feverish dreams, untended and sick, for how long I do not know.

Then a young girl, I believe following a stray sheep deep into the marshes, pushes open the door of the hut. She runs to fetch her mother, a goodwife who knows all too well the signs of a recent birth, but who does not ask me where the babe has gone. She says that good will come of this for me, for Lady Ygurne Guerdon, the wife of the lord of the manor, is languishing after the delivery of her own infant son, John, and they are in need of a wet nurse to feed the baby.

'The master believes his lady has been charmed by the midwife, so listless and out of sorts she is,' says the woman, 'like many a poor wretched wife in childbirth before her. Witches, the lot of them, midwives are, knowing all them witchery things.'

So the goodwife brings me a draught, brings me clean garments and restores me a little, then takes me, feeble and weary, to the great house of Guerdon Hall.

I stand, swaying, before Sir Edmund Guerdon, a man

aware of the gleam of every gilded curl on his head and the lay of every hair of his carefully shaped beard. Even in my weakness, I see he is a man who likes to run his eyes over every maidservant who passes through his door, while, I learn later, his slender, moon-white lady, Ygurne, keeps to her rooms above. He speaks as if we two are alone together in the chamber, though the woman who brought me is there.

'By all that's good,' he breathes close to me, 'your eyes are as deep and dark as the Styx. I wonder what dreams my heir will drink in from you.'

He tosses a few coins to the goodwife, who scrabbles around on the floor, making sure she has recovered every last one from the corners.

'Go tell them in the kitchen to send up the laundry girl, Kittie Wicken,' he tells her.

His eyes remain on me while the woman leaves. The only sound is of our breathing – until a moment later, when there comes a soft rap at the door.

A young girl enters, fair head uncovered, eyes lowered to the floor. Her hands tremble, her shoulders hunch forward. She is all submission and fear.

He moves towards her, raises his hand. She flinches for a second. He runs his fingers from the top of her head downwards till they reach the twisted tip of her long plaited hair. She does not lift her eyes.

'Kittie, this is our wet nurse, Aphra Rushes. Take her below, would you, and feed her up well on good

34

vittles. Maybe now our little man will cease his grizzling.'

Without a word Kittie leads me down a winding, stone staircase into a large kitchen, where smoke, steam and smells from the fireplace rise up among the chains and hooks hanging in the huge chimney. A writhing child frets in a wooden cradle set to one side of the fire. Kittie lifts him out, rocks him a little, then places him in my arms. He smells the milk and squirms and struggles, pushing his small fist into his mouth. I look at his red puling face and see his father.

The sound of coarse laughter echoes around the stone stairs.

Two men push through the door, their faces creased with mirth.

'How he got the net off himself in the end I shall never know,' laughs the first.

'Ha!' cries the second. 'How many tides was he in the water this time – was it two? Where is Old Clowder, Kittie? Long Lankin the leper man has got himself away over the marsh. We need a draught of ale from the cask.'

'And his terror every time it rose up around his neck, Walter,' says the first man, grinning. 'The monster thought he was going to drown. Then, when the master ordered the slops to be thrown over him, that was the best sport I ever saw. And what was that bit of meat he carried? A coney skinned ready to be eaten?'

'The master let his dogs make quick work of it, that's for sure. How the leper blubbered over it. Ha ha!'

I think I will faint into the fire, my heart is so sick.

'Ha! He won't come crawling back this way again soon. Kittie, will that child never be quiet? Go fetch Old Clowder for the ale. Ezra must be sure to burn the net, and not to touch it with his naked hands.'

When they have departed in their merriment, Kittie sees that the men have left me in some torment of mind. She brings me good ale from the cask and some soft bread, sits quietly beside me and asks about my lost babe, that I have milk to feed this one. In my misery, and because of her gentleness, I tell her it was Lankin's infant, his and mine, that the master's dogs devoured.

Then I regretted I did not keep my own counsel, for I could see Kittie was overcome with revulsion, though she tried to conceal it afterward.

Late that night, I am alone, utterly derelict, unwell, suckling the wretched babe in the low chair by the embers. I catch a movement, the glint of golden thread and seed pearls on dark velvet, the gleam of finely tooled leather. I look up to find Sir Edmund watching from the doorway.

I might turn a corner and he will be there, descend a bend of the stairs and he will press in too close as he passes. He has found out where I am lodged, in a small stone-walled room next to the arched vault where the ale barrels are stored, just along the passage from the great kitchen. Sometimes he will catch me when I am utterly alone with no chance of avoiding him. His touch is loathsome, and my protests scorned. The servants are afeared of him, and have little concern for me.

He has no inkling of how much I have grown to hate him, and how I also despise the insipid wife I barely see, for she lies on her silken couch from morn till evening. I feel nothing but spite for his peevish, fretful child, who bawls hour after hour, arching his back and clawing at the air.

Little does Guerdon know what manner of woman he keeps in his hall, suffering his attentions until my strength returns, while my heart aches for the long man on the marshes, and the poor dead thing we made together.

MIDSUMMER DAY – 21st JUNE 1583

It is the solstice. The child will take no nourishment, but bites at me with his sharp little teeth and draws blood and will not let himself be comforted. I put him roughly down in his cradle and leave him with Kittie Wicken, who every day weeps in corners and wrings her chapped hands in her apron. The cook tells me the pot boy has got Kittie with child, the pot boy blames the groom of the stable, but they all know that the father is Sir Edmund. Timid Kittie is not bound or betrothed to any man, and always keeps to the house.

As for me, I cannot shake away the sickness in my heart, and cannot summon up the strength or will to cast spell or charm.

Despite this, I can see Kittie is nervous when I am about. I might be weak yet, but am still able to torment, with a thousand little barbs, the ill-natured child I have to feed. Kittie saw me give him a draught on a spoon to make him vomit so I would not have to bring him to church on the Sabbath. She watched from a corner when I pricked him on his fingers with a bodkin so he would be testy and ill-tempered when his high-born grandmother came to bless him.

Kittie will do whatever I ask of her. I pay her little heed, for she is sorely afeared of me: I told her I knew magic that would let me creep inside her head, look out from her eyes, make her hands do my bidding.

I climb the stone stairs and go up into the evening light of the garden to find white poppies to prepare a draught to quieten the babe. It is not for his good – I care not if he is in pain – but for mine, for his endless shrieking provokes me. I can hear him even outside, his cries loud over Kittie's coaxing for him to chew on an apple core with his swollen gums, or her gentle singing while she tries to rock him to sleep.

The tide is out in the creek. I wander along the bank in the last of the sunshine, searching for the flowers, and come upon a low, gnarled tree garlanded with dark red roses. I close my eyes to draw in their fragrance when I am surprised by a sound close by. I know it, and feel a moment's rush of joy.

'Aff-ra! Aff-ra!'

I turn to see Cain Lankin, looking up at me out of the dry channel. He is in a piteous condition, his face a mass of sores and lumps, his nose collapsed. He reaches out his arms to me.

'Soon, soon, my dear, and I will be able to help you,' I soothe him. 'Just a little longer and we will be free – you and I together—'

I feel eyes upon us, look swiftly back at the house, and see a face at an upstairs window. The casement opens. Sir Edmund furiously shakes his fist.

'Get away from here!' he cries. 'Leave my servant be! I've told you before – get away from my land, you filthy, diseased, worm-eaten monster!'

His face disappears. In a flurry of commotion from the house, the door across the cobbled yard bursts open. A number of servants, Francis Parkin, Old Clowder, Thomas and Walter, thunder across the grass brandishing an assortment of implements – billhook, axe and spear.

Sir Edmund follows, bellowing, 'I'll drown you alive! I would have done it before if you wasn't such a pole of a man, and stuck up out of the wretched water!'

Walter and Thomas grab my arms and begin to pull me away, thinking Lankin had intended to attack me, but Lankin mistakes their intent.

He raises himself to his full height, which is considerable, and lifts his arms. Curling his claw-like hands into two fists, he turns to Sir Edmund and shrieks, 'Kill you! Kill you!'

It tears at my soul to hear him.

'Threaten me, would you!' Sir Edmund reaches down for a rock, and hurls it at Lankin. It glances across his shoulder, ripping out a piece of flesh. I feel the jag of pain as if it were my own. Howling, spitting out a thread of bubbles, he begins to retreat across the hard mud at the bottom of the channel.

He stands up again on the far bank, calling, 'Kill you! Kill you!' once more.

'Don't you dare creep up on my servants, you monstrous hedge-pig!'

Francis Parkin, Old Clowder and Sir Edmund continue to rain stones and abuse on the helpless leper until he disappears among the scrubby bushes and thin trees beyond the creek.

'I've told you before – I'll kill you, you foul and pestilent base-born cur!' shouts Sir Edmund after Lankin. 'I'll send my men out to find you and cut you down – be sure I will!'

Thomas and Walter usher me back towards the house.

I do not sleep, but pace the floor in the night kitchen as the great fire cools to grey ash. I could steal away, noiseless as a wraith, and return to the hut on the marsh, but here in this house I am slowly spinning out a thread of hope for the long man, with Guerdon's wretched child its vital filament – an ancient spell that could cure Lankin's disease, requiring him to drink of the blood of an innocent, spilled by a silver dagger and caught in a silver bowl.

Everything I require for my purpose is at hand.

I am well-fed on Guerdon's meat, fish, milk and bread, clean-shod and clothed at his expense. Each day my cheeks grow a little rosier, my eyes gleam brighter. When my full strength returns, my powers will be restored also.

And I will lead the long man round the water, will find a path to take us away northwards, will help him over the hidden streams to a wilderness where no one will ever find us.

At Lammastide, the festival of the First Harvest, the first day of August, Sir Edmund Guerdon will ride to attend the Privy Council at Greenwich, and by then I will be ready.

It was upon this day a year past that our babe was lost to us.

I am tired.

This child pulls on my skirts to stand, clings to me, totters alongside me wailing, with his fat hands twisted in the folds of my apron.

Old Clowder comes into the kitchen with the dirty vessels from the supper which the master has shared – along with his best wine – with his friend Robert, Lord Myldmaye.

'For God's sake, woman, calm that poor boy!' He tosses the dishes onto the table, pulls the babe away from me, lifts him into his arms, jigs him, quietens him. 'Are you sore, little man? Shall we find honey for you, or make up some pap in the milk pan?'

The child pushes his fingers into Clowder's white hair, hushes his sobbing, smiles. The serving man turns to me. 'What manner of spiteful woman are you, that you give him no comfort? If the master were not so' – he spits out the words – 'not so bewitched by you . . .'

He narrows his eyes, sets his mouth. 'I will have you out of here, tell the master what you truly are – ungodly, corrupt. I saw it in you from the first. I am surprised the whole household has not been afflicted by some pestilence, the sheep and cattle plagued by a murrain since you sullied these walls with your presence here. The master is at a game of Fox and Geese with Thomas and my Lord Myldmaye, else I would tell him now. I – I would see you hanged.'

Old Clowder carries the child up the stone stairs. 'Kittie?' he calls. 'Where is Kittie? Let us find her, my little lad. She will care for you, love you with her own babe when it comes.'

Later, when the old house murmurs with snore, sniff and creak from straw pallet, strung truckle or curtained mattress, when out in the warm night air the white owl floats from barn to wood under a slice of moon, I light my tallow candle. By its wavering light I take three henbane seeds and crush them into a cordial, drop into it three hairs from Old Clowder's head that the sleeping child still clutched in his hand.

I call up the spirits. Will they come for me?

A wisp rises out of the flame. I think it will be Little Clim or Matty the Boy, but it is crafty Tilly Murrell in a feather of smoke – says she will see to it, see that he drinks the draught, will ward the cup so that no one else will even touch it.

In the morning, after his ale and pottage, Old Clowder does not die, for that is not my purpose, but sweats and vomits and howls that demons are clawing at his eyes.

Two days later the physician Harper comes from Daneflete, examines him, thinks it unlikely he will ever recover his wits, has him bound and taken away.

As the cart rattles off with Old Clowder and his belongings tied in a bundle next to him, Kittie prays and weeps, the cook wrings his hands and Walter wails on Francis Parkin's shoulder.

The old man will never be well again.

I am ready.

Dark-cloaked and secret, I steal out the next three nights and walk along the creek, seeking Lankin out on the far side. On the third I see his long shadow winding in and out of the rushes. I call softly to him across the quiet reeds, and whisper to him what we will do at Lammastide.

LAMMAS EVE – 31st JULY 1583

I take the child, John, up the staircase for a brief dandle on his mother's knee, and to see if he will show a step for her, though she seems to take little pleasure in him, and he will not refrain from holding out his fat arms and fretting for me to take him. While he whines and snivels around her, I stand behind the silken lady where she cannot see me in her looking glass and, with a practised hand, swiftly and silently lift the small silver bowl that sits tucked away on the buffet behind two greater vessels.

I bundle it up in my apron, take the infant, press his body tight against me in a pretence of affection so the basin does not clatter out. My lady waves me away with a listless hand and I hurry back down the stairs and leave the child with willing Kittie; then I conceal the treasure under the pallet in my little room, with the candles that have been secreted one by one over the weeks.

The crossguard of Sir Edmund's small silver dagger always protrudes from his belt. He passes me in the stone passage with his groomsman to check the condition of his chestnut mare, Barbary, for the journey to London in the morning. I glance up at him from under my lashes. He enfolds my waist with his arm and I reach for the little knife, but the groomsman is watching. I lower my hand and push Sir Edmund lightly off. He looks back over his shoulder to see the curve of a smile on my plump, crimson lips as I turn away.

He returns from overseeing the stowing of his trunk with its carefully folded linens, fine woollens and embroidered velvets, and his strong box with the concealed lock that guards not only his sovereigns, but also his jewelled court doublet, cape and gold-threaded hat. He comes into the kitchen where I sit rocking the cradle with my foot. I do not look away.

In the dark night watches, footsteps approach the door I have left ajar. Lying on my pallet, in a thin shaft of moonlight, I steel myself to bear him, my heart fluttering with anxiety.

'How cool your flesh is,' he whispers as he takes me to him.

Instantly, I am by the black pool of years ago, Rufus Goode striding towards me, grabbing my arms in his huge hands. I feel my chest tighten, my head begin to pound.

I must not veer from my course.

Around Guerdon's back, I reach into his belt for the little silver dagger, draw it out, and slip it under the pallet.

As the rosy light creeps in from the small barred window almost at the ceiling, I hear the sound of hoof beats on the wooden bridge, Barbary carrying her master to London, and Thomas on the young filly, Marian, riding alongside. A little later comes the jingle of the two carriages clattering behind.

I look down at my half-covered body in the soft early morning, and all the world changes, for there on my stomach is a little round patch, light in colour. When I gently run my finger across it, there is no sensation. Another patch lies just near it, at my side, and as I search, I find another two just the same, on my calf and on my thigh, just above the twisted skin burned in the Balefire.

Zillah and Damaris restored me then, but I know that now there can be no healing, for there is none to do it.

So here is the changed world. In truth I see that the creature can never escape away with me, for there will always be water in his path and I will never persuade him over it. Alone, I might run for a while, but before very long, the festering and rotting will begin in earnest, and even those who once sought my enchantments will shun and abandon me. Where will I go then?

All that is left to do is lay the spell and save the man who once saved me.

All is set – there will be healing for Lankin, and a double reckoning for Guerdon, for there are two deeds of darkness to be done this Lammas night. I will do the one deed for Lankin and he will do the other for me.

The hour is late. The tide is out and the house slumbers. I stand to the side of the great fireplace in the kitchen and pull on the chains that open the trapdoor at the top of the log shaft. The kitchen is almost completely below ground and the huge logs for the fire are thrown down the brick-lined shaft from outside. With his long arms and legs it is no hardship for Lankin to clamber down, crawl through the small tunnel at the bottom and out into the kitchen, without disturbing the household.

He stands there on the flagstone floor with the firelight at his back, and the flickering candlelight from the table playing on his disfigured face. This creature of the marshes looks around in bewilderment at the array of heavy pots and vessels hanging from blackened hooks, the pitchers, jugs, knives and spoons, and the pewter dishes held in their rows on the wall by long wooden bands.

The silver bowl and the silver dagger, both edges of its blade clean and sharp, lie together. I fetch the sleeping child from his cradle, place him on the table beside the bowl and unfasten his soft, warm wrappings.

Under my breath I chant the ancient words, pass the knife through the flames of seven candles, as all the while Lankin holds the infant down. I pick up the knife, raise it high . . . and there – it is done. Stop your shrieking, you wretched child! I chant again.

The long man and I catch the blood in the silver bowl.

A footfall.

Who is hiding behind the door? Kittie Wicken, the sneaking little laundry girl. Pull her out, hold the knife to her fluttering throat. You will do my bidding, Kittie Wicken. Fetch the mistress, or you and that unborn child you carry will not see the sunrise. I twist her hair in my bloody fingers. See what I can do, Kittie – see it!

Panting, in a fever of fear, she stumbles up the steps.

An urgent, breathy voice hisses close in my ear. 'Aphra! Aphra! He drinks!'

In a spiral of light the spirit, Matty the Boy, flits to the ceiling and vanishes.

I turn. 'Wait, Lankin! You must not drink till I finish the charm—'

But he drinks greedily, too soon. The pale-skinned lady comes down and sees it all, screams and reaches out to snatch her lifeless infant. Flicking his tongue over his wet, scarlet-smeared lips, Lankin grabs up the silver dagger. She takes a long time to die, reaches almost to the top of the stone stairs before she slips on her own blood and snaps her neck.

Kittie Wicken flees from the kitchen, but will not utter a word, she is so stricken with terror and fear.

Footsteps. A servant's cry as he sees the lady on the stairs – Francis Parkin. He howls for Walter.

Back to the shaft, Cain Lankin! Vanish away! Swiftly, vanish away!

The spell is incomplete. An unfinished charm spins the circle the wrong way. All is undone.

Lankin will not live for long. The crooked spell will sail its certain course.

I wait to be found.

LITTLE YULE – 13th DECEMBER 1583

The belfry is a torment to me. The iron anklet cuts into me almost to the bone. I pull at it all ways. The chain jangles on the floor. The air in this consecrated place is like hot knives in my skin. I try to pluck out the blades with my fingers – pluck, pluck, pluck out the blades . . .

Hillyard, the priest, hastens up the stairs, anxious to be gone before the early night falls upon All Hallows. I listen for the clunk of the key turning in the great oaken door and the rumbling as it grates over the floor. When Hillyard enters, he fastens the door behind him.

The rattle of keys, the click of the lock of the door in the tower, up the stairs, rattle again, search for the key to the trap-door. One side of the trap comes up. Hillyard holds his breath against the foul air and pushes a pitcher of water and a hunk of bread onto the wooden boards. The heavy chain slides noisily across the floor. From behind the door, I snatch at the water jug with my filthy hands, gulp it down, choke, and it spills down my chin and over my breast. The cold water eases the swollen, burning points where the torturers pierced my skin. I let the pitcher drop and it rolls slightly.

I speak from behind the wooden panel, next to the priest's ear. I can hear the thudding of his heart.

'Will I be hanged?' I whisper.

'I – I think they may burn you,' he says.

The air rasps in my throat as I take this in.

'I think you may be burned,' he goes on, 'because you used magic against your master. That is what they are saying . . . but I cannot tell for sure . . .'

My breath comes hard. He waits for a moment.

'Sir Edmund Guerdon,' says the priest, 'has taken another wife.'

I am astonished. I should have known the master would not be consumed with anguish, overcome with grief. I should have known it.

'Lady Ygurne, the pearl-white mistress,' I whisper hoarsely, my flaking lips close to the door the priest still holds up, 'has been only four moons in her grave . . .'

'Guerdon wants another heir,' says Hillyard. 'His new wife, Lord Myldmaye's daughter, Mary, is young and beautiful. It is believed she is already with child.'

I cannot speak.

Guerdon will yet possess that which was for ever lost to me – an heir, a babe.

Hillyard begins to lower the door, and reaches out for the empty jug. My mind runs quickly – the house in the wood – the second fire – Zillah and Damaris burned again. 'Well burned twice – or they'll come back,' I hear across the years. 'Make sure. Only takes a bit of skelton left unburned . . .'

My skinny fingers grip his arm. I feel him flinch.

'If I am burned,' I say, 'don't – don't let them burn me twice. It will' – what do I say to a man of God? – 'it will destroy my immortal soul . . .'

'If you are a proven witch,' says Hillyard, 'then you have no immortal soul.'

'Don't let them burn me twice – I beg you – for mercy's sake—'

Hillyard shakes off my hand, backs away a little down the stairs, then firmly secures the trapdoor.

I hear him at the bottom, the click of the lock on the small door, his footsteps crossing the tower floor, the grating of the huge studded door at the entrance, the turning of the great iron key. There on my thigh, among the dirty, weeping, untended sores, is the patch of burned, silvery skin. My anguish rises and leaves me in a hoarse screech I do not have the will to stop.

I am sorry, mother Zillah, that I cried out.

14th DECEMBER 1583

The pale dawn comes through the small slatted window. For the first time in days I claw my way up the wooden framework of the belfry and pull myself to a kind of standing. My bleeding knees buckle. My bruised, festering feet will not take my meagre weight until I clench my teeth and force them. When the chain is at its most taut, the anklet cutting at its deepest into my flesh, then I can glimpse a patch of sky and a little land.

Piers Hillyard comes with hard bread. He tells me I am to be brought to Lokswood in two days for trial, then, if found guilty, immediately returned to Bryers Guerdon for execution.

'You may still save yourself,' he says from his place behind the trapdoor. 'If you . . . if you tell the truth . . . that Cain Lankin was with you that night in Guerdon Hall, that he was complicit in those foul deeds, that he was a murderer . . .

'What happened there, Aphra? I might be able to spare you the flames . . . It must be a terrible – terrible way to die.'

But I have already seen through the corner of the window the faggots and brushwood being brought for the fire by cart and by shoulder. I have heard the men shout, the clunk of axes, heavy branches splitting, and seen, on a wagon drawn by an ox, a barrel oozing pitch. They have gone to great cost to bring it here, to coat my body and thus increase my suffering.

'And who is to be my judge?'

He waits a moment.

'Lord – Lord Robert Myldmaye will preside,' he says at last.

Lord Myldmaye, the father of Mary, the new Lady Guerdon.

I am condemned.

Yet a little spark burns within me when I think on the power of this place, the enchanted portal of the lychgate.

'Lankin is innocent,' I lie to the priest, my lips close to the trapdoor. 'He was not there.'

'Can I believe you?'

'Would you not try to save yourself – knowing you were about to be burned alive? I alone am guilty. I killed the babe and his mother.'

'I will give you absolution.'

'I am beyond your absolution. But do not let them burn me twice.'

'I – I will plead on your behalf. That is as much as I can do.'

'And . . . and have you seen him – Lankin?'

'My man, Moses, gave me report that Lankin was seen by night breaking a way through the hedgerow on the southern side of the churchyard, but was sent off with stones. A few weeks ago he would not have been frightened away so easily, but it is believed he is fading . . .'

'When he dies, promise me you will bring his dead, guiltless body through the lychgate into the churchyard for Christian burial. I tell you again, he is innocent, and I beg you, as a man of God . . .'

When the morning comes, I vow to Belenos and Cernunnos, and to all the spirits of the earth, the air, the fire and the water, the last words I utter will be a curse upon the family of Guerdon through every generation that is to come.

I do not know if Hillyard can prevent what is left of my mortal body from being burned again.

And when Cain Lankin's own life ebbs away, as soon it surely must, for the spell was incomplete, will the foolish, trusting priest keep his word, and unwittingly allow the body of a murderer who has drunk the blood of an infant to move through the lychgate?

The Bonesmen taught me the secrets of the newly-dead.

Between their passing and their burial, they inhabit a half-realm that is neither of the earth nor of the spirit. For a short while Cain Lankin will journey through this mid-world on his way to hell. The power at the lychgate could keep him between worlds for all time, to become an enduring and terrible affliction to the house of Guerdon, and to all those who serve it and dwell near it, for ever.

I hear the scraping of earth, the soft thud of soil thrown on grass, a howl: 'Aff-ra! Aff-ra!'

The long man comes to dig his way in, with no tools but his bare hands.

It is too late. There is no more time.

'Lankin! Cain!' comes only in a dry whisper. I am hoarse

with crying out. The short chain slithers across the boards. I stretch out my hand towards the rope that moves the passing bell – stretch further, stretch – there I have it, pull a little – a rough clang of a chime, then another.

He hears the bell.

'Aff-ra!'

16th DECEMBER 1584

As scraps of snow fall onto the splintered planks at the bottom of the cart, Dr Fortyce, the divine they brought in at Lokswood, wraps a dirty piece of sacking around my shoulders, and another over my frozen knees twisted on the hard wood. Fortyce prays all the while, urging me to repentance, his voice rumbling all at one with the jolting wooden wheels, the creaking of the reins, the clatter of the chains, the steady clot, clot *from behind – Myldmaye and Guerdon and their men on high steeds, all closely wrapped in winter furs.*

On and on we lurch along the high roads and icy tracks, back from the Moot Hall. My oozing sores chafe with each stone, rut and turn. The manacles cut through my skin, but I clench my mouth to endure the torment, as I must endure the greater torment to come. Terrors pounce in unwelcome – Zillah and Damaris screaming in the flames in the house in the wood, the sweet stench of roasted flesh, the crackle of sizzling fat. My limbs stiffen, begin to tremble. I stifle a whimper of fear. When unwanted tears spill from my eyes, I lower my head, blink them hard away.

Ahead and beside ride rough guards on shaggy ponies. Behind them along the verges, close-cowled men, women and children gaze out at me, their faces blue and red-veined with cold, as the witch in the dung-cart passes by on her way back to Bryers Guerdon to die.

As we pitch and tilt down the slippery hill towards All

Hallows, I hear below the bellman summoning the marsh-dwellers from their labours.

Before the lychgate the horse lurches to a halt.

A drummer stands on a stool, a thin layer of snow covering his hat. He beats out a roll, then a throb like a heartbeat, waits, a roll and a throb, a roll and a throb.

In front of him a wooden stake, laced with heavy chains, rises up from a monstrous stack of interlaced branches, faggots and bundles of twisted straw.

A large crowd has gathered, all eyes turned towards me, in silence, save for the heartbeat of the drum. The cart scrapes over the rough ground, then stops. I slide across the coarse planks and the anklets bite into my bruised and blistered skin.

I raise my head.

Behind a spitting brazier, ready to light the torches, a huge man stands in the wavering, smoky air. I remember him – Slater, the brute from Hunsham who tried to spike my ear for a vagrant when I was hardly out of childhood, brought here to do this wretched, filthy work. He will not throttle me first for a mercy. He will make the agony last.

My gaze moves from Slater to the priest, Piers Hillyard, who looks on with pity and mutters prayers. Guerdon on his high saddle cannot meet my eye, but turns and makes some aside to his lordship.

Rough hands pull at my arms, but my feeble body will not support me. A rush of fear sweeps over me. My head pounds. My legs buckle. Around me blurred faces sway, leer forward, *fall back. Powerful, filthy hands hold me upright. I cannot stand on my deadened feet, can barely feel the boards of the cart. Dr Fortyce reads from a parchment but I do not hear the words.*

As the learned man's mouth opens and shuts, I look across to the church. With half-closed lids, my eyes roam over the top of the leafless, spiked hedges.

A point of light moves in the glimmering air, then another. I look along the trail of little stars and see him, the long man, leaning into the topmost branch of the double-hooked tree that overhangs the marshy pool on the far side of the churchyard. His face is disfigured, his body corrupted. He clings weakly to the branch with his poor shredded arms and gazes at me, and the dying lights lift off him, up into the falling snow.

Looking at him, I draw myself up and stand.

A bitterly cold wind begins to blow so the snowflakes spin and fly back upwards to the dull grey sky. The people wrap their woollens tightly about them.

The drum begins again.

They pull me down from the cart.

Under Lankin's gaze, I will endure.

WEDNESDAY 31st OCTOBER 1962

I am the dust of charred bones and ash.

While the embers were yet smouldering, red eyes of heat still glaring out of the blackened wood, charred bone and burned flesh too scorching hot to be touched, a mighty winter storm swept in. The winds blew and blustered from all four quarters to scatter me, but it was the north wind that gathered me up. In a whirl of icy rain, it pitched and flung me, hurled me against wall, stone and tree, broke up all that remained of me and carried me across the empty spaces. Writhing in its fury, it began unravelling the thatches of the meagre huts on the marshes, spitting out the sticks of fences and sheep-pens, snapping the reeds and foaming the pools. Then, when the wind had spent its mischief here, it raged off southwards to be spiteful on the sea.

With the fragments of crackling brown leaves, scraps of feathers, twigs and shreds of dry, white grass, I bobbed and twisted to the ground, each little part of me knowing, and seeing, and being.

The people were in turmoil that I had been taken up into the air, and none more afeared than Sir Edmund Guerdon himself.

He planted the sacred trees to keep me out of his garden, the elders and rowans, for I had cursed him.

'Do not cry out, Aphra. Use the pain for your hate.'

In my last agony, with my throat swollen and blistered, the flames scorching my flesh and boiling my blood, I cursed Guerdon and all his family that were to come and through all generations, cursed them and their infants with bitter suffering in mind and body, until the line was no more. I cursed Guerdon until my spitting, hissing body twisted out of the chains and rolled down into the raging wood.

And now I am being pulled out of the earth. On this night, in this place, I am drawing together.

Up between the stones and through the soil I come, from under the roots of the sleeping plants, squeezing past the blindworms, the soft black moles, the snails, slugs and grubs that dwell deep in the clay-cold ground.

I am rising out of the water of fresh spring and salty mud, out of the moisture of the air, puffed out and blown in a string of tiny, crumbling pieces that swirl and gather close.

It is the Eve of All Hallows. The shroud between the world of the living and the otherworld of the dead ripples and grows sheer, allowing flow and passage from one side of itself to the other.

I move towards the house.

Once it lay under a mantle woven of sturdy threads spun with spells and enchantments to keep me out, but like the shroud between the worlds tonight, the cloak has become gossamer-thin. The guardian trees are felled, the runes gone, the devices lost. A few silken strands yet hold the weakened fabric together, but a silken strand is easily cut.

Now I can sense them, behind those ancient walls — two

hearts plump with cursed Guerdon blood. I am bound here, for as long as there are Guerdons in the world, I must be in it. And they have returned to the marshlands – to me.

But in this stillness another Guerdon heartbeat thrums faintly, somewhere far-off – a thin, meagre pulse wavering on the edge of life.

I will find it.

In my time.

CORA

My new navy gymslip hangs on the outside of the wardrobe. On the chest of drawers are a stack of crisp white blouses with nametapes sewn on the inside of their stiff collars. *Cora Drumm. Cora Drumm. Cora Drumm.* Dad chose the embroidered blue copperplate, thought it looked posh, but Auntie Kath could only find grubby brown thread, and her stitching's all over the place – ruins the effect entirely.

I look at them and sigh.

Girls of my age don't wear brand-new uniforms, just as they don't start another school halfway through the term, or at the back end of the week, but Dad didn't take me to the outfitter's in time and the stuff didn't arrive until yesterday.

I take a pair of grey woollen stockings out of their cellophane wrapping, ready for the morning, and hear Mr Blezzard's raised voice over the wind outside.

'I told you, it's what Drumm wanted. He said to get rid of it all.'

I peep round the side of the new curtains and look down into the garden.

Stout Mr Blezzard, in flat cap and worn tweed jacket with elbow patches – proud owner of the dented green van standing on the other side of the creek with the bright yellow hand-painted lettering: E. BLEZZARD – BIG OR SMALL WE DO IT ALL – TEL: HILSEA 317 – is towering over little Mr Wragge.

'Well, I told *you*, Ed,' Mr Wragge whistles through his three yellow teeth, one at the bottom and two at the top. 'Over and over I told you, there are some things best left well alone. These trees is special. They was put here for a reason. You shouldn't have gone chopping them down. The same with all that stuff you've chucked in the barn and broken. You shouldn't have meddled. They could have stayed where they was and Drumm would have been none the wiser, but you wouldn't take no blimmin' notice. I wish to God I hadn't gone and got that flippin' jippy belly. I'd have stopped you doing it if I hadn't been laid up.'

'Stop being so ruddy daft, with your silly witchy trees, Gideon. It's what Drumm wanted, all modern, central heating, fireplaces boarded up. When you find a load of daft nonsense, you don't just put it all back again, you get rid of it.'

'That's opinion, that is,' says Mr Wragge with a phlegmy cough. 'And what's Drumm doing coming here anyway? He had no business turning it all around, an old place like this. Should have stayed in London, or bought hisself a house on one of them new estates instead. More money than sense.'

'Well, it's too bloody late now, so stop going on,' says Mr Blezzard. 'Anyway, Drumm didn't buy it. Them girls of his were left it all from Ida Eastfield – leastways he's in charge of the money till they get to twenty-one. I think Mrs Eastfield didn't have no other family but it took them lawyers a long time to sort all the ins and outs.'

It's quiet for a moment. When Mr Wragge speaks again, I can hardly hear him.

'They're the last of the Guerdons, then?'

'I suppose so, even though their name's Drumm. Maybe it's something on their mother's side, though she must be dead 'cause this woman who's come from London with them isn't their mum.' He leans in to the old man, looks about and taps the side of his nose meaningfully. 'Them girls call her Auntie Kath, know what I mean? Anyway, I'm off home for me tea. Sometimes it puts the wind up me, working down here, even in the daylight. I don't want to be hanging around in the dark. We'll come back and finish clearing up when Drumm's paid me what I'm due. I'll leave me big wheelbarrow and the crates and give you the word when to start loading. Let's go round to the van.'

'I'll get the bus.'

'For God's sake, Gideon, don't make it flippin' personal. I'll take you home.'

'I'm telling you, Ed,' I hear Mr Wragge mutter as they make for the gravel path, 'you should have left all that stuff where it was.'

'Oh, leave off, will you,' says Mr Blezzard, 'or I'll change me mind about the lift. Here, have a peppermint, warm yourself up.'

I look out over the garden, still encircled by the shifting tides. Most of the old shrubs have been hacked to stumps. The bare ground left behind by the purposeless clearing is covered with felled trunks, lopped-off branches and splinters of wood, all that's left of the trees that grew around the creek before.

On the other side of the bridge Mr Blezzard's van coughs, coughs again, then rumbles off.

I still can't quite believe we are here.

Back in Limehouse – maybe half a year ago, I don't know exactly – Dad began to stay away the odd night or two. Then, every so often, I would catch him looking out from the edge of the nets into the street, fingering the long scar on his cheek. He and Auntie Kath would have muffled arguments behind closed doors, and she'd go off to her mother's for a couple of days.

Around the same time the council inspector, then the medical man, turned up and said our houses had to be pulled down. Slum clearance. No bathrooms. Outside privies. When our neighbours started leaving for the new blocks of flats or the estates built out towards the countryside in Bexleyheath, Dad hurried up the lawyers, who were taking years to sort out Auntie Ida's money. It was difficult – difficult because of Mum. In the end something was sorted out, and Mimi and I seemed to be in line to get it – and Guerdon Hall – and Dad decided we were going to come out here and live in it, and be grand.

But I never wanted to see the place again.

THURSDAY 1st NOVEMBER

I meet nobody's eye, just lower my head under the wide brim of my school hat and stare at my sturdy black outdoor shoes. I may be dressed the same as all the other girls – silk-lined navy coat and every layer inwards down to the regulation blue knickers – but it doesn't make me the same, not in any way.

The Judys, Patsys and Carols in my new class only had to hear me answer our form teacher, Mother Anselm, in registration to decide that I was nothing more than a curiosity – Cora Drumm, the new girl from the East End of London. They weren't unkind to me, just indifferent. The stiff knife-edge of my collar has cut into the back of my neck all day, reminding me of the scrappy stitching around my name.

I stand well back into the fan-shaped entrance of the ironmonger's, G. H. Firestone & Sons, in between the neat rows of drawer handles in the window display on one side, and the spades and saws on the other. One by one the green buses come along. Girls surge onto the platforms, disappearing upstairs and inside. When there is nobody left at the bus stop, I emerge from my place and wait for the next 2A, standing on a flattened mat of damp brown leaves blown off the tree overhanging the shelter.

The bus turns left at The Anchor and runs along the

Wrayness promenade, past the candyfloss and hot-dog stalls, closed for the coming winter, and the children's rides, tightly covered in weatherproof canvas wrappings. Wide-mouthed bloody skeletons, needing a good coat of paint before next season, leer down from the hoarding around the entrance to the Ghost Train. Old cigarette packets, crumpled oily pages of newspaper discarded from fish and chips, and small, squashed empty cardboard tubs that once held cockles, prawns and winkles have blown into grubby piles underneath the padlocked fortune-teller's booth, the bolted rifle range and the rickety wooden scaffolding holding up the Wall of Death.

The bus trundles on beyond the attractions, past the cockle boats waiting in the mist for the turn of the tide, and the Victorian boarding houses and shops, then bends right into Strand Drive. It stops in front of the row of smart mock-Tudor detached houses with their large gardens running down to the road that skirts the seashore. I know that many of the girls in my new class live in expensive properties like these.

When I get to twenty-one, I will come into enough money to buy every house in Strand Drive – if I wanted to.

Wrayness is left behind. Under a darkening sky, the bus rumbles on into Lokswood, then through Daneflete.

A few miles further on I can see the pub, the Thin

Man, rising up out of the gloomy distance, the street-lamp in front of it already on. There is no other building close by, just endless flat grey fields stretching away from the road on either side, bounded in the distance by straggling, almost-winter trees, rising up, just visible out of the darkening haze.

I force myself to get up from my seat, ring the bell, drag my feet down the stairs and step off the platform. As the empty bus moves off towards Hilsea, I look back in the direction of Daneflete to Ottery Lane, over the road on the same side as the pub. The tall, arching trees on either side of the lane lead, in a long bristling line, to Bryers Guerdon.

I wonder if Roger and his brother, Pete, still live there, in the wooden house with the veranda and the huge wild garden, with their mum and dad, two younger brothers, Dennis and Terry, and Baby Pamela. Of course, she wouldn't be a baby any more. She would be four or so, the same age Mimi was when we came here before.

For a long time I haven't been able to picture Roger's face at all, not properly. I have flashes of remembering the colour of a shirt, a hand-knitted jumper, a pair of shoes, but not his face. The harder I try to recall it, the more blurred it becomes. If I saw him now, I'm not sure I would recognize him at all, especially as he must be all of sixteen.

I approach Old Glebe Lane – bold words on a new

sign, crisp black letters on white metal. The hawthorn hedges on either side of the road have been neatly cut, the gaping potholes repaired with patchy tarmac.

I pass the rectory, Glebe House, on my right. Beyond the wrought-iron gates, sturdy trees line the drive to the huge house. The warm lights are already shining brightly downstairs. Mr Treasure, the headmaster of Lokswood School, and his family used to live in the front half, with its pillars and glossy black door. Father Mansell, the rector, and his wife, lived in rooms at the back; probably still do.

I walk on beside the high garden wall until it stops at the edge of Glebe Woods. The hissing trees send drifts of crumpled brown leaves down onto the dry earth.

Moving on to the brow of the hill, I stand there in the dying light, looking down at the steeple of All Hallows, the little church all on its own, rising up out of a knot of trees on the edge of the marshes.

I tighten my school scarf and make my way down the hill. At the bottom I take the right turn into The Chase, lowering my head to avoid looking forward where the track continues on to the church.

A cold wind is beginning to blow from the distant river, making the trees that line the left side of the road bend and squirm above the overgrown ditch at their roots.

The muddy holes in The Chase have been filled with

stones, so vehicles can come up to Guerdon Hall. Dad drove off to London in his blue Zodiac yesterday, for all I know to avoid paying Mr Blezzard the money he owes him for doing up the house.

I'm not sure when Dad's coming back – sometime over the weekend, I hope.

I walk past the front door, in shadow under the ancient tiled porch, and round the corner of the house.

A table lamp glows through the diamond panes of the sitting-room window. I glance in. Mimi is sitting on the settee watching *Crackerjack*, eating something off a tray on her lap. Auntie Kath is standing by the lamp putting a cigarette to her lips. She looks over at me as I go by. Her eyes are unsettled and her dimpled hand shakes slightly.

'Do you want beans on toast?' she calls as I come through the back door and into the stone passage. 'There ain't no bacon left, though. We've had it all.'

'All right,' I shout back. 'But don't worry. I'll do it.'

On the right, just where the passage turns into the hall, is the old warped door that used to open into Auntie Ida's kitchen, now locked. The key pokes out of its hole, the room no more than a turn away. Dad says he's going to get the doorway bricked over next year.

I don't want to be here next year.

I turn into the hall, still slightly shocked by the bright green wallpaper with big yellow flowers pasted over boards covering the old wooden panelling.

I go into the new kitchen opposite the staircase – two rooms Auntie Ida never used, now knocked into one. I switch on the fluorescent light and, while it flickers and settles into its harsh glare, draw the vivid orange curtains to shut out the garden.

Sliding open one of the frosted glass doors above the counter of the glossy dresser, I take out a cup, fill it with water, drink it down, and leave it on the gleaming Formica worktop.

Two slices of bread under the eye-level grill of our New World gas stove, the other half of the tin of baked beans into a stainless steel pan. Strike a match. Spread the butter. Pour out the hot beans. Take it into the sitting room in time for *Double or Drop*.

'That Mr Blezzard came for his money,' says Auntie Kath. 'Said he wasn't clearing out the barn till he's been paid. I said he'll have to come back when your dad's here.'

'School all right?' I ask Mimi. 'You finished with the tray?'

'Everyone's calling me Lizzie,' she says, staring at the screen. 'Don't like it.'

'I suppose you had to expect that, with your name being Elizabeth on the register. Didn't you tell them you prefer Mimi?'

'No.'

'Made any friends?'

I know what the answer will be.

'Don't like no one. This girl Denise asked me to go over and play. She's in Ottery Lane.'

'You going, then?'

'No. Don't like her.'

I think it's my fault. When we got back to London after all that had happened at Guerdon Hall before, I found myself haunted by the fear of her being snatched away again. Before Auntie Kath came, there was only her and me when Dad was out. I always had to know where Mimi was, wouldn't let her out on her own. I know I should have done, but I was scared when it was just the two of us in the house alone. In the end her friends stopped knocking for her, and she gave up asking to go out to play.

I cut a mouthful of toast and squash some beans onto it with my fork.

'Is that a new dress, Auntie Kath?'

'I went to Lokswood on the bus. What do you think? Maybe it's a bit low in the front.' She pulls the bodice up a bit, smoothes it over her full bust.

'You can always wear a scarf if it gets too nippy.'

'Do you think your dad will like it?'

'He'll love it. Shows off your curvy bits.'

'Nice pattern, innit?'

'Nice colours.'

'You got any aspirins, Cora?'

'Ain't there any in the bathroom? You got a headache?'

'Feeling a bit funny. Must've been the coffee I had at this place – Wren's Coffee House, they call it. I was looking for a tearooms, but this Wren's smelled lovely from the pavement so I thought I'd give it a go. Never been in one before. We never had nothing that posh in Limehouse.'

'You should go again.'

'No, I don't think so. This waitress come up and asked me what blend I'd like and I said a cup of Nescaff with a nice slosh of milk and three sugars. Soon as I opened me mouth, she raised one of her painted eyebrows right up to her lace cap and said they didn't do no Nescaff. In the end I asked for a cream slice and she brought it on a little plate with a doily and a silver fork and it was real cream; then I had a coffee after all to be polite, and it was that strong and bitter I could hardly drink it till I noticed this china bowl with fancy brown sugar lumps I had to put in meself with these tong things. When she brought the bill, me mouth dropped down halfway to Australia – cost a blimmin' fortune.'

When we go up to bed at nine, Auntie Kath won't stay downstairs on her own, even with the light on.

Dad's only had one half of the house done; the rest is shut off. Still, he doesn't have a clue what to do with all the rooms he's had opened up. After a while they'll be just too bothersome to heat and clean, and it won't be long before they're locked up again, like they were in Auntie Ida's time.

At the end of the landing upstairs a new wall blocks off the other wing of the house. It makes the landing feel all closed in, even gloomier than it was before. The window that used to be at the end of the passage is behind the wall now, spreading its milky light over floorboards, timber beams and plaster that no one will ever see again.

Mimi and I are in the same bedroom, but with twin beds instead of the huge grown-up bed we shared last time. I can't stand the wallpaper. It's all zigzags with red splashes – makes your eyes go funny.

The rafters have been covered with plasterboard so the ceiling's much lower. There's another panel of it, painted white, pinned over the opening of the old fireplace. The boarding's everywhere in the house now. Mr Blezzard must have got a job lot of the stuff from the factory.

But I only have to shut my eyes and draw a veil aside to see the room as it was before – taste the dust, watch the spiders in the shadows, hear things ... like the ghosts of ghosts.

It's all there still, behind the veil.

I look over at Mimi's bed, at the soft curve of her

under the eiderdown. The unspoken memories of the past hang forever in the air between us, and because the words remain unsaid, I fool myself into thinking that Mimi has forgotten. Perhaps she has. She was so little then.

But for me, in some small moment of every day, that horrifying summer of four years ago forces itself into my mind to be remembered.

FRIDAY 2nd NOVEMBER

'It's getting so blimmin' dark in the evenings now,' says Auntie Kath, carefully slipping the crumpets off the grill pan onto a plate. I put the butter and strawberry jam on the tray and we go down the hall to the sitting room where Mimi is drawing, her new red exercise book propped up on her knees as she lies back on the settee. She's never been much of a one for drawing before, but she asked Auntie Kath to get her a book when she went shopping.

'Went to the pictures in Daneflete today,' says Auntie Kath, spreading the crumpets with thick butter.

'Go on your own?'

'Not much choice, have I?'

'You could've waited for Dad.'

'Never know when he's going to be around. Can't just hang about on the off chance, can I? Anyway, I like a bit of romance, meself. James Bond is more your dad's cup of tea. I can never work out what's going on in them films – you know, spies and things.'

She puts the tray down on the little table, takes the lid off the jam – 'Want a crumpet, Mimi?'– and plunges in the buttery knife.

Mimi shuts her drawing book, stuffs it behind a cushion and comes over.

The sitting-room curtains ripple a little as the

cold wind outside finds a chink to blow through.

Auntie Kath shivers and goes to the window. She stands there a while, I think in hope, listening for the car, but there is no rumble of an engine coming down The Chase; just the murmur of the telly in the corner and the moaning of the wind in the chimney.

'This bloke in the film,' she says, still with her back to us, 'he wasn't keen on this girl, not really, not like she was on him.'

Auntie Kath is wondering what Dad might be getting up to these few days in London. He was very cagey about why he had to go back, and he's always had an eye for the ladies. She's worried he's got some fancy woman somewhere, because she was his fancy woman herself once.

I look up. 'Come and have the last crumpet,' I call.

She half turns, stiffens, then looks back out.

'Auntie Kath?'

I can see her reflection in the glass, face motionless, eyes fixed on something outside.

'What is it?'

She shudders. 'Nothing . . .' she says.

She comes back to the table, and with shaking fingers reaches for her cigarettes, then changes her mind, picks up the knife and spreads jam quickly over the crumpet.

'You all right?' I ask, licking melted butter off my chin.

'Yeah, fine,' she says, biting in, then taking another chunk before she's swallowed the first. She looks back at the window.

'What's the matter?'

A few seconds go by.

'Nothing – it's nothing,' she says.

Mimi gets up, goes to the window and peers out.

Much later, in the night, I am woken by knocking on the door. In the thick fog of a half-dream I think I am in my bed in Limehouse.

The knocking comes again, still quiet but more insistent.

'Cora!'

I crawl out of bed, go to the door and open it slightly. The landing light is on. It makes my eyes hurt. Auntie Kath stands there in her curlers and pink nylon babydoll pyjamas, the ones with the short frilly knickers that don't do her any favours.

'Cora, was it you?'

'What?'

'Was it you?'

'Ssh.' I look back at Mimi, the light from the landing ceiling lying diagonally across her bed. I step out of the room and close the door behind me. 'What's the matter?'

'Have you been up?'

'Don't be daft. Of course not.'

'You weren't whispering . . . outside?'

'What would I be whispering about? What do you mean – *outside*?'

She glances sideways down the landing towards her bedroom, her eyes wide. 'Outside – outside my window . . .'

'How could I have been outside your window, Auntie Kath? We're upstairs. You must have been dreaming.'

'It – it wasn't dreaming.'

'The wind's getting up. When it's blowing through the trees over the creek, it sounds just like whispering.'

'Maybe.'

'Leave the light on.'

She hesitates. 'I did – the bedside lamp, I mean,' she says. 'I'll – I'll put the main light on an' all.'

'Night-night, then.'

'Night-night.'

When the front door opens, the afternoon air smells of autumn, of Bonfire Night just round the corner.

'Two drop goals!' Dad shouts as he and Pete come in from the rugby. 'Two! In his first tournament for the County! The last one won the ruddy championship! Put the kettle on, Rosie!'

Pete preens in, smelling of mud and sporting a spectacular graze down his face and a half-closed black eye. Mum, cooing and clucking, tries to press his cheek with a cold wet flannel as he sits in the middle of the kitchen holding court, letting excited Pam and round-eyed Terry take turns at wearing his medal while Dad stands proudly by. Pete flaps the flannel away with a sigh, pretending to be all plucky and long-suffering, but I know it's because he wants to flaunt his impressive injuries at school on Monday – wouldn't do to have it all heal too soon.

I go out to the shed with Dennis, who isn't impressed either.

'Blimmin' Saint Peter,' he mutters. 'Dad never came to watch me when I got third in the swimming gala.'

We find a pile of old newspapers to stuff our guy for Bonfire Night. Dad has laid out the fireworks on his workbench and covered them with sacking, all ready for Monday. We can't resist lifting a corner and taking a look.

'What are you doing?'

A rocket almost jumps out of Dennis's hand.

Pam is standing at the door.

'We're getting things for the guy,' I say. 'Come with us and choose a mask at Mrs Wickerby's.'

Pam whoops with glee, then skips great hopping skips around the house and down Fieldpath Road so the bobbles on the ends of her scarf bounce up and down. In the post office she picks out a warty mask with a hooked nose that Mrs Wickerby, the shopkeeper, most probably made herself, looking in the mirror for inspiration.

When we get outside, Dennis puts it on and chases Pam back up the road. 'Ha ha! I'm Guy Fawkes! I'm coming to get you!'

Pam shrieks and shrieks, even though she knows it's only Dennis.

'I always feel sorry for poor old Guy Fawkes,' he says, taking off the mask and looking at it as we near the house, 'getting the most absolutely horriblest death there ever can possibly be.'

'I think the worst thing must be having to watch your own guts being pulled out,' I say, 'and thrown in the fire.'

'You'd think after the hanging you'd be too dead to look.'

'Well, if you were still alive after they burned your innards, you'd definitely have had it after they chopped you up.'

Unfortunately we use the wrong trousers for the guy's legs. Turns out they're Dad's best ones. By the time he notices, we've already cut off the bottoms and stuffed them with balls of newspaper. He shouts till his cheeks go red like apples, and disappears off to the shed until dinner time.

It's a great guy, though, the best ever, maybe because the trousers are so smart. Pete humbles himself to join us, and we pad out an old jumper for the body and Mum sews the top of the trousers to it with her darning needle and some strong thread. She even finds a pair of old holey gloves to stitch on for his hands.

I empty out the old go-cart of wet brown leaves and other rubbish, and drag it down the garden to put the guy in.

CORA

Auntie Kath comes into the kitchen in her coat and takes the big shopping bag off its hook behind the door. Her lips are bright with lipstick and she's put a thick layer of Pan Stik under her eyes to try to hide the dark shadows.

'I'd better go up for some shopping,' she says, 'before they shut. Do you want to come?'

'I was going to do some homework.'

'All right, I'll take Mimi. She can help with the carrying. Will you be here when we get back?'

'Yeah. I said I've got homework.'

'You *will* be here, won't you?'

'Where on earth would I go to, Auntie Kath? I said I've got Maths to do.'

'Ta-ta, then.'

'Ta-ta.'

I hear their footsteps going down the stone passage and the thud of the back door closing behind them.

Through the kitchen window a huge, jagged blood-red streak stretches across the darkening sky like a wound.

I switch on the light, sit at the table and reach down to my school bag for my Maths exercise book, new log book, pencil case and textbook.

We have been here a week, and it's the first time I've been alone in the house.

The clock in the hall chimes like Big Ben at the wrong speed, too high and too fast. The last four strokes, marking the hour, echo off the wooden stairs and ring around the landing.

Then everything goes still.

I stare at the blue cloth cover of my log book, open it, sigh, think maybe I'll make a cup of tea.

Outside, the darkness is deepening.

I think something passes the window.

My heart stops for a moment. I tell myself Auntie Kath and Mimi must have come back for a torch; wait for the back door to open.

'Mimi?' I call, and wait, slide my eyes and turn my head slightly, hold my breath – no sound but a hiss under the silence.

I try and get on with the Maths.

Auntie Kath's affecting everything with her hearing things and seeing things – a bag of nerves and she's making me the same.

But the memories slink in.

The film rewinds.

This place is not like other places.

My eyes flicker up to the window, to the louring sky and the reflection in the glass of the cold, yellow strip light on the kitchen ceiling.

I get up and yank the orange curtains across, so quickly that the right one sticks halfway.

I look up slowly and peep through the gap.

The shadowy garden stretches away to the dark curved gash of the creek. A low mist rolls in towards the house from the marshes.

I tug the curtain closed, reach over to the radio and fumble for the switch.

The Light Programme – a football match. I leave it on, increase the volume.

Is the back door locked?

Where is Auntie Kath? Why aren't they home?

I fill the kettle noisily at the sink, light the gas ring, put the water on to boil, sit back down and take out a pencil. The columns of numbers swim before my eyes and under my running finger – tangents, sines, cosines. I write furiously – anything, hardly bothering to work out the questions.

Steaming water starts to bubble out from under the kettle lid. The whistle starts, rising and rising in pitch till I turn off the gas.

Westminster Chimes tinkle out the quarter while I make myself some tea.

Holding the cup against my bottom lip, I find myself staring at the curtains, as if they are transparent.

There is a lull in the football game.

I can hear something, hold my breath, listen.

The iron ring of the front door knocker is clacking, ever so slightly; lifting then lowering, lifting again.

It must be the wind.

A cheer from the radio. Bert Murray has scored a third goal for Chelsea.

There is no wind.

As the cheering dies down, I hear a scuffle against the door.

Someone is in the porch.

It must be Auntie Kath and Mimi. No – they will come round the back. Nobody uses the front door. We don't even have our own keys for it. There's only the one, hanging on a hook on the wall.

My knees feel hollow. I should get up but I can't move. I can never shake it off, the fear of opening the doors and windows in Guerdon Hall, the sound of long hard nails scratching on the wood in the night.

I hear the dull clatter of metal – the flap of the letter box rising and falling again.

Someone is there. No doubt.

I think to myself it must be the postman.

At half past four on a Saturday afternoon?

We haven't had any post since we came. Perhaps out here it comes much later than it did in London.

Heart thudding, I force myself up out of the chair and into the hall.

There is nothing on the floor – no envelope, no postcard.

I move towards the door, listening.

Towards the top there is a sturdy iron bolt. Slowly I reach up with my thumb, push hard and slide it back.

Swallowing, I take the key from its hook. It scrapes as it turns in the lock.

With both hands, I pull the heavy wooden door open. The rafters under the porch roof are laced with cobwebs and the mossy flagstone floor is piled high with brown leaves blown in from over the creek. As the cold, clammy air seeps inside, a few of the leaves spill onto the carpet.

I shiver.

And catch my breath.

Tied onto the iron ring of the knocker, with red twine, is a bunch of bare twigs.

I gasp, don't know what to do – don't want to touch it, but don't want to leave it hanging on the door.

My eyes sweep to the creek. The bridge is almost hidden by the curls of vapour rising from the water. When are Auntie Kath and Mimi coming back?

My heart thumping wildly, I snatch at the bundle of twigs, pull frantically at the red string, but it's tied with a double knot.

Unnerved, I shut the door, go back to the kitchen and, in a panic, open every drawer searching for the scissors. In the end I grab the breadknife, go back, open the door and clumsily saw at the knot until the twigs fall to the ground. At arm's length I pick the bundle up by the cut string and toss it as far as I can out into the darkness, then slam the door shut and go back to the kitchen.

My tea has gone cold.

I am all fingers and thumbs, snap two matches trying

to relight the gas under the kettle, notice something and look up. A small piece of wallpaper is peeling off near the ceiling.

I can just imagine what Mr Blezzard was thinking: nobody here, doesn't matter if it's shoddy, charge the bloke a fortune, move on to the next job. Or maybe he wanted to finish quickly because he didn't like being in the house. What did he say? *It's put the wind up me, working down here, even in the daylight.*

Please hurry back, Auntie Kath, Mimi.

ROGER

Pete writes the sign on a piece of cardboard with a black crayon – PENNY FOR THE GUY – and off we go down the road pushing the guy in the go-cart.

Outside Mrs Aylott's shop we group ourselves on the pavement under the streetlamp. We know not to go outside Mrs Wickerby's at the post office because she's likely to come out and shout at us for begging, most probably sweeping us off the pavement with her broomstick at the same time.

The sky is darkening. There are few people about.

'Should've come earlier,' Pete says.

We never usually get much. This year's no different.

The guy's arm flops out over the side of the go-cart. I don't bother to tidy him up.

Definitely beginning to feel too old for this.

After a few minutes the shop bell tinkles and a woman comes out looking a bit flustered, with a fair-haired girl of about Terry's age, eight or so. The girl looks in our direction, then whispers something in the woman's ear. The woman grabs the girl by the arm and hurries her over the road to the post office.

The girl turns and looks back at us over her shoulder a couple of times as the woman marches her along.

It's almost dark now, but in the light of the streetlamp the girl looks vaguely familiar, though I can't think where I could have seen her before.

CORA

Auntie Kath takes off her coat, slings it over the back of the chair, then starts to unpack the shopping. Mimi walks past the open door but doesn't come into the kitchen.

'Got some fish fingers for dinner,' Auntie Kath says, her voice slightly brittle. She pushes the packet into the little ice box at the top of the fridge, 'and sausages for to-morrow – oh, and a couple of fireworks for Bonfire

Night, all they had left in the post office. There was these kids on the pavement doing Penny for the Guy, otherwise I'd have forgotten all about it. Mimi wanted sparklers. Lucky they had one last lot.'

The ice-box door doesn't close the first time. Auntie Kath slams it hard with her knuckles, then shuts the fridge with a grunt of irritation.

When she turns, she runs her fingers through the front of her hair. I notice a tight look about her eyes. She picks up her handbag, thumps it down on the table and rummages noisily inside it for her cigarettes.

'What's the matter, Auntie Kath?'

She sits down heavily. The chair legs squeal. 'Flippin' funny people round here,' she says.

'What funny people?' I sit down opposite and begin to move my books back into my bag.

'There was these two women we passed up at the main road,' she says, 'the oddest-looking pair I ever saw – tall, they were, you know, and the old one had this pointy hood on. Honest, it was enough to give me the flaming doodahs. I said "Good evening", as you do, and she mumbled something, but I couldn't quite catch it. And then . . .'

'Then what?'

'Then I carried on, and turned to say a word to Mimi – and realized she wasn't next to me. I looked back, and there she was, stock still in the middle of the blimmin' path, staring at the two of them, and they was just standing there staring back, not ten feet away. I grabbed Mimi and muttered something like "Excuse me, we're in a hurry," and dragged her off. I asked her what on earth she was thinking of, looking at peculiar people, but she wouldn't say a blimmin' thing and hasn't opened her mouth since.'

I look towards the door, hear Mimi moving away down the hall.

'Never had this sort of trouble in London,' Auntie Kath goes on. 'Didn't have no weird people there.'

SUNDAY 4th NOVEMBER

The low mist is clinging to the muddy grass.

I walk down the garden, halfway to the creek where the slow-moving, foamy water is draining out on the ebb tide, then turn back and look at the house.

I think about the bunch of twigs on the front door, about the two women.

The angles of the walls of Guerdon Hall, the window frames and timbers are softening in the thickening grey air.

We were expecting Dad back but he hasn't come.

The house is now in two distinct sections. The ivy has been stripped off the side we are now living in, but a few long trails of clinging stems are left behind and have been painted white, along with the rest of the walls and the wooden framing. To the right of the cobbled yard, the other side of the house is unchanged, the cracked timbers greyish-brown. The ancient leafy walls seem to have sunk even more deeply into the ground than before, and appear now to be attached to the rest of the spruced-up building like an infected boil.

Inside, Auntie Ida's kitchen is on the other side of the locked door at the end of the hall, but its dark, crooked window is along the wall there, set into the old brickwork.

If I screw up my eyes, I can almost see her in her

headscarf behind the leaded diamond panes, filling the heavy cast-iron kettle from the tap over the stone sink, then moving back to set it down on top of the big black stove. For a silly moment, as she crosses in front of the table, I fancy she turns and looks at me, even gives me a little smile. I don't try to be sensible and shake off the small lift this imagining gives me, a shred of comfort in this cheerless place.

My gaze moves down to the bottom of the wall. Below Auntie Ida's kitchen, almost completely under the ground in the old, dark roots of the house, is the other, ancient kitchen, where the leper, Cain Lankin, and the witch, Aphra Rushes, killed Lady Ygurne, the wife of Sir Edmund Guerdon, and their baby son, John. How can I ever forget that room is there? Sometimes I visit it again in unsettling dreams, see the low arch over the fireplace, the thick, grimy chains and hooks hanging from the chimney.

A thread of wind blows across the grass. The mist shifts.

I feel a little shiver on the back of my neck.

I should have worn my gloves.

A movement draws my eye to another window upstairs. A pale moon face appears between our bedroom curtains, a real face – Mimi's, her hair like a fair, hazy ring.

I wave.

She is looking in my direction, slowly raises her hand, then brings it down again. Her eyes shift. Are they fixed on something over my shoulder?

I know there is nothing behind me, just the creek and the empty marshes, but why is there a prickle on my skin, a tingle in the roots of my hair? What is Mimi looking at?

The child has Guerdon's face, his hair, the lift of his chin. I saw him standing at that very casement, the day he and his men hounded Lankin away.

She sees me, sees me as I saw the spirit children – Matty the Boy and Dorcas Oates – as I saw the phantoms in the Bonesmen's house: a glimmer, a change in the substance of the air, a faint likeness in a misted mirror.

She does not turn away.

She sees me because upon her soul is the mark of Cain. She was touched by him, taken by him to the fringes of the half-world, and can never wholly return to this one.

Others did not escape him. Lankin hunted them, feasted on them for his sustenance.

All that stood in his way was a locked door and the rise of the tide – but a locked door can be opened, and the tide goes out . . .

I pull up my collar, turn slightly, and see nothing at the edge of my eye but the water in the creek and the tufted reeds.

'Cora! Cora! Where are you?'

It's Auntie Kath, sounding frantic.

I sprint across the grass, dash across the cobbled yard, through the door and along to the kitchen.

'Auntie Kath. What's wrong?'

'Oh, Cora, where were you? I couldn't find you nowhere.'

'I only went outside for a minute, not to Timbuktu.'

'Sorry. I'm sorry, Cora.' She reaches for her cigarettes.

'Mimi's here,' I say. 'She's upstairs.'

Auntie Kath is quiet for a moment. 'Oh, you know Mimi,' she says. 'Even when she's around it's a bit like you're by yourself, if you get what I mean – no offence.'

She points to the wall. 'Look.'

An entire sheet of wallpaper has rolled down the old plaster and has come to rest in graceful folds across the sink.

'The next one's unsticking an' all,' she says.

'I saw it beginning to go yesterday,' I say, gathering it together. 'What shall I do with it?'

'I dunno – it's too big for the bin,' she says, striking a match. 'Chuck it in the passage. That blimmin' Blezzard bloke must've used cheap paste. Crikey, there's another bit coming down.' She puts her cigarette down on the draining board, climbs onto a chair and starts pulling the paper off the wall.

'Watch your elbow on the shelf,' I say, giving her a

hand. 'Do you think we should phone him – Mr Blezzard? I remember the number from the side of his van.'

'Leave it for your dad to do,' she says. 'Blezzard won't take a blind bit of notice of a couple of females. That's men's business, that is.'

I go down the stone passage and bundle the paper under the sink in the downstairs toilet.

When I get back, Auntie Kath is standing in front of the window blowing out a swirl of smoke. I sit down at the table.

'Look at that fog coming up,' she says, flicking a bit of ash into the sink.

I almost don't want to ask it. 'What . . . what do you think of this house, then?'

She doesn't speak for a while, picks a bit of tobacco off her tongue. 'It wasn't what I thought it was going to be, that's all,' she says. 'Your dad said a big house with central heating, a big garden.'

Auntie Kath was thinking Strand Drive.

She was so excited that first day, getting into the car in London, in her blue 'I'm going up in the world' pillbox hat like Jackie Kennedy's, swingback coat and clicking shoes, waving at the neighbours peeping round the edges of their net curtains, while Dad stowed her huge case and blue-spotted vanity bag in the boot, looking over his shoulder all the time and telling her through gritted teeth to keep it quieter. Her mood began to dampen as we left the city behind, perked up a little as we slowed down to look at Glebe House through the wrought-iron gates, then lowered again as we drove straight past it, down the hill and along The Chase.

When we came to Guerdon Hall, Mimi and I trailed around after Dad as he proudly pointed out to Auntie Kath the things he'd had done in the house, showing off the new furniture and the radiators, ignoring the bleak expression on her face every time she looked out of a window over the wasted garden, the creek, and the empty marshes beyond.

'He said it'd be posh,' she says. 'He said the lawyers had let him have some of the money to do this house up for you and Mimi. We'd all be posh and you was going to go to a posh school with a nice uniform an' all. It wasn't what I expected – this, you know. There's nobody to talk to. And there's, well . . .' Her voice trails off for a moment.

'What?'

Then she adds, 'I – I don't like it here, Cora.'

She puffs out some smoke and joins me at the table. 'Your dad, um, wants to invite them people in the big house for dinner – them people up the hill, that head-master bloke and his missus.'

'Crikey. The Treasures? Why?'

'Dunno. Must be bonkers. Wants me to cook

something posh – you know, French or something – and have it in the other room over there' – she jerks her thumb behind her – 'where he's put that new teak table and all them uncomfy chairs.'

'Can you do French food?'

'Dunno. They've got them volervonts in that fancy grocer's in Lokswood. I think you just warm them up in the oven. Or I suppose I could do a tin of soup, something a bit different. Heinz do a nice minestrone.'

'I think that's Italian.'

'Is it?' Auntie Kath draws nervously on her cigarette. 'See, I'd be no good at it. I'd be a nervous wreck. Don't even know how to put the knives and forks out proper.'

She taps the ash into the ashtray. It's got TAKE COURAGE running round the rim – must have been nicked from the Half Moon in Limehouse.

'It just ain't my sort of place,' she says as another sheet of wallpaper over the door curls down over the lintel and flops onto the floor. 'Oh no, not another blimmin' bit.'

'Dad's going to be mad with Mr Blezzard when he comes back.'

'Better get the stuff out the way so he can't see it the moment he comes in,' says Auntie Kath. 'Where shall we put it all?'

'I put the other lot in the toilet.'

'We can't leave it there,' she says. 'Don't fancy

climbing over a load of paper every time I need to go.'

'We could chuck it in the barn with the other rubbish,' I say. 'Then Mr Wragge can take it away when he comes. Fancy doing it together?'

Auntie Kath gets up quickly and puts a match to the gas under the kettle. 'Tell you what,' she says, avoiding my eyes. 'You go and I'll make us a nice cuppa.'

'I can't carry it on my own.'

'Oh, it'll squash up all right.'

The freezing mist clings to my coat, its moisture crinkling my hair as I walk with a muffled crunch through the gravel round the house. The only other sound is the creak and rustle of the thick crumpled paper in my arms. It is an unsettling quietness, and the air is clammy, with a curious, unpleasant taste, so bitter it makes my eyes water.

The margins of the garden have faded to nothing. I stay near the walls until the wooden struts of the porch appear out of the slowly swirling grey, and I know I must turn towards the creek. As I narrow my eyes, squinting for the edge of the bridge, I tread more lightly on the stones; don't want to make too much noise.

The mud under the bridge cracks.

I shiver, cross carefully, make my way over the old farmyard.

Peering over the mound of paper, I move hesitantly towards the dark, gaping mouth of the barn entrance where the huge door is hanging at an angle, one of its hinges broken off.

Tendrils of mist follow me in, turning to nothing a foot or so inside.

I run my eyes over the humdrum builders' rubbish littering the dirty straw – discarded paint tins, broken-off pieces of kitchen tiles, the ends of carpet grippers and off-cuts of wallpaper – the brown and black squares in the bathroom, the awful zigzags in our bedroom – all waiting for Mr Wragge to get rid of.

After tossing the bundle of paper by a stack of dusty logs under a grubby window in the far wall, I move back and my foot twists over something hard. I bend down and see pieces of broken earthenware half hidden in the straw, like the smashed remains of old jugs, or bottles. I bend down and uncover an intact cup-shaped pottery base. Inside, fused together into a spiky lump, are long rusty iron nails and a tangle of what appears to be coarse brown wool. When I tip it slightly, the lump flops slowly in a thick brown sludge that coats the bottom. I put it to my nose. It smells nasty.

There are so many bits of earthenware on and under the straw, I fetch a long length of wallpaper to spread it all out on. The pieces are coloured a mixture of browns, greys and brick-reds. I guess which bits belong together, and there seem to be the remains of seven, possibly eight earthenware bottles, with swollen, rounded bottoms and narrow necks. Some are nearly nine or so inches tall.

One smaller grey pot is almost complete, just missing its neck, which lies close by. The top is stopped up with a lump of hard wax tightly wrapped around with string.

I shake the pot over the paper. It makes a dull rattle and a couple of bent rusty nails drop out with some pieces of sharp-edged green glass. Behind them, a tangle of brown fibres like chair stuffing sticks in the broken opening. I peer more closely. Swallow. It looks almost like matted human hair. I pull it away from the hole. A little hard yellow thing pops out, about half an inch across, shaped like a crescent moon.

Teasing it out onto my palm, I lift it to my eye.

And gasp.

It's a fingernail clipping.

A rustle.

I look up. Something is at the entrance.

The mist curls around the doorpost like a thin white hand.

Sweat needles my skin.

'Auntie Kath?'

With a sharp intake of breath, I flick the nail away into the straw and stand up, heart hammering.

'Mimi?'

Something rolls across the barn entrance from one

104

side to the other – the bundle of twigs I'd flung away yesterday, still tied with a scrap of red twine.

I blunder out of the barn towards the creek, slide over the slippery bridge and stumble my way round the house to the back door.

MONDAY 5th NOVEMBER

I wait ages for the bus home, so cold my breath streams out white and my toes grow numb.

When it comes at last, I go to the seat in the back corner upstairs, away from everyone else. Looking down, as the frosty evening deepens I catch glimpses of fathers putting the final touches to the bonfires. In one village a fire has been built on a green space surrounded by houses. Several men stand around rubbing their hands, grinning, drinking tea from Thermos flasks, setting out fireworks on a long trestle table.

Out of Lokswood I can see over a row of fencing into back gardens where excited youngsters, in hats and mittens, their faces glowing, are writing in the air with glittering sparklers, shrieking with delight as fiery rockets streak upwards into the star-spattered sky like whistling spears, then burst into flaming balls of blue, red and green. I see columns of white-hot gold and emerald sparks rising, soaring, dying, merrily shooting out dazzling, whirling bolts of silver fire before fizzing away on the grass; bangs, crackles and whizzes; mums coming out of warm kitchens, trays laden with plates of burned sausages and steaming cups of cocoa.

Then the empty blackness beyond Daneflete, seeing only my own face in the window, unnaturally pale under the harsh bus lighting, the brim of my school hat casting a hard shadow above the dark-ringed eyes that peer out into the cold, bleak night.

At last I make out the gleam of the single distant streetlamp that stands outside the Thin Man. I shift in my seat, loop the strap of my school bag over my head and across my chest, press the bell.

The conductor tips his hat as I step off the platform, his last passenger. I watch the bus for a while, its luminous yellow windows moving away in the darkness towards Hilsea. The popping of distant fireworks from Bryers Guerdon rolls over the damp, curling air that smells of smoke and gunpowder.

At first I think the road is deserted, but as I walk towards Old Glebe Lane, I glance up and notice two women standing, still and silent, outside the Thin Man. The streetlamp is casting their slightly elongated shadows across the main road and down the top end of the lane. The taller woman is wearing a peaked hat that juts out like a beak under her hood.

I feel a tightness in my chest as I turn into the road and step for a moment onto the shadows.

Picking out my way in the starlight, I hear footsteps behind me on the uneven surface, and quickly press on until I draw level with Glebe House.

Passing the gloomy mass of the woods on my right, I slacken pace slightly, listening over the thudding of my heart, telling myself the women will go through the wrought-iron gates – that they are simply friends of the Treasures, acquaintances of the Mansells . . .

But over the hissing of the trees still they come, here glancing on a stone, there sidestepping away from a patch of mud.

I move faster, trip as I run blindly down the hill, recover, trip again, arrive at last where the lane divides. I stop for a moment, hearing no sound other than my harsh shuddering breathing.

But something draws my gaze upwards to the brow of the hill.

The two women are standing there, black against the night sky, watching me intently. In long, dark-hooded coats, with sleeves resembling ragged wings under hunched shoulders, they're like a pair of monstrous crows – menacing, and waiting.

At a run I turn into The Chase and lurch and stumble on to Guerdon Hall, not pausing until, with a shaking hand, I push my key into the back-door lock.

Panting, I throw my bag down onto the kitchen floor, my breath rasping sore in my throat.

Auntie Kath glances up from peeling potatoes. 'You been running?'

'Thought I'd be late.'

'Oh, you needn't have worried,' she says. 'We'll have the fireworks after dinner. Go and fetch Mimi. She's watching telly.'

Mimi is on the settee, bent over her exercise book. She looks up and slaps it shut.

'Coming for tea?' I ask, then, 'What are you drawing?'

'Nothing.'

In the kitchen I sit with my back to the window while we eat mash with a bit of cheese on top.

The Light Programme is playing softly in the background.

Then I hear something – a light *tap-tapping* – from outside.

It stops.

Clink-clink.

I glance at Auntie Kath. She has her head down, squashes cheese onto her fork.

Tap-tap-tap.

'Can you hear that funny noise?' I ask.

Auntie Kath puts down her fork and knife, leaves her chair and turns up the volume on the radio. 'You're always the one saying I shouldn't take no notice of funny noises round here,' she says.

I look across at Mimi. Her eyes are lowered as she swallows her mash.

Pam's nose is squashed up against the window of her

new little room in the loft as she and Mum cuddle up together with cups of cocoa and a bag of rainbow drops, looking down excitedly into the garden while Dad finishes his preparations. The last rocket-launcher milk bottle is half buried in the grass and the final Catherine wheel pinned to the overhanging roof of the shed. Dad gives it a final test, spinning it round with his finger.

'Ready for the guy!' he shouts, moving over to the bonfire we've been building for a couple of weeks, mainly from old fallen branches, prunings and cuttings from the garden and wood from the shed, as well as the old kitchen chair Dennis swung on and broke and got a clout for.

Pete and I pull the guy out of the go-cart by its arms, and Dennis and Terry carry the feet. I shine the torch for Dad while he climbs up the stepladder, takes the guy from us and pushes it firmly into position at the top of the bonfire, wedging its arms behind two large branches. He twangs the elastic on the mask to bring the ugly face round to look at us, and tugs down the old felt hat we bought for a halfpenny at the jumble sale in the Scout Hut.

'Here are the spuds,' calls Pete, bringing the potatoes to put in the fire.

'Leave them there by the tree,' Dad directs him, 'and we'll put them in when it dies down a bit later. All right. Move back.'

We stand well clear while he holds the ends of some twisted sheets of newspaper to his lighter. As they catch, he pushes them into the bottom of the bonfire towards a bundle of rags he's already soaked in paraffin and shoved in earlier on a long stick.

At first there's nothing but a feeble smouldering, then *whoosh!* – the rags ignite with a mighty burst of flame right up the middle of the wood.

We cheer. Dennis and Terry whoop and jump about, while Dad, pouring himself a glass of Double Diamond, mutters something about his favourite trousers going up in smoke.

At first, as the flames creep up the wood behind the guy, his arms and legs hold their shape, but as the crackling fire blazes and spreads and eats into his paper stuffing, he begins to writhe and bend. It's as if he's dancing.

The mask remains for a long time, a dark face with a long nose under a fiery felt hat, the empty eye-holes glowing red. But after a while it curls in on itself and burns away into a few light ashes that rise into the air and float off among the trees.

CORA

Mimi and I stand in our coats on the cobbles between

the two wings of Guerdon Hall. Behind us the shaft of light from the open door sends our long shadows swooping down the garden towards the creek, which is all that separates us from the bleak, deserted marshes, now swallowed up by the black night.

I can't stop my eyes going to the corner of the building, straining to peer into the darkness, running along the dark margin of the garden where the freezing water laps against the mud, searching the shadows for any movement. Did the women follow me down? Are they watching us?

Auntie Kath, headscarf tied under her chin, excitedly lights a match and puts the flame to the end of Mimi's sparkler, which flares into life, shooting out its brilliant little spangles into the chilly night air. I light mine from Mimi's, then Auntie Kath sets hers going, and we swirl our names in glowing red trails into the dark until the packet is used up.

Auntie Kath goes out onto the grass, the torch glaring in front of her, the soil sucking at her narrow heels. She stoops down, scoops out a bit of earth with a kitchen knife, then pushes in a two-inch-high cone optimistically called Mount Etna.

'You got the matches, Cora? Hold the torch for me and I'll get this lit.'

I take the box over. Auntie Kath strikes one and it splutters into flame. She bends and touches the flare against the twist of blue paper until it begins to fizzle red.

'Quick! Quick!' she giggles.

I run back to Mimi with Auntie Kath hanging onto my arm; we all snuggle together and wait in suspense. For a moment I almost forget the women on the hilltop.

Little Mount Etna splutters out one feeble, sizzling spurt of sparks, then dies.

Our laughter echoes off the walls of the cobbled yard.

The Roman candle is much more impressive, crackling into the air, six inches high, one foot, then two, a fountain of blazing light. *Bang!* Out bursts a golden star. *Bang!* Then another. *Bang!* And another. The grass, the weedy beds, the old tree stumps glow silver bright.

The firework collapses into a long hissing tongue of fire and smoke.

'Come on, girls, let's go in now. I could do with a fag,' calls Auntie Kath. When I look round, I see that she has been picking up the spent sparklers and is holding them in a fan in her hand. I glance back. Mimi is facing away from the house, her head moving slowly from one side to the other as if she is searching the shadowy garden. Then her gaze seems to settle just beyond the empty cardboard tube sticking up out of the grass, the remnant of the Roman candle.

'Mimi, it's finished.' I put my arm round her shoulder and lead her towards Auntie Kath.

The wind springs up a little, sending drifts of fallen leaves across the cobbles.

Clink-clink, clink-clink.

We stop. Look up.

Clink, clink, clink.

Hanging above us, from nails in the wall above the lintel, are a few lengths of red twine, and knotted to the end of each one is a small white-painted stone with a hole through its middle. As they sway on their strings, the little stones knock against each other.

Clink-clink.

'What the bloody hell's going on now?' Auntie Kath cries in a burst of anger. 'What bloody joker's stuck them bloody things up there?'

She stands on her tiptoes and tries to catch hold of one, but she can't reach and swipes at empty air.

With a grunt, heels clicking, she storms off down the stone passage.

Mimi stares up at the little stones, turns back to the dark garden, then up at the stones again.

Auntie Kath comes back with a kitchen chair, rests it dangerously on the uneven cobbles – 'Hold this steady, will you, Cora?' – and begins to climb up, snatching at the red strings and yanking them down.

'I think we should leave them there,' Mimi says.

'What! You must be ruddy joking!' Auntie Kath flings

the stones away onto the grass, where they land with a dull plop, one by one.

I feel a gloved hand on my sleeve, glance down. Mimi is looking up at me with an odd expression.

'Can't we leave just one?' she asks.

But Auntie Kath won't stop until they have all been pulled down and thrown away.

She marches back down the stone passage with the chair, and I push Mimi inside in front of me.

Just as I am closing the door, I hear another sound, but I'm not sure if it's the sighing of the reeds as they move with the wind on the far bank of the creek, or if someone is whispering in the garden.

With a shiver I follow Mimi down the passage, along the hall and into the kitchen.

Auntie Kath is sitting under the harsh strip light, still in her coat and headscarf, rubbing her forehead with an unlit cigarette between her fingers.

'You all right?' I ask nervously.

She looks up. 'What do you think?' she says. 'Course I'm not bloody all right. What sort of ruddy place is this, Cora? Close the curtains, Mimi.'

Mimi takes a curtain in either hand and begins to pull them slowly towards each other. In the last moment before they come together, she peers out through the gap into the darkness.

TUESDAY 6th NOVEMBER

In that drowsy moment just before the alarm rings I think Auntie Kath is knocking at the door again, but it's the wind whining in the chimney, bobbing at the plasterboard pinned across the fireplace. The radiator sends out its feeble heat into a crisscross of freezing draughts.

As I get into my uniform, quickly in the bitter cold, the sound of the radio booms up the stairs from the kitchen, waking Mimi, who sits up in bed, dazed, rubbing her eyes then her arms for warmth. Knotting my tie, I clatter down the stairs.

The music is unbearably loud. The cups are chinking together on their hooks on the shelf, the empty milk bottles rattling on the stainless-steel draining board. I reach over and turn off the radio.

'Blimey, Auntie Kath, are you going deaf?'

'I was listening to that,' she says, staring out of the kitchen window, loose threads hanging from the cuffs of her blue candlewick dressing gown, twisting a half-smoked butt into a saucer where there are already enough squashed cigarettes to supply a whole ship of sailors.

She fumbles in the packet for another and lights it while the sparks still smoulder on the tip of the one before. 'I don't like it quiet,' she mutters.

'Is it the noise of the wind? Does it bother you?'

She turns her head towards me. I am shocked. Her skin is pasty and her eyes slightly bloodshot, surrounded by deep dark orbits. She half opens her mouth, then shuts it and looks back at the garden.

'Didn't you sleep?' I ask.

But she doesn't answer, just continues to gaze out of the window.

I have no substance. I need flesh and bone, hands, feet and fingers for my purpose.

This woman is no use to me. She will not yield. The dying lights are not on her.

'. . . led to the Great Reform Act of 1832 . . . abolition of the rotten boroughs . . . parliamentary reform . . . repeal of the Corn Laws . . .'

Heads bent, weary, our pens scratch on and on as we write in our exercise books from Mr Heygate's endless, mind-numbing dictation.

'. . . Lord Russell's reform bills of 1851 and 1854 rejected . . .'

Under the monotonous drone of his voice is a shuffle of sounds – knuckles cracking somewhere near the door, a long sigh to my right, Neil Preston's cat-like sneeze, me yawning.

Then a moment of unexpected joy.

'Snow, sir! Look sir, it's snowing!'

A few boys rise excitedly up from their chairs, stretching their necks.

'Sit down! You've all seen snow before! Sit down, Foster! The Second Reform Act of 1867 . . . householders with twelve months' residency . . .'

I am sitting under the window with my left hand resting, almost unbearably hot, risking third-degree burns, or chilblains at the very least, on the wide metal curves of the ancient iron radiator next to my desk. I look up at the thick grey sky beyond the clear upper windows. The snowflakes fall out of it like small dark dots, then grow fatter, whiter and lazier as they approach the ground before disappearing behind the frosted glass of the lower sashes, where I can barely see them pass.

'Third Reform Act 1884 . . . two million labourers given the vote . . .'

I miss a bit. My brain's gone dead.

Can't think why she's in my head all of a sudden – that girl who came out of Mrs Aylott's with her mum when we were doing Penny for the Guy on Saturday. It was quite dark. The light from the shop was behind her. It was her hair, fair and fluffy, and the way she kept looking back at us over her shoulder. Mimi had hair like that.

The snow thickens as Mr Heygate's dreary voice moans on and on.

Surely it wasn't Mimi.

I feel my palm go moist under my pen. My heart begins to hammer too fast.

'Jotman!' Mr Heygate snaps. I jump. 'You've been staring out of that window for the last five minutes! Detention. After school. Outside the staff room at four o'clock!'

'Oh, *sir.*'

CORA

I can hear it from The Chase. By the time I reach the bridge, *Jailhouse Rock* is blaring out from the house, almost as loud as the squalling wind that scatters snowflakes in all directions.

I rush round the end wall. Even the windows seem to be vibrating.

I stand at the back door, fumbling in my pocket for my key; then, in the space between songs, hear feet running down the stone passage.

'Oh, thank goodness you're here,' Mimi cries, flinging open the door. 'Auntie Kath won't blimmin' well turn it down. I used to like Elvis Presley an' all, but it's the third time that LP's been on since we got back from school.'

I stride quickly along the passage and into the hall, tossing my hat and bag down on the carpet by the staircase.

'I think she must've had music on all day,' Mimi says. 'There's records all over the place.'

The sitting room is hazy with smoke. *Heartbreak Hotel* is now blasting its way out of Auntie Kath's red mock-crocodile-skin Dansette record player, which stands with its lid up on the small table. Auntie Kath herself is sitting on the floor, her wide pink skirt spread out in a circle around her, holding a lighted cigarette in one hand and the Take Courage ashtray in the other. Looking up from their scattered LP covers are Tommy Steele, Russ Conway and a host of other Auntie Kath favourites.

I pick my way carefully over the records and turn the volume knob so far down that poor Elvis sounds as if he's singing outside in the garden.

'Oh, hello, Cora – you're home, then,' Auntie Kath says, standing up and smoothing down her skirt, as if everything is all perfectly normal.

'Are you all right?' I say. 'Do – do you want me to do tea? Did you go to the shops?'

'What? The shops?' She rubs her forehead, and in her other hand the ashtray tips, spilling ash down her skirt.

'There was a bit of bacon in the fridge yesterday,'

I say, taking it off her, 'and some eggs. I'll go and get started.'

'It's all right, love,' she says, flicking off the ash. 'I'll do it.'

Under the bright light in the kitchen, Auntie Kath looks washed out, the vivid lime-green of her cardigan showing up the dark crescents under her eyes. She clumsily drops large pieces of eggshell into the pan with the eggs, and almost burns the fried bread while I'm making us a pot of tea.

When we go to bed, Auntie Kath comes up too, and won't let me switch off the landing light.

Music comes wafting down the landing from the clock radio on Auntie Kath's side of the bed. I've never known her play it at night before. I drift off to sleep with Bobby Vee singing *Take Good Care of My Baby*.

WEDNESDAY 7th NOVEMBER

'Enter.'

My hands shake as I push open the door.

The room is long and narrow, with no lamp lit to warm the cold grey light.

Rows of leather-bound books to the ceiling. Dark oak filing cabinets. Religious pictures of saints I don't know – martyrs dying serenely in a haze of holy radiance.

Through the glass of the small sash window the snow falls gently on the netball courts, melting on the wet tarmac before it has a chance to cover the lines.

Madame Mary St Bernard – white tunic, black scapular, white wimple, black veil – rises tall out of her chair behind the desk in the shadows at the far end of the room.

The huge silver and ebony rosary beads looping from her belt to the floor click against each other as she stands.

My hand coats the doorknob with a film of moisture.

'Good morning, Cora. Please close the door.'

The walls are so uncomfortably high that the foot of the large crucifix hanging behind the nun is still a good few inches above her head.

'Good morning, Miss – Mother—'

'*Madame*. Come forward.'

'Madame – sorry, Madame.'

In their long walk to the desk, my soft indoor shoes

make barely a sound on the hard wooden floor. When I get there, I bob an awkward curtsey, having been warned I must never forget that the headmistress is the sister – or cousin, is it? – of a duke – or an earl . . . I don't remember.

My eyes flicker up, catch hers, then drop down to the parquet. My hands are now so sticky, I wipe them on the back of my gymslip.

'Mother Anselm and I have been discussing your progress,' Madame Mary St Bernard says in her clipped voice.

'Yes, Madame,' I say, my eyes fixed on the floor.

'You have been here at the Abbey for a week now, and I have here a report on your general progress and effort and a list of your marks.'

'Yes, Madame.'

'Even taking into account the fact that you are new to the school, they are nowhere near the standard we expect.'

I swallow, feeling sweat moisten my fringe.

The nun shuffles papers. 'Your weekend Maths homework was particularly poorly done. Can you explain this?'

I am hunched over my Maths book in the kitchen table in Guerdon Hall, half listening to the football match on the radio, hearing the scuffling in the porch, throwing away the bunch of twigs.

I say, 'I ain't – sorry, *haven't* done a lot of that stuff before, Mother – Madame.'

'Your father was most anxious to tell me how diligent you were. This was one of the reasons I agreed to take you mid-term. That, and the fact that your mother is – is in an asylum. Incidentally, I have kept that information to myself. It isn't the sort of thing you would want bandied about, I think.'

I stare at the herringbone wooden blocks around my shoes.

'I can assure you,' she goes on, 'there are many girls who would give their eye teeth to enjoy the education you are privileged to be receiving within these walls.'

I glance up at her. Swallow. Look down.

'I am also given to understand that you are making no effort whatsoever to get on with your classmates.' I hear the papers twitch. 'The words I have here are *sullen, morose, unfriendly*.'

She waits for me to take this in.

'Is anyone being unkind to you?'

'No, Madame.'

'I am writing to your father about all this.'

My heart flutters with alarm.

'Look at me, Cora.'

My eyes flick from the desk leg to the leather blotter, to her face. Her expression is unreadable, as cool as the wall behind her.

'I understand you have a younger sister?'

'Yes, Madame. Mimi – Elizabeth. Sorry, she's Elizabeth.'

'Well, if I'm expected to take Elizabeth in the future, as things stand now that would be a vain hope. You have until the end of term to improve this situation. If things remain as they are, I will have no choice but to ask your father to find you another school after Christmas. I will be writing all this in my letter. Do you understand?'

'Yes, Madame.'

My legs go weak. A letter to Dad. I swallow, slide my eyes to the bookshelves.

The volumes stand perfectly vertical: *The Cistercian World: Monastic Writings of the Twelfth Century*, *The Life of Bernard of Clairvaux*.

Four whole shelves of *Sorrel and Brassock's County Records*. Brown leather spines. Gold lettering.

Vol. 3: Wrayness Hundred inc. Merham St Michael & Merham St Peter, 1498–1600.

Vol. 11: Lokswood Hundred inc. Corsey Island, Longcreek, Gitting & Whitestone, 1710–1807.

Vol. 20: Daneflete Hundred inc. South Fairing, North Fairing, Bryers Guerdon & Hilsea, 1409–1519.

Vol. 21: Daneflete Hundred inc. South Fairing, North Fairing, Bryers Guerdon & Hilsea, 1520–1625.

'Cora – are you paying attention?'

'Yes, Madame.'

She glances at the books, then back at me.

A small moment of warmth.

'Do you like History?'

'Yes, Madame. I'd rather have done it than Geography, but there wasn't no more room in the class – me coming late an' all.'

My eyes steal their way back to *Vol. 21: Daneflete Hundred . . . 1520–1625.*

Again she follows my gaze. 'Do you live in that area?' she asks, then runs her finger down a paper on the desk. 'Ah yes, Bryers Guerdon. You must be our most distant pupil.'

'What – what's a Hundred please, Madame?'

'It's an old administrative district, Cora, somewhere in size between a parish and a county. We are most privileged to have a complete set of *Sorrel and Brassock's* here in the Abbey. The only other whole set is in the County Archives.' She moves over to the bookshelf and places a long slender hand on one of the spines. 'These books are most valuable, containing copies of a wealth of historical documents, important letters and deeds, trial records, that sort of thing. Hardly a week goes by when I am not contacted by an academic or historian requesting permission to resource material in one or other of these volumes.'

She strides back to the desk.

'From time to time we even afford sixth formers who

are studying A-Level History the privilege of accessing these books under supervision. It is a great honour, and a measure of the quality of the education we provide here at Wrayness Abbey.'

My eyes linger on *Vol. 21* . . .

'Which reminds me,' she continues. 'A week from today, Wednesday the fourteenth, we have Prizegiving. You know what that is, I take it?'

I return to her still, pale face.

'No, Madame.'

'Why am I not surprised? It is a ceremony in which our high achievers are awarded prizes for conspicuous attainment and scholarship. Traditionally girls in the fifth form who are not members of the school choir act as stewards, showing guests to their seats and handing out programmes . . . Cora?'

'S-sorry, Madame. Sorry.'

'I have already added your name to the list of stewards, Cora. It will begin at half past seven and your uniform must be spotlessly clean and pressed, shoes polished, hair neat and tidy. I expect your complete commitment and shall be watching you most carefully. Is that clear?'

'Yes, Madame.'

'And I would prefer it if you do not engage in conversation with guests; in fact, do not open your mouth at all. Just smile and indicate seats by gesture. Lazy enunciation is unbecoming in an Abbey girl, and other parents may be shocked to hear we have a pupil who speaks as you do. From now on you should make an effort to improve your diction. Take note of the pronunciation used by the other girls in your class and practise at home until you have rid yourself of those appalling consonants and ugly vowels. You are dismissed.'

'Yes – yes, Madame.'

She remains standing, still and upright behind her desk, while I make my way to the door, my face hot with humiliation. I fumble for the doorknob, slippery in my clammy fingers, turn it at last, and sidle into the corridor, mercifully empty so I am spared the shame of anyone seeing my flushed cheeks.

Half a minute after I leave Madame Mary St Bernard's study, the dinner bell clangs throughout the building, from staircase to classroom, from gym to cloakroom.

Before the corridors fill with rushing feet, I hurry out through the nearest door into the snowy playground and head round the back of the refectory to the small yard outside the entrance to the kitchens, where they keep the huge metal bins.

It stinks of cabbage and chocolate sponge.

I lean my head against the brick wall in the corner, out of sight. My stomach churns. I feel dizzy, and hungry. The snow dissolves the moment it touches the hard ground, but clings like sugar to the tufts of grass sticking up around the bottom of the walls.

As the headmistress's words buzz and spin in my head, I try desperately to swallow down the lump rising in my throat, to squeeze my eyes so the tears won't come. But I can't stop them. They spill out, stream down and bite into my cheeks as they cool in the icy air. I have no handkerchief, pull up the hem of my pullover and scrub my eyes and nose on it, then rub my freezing hands hard together.

There is a clattering noise. The green door is pushed open by the back of a plump woman in a white overall and netted cap. She struggles with two buckets full of slops.

Quickly I wipe my eyes with my palms, lower my head and turn away. She empties the buckets into one of the big bins, then mutters, 'You'll catch your death out 'ere, love.'

As the door clunks shut behind her, I notice, through watery eyes, the crates stacked nearby, full of the small milk bottles given out at playtime. Among the empties are a couple left unopened, still full. I take one from the crate, brush the powdery snow off the cap, press it in, then gulp down the icy milk so fast it hurts. I put the empty bottle back and wipe my face again.

My stomach aches with crying.

The snow eases off, but the cold has crept through my pullover and under my blouse to my quivering skin. I blow on my numb fingers and stamp my wet, throbbing feet in their soft indoor shoes.

I wait and wait, tense and shivering, until I can bear the cold no longer.

Slipping round the corner, I sneak into the cloakroom on the other side of the refectory, push my outdoor shoes on over my wet stockings and pull on my coat, scarf and hat. Skirting round the high playground wall, I open the heavy wrought-iron gate and head up the road to the bus stop.

Beyond the shoreline at Wrayness, the dark, heaving waves are tipped with ragged white curls. Overhead, steel-grey clouds threaten more snow. I try to imagine what that might look like, snowflakes whirling over the sea, but the bus turns inland and I don't find out.

I think of the other girls settling down to afternoon lessons, searching in their desks for the right exercise books – blue Maths, pink English, or green Science . . . ah, yes, it's Wednesday afternoon – yellow French, followed by brown Geography. Desk lids will be clunking down, the books spread open next to the shiny-lidded fountain pens, sharpened pencils, wooden rulers and smooth, clean rubbers.

In the bleak fields between Daneflete and Bryers Guerdon, the snow has settled in the hollows between the lumps of mud or collected around the tufts of wiry grass. It is much colder here than at Wrayness.

I get off the bus and walk towards the turning.

A few white flakes fall gently on my navy coat sleeves and touch my shoes before melting. By the time I reached Glebe House, the snow is dusting my coat and must be making quite a layer on the crown and brim of my hat.

Glebe House stands solid and confident behind the black railings of the tall gate, protected by sturdy trees and bushes, the snow already rounding and smoothing them like iced cakes.

I make my way down the hill, stand where the road parts, and look down The Chase.

The large flakes form a flimsy curtain, parting to reveal the way to Guerdon Hall, then drifting back together.

As I move on, my mind cloudy with worry about the headmistress's letter, I see something blue coming in my direction, hear someone walking awkwardly, in the wrong footwear for the weather. I draw back slightly along the track to All Hallows and stand still as still, half hidden by the hedgerow.

It's Auntie Kath, in her shiny court shoes, ankles twisting all over the place on the slippery stones. She must be going up to North Fairing to collect Mimi from school.

For a second I think I might go and join her, but she'll ask why I'm home early, and will see that I've been upset – all too difficult, so I stay where I am and watch her. Then, as she passes quite close to me and I see her more clearly, I'm glad I didn't come out. She's holding one of Dad's big hankies up to her face, looking nervously all about her, making whimpering noises, and crying.

Quietly, slowly, I move back and back again, keeping close to the hedge, watching Auntie Kath making her awkward way towards the hill, hoping she's too upset to notice my footprints. I turn and see I have come quite a way down the track. It is narrower than I remember; the light covering of snow clings to the grass spreading into the road, softening the edges so it's hard to tell where the verges begin.

There is no sound but the dull creak of my shoes as I walk towards the church.

The lychgate is smothered in a jumble of purplish brambles, stinging nettles and thorny briars, on which a few shrivelled rosehips still hang. A vicious barrier of barbed branches has grown up where the old wooden gates used to be, so dense I could not have passed between the pillars. Oddly, a young tree has sprung up in the middle of them; its thin arching branches, still bearing tight bunches of red berries, scramble under the roof, little by little pushing up the mossy tiles with their tiny probing shoots. I take one of the thicker boughs in my fingers and shake it. The snow wafts from it like a cloud of flour through a sieve.

I walk on and try to open the metal gate to the church-yard, having to push at it over and over, wetting my chilly hands. At last it gives. The grass has grown quite tall under the lower bar and it showers my shoes with snow as it springs back.

Further up, the path near the church porch is a stack of bricks and a heap of sand. A few of the bricks have tumbled down and the dull orange sand has blown about and spread itself over the flattened grass and among the tombstones. A rough stake and wire fence runs from the corner of the tower wall across the entrance to the porch and down the length of the build-ing. A crudely painted wooden sign is tied onto the fence with a piece of frayed string – DANGER KEEP OUT.

The falling snowflakes start to thin.

I glance to my left. In the Guerdon plot is an upright gravestone overhung by the branches of the old elder tree. The gravestones and crosses round about are lean-ing, half buried, knotted with ivy, unreadable, but this stone is plain grey and starkly new, only matching the others with its capping of light snow.

I stare at the stone for quite some time, then step over the low wrought-iron railing, and approach it through the long grass. The snow is slowly melting, leaving a thin layer of icy water over the wet leaves, brown, golden and red, that have settled against the stone.

I am utterly unprepared for the blinding shock of sudden grief that engulfs me at the sight of Auntie Ida's name. With a groan, I drop to my knees on the cold wet grass, and find myself choking and shuddering, as flood upon flood of tears overflow my eyes and course down my cheeks, unchecked and unwiped, through my trembling fingers and onto the grass. I would not have believed I had so many more tears left in me. I wrap my arms around the gravestone, as if the hard, unyielding slab were Auntie Ida herself.

. . . This then, is Ida Guerdon, the woman who wrenched him back through the portal of the lychgate and ripped him out of the world.

I am drawn to the flesh that last touched his, find my way into this grave, squeeze in with the hump-backed coffin flies through the fine cracks in the wood of her casket, and see her lying there, her waxy shell unspoiled by the worms and burnished beetles. If it were not for the stillness of the silken veil that covers her face, I might have thought she was only under the spell of sleep in this wet, uncorrupting mud, and that it was the weak, distant murmur of her blood that I sensed on the air beyond the hammering of theirs.

But no blood runs in these cold limbs.

So peaceful is she that I lament, because she is clearly at rest, while I am not.

And so it must be – as long as Guerdon hearts continue beating – one now so close that I can hear its drumming against the stone above.

As I cling there, wave after wave of half-smothered memories pour into my head in sharp, livid colours and with harsh sounds. In the bitter-cold November church-yard I seem to feel again the intense heat of that terrifying summer, see Long Lankin shriek for the last time, see the little ghostly children and, kneeling beside Auntie Ida's motionless body, not more than a couple of feet from the spot where she lies now, look up to see Roger wiping tears from his filthy cheeks with the heel of his hand.

I remember his face at last.

I gaze in horror at my reflection in the piece of mirror wedged behind the water heater over the sink. Pete comes through the kitchen door and hoots with laughter. Dennis and Terry run in to swell the merry gathering, and they all stand there, roaring with mirth.

After dinner Mum decided to get her clippers out. Unfortunately she can't cut hair as well as she cooks fish pie. She only does one style, the Jotman Conscript – short back and sides and a bit off the top – with clippers so ancient they pull at the roots and make your eyes water. We all sport the Conscript, even Dad, but Dennis has a double crown and a cowlick, and no matter what Mum does, it always looks as if a cat has gone to sleep on his head.

Pete went first. Afterwards, he threw the old towel off his shoulders and emerged smooth and sleek as a matinée idol. Pete always manages to look spruce regardless of anything Mum does. I shook his hair off said towel, wrapped it tightly around my neck and perched on the stool of doom.

'Everyone's wearing it longer now, Mum,' I pleaded as she came towards me brandishing the clippers. 'Can you not take so much off this time?'

'I can only do short with these,' she said.

'What about the scissors?'

'The paper scissors are a bit blunt. Wait and I'll get my dressmaking shears.'

Ten minutes later and I look like a monk. Thank God she didn't go the whole hog and give me a tonsure while she was at it.

Pam doesn't laugh, bless her, but just reaches up and touches the shorn ends at the back.

'Liked you best before,' she says.

Wish I didn't have to go to school tomorrow.

CORA

My key won't open the back door. It's bolted on the inside.

Through the windows every light is blazing with a harsh glare.

I bang on the wood with my fists. 'Auntie Kath! Mimi!' I shout. 'Let me in! It's me, Cora!'

I wait.

Nothing.

'Mimi! Where are you? Mimi?'

I run back round the house to the sitting-room window. The curtains are roughly pulled across, but there's an untidy gap of a few inches where they haven't been completely drawn. I cup my face with my hands and press it to the glass.

I can see Mimi's fair head above the back of the settee, facing away from me, looking at the doorway, the padded folds of her eiderdown around her shoulders.

I bang on the window.

A jolt of fright shoots through her body. I hear a gasp.

'Mimi! It's me!'

She turns in my direction, her eyes wide with terror.

When she sees my face, she pushes off the cover, jumps down off the settee, runs towards the window and jerks back the curtain, her eyes filling with tears.

'Oh, Cora . . .'

'Let me in! Unbolt the door!'

I run back round the house, hear the bolt being drawn back, thrust my key in the lock and push open the door.

Mimi throws her arms around me, burying her face in my coat.

The house is so bitterly cold, our breath streams out white along the stone passage. I bend and cup Mimi's chin in my hands.

'What's Auntie Kath doing? Where is she?' My teeth begin to chatter.

'She's gone,' Mimi says.

'What do you mean *gone*?'

'You know, like she used to do sometimes back in London. She came to collect me from school, and when we got back here there was this car waiting – a taxi to take her to the station, with . . . with all her stuff. She's left a note for you – in the kitchen.'

'Mimi, this is serious. What are we going to do?'

'Will she come back, like she always did in Limehouse – you know, when Dad and her used to squabble?'

I avoid the question.

'Why's it so freezing in here?' I say. 'Has she taken the blimmin' boiler an' all?'

'The radiators are stone cold.'

I run my hand along every one I pass until I get to the kitchen – hoping, I suppose, to find one of them warm. Auntie Kath's note is propped up on the table against the sugar bowl.

Dear Cora,

Gone back to London. I'm really sorry. I hung around for you as long as I could. I didn't want to leave Mimi all by herself but I had to get the train and the taxi man was charging me for the waiting. There's bread in the bread bin and some cheese. Your dad's supposed to be coming back tonight. Tell him sorry but I'll go up the wall if I stay here any more.

Love Auntie Kath xxx

P.S. I think the pilot light's gone out in the boiler. I took the front off and had a look but I didn't know how to fix it.

Auntie Kath always came back before. She couldn't stand being with her mother for too long, and we were only round the corner. She'd only be gone for a day or so. I'd come home and she'd be doing dinner, as if nothing had happened. But this is different. She and Dad haven't had a scrap, and we're a long way from London. In the sitting room there's a gap on the small table where her record player stood, and her stack of records has disappeared from the top of the sideboard. She never ever took all her stuff with her when she left us before in London – never.

Mimi and I watch television squashed together under the eiderdown, our cheeks and noses numb, but I don't take in anything that's happening on the little grey screen. The worry wriggles around worm-like in my stomach.

At half past eight we hear the crunch of Dad's feet on the gravel outside. The back door opens. An icy gust of air sweeps down the hall.

He will be so angry.

I feel Mimi go taut. I can't stop my own limbs stiffening.

'Bloody hell, it's freezing in here,' he says, coming in, rubbing his hands together. 'Blimey, the pair of you look like a camel with two humps under that thing.' He reaches out and feels the radiator. 'Flaming Nora, what's happened to the heating? Has Auntie Kath been fiddling with the bloody boiler? And what's she done for dinner? I'm starving.'

I swallow. Mimi blurts it out – the heating's broken down and Auntie Kath's gone back to London – then she pulls the eiderdown up over our heads so we're dark and padded while he shouts and thumps his fist against the back of the armchair.

For the rest of the evening Dad spends a lot of time crouching in front of the boiler, cursing the pilot light and Auntie Kath. No sooner does the little flame flare into life than it goes out again. Three times he gets up and tries ringing her on the telephone, but judging by the swearing and the flinging down of the receiver into its cradle, she either isn't there or doesn't answer.

The fourth time he speaks to somebody.

'Tell her to bloody ring me. What do you mean *Miss World*'s on the telly? Sod bloody *Miss World*. Tell Kath to bloody well get up off her backside and explain herself. And don't let her pretend she's forgotten the ruddy number. It's North Fairing 248. Write it down – no, not bloody 348 – 248! Put your hearing aid in when you answer the blasted phone!'

Later, Mimi climbs into bed with me but we can't sleep for the cold, even jammed together. We keep our uniforms on as we can't bear to get undressed, though I make Mimi take off her tie in case she strangles herself by accident in the night.

As I lie there, sleepless, my worm of worry becomes a great writhing, suffocating snake. What if Auntie Kath doesn't come back and Dad keeps staying away?

'There's a bit of the curtain open,' comes Mimi's little voice from out of the darkness.

'For heaven's sake, it's only a tiny gap – and move your blinkin' feet away. They're like ice blocks.'

'Please, Cora, please close it.'
'Mimi, it's freezing out of bed.'
'Please.'

I watched her coming and going over the bridge with her bags and boxes, slipping in her hard little shoes. The man stood impatient, grudgingly helped her, then took her away. She peered through the cloudy glass as she moved off, wiped a dark, wet smear with her glove, turned her face to where I was, misty against the scattered snow, and narrowed her eyes . . .

FRIDAY 9th NOVEMBER

Exhausted, frozen, muscles stiff and aching from shivering, I force myself to get up and pull the curtains aside. They feel damp. Swirly ferns of grey frost curl across the inside of the glass. I blow on the leafy patterns with my icy breath and rub them away with cold, stiff fingers.

Turning, I notice that the plasterboard panel covering the fireplace has come away on the left. I pull at it and the small pins on the right-hand side pop out one by one. I drag the whole panel sideways, and there is the old brick-lined hearth, just as I remember it.

Some of the little bricks at the bottom have been taken out and are lying in a pile at the back, leaving a dark jagged hole, as if something that was buried there has been taken out, but the hole not filled in again.

I lean the plasterboard up against the wall.

'It's coming off the ceiling an' all.'

Mimi is leaning against her pillow, each breath a spreading cloud.

A furious cursing starts up downstairs. I begin to tremble. Has the letter arrived from Madame Mary St Bernard? I creep out onto the landing and lean over the banister rail. A frantic hammering echoes up the staircase. I blow out with relief. Dad is trying to nail the boarding, with its wallpaper still half attached, back over the panelling under the staircase.

'What's going on?' I call down.

'Bloody hold this!' he shouts, his hair tumbling over his forehead.

I run down, spread my hands out over the panel and push hard against it. Dad is using a long three-inch nail to pin the corner down, but with each stroke of the hammer, it seems to bounce back out again.

'What's the bloody matter with it?' he grunts. 'Hold it better! Don't let it slip about!'

'Try a different place,' I suggest.

'I've tried all over the flippin' thing!' he yells, dealing the chipboard such a hefty kick at the bottom that it slides off the panelling, ripping the wallpaper even more. 'I'm going to have to bloody well start again,' he says. 'Help me lift it up.'

'Dad, I've got to go to school.'

In an explosion of temper, he punches at the board with his fists then kicks it twice more with his right foot. The small thread of paper tears completely and the panel falls forward, wedging itself against the opposite wall. In a burst of rage, he pulls it free, stands it up against the wall, then kicks it again.

My eyes slide to the panelling. There they are, the marks of the past – the long, deep scratches made by Lankin's nails when Roger, Pete, Mimi and I were in the priest hole under the stairs; the jagged gashes in the wood where Auntie Ida splintered it with the axe – and over them Mr Blezzard's bit of rough patching-up with some strips of ply.

When I get back from school, Dad has got the boiler working, apparently with a great big kick. He's in the sitting room, restless, tapping the wooden arm of the chair with his fingers.

'Are you all right, Dad?'

'No, I'm not all right,' he says. 'I'm flamin' mad with Kath, just waltzing off like that. Won't even ruddy well come to the phone, and her bloody mother's pretending to be deaf.'

'She – she's always come back before,' I say.

'Look, I'm going to pop up to London, first thing in the morning, to bring her back. You'll be all right with Mimi for a day or so, won't you.'

'I expect so.'

He reaches out from the chair, I think to put his arm around my waist, but I sidestep and he drops it. He coughs awkwardly. 'You know, er, you know I think the world of you and Mimi, don't you?'

I stare at the floor.

'I . . . er, I know you didn't want to come out here,' he adds.

The light from the table lamp shines across the scar running down the length of his right cheek, a thread of shadow showing up the slightly raised edge. I gaze at it for a while, at the little white dots where the stitches were.

'Um, did they ever get the man who did your face?'
I say.

He lifts his hand and runs a finger down the white
line. 'Nah.'

'I thought you knew him.'

'Yeah, well – doesn't mean you can grass on someone,
does it? Can open up a whole tin of worms, that lark.'

His fingers go back to tapping the wooden chair arm.
'Sorry if things have gone a bit skew-whiff,' he
says, trying his smile. 'I'll come back with Auntie Kath.
Promise.'

'Lay on the charm, will you?'

'Do my best.'

SATURDAY 10th NOVEMBER

'There isn't much in the cupboard, Mimi. We've got to go down the shops,' I say, walking into the sitting room. 'Dad's left us five bob. Go and get your coat.'

She looks up, an odd, almost guilty expression in her eye, quickly closes her exercise book and takes it with her. She spends so long fetching her gabardine mac, I know she's hiding the book somewhere.

I hear the clatter of the letter box and go into the hall.

On the carpet by the front door is a large cream envelope addressed to *H. Drumm Esq.* in perfect sloping handwriting. I turn it over and pull open the flap embossed with *Wrayness Abbey School.*

I run my eyes down the long letter, catch a few words, then rip the piece of paper into shreds, even trying to tear the pieces that are too small to tear any more. I don't notice Mimi is standing there until she speaks.

'What you doing?'

'Nothing.'

I stuff the bits of paper into my pockets and we leave the house. I notice Mimi's eyes searching the garden before we turn the corner, bracing ourselves against the cutting wind.

'Let's make some snow,' I say as we cross the bridge. I give Mimi some of the paper scraps from my pockets. When we're a bit further up The Chase, we hold up our arms, open our hands and let the wind take all the little pieces. Off they whirl, soaring and spinning through the scraggy trees to scatter themselves on the marshes.

In Ottery Lane, as we draw near to Mrs Aylott's shop, I pull my scarf up over my nose.

'What's the matter? What you doing that for?'

'Don't know. I'm cold.'

'Don't you want people to know who you are?'

I don't answer her. Of course I don't want Mrs Aylott or the huddle of women who always seemed to be in there before to remember us, and look sideways. And what if we were to see Roger, or Pete? What would I do?

I glance quickly through Mrs Aylott's window – just a couple of women inside, and a boy in blue National Health glasses.

I pull my scarf up even higher so that only my eyes show, and push open the door. At the tinkling of the bell, the two women at the counter turn and look, let their eyes linger on us for a moment, then carry on chatting with Mrs Aylott.

I stare at the floor while we wait.

All at once the boy's voice rings out.

'Hello, Mimi! You come back, then? You've got big.' He comes out of the corner towards us.

'Hello, Terry!' cries Mimi. 'Yeah. We're at Auntie Ida's again.'

In a blur of shock, I am aware of the women swiftly

turning and Mrs Aylott looking up. Grabbing Mimi's hand, I pull open the door and drag her out. She runs beside me as I march her back up Ottery Lane.

'What's the matter? We didn't get no food!'

My eyes look straight ahead.

Mimi hasn't forgotten at all – any of it.

We are almost at the top. A bus is coming from Daneflete on its way to Hilsea. We stand on the verge and wait for it to rumble by.

Then I feel the pull of someone's eyes and see the two tall women who followed me down Old Glebe Lane on Bonfire Night standing motionless at the bus stop, turned in our direction. The taller one is clearly older than the other. Again I am reminded of scavenging birds – billowing coats flapping out like wings, high shoulders curving backwards, the older woman's beak-like hat under the black hood. She turns to say something behind her hand to the other woman, whose large round glasses glint in the light; then she seems to make some kind of curved sign with her hand in the air.

My fingers clench inside my gloves.

Then I see they appear to be looking hard at Mimi. I glance down and catch her mouthing something and moving her hands. Her eyes flicker up to mine. She quickly drops her hands, presses her lips shut.

The bus growls to a halt between us.

A man and a boy step out from behind it and cross

for Ottery Lane. The bus moves off. The women have gone.

'Mimi, who are they – those two women?'

She is watching the bus move away towards Hilsea; doesn't look up at me at all.

'Mimi, say something!'

She starts to cross the road.

'Mimi!' I call after her. 'Why do you always do this? Why don't you flippin' well say anything?'

ROGER

Terry runs though the back door and dumps a shopping bag on the table.

'Guess who I just seen, Pete.'

'Popeye the Sailor Man.' Pete is leaning over the kitchen sink, picking the dried mud off the studs of his rugby boots with a meat skewer.

'Guess again.'

'Mrs Droopy Drawers.'

'Nah – guess really.'

'Rin Tin Tin in a dress.'

'Stop it! You're a big nit!'

'*You're* a big nit!'

'*You* are!' Pete wipes his boots with the dishcloth and

throws it back in the sink, then pulls his blue and white striped socks and shirt off the airer, stuffs them in his kit bag and leaves the kitchen.

'*You* are!' Terry calls after him. 'Guess who I just seen, Roger!'

'A giant tortoise called Prince Philip.'

His lower lip begins to wobble. 'I'll hit you on your arm!' he cries.

'Don't care.'

'Don't care too.'

Terry goes into the sitting room. 'Mum!'

'What is it, Terry?' I hear her ask.

'Guess who I just seen.'

'Who did you just see, sweetheart?'

'That girl who was here before – that girl who used to play with me – but she's got bigger – that girl with the big sister.'

I can almost see Mum sit up in her chair.

'What?'

'She said she was down at her Auntie Ida's again.'

'What? I don't believe it!'

'Honest,' cries Terry. 'That Mimi girl, and her big sister, in Mrs Aylott's.'

I am at the sitting-room door before I know it.

'Are you sure you weren't seeing things with those new glasses?' I say.

'Promise. When I said hello, that big girl pulled Mimi out the shop.'

Mum looks over at me, but I quickly turn round, head for the bedroom I share with Pete, climb up onto the top bunk and lie there, not knowing what to think.

After a while there comes a soft knocking on the door.

'Cup of tea, Roger,' says Mum's voice, softly. 'I'll leave it here.'

I hear the chink of a cup in its saucer as she places it gently on the hall floor, then the car engine starts up outside and the horn beeps twice.

'Bye, Mum!' Pete shouts. 'Just off to the match!'

'Good luck! Up the blues!' Mum calls as the front door slams behind him.

One by one, I bat the three model Spitfires hanging from the ceiling. They are the first things I see when I wake up from a nightmare. And I stare at them, lying as still as I can, pretending I'm asleep when I've been woken by Pete in the lower bunk, crying quietly in the night, remembering too what happened to us four summers ago.

CORA

Glad to get out of the cold wind, Mimi and I round the corner of the house. I've given up trying to get her to talk to me, and am seething with irritation. I take the back-door key from my pocket, wondering why we bother to lock the house at all. Just as I'm thinking it, we turn into the cobbled yard and I stop dead. Something has been chalked on the back door – a mark like an M, the two halves crossing over at the bottom. Just touching the two points at the top is a circle like a white moon.

I blink. Swallow. Look down at Mimi, ask the stupid question:

'Did . . . did you do that?'

'I've been with you, ain't I,' she says.

'I'll have to get a rag to it,' I say.

'Maybe . . . maybe we should leave it,' she says.

'Why?'

'Maybe, just for now.'

'Are you sure you didn't do it?'

I turn the key in the lock. Mimi goes up the stone passage and takes off her coat.

'Was it those two women?'

She doesn't answer me.

'Mimi! You're driving me up the flippin' wall!'

ROGER

I cross the main road, make my way to the top of Old

Glebe Lane and start walking down, for the first time in over four years. It's been done up a bit, a lot of the potholes filled in, the bare hedges trimmed of their tops.

I feel a wash of cold sweat on my forehead.

Keep going.

Standing for a while on the brow of the hill, the bitter wind at my back, I gaze down at the little steeple of All Hallows rising up out of the tangled black branches of the elms, a triangular patch of snow clinging to its north side. The marshes beyond are a colourless expanse. Under a low grey sky are grey pools of still, half-frozen water edged with grey grass patched with clumps of white, and stiff grey reeds.

To the right the salt creek leaves the river on the horizon to feed the tidal channel around Guerdon Hall, the twisted, snow-topped, red-brick chimneys of the house visible behind the bare trees of Glebe Woods.

My heart thumps. I shut my eyes tight, trying to squeeze out the memories, but they leap even more vividly into the darkness.

How could Cora and Mimi have returned to this dreadful place, after everything that happened here?

I wipe my glove across my forehead, turn slowly and make my way back to the main road.

Dad throws his keys down on the kitchen table, takes off his overcoat, puts it over the back of the chair and fishes around in the pocket for his cigarettes.

The creases around his eyes seem deeper.

'Could do with a cuppa,' he says, sitting down, flicking his lighter.

I put the kettle on.

'She didn't want to come back, then, Auntie Kath?'

He draws in deeply, blows out the smoke. 'Wouldn't even let me in the bloody house. Kept me standing on the ruddy doorstep – wasn't even enough room for me to get me foot in – said through the flippin' crack she wouldn't come back here for all the tea in China.'

'Did – did she say why?'

'Shut the door on me, she did. Then that blimmin' old cow, her mother, shouted through the ruddy letter box, said Kath had told her this house was falling to bits, and was bloody haunted. I ask you – haunted! You seen any ghosts? Well, *have* you? On my life, I ask you.'

I empty the tea leaves out of the teapot into the sink,

and feel like the world has closed me in so tightly it's like wearing a coat three sizes too small.

Nobody ever wants to stay with Mimi and me.

I talk to fill the moody silence, but know even as I speak that I should have waited for a better time, or maybe I realize there may never be one.

'Um, it's the Prizegiving thing at school on Wednesday. I've got to stay behind, show people to their seats and things. I won't have time to get home for tea first, probably won't be back till really late.'

'Ruddy hell!' Dad thumps his hand on the table top. 'Why do *you* have to ruddy do it? Didn't you say you lived too far away? Use your nonce, Cora – tell them to get somebody else who lives round the corner.'

'I – I've *got* to do it.' I look down at the lino. 'Just wanted to make sure you . . . you'd be here for Mimi.'

'For Pete's sake, it's not a bloke's job to be looking after flaming kids.' He stubs his cigarette out furiously in the ashtray. 'All this molly-coddling – getting her from school. Why doesn't she walk up the bloody road with somebody else? How long is it going to take her to make some ruddy friends! What is she? Eight ruddy years old. I took myself all over the place when I was a nipper half her age!'

He takes out another cigarette. His hand is shaking.

'And what's she bloody doing scribbling with chalk on the ruddy back door? I'll give her a ruddy good hiding mucking things up when this place cost an arm and a leg to do up!'

'She said she didn't do it.'

'Who else would it flippin' be? Get a rag and wash it off for me, would you? And where's that tea? I'm bloody parched.'

A bit later, I pull open the back door and scrub out the drawing with a damp dishcloth. The cold wind stings my wet hands.

I run my eyes over the garden as far as the creek. The last of the snow has disappeared and the water is sloshing high up against the muddy bank overhung with drooping spears of pale reeds. Just on the edge of the cobbled yard, a little white stone, still knotted with red string, lies in the grass. I walk over and pick it up.

The bundle of twigs . . . the stones . . .

I think I might just go and look at the front door too.

I walk round the house to the porch, step inside and up to the door. The mark is there – the M crowned with a circle, just like the other one. I rub it off with the cloth.

I shiver. The evening is drawing in quickly.

Going back round the house, I think about Prize-giving, imagine Mimi having to walk home in the darkness alone.

For four years, sometimes in waking moments, more often in dreams, I have lived in two worlds, the one where Mimi was saved, and the other, almost more vivid, where she wasn't; where Auntie Ida, Roger and I got to the crypt too late. And in that ghastly second world, I am engulfed by the same ocean of grief and terror I would have drowned in if it had been true. The division between the two worlds is fragile, like a film of frost, easily melted with a breath.

When I get back in, Dad says, 'Look, I'm sorry I got cross with you, Cora. Don't worry about that Prizegiving palaver – all right? I'll be here.'

I feel such a surge of relief that I reach up and kiss his cheek, just beside the scar.

'I – I'll sort something out for you – try to get someone to come and help out. It isn't easy for a bloke on his own, all this . . .'

I go to the sink to rinse out the cloth when Dad says, 'Oh, by the way, has Mimi made a friend at long last?'

'I don't know. Why?'

'When you were out just now, I could have sworn I heard her talking to somebody on the telephone.'

I go to the door, look along the hall to the small table where the telephone sits solid and solitary opposite the clock.

Dad says behind me, 'I didn't even think she knew how to make a call.'

ROGER

Mass in the school chapel. Phil Chisholm makes a great big thing about pointing out in a loud whisper to everyone the similarity between my barnet and the hair of St Dominic, standing in his stone niche on the wall. Even I have to grin from the row behind: the likeness is uncanny. Father Bartholomew spots him, and Chisholm gets his whole row a detention for laughing at a holy statue; then notices me smiling and ropes me in as well.

Fortunately Mum's given me half a crown to go to the barber's on my way home. Hope I'll be out in time to get there.

I jump off the bus in Daneflete, nearly go over on the slippery pavement, shiny under a thin layer of ice, leg it past The Longship, down Paxton Street, up to the Happy Plaice fish-and-chip shop with its tantalizing smell of greasy chips wafting out onto the road, and on to Monsieur Antonio's, the barber's next door.

I groan with frustration. Monsieur Antonio is behind the glass, turning the card from OPEN to CLOSED. I bang on the door, and jab my finger at my ghastly hair. Monsieur Antonio points to CLOSED. I hold out my hands in supplication. He shakes his head and points to CLOSED. I join my palms and wring them in prayer, hold my head to one side, and try to form an expression of mute desperation.

He raises his eyes to heaven and bends to unlock the door.

'Oh thank, thank you,' I gush as I bluster inside, restraining myself from grabbing his hand and kissing it.

'Who did this?' He curls his fingers around a lock of hair and flicks it back in disgust.

'Mum,' I say.

'What with – a knife and fork?'

He steers me over to the big chair and wraps a huge, yellowing white nylon cape around my shoulders. A few of someone else's blond curls are still clinging to it with the static, and it crackles whenever I move.

'How short do you want it?' he says, with a touch of south London in his voice.

'Do I have a choice?'

He clicks his scissors and lays out his clippers.

'I thought you'd be Italian – or, um, French?' I say, once he begins snipping.

'No – come from Peckham. I started out French, like, with *Antoine*, 'cause me name's actually Tony; then the ruddy man who painted me sign went and put *Antonio* and was going to charge me an extra ten bob to put it right, even though it was only three blimmin' letters.

He'd just done the ice-cream shop down the road, and had Italian on the brain.'

'Why didn't you just stick with Tony?'

'Ooh no, no, no. It's class, mate. French is classy. *Monsieur*'s got a ring to it. I get a better sort of clientele in here than Bill's Barbers round the back of the garage.'

When Monsieur Antonio has finished, I might not look like suave and sophisticated Paul Newman gazing out from a framed photo standing next to the tins of pomade, but glancing in the mirror – no, definitely not Paul Newman – I feel I can at least hold my head up again without shame. My hair even seems a bit longer. I feel quite cheery.

I fumble around in my blazer for the half-crown and hold it out for Monsieur Antonio.

His mouth withers under its little black moustache. 'It's three bob,' he says, 'and I stayed open special.'

'Oh, I'm really sorry. This is all Mum gave me. I could call in tomorrow with the extra sixpence.'

''S all right,' he says, vigorously shaking the cape to try and dislodge the clinging hair, then reaching for his broom. 'Off with you, now – and mind how you go. Pavements are getting slippy.'

When I get off the bus at Bryers Guerdon, the air is raw and it's long past dinner time. I put my head down, wrap my arms around my chest against the biting cold, and set off down Ottery Lane. All the way home, passing the lighted windows of the little houses, their chimneys belching out grey smoke against the black night sky, I count my steps in groups of fifty, then twenty, then ten, hoping dinner will either be sausage stew or shepherd's pie, with apple crumble and custard for afters. I'm praying it won't be tinned prunes.

CORA

As I go into the sitting room, Dad screws up a brown envelope and tosses it across the rug into the fire, which flares up for a moment, leaving a scrap of black, feathery ash.

I put his cup of tea down on the little table. 'Do you want me to get you a biscuit?' I say.

'No, it's all right.'

He taps his fingers on the arm of the chair, seeming a bit far away. I expect he's still annoyed because Mr Blezzard came round for his money, caught Dad on the hop. They had a big row about the wallpaper coming off. Every morning we pick more up off the floor where it's rolled down in the night and have started shoving it into a pile in a corner of the dining room with the fallen plasterboard. Mr Blezzard is going to have to order some more, and get better paste, and start clearing out the barn as well, or he won't get a penny.

Dad's cross about everything at the moment. I think that for all his fancy plans, he had no idea what he was going to do with himself in this worn-out old house in the middle of nowhere. He's used to the city. He doesn't fit in. And he's bored.

I notice him stuff some creased paper down the side of the chair before reaching for the cup and saucer.

'It wasn't my fault, you know,' he says out of the blue, 'about your mother. It makes my life bloody hard, I'll tell you that.'

I take a deep breath, say nothing.

I go into the hall and push open the door into the cold wooden bareness of the dining room, with its heap of wallpaper piled up in the corner.

I hold my hands out over the unscratched teak table top. My fingers are trembling.

I think of my mother in the only photograph we've got of her – getting married to Dad just after the war. She's wearing a dark suit with a fox fur around the neck, its legs dangling down the front of the fitted jacket. Her fair hair's all wavy under her hat, and she's holding a bunch of carnations – only a handful of flowers, but lots of fluffy leaves to make it look bigger and more expensive.

It's four years since I last saw her, and now I only seem to remember her as she looks in the photograph. Whatever she's doing – washing the clothes in the sink, pegging them out in the yard, cooking spuds, scrubbing the doorstep, on a bad day sleeping on her bed with the curtains drawn – she's wearing that suit with the fox fur, and the hat, and the smile, and the carnations are somewhere next to her, and everything is in black and white as it is in the photograph, even the flowers.

When we came out here, I felt as if I was leaving Mum behind. All my memories of her are in our old house, and they are fading. I want to stop myself imagining how it would be if we heard she had died in the asylum. Would it make any difference to us at all?

She is only there because of what happened here in the war; because she thought she was to blame when Lankin snatched away her little sister.

From the dining-room window I can see out to the creek at the front. With no light on in the room, I should be invisible to anyone outside as I peer through the glass into the half-darkness. With a shiver I see that it isn't so. Old Mr Wragge is on the bridge, bent slightly to one side, pushing a wheelbarrow towards the house. Even in the gloom of the wintry evening, it is obvious that he is looking at me. Seeing him makes me think of the broken pottery in the barn.

I hear the squeak of the wheel as he approaches the front door. The knocker thuds twice.

I wait for Dad for a moment, but in the end go to unbolt and unlock the door myself.

In the shadow of the porch roof, Mr Wragge stands among the leaves on the flagstones.

'Your dad said I was to come for the wallpaper what's fallen off,' he says. His dark little eyes gleam out from under a furry hat – their gaze steady and unnerving.

Dad's voice bellows down the hall, 'Can't you close the ruddy door? There's a gale blowing in.'

'Come for the wallpaper, Mr Drumm,' Mr Wragge says again as Dad appears.

He points to the dining room – 'It's in there' – then goes back to the sitting room.

I follow the old man. 'Cup of tea?' I say. 'There's some in the pot.'

'No, don't worry, thanks. I'll just get this loaded, then I'm off back home. It's too dark to do no more.'

He gathers up the paper.

'You cleared the barn yet?' I ask.

'No. It's going to take a while, and Ed – Mr Blezzard to you – will have to bring his van down.'

'Funny old stuff in there,' I say.

'You don't want to go rummaging round with that lot,' he says. 'Best left alone.'

'I've seen it already,' I say. 'Those old broken bottles and things.'

''Scuse me,' he says, trying to get past me with his bundle.

I follow him back down the hall and open the front door for him.

'What are they – those bottles?' I ask.

'None of your business,' he says.

'You know what they are, don't you?' I say, the cold beginning to creep into my sleeves as I stand in the porch.

'Not saying nothing,' he says.

He turns his back and I watch him trundle the barrow away down the path.

I run after him. 'Mr Wragge—'

He stops, irritated. 'What do you keep pestering me for?' He purses his lips, moves on.

'If you won't tell me about the bottles, what about twigs tied with red twine . . . little white stones . . . chalk marks on the back door, a big M with a circle on top—'

'Must be getting on,' he mutters, walking faster.

'Mr Wragge . . .' I hurry alongside him towards the bridge, beginning to freeze without a coat. 'I'm going to keep asking you – every day till you tell me.'

'I'm not going to be here, so there,' he says. 'I'm doing some work down the Patches from tomorrow.'

I stop. 'The Patches? You don't know Mr Thorston, do you, in the thatched cottage?'

He stops. 'Hal Thorston? How do you know Hal Thorston?'

'I knew him a few years ago. He helped me out, told

me things nobody else would, because round here people don't tell you flippin' nothing.'

Mr Wragge lifts the handles of the barrow and, without another word to me, trundles it over the bridge.

I stand there for a while, cold and annoyed, watching the old man as he moves away towards the barn.

He wheels away the paper the scarred man had them put on the walls to cover over the ancient wood.

The old, tired house has sloughed them off.

It did not want to be made new.

TUESDAY 13th NOVEMBER

I cook us some fish fingers, call Mimi and Dad.

'Don't worry about me,' Dad says, putting his arm in his coat sleeve, that elsewhere look on his face again. 'I'm going down the pub.'

'Oh.' I don't know why I'm so surprised. He was always in the Half Moon in Limehouse. 'The Thin Man?'

'Yeah,' he says. 'That Blezzard bloke said they do a good pint.'

As the Zodiac grumbles away over the stones in The Chase, Mimi and I eat all the fish fingers between us.

As the clock strikes nine, I remember I need to forge an absence note for Mother Anselm, my form mistress. She's been nagging me for it ever since I walked out of school last week. I told her I'd been sick. She said I had to bring in a letter from my mother.

'Mimi' – I squeeze her shoulder – 'you must go to bed now. I won't be long. I've just got something to do.'

'Ain't going up on my own,' she says. 'I'll wait till you've done it.'

'I might be ages.'

'I ain't tired.'

I see the dark patches under her eyes. 'You look it, sis.' I take my arm from round her. 'Tell you what, I'll make us a nice cup of tea and some toast.'

'Need the toilet.'

'That's all right. You go and I'll put the kettle on.'

'You've got to come an' all.'

'For heaven's sake, Mimi!'

She lowers her eyes and says nothing.

When we come back, we munch our toast and drink our sweet tea.

'Now don't forget I'm going to Prizegiving tomorrow. Don't be a pest for Dad, all right?'

I find a pad of cheap notepaper and some scruffy envelopes in the kitchen drawer and take out my pencil case.

Dear Mother Anselm . . .

As I write, Mimi's head begins to droop. After a short while she lies fast asleep on the table, her head resting on her folded arms. I stroke her hair and run my finger down her soft, flushed cheek.

It's easy: black biro instead of school fountain pen and washable blue ink, a slope to the right, a few little flourishes, a bit of fun with the capital letters. Nobody is ever going to read Mum's writing – possibly nobody in the world ever again. I don't suppose she writes any-thing in the hospital. I wouldn't know. Mimi and I were never allowed to go and see her.

. . . she felt a lot better after a good nights sleep.
Yours sincerly,
Mrs S. Drumm

I fold the paper, seal it in a brown envelope and write *Mother Anselm, Wrayness Abbey High School* on the outside.

I lean over Mimi and blow on her eyelashes. 'We've got to go to bed, Mimi. It's getting really late.'

Her head flies up. Her eyes stare wildly although clearly; she hasn't quite woken up. 'She's looking in,' she cries.

'What? Wake up, Mimi!'

'She's trying to get inside . . .'

'Who? What are you talking about?' I shake her arm.

Mimi blinks violently and rubs her forehead. 'My head hurts,' she says.

''S all right, Mimi,' I say gently. 'Let's get to bed. We won't turn the lights off.'

She stands on the bedroom floor, her eyes half closed, and raises her heavy arms for me to lift her gymslip over her head. Something falls out of the pocket and rolls a little way along the floor. I get her into her nightie and tuck her into bed, then begin to pick up her clothes. My foot crunches on something. I look down at a broken stick of white chalk.

Was it Mimi who scrawled the mark on the doors?

I glance at her sleeping face, then crouch down and gather up the pieces.

She's looking in. She's trying to get inside . . .

Mimi's words circle inside my head while the ceiling light glares above us all night long.

What are all these things that Mimi knows and I don't?

And why won't she ever tell me?

I look up at the clock above the blackboard.

Ten past three. Dad should be waiting outside school for Mimi, like he said.

Early this morning I crept into his room. He was still in his shirt, lying back on his pillow with his mouth wide open, stubbled, snoring, smelling of stale beer and sweat. His jacket was lying across the foot of the bed with a crumpled piece of paper attached to the pocket by a safety pin. A scrawl of biro said: *Angela Russell, The Cosy Café, Hilsea 463.*

Trying hard not to feel sickened, I shook him, whispered loudly in his ear to remember I'd be at Prize-giving. He stirred and mumbled, but didn't waken.

I was worried he wouldn't get Mimi to school so I hauled her out of bed, hurried her ready and towed her, still half asleep, all the way to North Fairing. I ran like the clappers back up Ottery Lane, only to see my bus pulling away from the bus stop, and got a late mark.

Forty minutes later, the bell rings. We stand and push our chairs under the desks.

'Good afternoon, girls.'

'Good afternoon and thank you, Mother Mary Dominic.'

I've got about three hours before I have to come back to school for Prizegiving.

It's cold.

I wander around Wrayness, from one shop to another, to keep warm. The man in the television rental place lets me watch some of the children's programmes before chucking me out.

As the shop doors begin to close and the shutters lower, I walk down to the seafront, my head bent into the bitter wind blowing off the sea, school scarf tight around my neck. I'm looking for a café, but they're all shut for the winter, except for one grubby fish-and-chip shop at the end of the promenade, with a couple of teddy boys in drainpipe trousers standing outside, eating saveloys out of newspaper.

'Just some chips, please,' I say to the man. 'Can I eat them in here?'

'If you like,' he says. 'But stand in the corner. I don't want you blocking up the counter. Salt and vinegar?'

'Yes, please.'

The corner is freezing, in the line of an icy draught.

I eat the chips one by one, chewing them slowly, and watch the clock, wondering what Dad and Mimi are having for tea.

I swallow down a little niggle of unease with my last chip. What if Dad stayed drunk all day and didn't go to pick Mimi up? It wouldn't be the first time, by a long chalk, that he'd promised one thing and done another.

'Would you like some scraps?' the man calls over.

173

'Yes, please.'

He pours some curls of crispy batter into my piece of newspaper.

At quarter to seven I make my way back to school. Not long afterwards, choir and prizewinners begin to arrive in their white dresses, gloves and shoes. Thank goodness I didn't have to have a white dress. Where would I have got one from?

I stand at the door giving out programmes, smiling politely, not opening my mouth.

My eyes rove over the honours boards hanging on the walls.

1956. Josephine Cardwell. Major Open Scholarship in Mathematics, Girton College, Cambridge.

Penelope Burne. County Major Scholarship to Birmingham University.

Mothers sit straight-backed, attentive, in neat two-pieces, gloves and court shoes, next to dark-suited, starch-collared fathers. The front row is a line of nuns in white habits, long black scapulars spilling apron-like over their knees, their smallest tic or twitch marked by the chink of rosary beads.

Madame Mary St Bernard gives a speech – something about humility in victory.

1957. Margaret Anderson. Open Exhibition in Chemistry, Imperial College, London.

Subdued clapping.

Jacqueline Bonville, head girl, swishing in a sumptuous full-skirted dress with a creamy silk rose to one side of the sweetheart neckline, gleaming hair swept up and set with a perfect white bow, breathes in through her nose, opens her mouth and sings:

> *'There once was a Vilia, a witch of the wood,*
> *A hunter beheld her alone as she stood,*
> *The spell of her beauty upon him was laid;*
> *He looked and he longed for the magical maid!'*

The choir joins her. The music swells.

> *'Vilia, O Vilia! The witch of the wood!*
> *Would I not die for you, dear, if I could?'*

The pieces of pottery in the barn come into my head, the hard yellow fingernail, the bundle of twigs tied with red string, the mark chalked on the back door, the little white stones – *clink-clink*, Mimi . . .

The niggle I felt before is becoming a pang of anxiety.

After the applause ends, a very important man, Marmaduke or Montague or Montgomery Bolsover, in highly polished squeaking shoes, with a red carnation in his left buttonhole, clipped moustache, thinning hair, rounded stomach pushing against his waistcoat, rises to speak.

My gaze settles on the slowly moving hands of the clock between the two double doors. Nearly nine.

I can't swallow down the huge knot growing in my chest; tell myself that Dad *did* collect Mimi from school, the boiler *will* be working, and the lights . . .

'. . . more opportunities for girls than there have ever been. These days they can be secretaries, nurses and teachers. One day we may even find young ladies in the engineering profession – yes, you may smile . . .'

Mimi *will* have had some dinner – in fact, should be asleep in bed by now.

The knot tightens.

I should have telephoned home from a box to make sure she was all right. Why didn't I think of it when I was wandering around Wrayness earlier? I lean against the doorframe, feeling sick. I shouldn't have come to Prizegiving.

But I had to.

A burst of clapping. Mr Bolsover moves back and sits down. His chair makes a rude noise. A couple of girls giggle behind white-gloved hands.

The presentation of prizes starts. Mr Bolsover hands out one book after another, from time to time mopping his forehead with his silk handkerchief.

Madame Mary St Bernard is watching the prize-winners, smiling grimly, not looking at me.

I slip backwards quietly between the double doors,

dump my leftover programmes on a bench, turn a corner.

Distant clapping. The choir begins the school song: *Sing We the Praise of Our Glorious Abbey*. I move quickly through the corridors to the cloakroom for my coat, hat and outdoor shoes, and make my way out of school. Outside, the road is lined with glossy cars.

At the bus stop the 2A sign shines out of the darkness. I climb upstairs and settle into the corner seat. The heater under it blows out hot air.

I'm tired.

A gentle shake on my shoulder. 'Sorry to wake you, love. The bus terminates here.'

'Sorry?'

'We're not going any further.' The conductor's uniform smells stale. 'You'll have to get off, love.'

Where am I?

I look out of the window into the night. A couple of drunks, shoulder around shoulder, are swaying down the pavement outside The Longship.

'But we're only in Daneflete.'

'We don't go no further this time of night.'

Next to the pub, the clock on the wall of Galleywell's Garage says twenty past ten.

'Aren't you going to Hilsea?'

'Nah. The bus before this was the last one.'

'I've got to get to Bryers Guerdon.'

'It said "Daneflete" on the front, clear as day. You'll have to walk it. Sorry, love, but can you hurry up? Me and the driver want to get home. We're on earlies tomorrow.'

I stumble down the stairs, clutching my school bag.

How long will it take me to walk? An hour?

'Give us a kiss, love!' leers one of the drunks as I step off the platform. The other laughs and belches and kicks a bottle into the gutter behind the bus.

I move quickly on, crossing over the South Fairing road, and start walking to Bryers Guerdon, my shoulders already stiffening with cold.

The streetlamps run out not long after I pass the last house, and then the pavement disappears into a verge, the ground hard, the grass stiff with frost, dropping sharply at the side into a ditch running under a spiky hedgerow.

When at last I get to Old Glebe Lane, I start to run on my numb feet, veering off the track in the darkness, slipping on the black glass of the frozen puddles, the fear for Mimi increasing with each step. My school bag bounces from side to side across my back as I stumble down the hill and along The Chase. I run with my mouth wide open, gulping in the cold air, the pain from the back of my tongue all the way down to my stomach so sharp it feels as if my throat has been sliced. Within sight of Guerdon Hall I have to stop and knead the stitch under my ribs with a clenched fist.

And look up.

There is no car and not one light in any window to break up the solid black bulk of the house.

Tense, my heart thumping, I dash across the frosty bridge.

On the other side of the cobbled yard, the back door is slightly open.

Dizzy with fear, I push through into the stone passage.

'Mimi! Mimi! Dad?'

I feel for the light switch, push it down – up – down again – up – down.

Nothing.

Complete darkness.

I move further down the stone passage, fumbling for the next switch.

No light.

I stumble over something, pick it up – Mimi's satchel.

'Mimi! Mimi! Where are you?'

A wave of utter panic floods me.

Moving further down the passage, feeling my way along the wall, I turn into the hall.

'Mimi . . .' The sound leaves my throat like a whimper. 'Mimi . . .'

I hold my breath – listen.

Against the steady ticking of the clock, the layer of silence hovers over the dark, jagged slope of the staircase and steals out into the hall through the open doors of the empty rooms.

I move blindly down the hall and into the kitchen, barging into one of the spindly dining chairs. It collides with the table, the legs squealing on the lino. Startled, I pause for a moment to catch my breath, listening, every nerve pricking, for any tiny noise in the noiseless house, hoping to hear Mimi call for me.

I inch my hand along the top of the dresser, over the bin and across the wall beside the window until I reach the sink. I bend to push open the sliding door of the cupboard underneath. In sightless confusion, I grope my way along the shelves, dislodging packets and bottles that clatter one against the other. A couple of tins drop out onto the floor, each jarring clunk echoing around the panelling in the hall outside – every one stopping a heartbeat.

At last, towards the back of the bottom shelf, my fingers grasp the familiar shape of the torch. I draw it out and, trembling, push the switch with my thumb. It won't move. Frantic, I push again.

The light flares out like a fan, and the straight-edged shadows of the cupboards, chairs and table leap up the walls.

'Mimi . . .' I am so gripped by dread, the name hardly escapes my mouth.

I must search the house – every murky, shadowed corner of it.

The crunch of footsteps on the gravel. A bobbing light moves outside the window.

Mouth dry, skin bristling, I slide my eyes up.

The black-dark shape of a head is peering through the glass.

She's trying to get inside . . .

I've left the back door open.

Dizzy with fear, I slide down to the floor – sit there with my back to the cupboard, clutching in my hand the torch that throws its beam quivering across the floor.

I don't know what to do.

A furious knocking rattles the window.

I gulp in a breath, feel for the switch on the barrel of the torch, then press it backwards. I am engulfed in darkness, save for the glimmer from the path.

A loud whisper from outside.

Footsteps on the gravel – moving away from the kitchen window.

Voices.

The creak of the back door.

Heavy footfalls in the stone passage – getting faster – now in the hall.

'Cora! Cora! Where are you?' a man shouts.

'Cora! We saw your light!' someone else yells. 'Tell us where you are!'

'Who – who is it?' I stammer, my voice catching in my sore, dry throat.

The voices draw nearer. I gulp – switch the torch back on.

They are at the kitchen door – two men – behind wide beams of dazzling light that crisscross the room.

'Cora, Cora – it's all right, it's all right . . .' the first man says, coming in, crouching next to me.

'Who – who are you?' A wave rises up through my chest and bursts out in tears.

'Here, hold this a minute, Roger,' the man says, handing his torch to the other, and fishing in his pocket for a handkerchief which he presses into my hand.

'It's Mr Jotman – do you remember me? And Roger – Roger's here.'

'It's me, Cora,' Roger says. 'You all right?'

I look up but can't see him beyond the torch light.

'We're taking you back to ours,' says Mr Jotman.

One of them – I think it's Roger, but he's so much taller – takes hold of my hand in a firm grasp and pulls me up off the floor.

'You can't – you can't – Mimi's gone. I've lost Mimi—'

'She's at our house,' Roger says.

'What?'

'She was here all by herself and the lights went out,' says Mr Jotman, holding out his handkerchief. 'She was terrified – ran all the way up to the village, to us. It was probably the only place she could think of.'

'She's at your house . . . ?'

'Eating sausages,' says Roger. 'We've saved some for you.'

I wipe my eyes on the hanky.

'I've brought some fuse wire,' says Mr Jotman. 'Do you know where the junction box is?'

'Um – I think it's near the back door, up on the wall.'

'I'll see if I can fix it. You go up with Roger and get clean school stuff for tomorrow, for you and Mimi, and your night things and toothbrushes . . .'

'What?'

'You're staying with us tonight.'

'But there's no room—'

'Oh, we can always make room. Go and get your stuff. I'll see if I can sort out the electrics.'

Our torch lights play on the worn wooden treads as Roger follows me up the stairs. The shadows of the carved banisters stretch themselves up the wall and bend across the ceiling above our heads – black parallel lines, moving as we move, like a living cage.

I push open my bedroom door to get some clothes, and a light flickers on in the hall downstairs.

Mr Jotman shouts up, 'I've got them going down here. Try the landing!'

Roger flicks the nearest switch and the ceiling light outside my bedroom comes on. 'Brilliant, Dad!' he calls down.

He sounds so different.

We walk quite a way into The Chase before we reach the car. Mr Jotman settles me into the front and we drive bumpily up Old Glebe Lane, over the main road and down Ottery Lane to Bryers Guerdon. As we turn left into Fieldpath Road, I notice in the glare of the head-lights two new bungalows on the other side of Bull Cottages, where old Gussie lived and, next to her, Mrs Campbell.

'Is old Gussie still alive?' I ask, straining my eyes through the car window to see if the front garden of number 1 is as neglected as it was before.

'She died a couple of years ago,' Roger says. 'Mrs Campbell found her.'

'What happened to all the cats?'

'A van came from the RSPCA,' says Mr Jotman. 'Probably all put to sleep – riddled, most likely.'

'The cottage has all been done up,' says Roger. 'There's this young couple in there now. They've named it Rhondadon.'

''Spect he's called Rhonda and she's called Don,' says Mr Jotman.

Roger laughs. 'Rhondadon – sounds like a dinosaur,' he says.

'Or a medicine for excessive wind,' chuckles Mr Jotman.

I can't believe I'm smiling. It feels odd.

'Must have smelled awful when they first moved in,' I say.

'Because of the cats or the wind?' Mr Jotman laughs as we draw up outside the house.

The Jotman house is much as it was. Even in the darkness the wooden walls, veranda and large wild garden are comfortingly familiar.

We walk up the veranda steps and Mr Jotman pushes open the back door. There is just a little sidelight on in the kitchen. Mrs Jotman gets up quickly from her chair, comes over, her concerned eyes searching my face, and rubs both my arms warmly.

'It's lovely to see you again, Cora,' she says with a nervous smile. 'Look at you in your nice uniform. Roger, take Cora's hat and coat and hang them up in the hall, would you, and I'll make a pot of tea.'

She turns back to me. 'You and Mimi are sleeping in Roger and Peter's room,' she says. 'They'll be all right in the sitting room. Mimi's already in bed, on the bottom bunk. I've saved you some sausages. Do you want me to warm them up?'

'I'm all right with cold, thank you, Mrs Jotman.'

Mr Jotman asks me if I've got a telephone number for Dad.

'I've only got the number for the Half Moon, our local in Limehouse. Alf will take a message.'

Mr Jotman looks at his watch. 'It'll be way past

closing time now. I'll ring tomorrow, find out what's happened.'

Roger sticks his head round the door to say goodnight.

So odd – every room in this little house is occupied. In Guerdon Hall they are nearly all empty.

A short while later I am snuggling down under the woollen blankets on Roger's top bunk, in clean cotton sheets, my feet on a hot-water bottle with a knitted cover.

It feels strange lying there in the half-darkness under some little painted aeroplanes dangling from the ceiling on bits of dusty string. A few books stand between some wooden book-ends on the chest of drawers under the window – *Biggles*, *Billy Bunter*, *Five on a Secret Trail*, *The Four Feathers* and, on the end, *The Last of the Mohicans*.

Dad told me that when he was a boy, Nan had taken him to see the film starring Randolph Scott and he'd taken a shine to the girl playing Cora Munro, so when I came along that's what he wanted my name to be. Mum insisted on Agnes, after her mother, but she wasn't well after I was born so Dad went to register me on his own and made me Cora.

Mimi whispers up, 'Cora? Are you awake?'

I lean over the side.

'You ain't cross, are you, sis, me coming up here?' she says. 'I didn't know what to do.'

I hang my hand down and she touches my fingertips.

'That was really clever,' I say. 'Ten out of ten with a gold star on top. I'm so sorry I wasn't there, Mimi.'

'It was horrible, specially when the lights went out, and—'

A few seconds go by.

'And what?'

She turns towards the wall.

'Nothing.'

I feel Pete's foot in my back.

'It's quarter past seven, mate,' he says.

'Flippin' heck!'

It takes a few seconds for me to remember I am on the settee in the sitting room. Pushing down the top of Dad's itchy old army blanket, I peer at Pete, already in his uniform, with a cup of tea in his hand.

'Mum said to give you this. You'd better hurry up or we'll miss the bus.'

'Is the bathroom free?'

'Dad's in there.'

I roll myself up to sitting, my back aching from being bent out of position all night, my eyes sore and heavy with tiredness, and take the cup and saucer.

'It's hot,' he says. 'You'll have to blow on it.'

There is a slight edge to Pete's voice.

'What's the matter, mate?'

He starts smoothing his hair in the mirror over the mantelpiece. 'Nothing.'

'Come on, Pete. What is it?'

He turns slightly away. 'Why did you flippin' well have to bring them back here?'

'Who?'

'You know, them two.' He jerks his thumb towards the door. 'We were all right, Roger. Everything was all right again. Why did they flippin' well have to come back?'

'Are – are they still here?'

'Cora must have left for Wrayness. I haven't seen her.'

He goes out of the door, and I sigh.

Say nothing. Don't talk about it.

CORA

After school I come through the Jotmans' back door. The family are around the table, scooping up the remains of their meal. They freeze, spoons halfway to their mouths, all eyes on me as I walk in, but it lasts no more than a moment. They've grown so much, they make the kitchen seem so much smaller than I remember. I just about recognize Pete, looking as if he may be almost as tall as Roger, and both of them bigger than their dad. Pete lowers his eyes and goes back to scraping out his bowl, but I catch him looking up at me quickly from under his eyelashes, then as quickly away. A little girl, grown up from Baby Pamela, sits next to Mimi at the table, studying me curiously.

'Hurry and finish your semolina,' says Mrs Jotman busily. 'We'll have to be quick if we're going to get to this show in time. Roger, can you get the cloth and wipe the table down? Did I say we're going to see *The Desert Song* tonight, Cora? My friend Barbara's in it. You can always tell it's her on the stage because of her big nose. Oh dear – don't tell her I said that, will you?'

'Ruddy waste of time, this blimmin' show,' says Mr Jotman. 'Can't you tell Barbara we were all sick?'

'No, I can't. They've been rehearsing for weeks. You can't just let people down.' The doorbell rings. 'That's Nellie come to babysit, and I've already paid for the tickets.'

Mr Jotman sighs. 'Cora can have mine.'

'No, she's having Dennis's,' says Mrs Jotman. 'He's gone swimming. Peter, can you let Nellie in and go and get your shoes on.'

'I'm not going.' He scowls.

'What? Why not?'

'Just not.' He slopes out of the room.

'Peter!'

Mrs Jotman goes after him. Low, agitated voices in the hall move into the sitting room. The doorbell rings again.

Mr Jotman, irritated, goes to the front door. 'Sorry,

Nellie, we may not need you after all. Rosie, what's happening?' he calls.

'Oh, Nellie,' says Mrs Jotman. 'Here's your half-crown. So sorry. Peter's staying at home after all.'

She comes into the kitchen, says, 'It's just the four of us. Coats on. Let's be quick.'

Nothing more is said. Mrs Jotman busies herself putting on her hat in front of the scrap of mirror tucked behind the water heater. Roger, clearly feeling awkward, reaches for his gloves dangling over the airer.

Outside, Mr Jotman holds open the car door for me and says quietly, 'I nearly forgot, Cora. I've spoken to your dad on the telephone. Said he had to go up to town quickly yesterday, and got held up.' He and Mrs Jotman exchange a look over the roof. They think I don't see it. 'Oh, and he's sorted something out for you and Mimi. He's coming back tomorrow – with a surprise, he says.'

ROGER

On the way to South Fairing, the headlights pick out a bit of sleet.

I'm sitting in the back with Cora, still in my uniform. I didn't think it was fair if she was the only one wearing her school things to a show.

Dad breaks the slightly uncomfortable silence. 'I hope that blimmin' Audrey Finch isn't doing the lead again,' he says, peering through the windscreen as the wipers clunk back and forth.

'She's got a lovely voice,' says Mum. 'She used to entertain the troops during the war.'

'The Second World War, or the First?'

'Oh Rex, don't be rude. She's the only one who can reach the top notes, Barbara said.'

'Like that ruddy Ken Pewsey. If he's doing the Red Shadow, I'm asking for my money back.'

'Ken Pewsey used to be at Sadler's Wells Opera,' says Mum.

'Selling ice creams or behind the bar?' says Dad. 'Honestly, Cora, he's been the flippin' romantic lead for the last thirty years. You should have seen the pair of them doing Carmen and Don José last year. It was like a bit of late-flowering hanky-panky at the Over Sixties' Club.'

'Rex! Anyway, they're lucky to have people who can sing at all. It's only a little company.'

'Then they shouldn't flippin' well do musicals, should they? They should stick to plays. And is that Hilda Fenton going to be conducting again? When they did *The Gondoliers*, Cora, she was wearing this straight dress like a tube—'

'Rex – you shouldn't be telling Cora about that!'

'For heaven's sake, woman! As I was saying, Cora,' Dad goes on, 'this Hilda Fenton was standing on this podium, and every time she lifted her arms, her dress went up and everyone got an eyeful of her suspenders.'

Cora hoots with laughter.

'Rex! That's enough!' Mum cries.

We pull into the small car park of the South Fairing Community Hall.

'What's this *Desert Song* about, then?' Cora asks. 'I ain't never been to the theatre.'

'Well, this Pierre is in love with this girl called Margot who's just arrived in Morocco from her convent school in France,' Mum tells her, 'but she doesn't know he's really the Red Shadow in disguise. It's so romantic.'

'Romantic – my foot!' says Dad. 'If she can't see it's the same ruddy bloke, when the only difference is, one's got an old red towel over his head!'

'It's the magic of the theatre,' Mum mutters as we hurry up to the hall. 'Don't spoil it for Cora, Rex.'

Dad shows the tickets to one of the two permed ladies sitting at a table in the entrance, who shout out, 'Shut the door! It's perishing here!' every time anyone comes in.

We push through the swing doors into the hall, find our places – halfway back on the right – and settle into the khaki canvas and chipped metal chairs.

Pete might as well have been here, his empty seat a

constant reminder of his refusal to come. Mum puts the box of fruit gums on it.

Dad is looking at the programme. 'Flippin' heck,' he cries. 'It *is* flaming Ken Pewsey and blimmin' Audrey Finch.'

'Not so loud, Rex.'

'Well, honestly, how are they going to get her to look like she's just come out of school?'

'Maybe they'll put a lot of make-up on her,' Mum whispers.

'They'll need a ruddy cement mixer.'

Cora giggles. When she laughs, it makes me laugh.

At exactly half past seven, the show begins.

Dad causes a bit of a stir when the Red Shadow comes on, all in livid scarlet.

'Who does he think he is – ruddy Father Christmas?' he whispers to Mum, but so loudly that the tittering spreads for at least three rows in front and behind us.

CORA

Back under the dangling aeroplanes, even with the warmth of the hot-water bottle spreading up from my toes, I can't seem to settle to sleep. In a flash I remember why – I haven't done my Geography homework: two pages on the industries of the Ruhr Valley, to be given in on Friday, tomorrow. I must do it, or a report will land on Madame Mary St Bernard's desk in the cold room with the parquet floor. She may already know that I slipped away early from Prizegiving and was late for school yesterday morning.

I groan with irritation, throw back the covers and swing my legs round, searching for the ladder with my feet. I don't want to put the light on again and risk waking Mimi. I fumble about until I find my school jumper and pull it on over my pyjamas, stretch Mimi's old socks onto my feet, then drag up my school bag, open the door as quietly as I can and tiptoe into the hall. Noiselessly, I creep past the sitting room, so as not to disturb Roger and Pete.

A light is coming from the kitchen. The door is ajar. I push it open and step backwards in surprise.

'Blinkin' heck!' Roger cries. 'You scared me to death.'

'*You* scared *me*.'

He is sitting at the table in a navy-blue dressing gown, pen in hand, books spread out in front of him.

'You doing your homework?'

'It's got to be in tomorrow,' he says, lowering his eyes, a little flush of pink creeping over his cheeks. 'I didn't have time before, with – with, you know, the show.'

'Same here,' I say. 'What's yours?'

'History.'

'Mine's Geography.'

I stand there, pulling down the edge of my jumper, self-conscious in my pyjamas and Mimi's dirty socks.

Roger coughs awkwardly, then slides a couple of books across the table towards him, clearing a space. 'Um, why don't you sit down?' he says.

I sit in the chair opposite and empty my bag. 'Wish I'd done History.'

'You wouldn't have wanted to do this, honest,' he says. 'Flippin' nineteenth-century Acts of Parliament and Reform and things. When you choose History, you think you're going to do the Tudors or the Vikings – something bloodthirsty you can get your teeth into – then they land you with this.'

ROGER

We write, check, write again, acting busy and diligent to cover our discomfort, as if it's somehow perfectly all right to be sitting here, alone together, at dead of night in our pyjamas, so obviously not the children we were before.

I can't bear it. I have to say something.

'D'you fancy a cup of cocoa?'

I can't believe that's the best I could come up with.

'That'd be nice.'

I drag myself up and, as I pass the bit of mirror behind the water heater, notice to my horror the front of my hair is sticking up, and there's a great splodge of dried Weetabix on the front of my dressing gown. I steal a glance at Cora in the mirror's edge. Her head is down in her book so I try to flatten my hair with my fingers. I let go. It flicks up again. I press it down once more and hold it there while I open the cupboard door with my other hand and look for the cocoa, but can't see it anywhere.

'Sorry, there's no cocoa – it's either Horlicks or Ovaltine.'

Cora raises her head and the corners of her mouth turn up. 'Horlicks would be lovely,' she says, shifting in her seat.

I realize I am still pressing down my fringe.

With a cough I reach for the tin, scratching my forehead furiously as if I have an itch.

I stick a pan of milk on the gas, spoon in some Horlicks and sugar and give it a good stir with a wooden spoon.

'It'll be a bit hot,' I say when it's ready, putting the cup and saucer down by Cora's arm.

'Thanks.'

Cora sips at the cup. 'You've put an awful lot of Horlicks in.'

'Sorry. I like it strong.'

The clock ticks away on the wall. We scribble in our books, drink, yawn, sigh, cross out, turn a page.

Then, without warning, a moment from *The Desert Song* comes into my head. I can't stop laughing to myself.

'Roger! You'll wake everyone,' Cora hisses.

'I just thought of that Ken Pewsey, when he had to do that quick change from the Red Shadow to Pierre . . .'

Cora's face lights up. 'And came in without his little wig,' she chuckles.

'It was that look on his face when his hand went up to his head . . .'

'. . . and he realized it wasn't there.' Cora laughs.

Still smiling, I rub my eyes. They feel sore.

'What do they keep them on with?' Cora says.

'What – toupees? I don't know – special glue, I suppose.'

'I wonder what happens in a strong wind.'

'Most probably blow off into the trees, then the birds use them for nests.'

We laugh for a bit, then carry on writing. The hands of the clock are at five to twelve.

'How's it going?' I say. 'I'm almost done.'

'And me. Grammar's all over the place. I'm so tired.'

With a flourish I finish my last sentence, slam the book shut and exhale loudly. A couple of minutes later

Cora closes her own book and starts to put everything back in her bag.

We sit in silence for a moment. A little click comes from the kitchen clock as it hits midnight. The one in the hall chimes twelve whirrs and clunks.

'The spring's gone,' I say.

Cora yawns. 'I'm going to be like one of the living dead tomorrow.' She realizes what she's said, shoots me a look, then drops her eyes and stares down at the table.

I gaze at the empty cup in front of me, at the frothy cream-coloured ring of dried Horlicks just below the rim.

'Do – do you ever think about what happened before?' I ask quietly.

The clock ticks on.

It's ages before Cora speaks.

'Think I'll go back to bed,' she says, getting up, taking her bag and heading for the door. 'Night-night.'

I glance up. Swallow.

'Night-night,' I mutter.

CORA

I pull off my jumper, lay it on the chair, and notice Mimi's blankets have slipped down. I reach over to pull them up, and the sheet catches on something. I lean over. It's the red exercise book, clutched to her chest. She didn't leave it behind at Guerdon Hall, though she left everything else in her haste to get here last night.

I take hold of the corner between finger and thumb, wriggle it, try and pull it away.

Mimi stirs, hugs it even closer.

I sigh, let go, lift up the fold of the bedspread to cover her shoulders, and see that there is a loose piece of paper almost completely fallen out of the bottom of the book. I hold my breath, watch Mimi's face, and carefully, softly, slide it away. Then I gently tuck her in, tiptoe to the crack of the doorway, and unfold the paper in the line of light from the small lamp on the hall table.

An address is printed on the top right-hand side: *St Lazarus Hospital, Founded 1453, Church Road, Hilsea. Telephone: Hilsea 266.* There is a pencilled ring around the telephone number, and written in the middle of the page in spidery letters are two names: *Mrs Lailah Ketch* and *Miss Iris Jewel*.

In the lower corner somebody has drawn a curving M, and touching the two points at the top is a circle like the moon – the sign that was chalked on the doors at Guerdon Hall.

I stand in the half-light and look sideways at Mimi, lying in the shadows, and my heart beats so fiercely I think the pounding might waken her.

Along the hall the kitchen door opens. Yawning loudly, Roger makes his way back to his makeshift bed. When I hear the sitting-room door closing gently behind him, I tiptoe out to my coat and push the paper deep into my pocket.

Dad brings fish and chips – and Ange.

I am sitting across from Mimi, watching the television, pretending not to see her thumbing through her exercise book then holding out the covers and shaking the open pages over her lap. The car growls down The Chase, and from the window we see the sweep of the headlights over the creek. Relieved, we rush down the hall and along the stone passage to the back door. Footsteps crunch along the gravel path. I pull open the door, and a thin woman is standing there with a wary smile on her face.

Our mouths drop open.

She is wearing a drab, pink bouclé two-piece with an off-white Bri-Nylon blouse underneath, making her skin look sallow. The suit has definitely seen better days – like her, by the look of it. The woman's hair, a faded red, is backcombed into a beehive, half covered with a gauzy blue chiffon scarf tied under the chin.

I can't think what she is doing standing at our back door. Dad comes up carrying an old, battered suitcase. I smell the reek of vinegar and realize that the woman is holding, slightly at arm's length, four portions of fish and chips wrapped loosely in the *Daily Mirror*.

'They're from the chippy in Hilsea,' Dad says. 'Hope they haven't gone cold. Oh, this is Angela.'

I recall the scrap of paper pinned to his jacket when he was drunk – *Angela Russell, The Cosy Café, Hilsea 463*.

Surely not. She isn't Dad's type at all – far too skinny, and she must be the wrong side of forty.

'Ange – call me Ange,' she says, pulling off the pale blue chiffon. 'Got any red sauce?'

'In – in the kitchen,' I say.

'I could murder a cuppa tea,' she says, following my pointing finger and pushing open the kitchen door. 'Ooh, very nice, very modern.' She runs her lean hand across the counter. 'Is this that Formica stuff? Love them curtains – like a tin of mandarins, or sunset over Clacton-on-Sea. Need to get them walls sorted, though. Could do with a lick of paint.'

'The wallpaper fell off,' I say.

'There's a funny thing,' she laughs. 'Never heard of that one before. Still, I'm a dab hand with a paintbrush. We could do it together. Go to the paint shop and choose something nice and bright. Cheer the place up. Cold in here, isn't it?' With a little shiver passing across her shoulders, she runs her hand over the radiator.

'At least the boiler's working,' I say. 'Last week it went off and we didn't have no heating at all.'

'Crikey,' she says. 'Must have been like Captain Scott up the Pole.' She points to the kettle. 'Do you mind?'

I shrug, still bewildered.

Ange fills it, lights the gas and looks for the tea caddy, puts the sugar bowl on the table, opens a drawer and finds the teaspoons.

'How many sugars do you have in your tea, Cora? Do we want plates for the fish? Where do you keep them?'

'Don't bother, Ange,' says Dad, coming in. 'Why don't we eat it out of the newspaper in the other room.'

We sit in front of the television, pulling the fish apart with our fingers. *Dr Kildare* starts. Ange sings along with the theme tune, her mouth full of half-chewed chips: '*Laa, laa, la-la-la-la.*'

Dr Kildare strides manfully down the hospital corridor towards the emergency room, his white coat open and flapping behind him like angels' wings, his face, knitted with a sensitive frown, a study in concern. Behind him trot a group of nurses, all starched cotton and perky little caps, lipstick and flicked-up glossy hair.

'Ooh, he can take my temperature any time,' Ange squeals, and elbows Dad so hard in the ribs that he drops a piece of fish onto his knee. The laugh turns into a fit of coughing. A mouthful of chips flies out and Ange catches them in her hand.

'Ooh, look at me. Sorry.' She clears her throat self-consciously, pulls a lavender-scented hanky from her sleeve and wipes her fingers.

When we've finished eating, she gathers all the bits of vinegar-soaked newspaper and scrunches them together into a great big ball.

'More tea?' she calls as she leaves the room.

'No, thanks,' answers Dad; then he whispers, 'Do you like her?'

'Seems all right,' I say. 'Don't know her, do we?'

'Where did you pick her up from?' asks Mimi. 'What's she doing here?'

'That ain't a very nice thing to say,' I scold her.

Something smashes in the kitchen.

I jump up.

Ange is at the table, where she's been setting out the cups and saucers. Her hands are trembling as she fumbles in her bag and pulls out a packet of Capstan Full Strength and a box of matches. She shakes out a cigarette, and two more come with it. She squashes them back into the packet.

I pick the broken pieces of a teacup up off the floor and drop them in the bin.

Ange strikes a match so hard it snaps. She tries another, then another, until at last she manages to light the cigarette and draw it in, then lets the smoke out slowly through her nose in two thin streams. Her hands become still but her strained face remains colourless.

'What's the matter, Ange?'

'Sorry about the cup. I hope it wasn't dear.'

''S all right. We've got loads of them ones.'

'Sorry.'

'Shall I finish doing the tea?'

'Thanks. Yes. Thanks.'

I empty the tea leaves out of the pot, then, just as I go to put another teacup on the empty saucer, Ange stubs out her cigarette in it.

'Would you – would you shut the curtains, love?' she says, taking one of the squashed Capstans out of the packet and rolling it smooth in her fingers before lighting it.

I pull the orange curtains together – sunset over Clacton-on-Sea – happy to shut out the blank black miserable evening outside. When I turn back, I notice Ange staring at the window as if she were still looking through the glass.

'What – what happened, Ange? Why did you drop the cup?'

'We're – we're on our own out here, aren't we?'

'Yes, the nearest people are the Treasures, up at Glebe House, past the top of the hill.'

'They wouldn't come down here, would they?'

'Never,' I say. 'Not in a million years. Why? What's the matter?'

'Someone – no, maybe they didn't . . . I was over at the

sink just now, rinsing out the cup, and I thought – I thought someone was looking in – looking right at me.'

'What? What did they look like? You sure it wasn't your reflection – you know, against the dark?'

'Yes, most probably.' Her hand shakes again as she draws on her cigarette. 'Stupid, eh? I thought it was this woman. It gave me such a fright I dropped the blimmin' cup . . .' She blows out the smoke. 'Then – then I saw the face was mine after all. It was just me looking at myself.'

This woman is a gift to me. She does not know it, but the dying lights are on her. Her skin is thinning.

Patience, Aphra, patience and endurance – and you will get inside.

The kettle starts whistling.

Ange turns towards it, squashes the barely-smoked cigarette into the saucer.

'It's all right,' I say. 'You sit down. I'll make some for the two of us. Dad doesn't want any more.'

I pour the water into the pot.

Ange coughs, then we sit in silence for quite a while. So many questions I want to ask her, sorting them out in my head so they won't sound like prying. In the end I needn't have bothered because, out of the blue, she says simply, 'You're wondering what I'm doing here, aren't you?'

I lower my eyes. Ange pours milk into her cup. 'I come from near Mistleham way,' she says, 'but there's no work for a woman on her own up there. I saw this advert in the paper – a job with a room at the Cosy Café – you know, the transport caff on the other side of Hilsea, set back off the road, opposite the Hand and Flowers.'

'No, sorry.'

'Never mind. Anyway, I was getting really fed up with it, earning peanuts – the long hours on me feet all day, and living in this bedsit over the kitchen, with mould coming down the walls and smelling of grease.'

She takes a sip of tea, blows across the cup, sips some more.

'I haven't been feeling too good lately and the caff was getting a bit much, wearing me out, specially the evening shift, and I'm not really what you'd call the sort of woman lorry drivers like serving up their bacon and eggs. They like a bit of glamour – to be honest, I couldn't have been much good for business.' She stirs another spoonful of sugar into her tea. 'Mike, the owner, only took me on because he was desperate for a waitress quick when his wife, Beryl, ran off with the chap who delivered the baked beans.

'Anyway, I decided to look for another job that wasn't going to do me in so much, and put a card in the newsagent's window in Hilsea, and this barmaid, Muriel, who works in the Thin Man, telephoned me

Tuesday night, said she'd seen my card, and this bloke was in the pub and was grumbling about—' Ange breaks off, puts down her cup and reaches for her cigarette packet. 'Oh, listen to me, going on . . .'

'Grumbling?' I don't really want to say it. 'About Mimi and me?'

'About you and Mimi?' she comes in quickly, pulling out another cigarette and tossing the packet back on the table. 'No, no, dear, no.'

I decide to believe her.

'Was he grumbling about Auntie Kath, then? She came with us out here for a bit, but she went back to London – last week.'

'Yeah, that was it.' She strikes a match, sucks the cigarette alight, then shakes the match out and drops it into the saucer. 'This Muriel said your dad was having a moan about your Auntie Kath – all that sort of thing, you know – and was looking for somebody to mind his two kids – six quid a week in your hand, all expenses, board and lodging thrown in.'

She blows out a stream of smoke. 'Seemed too good to miss, a doddle really, and better money, and I've always liked kids, not having had any of me own. Thought you was a bit younger actually, the way Muriel was talking, though I don't suppose she would have known. What are you – sixteen yet?'

'Nearly.'

'Anyway, Muriel passed me on to your dad. He was happy as Larry, didn't even want no references, said he had to go up to London for a bit the next day, the Wednesday, and he could pick me up from Hilsea Friday night on his way back. I thought he sounded a bit squiffy, so I told Muriel to write down my particulars and make sure he took the bit of paper home with him, so he'd remember when he sobered up.'

She taps off some ash, wants to ask me something but doesn't quite know how to put it. At last she says, 'Your dad win the football pools, did he?'

'Sorry?'

'Just wondered how you came by this big house, as you're from the East End by the sound of you.'

'No, we – er – it was left to us,' I stammer.

'Family?'

'On – on my mum's side. They were Guerdons.'

She draws on her cigarette, her almost colourless eyes shaded with pity. I shift uncomfortably in my chair, look at the table top.

'Hard being a widow man, specially with kids,' she says, then adds, 'Oh, I forgot.'

She balances her cigarette on the edge of the ashtray, then bends down and rummages in her handbag, eventually pulling out a couple of little brown bottles. 'The doctor gave me these. Should've taken them this morning.'

She shakes out some tablets and swallows them down with a gulp of tea.

Thinking Mum is dead makes her mindful of her own health.

In the night the snow comes.

The boiler breaks down again.

Even when the radiators are working, Guerdon Hall is never really warm, but when they are not, freezing, biting air from the surrounding marshes flows like icy liquid under the doors, finding its easy way through the little gaps and spaces between the splitting wood, the ancient, ill-fitting glass, cracked and hairy plaster, and crumbling brickwork.

ROGER

Before I even open my eyes, I can hear that snow has fallen in the night – muffled stillness, broken by the soft crunch of the postman's boots on the steps of the veranda, the thud of the letters on the hall mat, the distant hum of the milk-float coming, late, carefully, up Fieldpath Road.

The phone rings. I turn towards the wall and pull the blankets up around my ears. Silence from Pete in the bunk below.

A door opens. The rumbling of Terry's feet on the runner in the hall.

'Hello. This is North Fairing 410 – yes, all right. I'll tell them.'

From the bottom of Terry's lungs comes a mighty yell, almost loud enough to send the walls vibrating. 'Pete! Rugby's cancelled!'

From behind Mum and Dad's bedroom door, a groan from Dad. 'Terry, for Pete's sake . . .'

A distant cry from Dennis: 'I'll blinkin' get you, Terry!'

Terry scuttles up to Pamela's bedroom and is

probably pulling off her covers. 'More snow, Pam. Get up. Come and build a snowman.'

I hear Pam shuffling down her little staircase and into Mum and Dad's room.

'Can Mimi come and make a snowman with us?' she calls.

'Pam, it's only half past six,' I hear Mum mumble. 'We'll telephone later. Go back to bed.'

'Not tired no more.'

The sound of metallic scraping. Someone in one of the new bungalows is already up and out with a spade, clearing their concrete path. The milkman climbs the steps in the postman's footprints, clinks the empty bottles out of the metal crate by the front door and clunks in the full ones.

Early in the afternoon, Dad phones Guerdon Hall, asks if Mimi wants to come and make a snowman with Pamela. He'll go and pick her up in the car if he can get to the house.

'Come down with me, Roger,' Dad calls, 'in case I get stuck.'

I pull on my boots, my big coat, gloves and scarf.

The car makes it along Old Glebe Lane as far as Glebe House, but Dad doesn't want to risk the hill, so we get out and walk the rest of the way.

At the bottom of the hill the road divides. Ahead of us

is the thickly covered track to All Hallows, under a network of snowy branches.

I feel a tingle of sweat on my forehead, a hollow feeling in my stomach.

Thank goodness Dad doesn't hang about, but tramps off to the right up The Chase.

'Why anyone would want to come back to this god-forsaken place, I can't imagine,' he says, stopping to wipe some snow dust off his glasses. 'I thought that after Mrs Eastfield died, the house would have been pulled down. Would have been the best thing for it.'

A heart attack in the graveyard – that's the story that went round in Bryers Guerdon four years ago. A small tucked-away paragraph in the local paper – subsidence in the old church, built on wet ground too close to the marshes, causing part of the crypt to collapse. In the village, whispers behind hands, knowing nods. Then, after a couple of days, nothing more. The village continued to do what it had always done – kept quiet.

Softly curved drifts on either side of The Chase close us in like a tunnel. At its end is the dark, looming shape of the old barn. Everything is densely silent, but for the noise of our breathing and the dull thump of our boots breaking through the flat surface of the snow.

The bridge is icy, the creek a narrowing channel – the ice, like jagged, broken pieces of frosted glass, creeping from the edges little by little into the sluggish water.

I'm feeling nervous.

The windows of Guerdon Hall are blank and unwelcoming, diamond-shaped mirrors of the cold, bleak sky. The newly-painted white walls on one side look grubby under the snowy roof.

'I'm all for history,' Dad mutters as we turn the corner at the end of the front wall, 'but this is a wretched place.'

CORA

Mr Jotman and Roger stand awkwardly in the hall, their white breath clouds mixing with ours – the house is so unbearably cold – while Ange pulls a second jumper over the one Mimi is already wearing. For a girl who doesn't normally seek company, Mimi is surprisingly biddable. Maybe she thinks Pam is too young to pry, won't ask the uncomfortable questions other girls might ask when they are on the edge of friendship.

'Breathe in,' says Ange, buttoned up to her neck in a thick woollen cardigan, 'or I won't be able to do your coat up.'

'Perishing, isn't it,' says Mr Jotman. Weather's the best bet when you've nothing in common. 'Wonder if that's the last of it – the snow.'

'Odd to have so much in November,' says Dad.

'Never seen the like,' says Mr Jotman.

Then Mr Jotman gets on to DIY, the other fail-safe.

'I'd have a look at your boiler for you,' he says. 'Could be something to do with the pressure, or a leak. That'd be a nuisance, having to lift floorboards. I'd hate to make a mess of it. You'd do better to get somebody in. There's this good chap in Daneflete would fix it, I'm sure. Jim's his name. I'll let you have his phone number.'

'Thank you, I'd appreciate that,' says Dad, knowing he's going to take the boiler to bits himself, shouting at all the parts as they come out.

I steal a glance at Roger, searching for the boy he once was in this tall, angular person he's become. I can't get used to it. I notice him gazing at the scratch marks on the wooden panelling where the priest hole used to be. He looks across. I lower my eyes, but the connection is made, the memories colliding in the seven feet of space between us.

'We might have a couple of paraffin stoves we could lend you for the time being,' Mr Jotman continues. 'Mr Aylott at the shop does paraffin, but I've probably got a spare can in the shed.'

'Thanks.'

'I'll get them down to you when I bring Mimi back.'

'Actually, I'm hoping to uncover the fireplaces in a couple of the rooms this morning and see if I can get them going. Maybe' – he sizes up Roger – 'maybe your lad here could give us a hand.'

'Of course. You don't mind, do you, Roger?' says Mr Jotman.

Roger shifts on his feet. 'That's all right,' he says quietly.

When Mr Jotman and Mimi leave for their trek up to the car, Roger helps Dad take the plasterboard off the fireplace in the sitting room with a crowbar. It was put up so badly, it pops off in no time, revealing the familiar bricked space, blackened by soot, under the heavy stone mantel. Even the fire basket is still there, propped up against the back wall.

'Tell you what,' says Dad. 'I'll tackle the fireplace in the dining room and you two can start bringing some logs from the barn. They're the old trees from the garden that Blezzard chopped up.'

'I'll put the kettle on for some tea,' Ange calls from the kitchen, 'and break open these digestives. Thank goodness the pipes aren't frozen.'

I put on my coat and boots while Roger leans against the cold wall of the stone passage, rubbing his arms and blowing on his fingers through his gloves.

'Who's that woman?' he says.

'Woman? Oh, that's Ange. She came last night, with Dad.'

'Is there . . . ? Um, are they . . . ? You know—'

'Ssh, she might hear. No, not like with Auntie Kath – you know, the one who went back to London. Dad's got her in to look after us. He goes away a lot.'

I pull down my woolly hat, uncomfortable with all this – Auntie Kath living with us, and her and Dad not married, not to mention Mum being in the hospital – always keeping quiet and separate so nobody gets a chance to find out about these things, telling Mimi not to say a word to anyone at school, just in case it gets around.

'Don't know anything about Ange really,' I say, 'except she worked in some transport caff in Hilsea.'

'Come on,' Roger says gently, moving away from the wall. 'Better get the logs. It's freezing in here.'

The huge barn door is leaning off its remaining hinge, but standing open enough for us to get through, though we have to climb over a heap of snow that's blown in across the entrance.

Among the rubbish in the straw – the paint tins, gripper rods and broken plasterboard – is the long sheet of wallpaper with all the pieces of pottery still laid out where I left them.

Roger stoops to pick up one of the curved pieces. 'What on earth's this?' he says.

'Don't know. I found all these funny old bottles. Look at this sludgy stuff – smells horrible, doesn't it? And this one's got bent iron nails in it – they're all rusty – and look at that, it's like hair, and . . . and I found an old fingernail clipping, all hard and yellow, but dropped it in the straw.'

'Ugh.' He screws up his nose. 'What are they? And where have they come from?'

'I think the builders must have found them when they were doing up the house, and chucked them out with the rest of the rubbish. They were stopped up at the top with wax and a bit of string. Look – like this.'

I show him the broken top. He turns it over in his hand.

'This old bloke, Mr Wragge, who's been helping out the builder, Mr Blezzard, he knows what they are,' I say, 'but he won't flippin' well tell me. Come on, better get the wood.'

The logs are piled in an untidy heap against the far wall.

When we come out of the barn, dragging the sack of wood between us through the snow, the sky has darkened to a deep iron-grey and a few flakes begin to speckle our shoulders.

'Cavalry's arrived,' calls Ange as we clatter in at the back door, stamping the snow off our feet. 'Kettle's on.'

Dad helps Roger carry the sack into the sitting room, where he stacks the logs to one side of the wide stone fireplace.

I twist some sheets of newspaper into kindling and

lay them in the fire basket, while Dad and Roger break little side twigs off the logs to mix with the paper, though some are too bendy to snap.

'I'll get the saw,' says Dad, leaving the room.

'I hope it lights,' Roger says. 'Some of this wood's really green and damp. We might end up with a house full of smoke.' He peels off a piece of bark and tosses it onto the kindling. 'When we lit our first fire after the summer, we all nearly choked to death till Mum opened the windows. It wasn't the wood 'cause we have coal, but this bird had built its nest in the top of the chimney pot, stupid thing.'

'It's most probably all right,' I say, leaning across the fire basket and peering up the black dark chimney. My shoulder brushes the soot clinging to the small herring-bone bricks at the back. Some of it dislodges and falls into the hearth.

'Give us that.' I point to the rusty old poker leaning behind the log stack.

Roger puts it into my outstretched hand. I push it up the chimney and wiggle it about. More soot falls, and dust and cobwebs, small stones and bits of rubble. I shut my eyes, feel the dirt on my face, in my hair, taste the soot. My hand and the sleeve of my coat are black.

'Just a minute,' I mutter. 'There's something here.'

Reaching up, I run the poker along the crusted edge of a ledge at the back of the fireplace, a foot or so above the opening. I scrape it along one way, then the other. It bumps over something lying on the ledge. I stretch out with the end, try to dislodge the thing and pull it towards the shaft. At first it won't move out of its bed of hardened soot. I scrape at it again and again.

'Flippin' hell!' coughs Roger. 'What are you doing?'

'I'm going to get it out. It's coming . . . Hang on.'

Forcing the point of the poker underneath, I manage to flip the thing up, then with two hands slide the poker backwards and forwards along its length. At last the object comes loose. In a shower of soot it falls down onto the filthy twigs and newspaper in the fire basket – a flattened, blackened, rectangular piece of thick dry leather, about four inches by five.

Snap! The last silken strand is cut. The cloak of enchantment has fallen to pieces. The house stands open.

'What on earth's that?' Roger says. I pick it up and run my fingers over its grimy surface.

Soft footsteps, muffled in sheepskin boots, come down the hall carpet. Teacups rattle on a tray.

Quickly I push the object deep down behind the pile of logs.

'Why are you hiding it?'

'Don't say nothing – all right?'

'How many sugars, Roger?' Ange backs into the room

and sets the tray down on the small table behind the settee. 'Goodness, Cora, look at the state of you! What on earth have you been up to? And how are you going to get a bath if the hot water's off?'

Dad comes in with more logs and the saw. 'Thought you'd have lit the fire by now.'

'I was just checking the chimney was clear and some soot fell down.'

'That was a bit stupid, wasn't it?' says Dad. 'Here, Roger – you saw off some more kindling and I'll try and get this started.'

Dad strikes a match and touches it to the ends of the newspaper, then another match, and another. He throws on more small twigs as Roger saws them off. They crackle into life, but thick dark smoke rolls into the room.

Ange fans her face with one hand, coughing till her eyes water, as she tries to pour the tea with the other. 'Crikey, it's like the bloody Black Hole of Calcutta in here.'

'It isn't going to work, Dad,' I splutter. 'We're all going to suffocate.'

He throws on one of the larger logs.

'I'm getting a bucket of water to put it out,' says Ange, breathlessly, heading towards the door.

'No, wait,' says Dad, his eyes streaming. 'This fire hasn't been lit for years, and in this sort of weather you can get this little cushion of cold air stuck halfway up the chimney. If we wait a bit, the smoke might start going up. I'll stick another log on.'

Eventually the air clears a little, but the acrid smell remains. Even so, as the fire begins to draw, the warmth is welcome, despite each fresh, damp log sending up a stream of hissing new smoke. When it's properly ablaze, we sit in our coats in front of the hearth, drinking our tea, feet stretched out so the rubber soles of our boots feel as if they might be melting, the front of our bodies burning hot, our backs frozen.

Just as it's getting dark, Mr Jotman passes by the sitting-room window with Mimi.

When Roger and I go to the back door, Mr Jotman sets a small stove down onto the flagstones and Mimi almost drops a can of paraffin.

'Carried it all the way down the hill,' she says, clawing and unclawing her hands. 'Nearly slipped twice.'

'Did you have fun?'

'Built this *huge* snowman,' she says, spreading out her arms, 'and made some fairy cakes with sprinkles on.'

Mr Jotman pulls a brown paper bag out of his pocket and looks inside. 'Sorry,' he says. 'Fairy crumbs.'

'You can still eat them,' Mimi says.

'Cup of tea before you go?' Ange asks.

'Ooh no, but thank you, must get back,' Mr Jotman says.

Roger takes his gloves out of his coat pocket, flicks up his eyes. 'See you, then,' he says.

'See you,' I say.

He sets off with his dad along the snowy path, two dark shapes disappearing into the twilight.

Later, Dad, Ange, Mimi and I eat egg on toast off our laps in the sitting room.

Dad says, 'Better let the girls have the paraffin stove tonight.'

'No, tell you what,' Ange says, 'why don't they sleep here in the sitting room? Shame to waste the fire. It'll be like camping, a bit of fun. What do you think?' Dad shrugs his shoulders. 'Go and get your blankets,' she adds.

'You'd better have the stove, then, Ange,' says Dad. 'I'll be all right. I've known worse, under canvas in a blizzard, training with the army in Yorkshire.'

I let Mimi have the settee and make up a bed for myself on the carpet.

When we settle down to sleep, the fire is burning steadily, lively, brilliantly red.

In a dream a bell tolls.

I find myself drowsily awake, stiff with cold, my hip and shoulder bones aching from the pressure on the hard floor, and the clock in the hall is striking three.

The fire is almost out. In the darkness the ash-grey logs settle in a shower of sparks.

I hear gentle breathing from Mimi, curled up on the settee under her mound of blankets, and Ange's distant coughing from upstairs.

What has woken me? Is it the sound of the wind in the chimney – a low, whirling rush as if the air is moving round and round inside the stack.

Something light falls into the hearth, too dark to see – perhaps another shower of old soot, blackening the remains of the embers.

Then a strange sensation passes over me, like a draught of icy air that steals slowly across my face, numbing my hands as they clutch the edge of the eiderdown. I pull it tight around me, but the bitter cold creeps around my shoulders, down my back and legs to my feet, chilling my toes through their socks. My teeth chatter. I am rigid with cold, and cannot seem to shiver off a sudden and crushing sense of dread.

I hear Mimi take a gasp of air, pulling her blankets closer in her sleep.

After a few seconds the freezing draught seems to subside and I can see once again the small glow of red in the fireplace.

Bent with discomfort, trembling, I throw off the eiderdown, reach for the poker and prod the embers till chunks of charred wood and ash fall through the fire basket. I lean over for another piece of wood and throw it on the dying fire, but for a few minutes it just lies there, as if too tired to take a flame. I poke again, until at last a small blue tongue licks up and over the curved coat of bark, and it begins to sizzle and crack.

When at last the fire flickers up golden and red with a little heat to warm my deadened face, I get up, reach behind the log pile and drag out the strange piece of dried-up leather I found on the ledge in the chimney.

I turn it over, brush off some soot and blow out the dust gathered deep in the cracks. I run my fingers across it, then realize it is folded tightly over in the middle. I turn it over once more and, holding it over the little flames in the grate, try to rub off more of the hard soot.

Leaning further in, I bring the hard leather close to my eye, and notice nail heads, evenly spaced, running all around the edge. Along the front and back of the smooth, folded-over side are scratched, blackened lines, difficult to make out in the half-light, but rather like letters – an S, an E . . . maybe a B – or is it an R? My eyes ache. Towards the bend of the fold, another R, perhaps a P – hard to say. I lick my finger and trace it over the marks.

SEHSURARHPA

Is it some ancient language – from Africa? Egypt? India?

A code? A message? A puzzle?

A name?

My sooty finger runs forwards, backwards, forwards once more. All at once I realize what the letters are – a name, scratched backwards.

APHRARUSHES

Aphra Rushes.

The witch.

A bristling sensation creeps along my arms.

I glance across to the settee and see two eyes peeping out over the blankets.

'How long you been awake?' I ask.

'Only a minute,' Mimi says. 'What's that there?'

'It was hidden up the chimney. I found it when Roger was here.'

Mimi stares, frowning, at the thing in my hand.

I think I hear a creak from the staircase. Mimi's eyes flicker towards the door.

'Put that thing back, Cora,' she breathes.

'What?'

'Up the chimney. Put it back again.'

'I can't now, can I? There's a fire going. I'll put it back in the morning.'

'First thing?'

'It's only a bit of old leather, Mimi.'

She is listening for something. I strain my ears, but hear only the rustle of the flames in the wood.

'Promise you'll put it back first thing,' she whispers again.

'All right. Promise.'

'Cross your heart.'

'Cross my heart. You warm enough with all them blankets?'

'Like a piece of toast.'

'Can I have one, then? I'm so blinkin' cold I can't sleep.'

Mimi jiggles to dislodge the top blanket. I begin to reach over when there is a cough from the hall.

My heart skips. Mimi jumps.

The door creaks open.

Ange is standing there, dressed only in her winceyette nightdress, the firelight flickering on her bony forehead and hollow cheeks.

Behind her the hall is black, unlit. She has come down the stairs in the dark.

'Ange?' I gulp. 'You all right?'

She looks at us – first at me, then at Mimi – but it is as if she doesn't actually see us. Her eyes are gleaming with a strange glassy sheen.

She says nothing, coughs again, moves backwards into the darkness and pulls the door shut. Mimi and I hold our breath and stare at each other as we hear her bare feet moving back towards the stairs.

I swallow. 'Must be sleepwalking,' I whisper, my heart fluttering.

I need no rush-light or candle. I have nothing to fear in this darkness.

She struggled against me a little, but was full of sleep, and weak. The fight went out of her after a while, and I felt once again the frame and set of hard bone, the coursing of bile and blood, and the slow, steady surge of breath.

I flex her fingers, stretch them, and run her hand along the panelling, touch the wood I touched then, feel the scratches made by Cain Lankin's nails. For a moment I brush those marks with her fingers and rest her cheek upon them, lingering for a while, fancying I can sense some remnant of him there. I move back down the dark passage towards the staircase and climb the self-same stairs I trod taking the child to his snow-pale mother for their last embrace.

'Please put that thing back when the fire goes down – that thing you found,' Mimi hisses, pulling her blankets around her with a last quick glimpse at the door.

I get up quietly and stuff the piece of leather well down behind the logs, grab the blanket Mimi has kicked out for me, and wrap myself up on the floor.

Unsettled, still shivering with cold, I turn over

towards the fire and see Roger's school scarf – navy with red and green stripes just above the fringe – on the floor under the small table near my pillow. I reach out with my fingers, pull it over.

It smells of bonfires, leaves, the outside, of the ease of Roger's house.

I wind it around my neck, roll myself in the eider-down and blanket, and tuck in my feet. The scarf lies crossed over my chest under my close-folded arms, a scrap of warmth.

I lie there with no hope of sleep. Troubled, I wait restlessly for the pale, cold dawn.

After church, Pete, Dennis and Terry turn off the main road and begin to tramp through the snow down to Bryers Guerdon. I stand for a moment, looking over at the white hedgerows that mark the line of Old Glebe Lane.

'You coming? Dinner'll be ready soon,' Pete calls, a tad touchily. 'Remember we're having it early 'cause Dad's going over to clear Grandma's drive.'

'I won't be a minute. I left my scarf down at Guerdon Hall yesterday. I'll need it for school. You go on. Unless' – I swallow – 'do you want to come with me?'

His face darkens. 'You've got to be joking, mate,' he mutters through clenched teeth, turning away.

'Woo-woo!' Dennis pouts. 'Roger's going to see that Cora.'

'Shut up, you flippin' idiot!' cries Pete, from nowhere landing a whistling thump on the side of Dennis's head.

Shrieking, 'What did you do that for?' Dennis lunges towards Pete, kicking out at his shins, then slipping on the snow. Pete seizes the moment to snatch his arm and twist it behind his back. Dennis struggles, howling, 'Get off me! Leave off!' trying to catch Pete's ankles with his heels.

'You're really naughty boys!' Terry taunts from a safe distance. 'Only just been to Communion an' all. Going to tell Mum!' He turns and runs off down the lane, almost coming a cropper on a patch of ice.

Dennis spits after Terry. Pete, in a fury, still holding Dennis's arm in a lock up his back, dishes out another clout, and Dennis bawls again, managing to land a backward kick on Pete's knee. 'Why're you so – flippin' – mad? I – didn't – say a – blimmin' thing! Let go!'

'Stop it, Pete! Stop it!' I yell, wrenching him off. 'Leave him alone!'

Without saying another word, Pete, panting, flexing his fingers, marches away.

'You all right, mate?' I ask Dennis.

Red-faced, a few angry, embarrassed tears welling, he shrugs me off and rubs and stretches his arm. 'What's the matter with him?' he mutters, kicking at a stone sticking up out of the thin crust of a frozen puddle, before crossing the road so he doesn't have to walk down on the same side as Pete.

What's the matter with him? It's best not to know, Dennis.

Shaken, I walk to the Thin Man, then cross over into Old Glebe Lane.

It is slightly warmer, and some of the snow has melted in the weak sunshine, but even so, large patches hug the bottoms of the trees and it's blown deep into the dark spaces under the hedgerows.

Ahead of me, a smart Rover noses out of the gates of Glebe House. It's Mr and Mrs Treasure, off to the service at St Mary's in North Fairing. Mr Treasure is surprised to see me on the road, turns into the wet at such an awkward angle that I have to move back onto the verge; the back wheel sprays a huge fan of cold slush around my knees, which then slops in an icy dribble down inside my boots. Mrs Treasure waves to me with her leather-gloved hand. I wave back with my big grey woolly one and force a smile through gritted teeth.

I shake one leg and then the other, but it only sends the freezing water trickling down my socks.

No sooner have I set off again than I hear the throb of a second engine and the squelch of another set of tyres. Father and Mrs Mansell's battered old Wolseley emerges from the drive of Glebe House, also no doubt heading for St Mary's. Father Mansell touches his hat to me as they pass. Again I raise my glove, then emerge from the verge into another shower of slush that shoots out from under the wheels. If Father Mansell had deliberately aimed at me he couldn't have done a better job.

As I stand there, drenched, cold and uncomfortable, I feel stupidly sorry for myself, and irritated with the never forgetting, with the past that's always tapping me on the shoulder – and Pete too, it seems.

I decide to turn back, get some hot food, some warm,

dry clothes, when I see Cora coming along the lane, muffled in her big blue duffel coat and red bobble hat.

'You left this!' she calls, waving my scarf.

'Oh, thanks.'

I wrap it gratefully around my neck. It smells sweet.

We stand there awkwardly for a moment.

Then Cora says, 'Coming down? Dad's got some fires going and we can make a cup of tea.'

'Mum's doing dinner,' I say, 'but I suppose I could come for a minute.'

We walk on past the woods and down the hill, and as we draw near to the turning for The Chase and I look down the track to All Hallows, I am filled with a sense of deep remembered dread. I think of Pete again.

I glance at Cora. She must see something in my face, turns slightly away.

'Do you want to see it again – the church?' she asks, still not looking at me.

'What's it like?' My voice cracks oddly.

'Well, they – they started to do some repairs, but the stuff's all been left – you know, the bricks and sand and things. There's this big fence round the church so you can't get in. And' – she pauses, looks down at her boots – 'there's Auntie Ida's grave, just a couple of feet away from where she . . . you know, where she died. Do you want to come? You don't have to, you know.'

I truly don't know what's best.

'Perhaps – maybe I *should* go,' I say, at last.

The sky above the stark black branches of the winter trees has turned a deep brooding grey, and the air seems ever more raw as we move down the track. Inside my gloves my fingertips are deadening.

'Feels like more snow's coming,' Cora says, rubbing her hands together.

My feet are heavy and unwilling as we approach the lychgate, bleak and miserable on the left-hand side of the road. A small tree rises out of the watery snow between the pillars, exactly in the place where Long Lankin fell.

And he haunts it all, every stone of this gate, each frozen leaf and twig and blade of icy grass around it. Somewhere behind that net of new branches there are words carved into the wooden beam holding up the roof – *CAVE BESTIAM . . . Beware of the beast.*

Something bitter comes up from my stomach. I swallow it down.

Then the snow begins to fall, just gently drifting at first, powdering our hats and our shoulders.

In silence, we tramp onwards to the metal gate and stand there, neither of us inclined to go through it into the churchyard.

I feel myself shudder.

'You all right?' Cora says.

'Just cold,' I pretend.

I look across the top of the gate at the new grey grave-stone, capped with a soft arch of snow. No need to ask who is buried there. Above it the elder tree has spread a shield of branches.

The freezing air stings my eyes. They begin to water. I should have been braver than this.

Through my coat sleeve I feel Cora's hand.

'We can always come again another day.'

We turn and walk back up the track in silence.

In sight of the bend curving into The Chase, I steal a sideways glance at Cora. She blinks the snow off her lashes, and in that fleeting, unguarded moment I am shocked to see how drained her face looks, how deep the shadowy smudges under her eyes appear in the steely air.

'Are *you* all right?' I ask.

She turns her head away.

'What's the matter?' I say; then, more gently, 'You can tell *me*, surely, after everything . . .'

She doesn't move. I try the breezy tack, stamp my feet and blow through my gloves. 'Honestly, I can't stand around here for too long. It's so parky I think my socks have frozen solid.'

She lowers her eyes. 'I don't want to trouble you, Roger.'

I wipe some snow off my nose. It's getting thicker. 'We're always going to be troubled, Cora, all of us – you, me, Mimi' – I think of Pete's outburst in the road – 'and even Pete. I think it would have been better if we'd talked, Pete and me' – I look at her – 'but we never did.'

'It's just that—' she begins, stops, begins again. 'This place seems, I don't know, not like other places. Even now, after everything, it's not right . . .'

'Just tell me.'

'Honestly, I really wanted to tell you before.' She blows out a long breath of resignation. 'You see, not long after we came, I was all by myself in the house when I found this bunch of twigs tied to the front door knocker with funny red string. It really scared me, Roger. Why should anybody put something like that there? Then, on Bonfire Night, someone hung little white stones over the back door, with the same red string. Auntie Kath threw them away.'

Then Cora takes off her glove and pulls a folded sheet of paper out of her pocket, pushes it into my hand.

'Look, I found this in Mimi's book – at your house, actually. See, it's from the St Lazarus Hospital in Hilsea.'

'The St Laz?'

'What is it?'

'Oh, it's not the sort of hospital that's got doctors and nurses and things; it's almshouses – really, really old, hundreds of years. It's little houses all joined together, five or six of them – I can't remember exactly – for old gentlemen to live in.'

Cora taps on a letter M crowned with a circle. 'And look, you see this little drawing? Mimi scrawled it on our door with chalk – least I think it was her. Dad made me rub it off, then I found one on the front door an' all. Do you know what it is?'

'No idea.' I try and puzzle it out for a few seconds, then give up. 'Have you asked Mimi about it? And these two?' I run a finger across the two names – *Mrs Lailah Ketch* and *Miss Iris Jewel*.

'To be honest, I didn't want her to know I'd pinched this paper from her. But when I do ask her anything, she clams up, like blimmin' everybody else – even like Auntie Ida did until the very end. It's like an infectious disease around here, everyone keeping flippin' secrets.'

'Come on, Cora,' I say. 'You're almost as bad.'

She sighs. 'Maybe I am. Maybe I've caught the disease an' all.'

I kick the snow off a tree root to see if I can feel anything through my boots.

'Do you know who these ladies are?' I ask.

'Of course I don't, but Mimi does.'

'Um, do you mind if we keep walking. Everything's gone numb.'

Cora puts the paper back in her pocket, and we trudge on without a word until we're almost at The Chase, then she says, 'Oh, you know that piece of leather we found up the chimney yesterday, before we lit the fire?'

'The thing you hid behind the logs?'

'Well, it's got a name scratched on it – backwards.'

'Crikey.'

'Do you remember the witch who killed the Guerdon baby with Long Lankin, the one who was burned here at Bryers Guerdon?' She turns and faces back down the track. 'Down there . . .' She points towards the lychgate. 'She was burned down there.'

'Aphra Rushes,' I breathe.

'It was winter.' Cora shivers. 'I wonder if they brought her down this track, and it was snowing, like this.'

A few seconds go by. Unsettled, we turn and plod on towards the bend.

'Why do you think her name's backwards?' I say.

'How should I know?'

All at once Cora gasps and stares straight ahead, her face colourless under the vivid blood-red of her hat. I follow her gaze. Through the flurry of snowflakes I can make out two dark figures struggling up the hill.

Cora starts to move quickly. 'We've got to catch up with them,' she cries, stumbling on. 'I'm sure it's the two women whose names are on the paper. They must come from Hilsea – I saw them catch the Hilsea bus last week.'

The snow is now sweeping down the hill towards us, reddening our cheeks, filling our mouths, settling in an icy crust on the front of our coats.

We battle up the slope, heads bent, hanging onto each other to stop slipping, but by the time we crest the hill and squint ahead through the white, gusting swirl, the two figures are way ahead, almost at the main road. Breathless, we plough on, but at the end of the lane their footprints are so heavily covered we can't see whether they turned left or right. What we hear, though, is the throbbing of a bus, just visible in the distance, labouring through the snow towards Hilsea.

Cora covers her cold cheeks with her hands and puffs out, 'I can't believe they've got away.'

'What were they doing at Guerdon Hall? They must have been there – there's nowhere else to go.'

'See if we can find out.'

The snow eases as we turn, stumble back down the hill and tramp along The Chase, and by the time we reach the bridge it is falling sparsely once more.

From across the creek comes the sound of a man shouting. Alarmed, we hurry on towards the house, round the corner and approach the sitting-room window. Cora pulls me in and we flatten ourselves against the wall.

'. . . upsetting Mimi like that!' Mr Drumm is yelling. 'She won't even let me in her room! Stuck a ruddy chair against the door or something! I won't have it, Ange, making her cry like that! She's had enough to bloody put up with!'

'I'm sorry, Mr Drumm—'

'And shrieking at them two women like – like a fishwife!'

'I've told you I'm sorry, Mr Drumm. I don't know what got into me. I don't even remember what I said.'

'I tell you, Ange, I don't want no crazy woman looking after my kids! I – I've had enough of it! You'll be out on your bloody ear!' Mr Drumm goes quiet for a moment. We peer round the edge of the icy window and see him distractedly running his hand through his hair.

He starts to speak again. We duck back.

'They must have got lost, the two of them – looked ruddy frozen,' he says. 'You could have made them a cup of tea, helped them get warm by the fire. What were you ruddy playing at, shouting at them like that, telling them to push off?'

'I told you – I think they were looking in the window, I think I remember that – then Mimi came down, tried to talk to them . . . I think—'

'This is a bloody awful start, Ange!'

Then, out of the corner of my eye, I notice something blue in the middle of a patch of watery slush, just a few feet away from us. Cora looks over as I crouch down under the window and steal towards it – a large drum of Cerebos salt lying on its side, lid off, contents spilled across the path in an arc, melting the snow.

I pick it up, shrug my shoulders.

Cora dips down and creeps towards me, takes the tin, turns it in her hand curiously, then, with raised eyebrows and an answering shrug, drops it back into the snow. Glancing cautiously at the window, she waves me to follow her round the house.

As we turn the corner I can smell roasting meat. My stomach growls.

Moving along the wall, we step over another spilled drum of salt turning the snow to a puddle.

'Has your dad, or Ange, tried to clear the path?' I whisper.

'Don't know,' Cora says under her breath, 'but we've never had that posh salt in the house. We have Saxa.'

She snatches a look to right and left, then moves out slightly and cranes her neck upwards to one of the first-floor windows.

She cups her hands around her mouth, tries to shout quietly: 'Mimi!'

She steps back, calls again. 'Mimi!'

A face comes to the window. In the same moment I take in Mimi's watery mouth and tear-streaked cheeks, the glass steams up, and she wrenches the curtains furiously together.

'Oh, Mimi . . .' Cora sighs.

'Should you go up and see her?'

'She's not going to let me in any more than Dad. She's . . . well, she's a bit odd sometimes.'

Cora thinks for few seconds, pats her pockets, then says, 'I'm sorry, but have you got any money?'

'What?'

'Have you got enough for the bus to Hilsea? I want to find those two women.'

'What?' I jingle the few coins in my pocket. I was going to get Dad the Sunday newspaper from Mrs Wickerby's on the way back from church. '*Hilsea? Now?*'

'Roger – would you come with me?'

The smell of sizzling meat with a hint of lemon fills my nose.

'Aren't you starving?' I ask, looking along the wall to the kitchen window.

'I've lost my appetite.' She looks at me imploringly. '*Please.*'

What's a chap to do?

We tramp back along The Chase and up Old Glebe Lane, but at the main road a car, snow halfway up its wheels, has stopped on the road facing Hilsea. A man with a spade is leaning in at the window talking to the driver.

'You won't get through,' he's saying. 'There's two cars stuck in a drift by Rushbottom Farm. A lorry's had to turn round and they're stopping the buses at Daneflete now. We've heard they're going to send out the snow-plough from Lokswood. Could be hours. Why don't you come in? The missus has done a big cottage pie if you'd like some.'

We can't hear what the man says, but after a minute he gets out, locks the car and follows the landlord across the road and into the Thin Man.

I look from the pub to Cora. Her face is bleak with disappointment, as grey as the snow-heavy sky.

I try to think of something, anything.

And all I can think of is going back to see old Mr Thorston. Four years ago he told us so many things – about Long Lankin, and even about witches. He had a chest in his cottage full of family papers and ancient documents. Surely he would know, if anyone did, about the twigs on the door, and the stones, and the broken bottles. He might even have some idea who the two women could be.

I suggest it to Cora. She flicks me a watery smile.

'His wife died a while ago,' I say as we cross the road. 'I was in the post office when Mrs Wickerby was telling someone about the funeral at St Mary's in North Fairing – hardly anybody there, she said, just Mr Thorston and a couple of old biddies . . . Oh, and a daughter – a widow . . . Margaret or Marjorie or something.'

'So he didn't just have the three sons killed in

the Great War, then. Must have had four children.'

We tramp down Ottery Lane, and thankfully the snow stops falling. Passing the end of Fieldpath Road, I wonder fleetingly if I might just nip up and borrow Pete's dry boots and some warm socks, maybe even snatch a roast potato, but I know if I go back now Mum won't let me out again. My stomach grumbles noisily. I hope Cora didn't hear it. Perhaps Mr Thorston will have some more of that nice seed cake he gave us last time.

I soldier on with Cora through the fresh, quiet snow, gallantry personified.

CORA

Before us, a seamless river of white stretches onwards under the arching trees.

Formless. Black in the hollows, grey in the shadows. The only sound in the stillness is the muffled crumping of our feet through the powdery crust.

No birds sing, no dogs bark.

The road is just the vaguest dip between the rounded banks.

On our right, the snow has drifted against the garden wall of North End, Dr Meldrum's house; the house that was once home to the Eastfields – Auntie Ida's husband,

Will, his sister, Rosalie, and also his brother, James, killed in the Great War like Mr Thorston's sons. There is no driveway visible, no gravel path skirting the lawn, just a glistening milky sea stretching away to the cream-coloured house. Rising up in front of it are the domes of the three huge willows, the snow clinging gracefully to the long, drooping branches.

The track to the Patches goes off to the left. The light wind blows fine, dusty clouds into our faces off the tops of the high hedges to either side; behind each hedge is a plot of land bought or rented by people from the East End of London between the wars – people desperate to escape to the countryside.

We make our way slowly, lifting our knees as we plough on, too cold to talk. The landscape is difficult to read, each wooden house just like the next. The markers are buried, distances hard to judge.

But still we manage to find our way. Round a bend is Mr Thorston's cottage, its deep thatch rounded and smoothed by the snow.

As we stand there at the open gate, an unexpected shaft of sun breaks through the thick grey clouds and moves slowly down the roof. In the new light, the glassy icicles hanging under the eaves begin to gleam and glister, and in the front garden, each little bead of ice on twig and stem and winter leaf flashes a sparkle.

We follow a trail of fresh footprints leading up the

path from the gate. When Roger knocks on the front door, it moves slightly inwards.

We wait.

'Mr Thorston!' Roger calls, then knocks again, and the door moves a few inches more.

'He must be there,' I say. 'He wouldn't leave his door open, and look – there's smoke coming out the chimney.'

Roger puts his head inside and calls again. When no answer comes, he turns back to me. 'Maybe he's hurt himself.'

'I suppose we'd better go in, then, just in case,' I say, pushing Roger through. The door opens directly into the sitting room.

Stamping the snow off onto the mat, I gaze around at the familiar low, blackened beams, the small windows set back in the thick whitewashed walls, the two large chintz-covered armchairs, rather worn and faded, on either side of the wide fireplace, where a log fire is burning. Mr Thorston's frail wife, Grace, used to sit in the chair on the right, but it's empty now, save for a hollow in the seat cushion, as if she has just got up to make a cup of tea. Against the side wall is the old chest full of Mr Thorston's family papers. Black with age, it is carved with a row of little wooden people. All these things remain the same, but in the middle of the room are a number of wooden tea-crates filled with books, some of which have slipped off onto the sloping floor.

'Looks as if he's decided to move out,' Roger says.

The deep windowsills are empty. I remember the faces under the army caps in the grainy photographs that used to stand on them; the faces of his three dead sons.

'Maybe he's lonely,' I say.

Although the fire is burning, there is a vacancy about the place.

'Mr Thorston?' I call, but nobody answers.

'Maybe he's upstairs.'

'Where are they, the stairs?'

I look around. In the corner of the sitting room is a full-length cupboard door, standing a little open. I peep in, and behind it there's a small winding staircase.

'Mr Thorston?' I shout up.

No answer comes.

I climb the stairs to a tiny landing, and push open the door on the left. A chest of drawers stands beside a stripped iron bedstead covered with shirts, jackets and trousers. In the room to the right there are more clothes spread out on a wooden bed – old-fashioned dresses smelling of mothballs, cardigans, coats, hats – but no sign of Mr Thorston. A door leads to a further room with a steeply sloping ceiling: two more beds with bare mattresses covered in faded ticking, a broken chair, another tea-crate, and books in stacks on the old worn rug.

'He isn't up here!' I call, making my way back down the stairs.

At the bottom I see Roger isn't where I left him. 'Roger? Where are you now?'

If he replies, I don't hear him. My eyes are drawn to the chest by the wall. The little carved people seem to watch me intently as I glance cagily at the front door, half open to the snowy garden, then at the small windows, making sure nobody is about. I take a few steps forward, and though I know I shouldn't be doing it, I grab the edge of the heavy lid and wrench it up with both hands.

Empty.

No notebooks or rolls of documents – nothing but dust and a musty smell.

Irritated, I stare at the bare wood for a few moments before dropping the lid back as quietly as I can. I take a hasty look into each tea-crate, move a few books aside, but see nothing that resembles a pile of old papers.

From somewhere at the back of the cottage Roger cries, 'Look here, Cora!'

Feeling a flush of guilt at having opened the chest, and now fearing the worst for Mr Thorston, I turn and hurry through the door into the next room, where Roger, Pete and I sat around the table eating honeycomb off little plates from the crowded dresser. Now the dresser is just empty shelves, the little dark circles in the dust showing where the cups and jugs once stood. I squeeze past two large cardboard boxes filled with crockery wrapped in crumpled newspaper, and go through the far doorway into the little kitchen.

'What – what is it?' I ask nervously.

'Biscuits,' Roger says, all excited, holding up a packet of digestives.

'What?'

'Chocolate ones,' he says. 'I'm so blimmin' hungry, do you think Mr Thorston would mind if we had one? It's already open.'

'I can't believe it!' I say. 'Flippin' biscuits? I thought you'd found him dead or something.'

'I don't think he's here.'

'I've just opened that old chest,' I say, 'and there's nothing in it – no papers, nothing at all. Perhaps he's put the stuff somewhere else, packed it all away or something. We'll have to ask him. He can't have gone far with the fire going.'

I stand on the red quarry tiles and look around the cosy little kitchen. There's something of our old kitchen in Limehouse about it.

Mr Thorston still cooks on a small black range, keeps his fresh food cool on slate shelves in the little pantry behind the small door, hangs his meat from metal hooks in the ceiling, and lights a fire under the copper to heat the water for washing.

At Guerdon Hall we have a stainless-steel sink, a new gas cooker with eye-level grill, easy-wipe Formica work surfaces, smart linoleum sheeting on the floor, and a fridge with an ice box you can keep a block of raspberry ripple ice cream in. But I would swap it all for this – so small, so simple.

'Or maybe he's in the garden,' Roger says.

'In this weather?' I go to the sink and look through the window.

I glance over the vegetable plot with the mounds of frosty cabbages standing proud of the snow, then across to the orchard with the bare knotted branches of the fruit trees reaching down almost to the roofs of the bee hives, which are all wrapped in tar paper. To one side, in front of the hedge, is a clapboard outhouse with a water butt attached to its guttering by a drainpipe, and next to that a greenhouse, the glass roof covered with snowy potato sacks, frozen rigid, weighted down with flat stones.

'Can't see him,' I say. When I turn back, Roger has peeled back the top of the biscuit packet.

'Honestly,' he says, 'if I don't have something soon, I'm going to go funny.'

'You can't just take people's stuff without asking, Roger.'

'It's only biscuits. Tell you what – if he doesn't come back soon, we could write a little note to Mr Thorston saying we hope he doesn't mind us taking one because we haven't had dinner yet.'

My stomach rolls. 'Well . . . all right, then, just one

each, but only if we do the letter, really polite, and say thank you.'

I am hungrier than I realize, and gulp my biscuit down so fast it gives me hiccups.

'Hold your breath,' Roger says. He counts to twenty-five.

'*Hic!*'

'Drink some water from the other side of the cup.'

I reach for an old tin mug on the wooden draining board and turn the tap. Nothing comes out of the spout.

'Flip, the pipe must have frozen. What shall I – *hic* – do?'

Roger, crunching his third biscuit, looks along a row of corked, dusty glass bottles on a shelf. He takes one down and looks closely at the yellow liquid inside.

'Remember we had some of Mr Thorston's home-made lemonade last time?' he says. 'Do you think this is some more of it?'

'Looks darker to me.'

'Might be a bit old, but it should still be all right, with the sugar in. Shall I pull the cork out?'

'Only – *hic* – if we mention it as well, in the note to Mr Thorston.'

Roger wiggles out the cork and puts the bottle to his nose. 'It's not lemonade,' he says. 'Smells a bit like honey, and wine or something.'

'Won't do us any harm, then,' I say. 'Honey's good for you.'

'Shall I try a bit?' he says, pouring some into the tin mug.

'Go on, then.'

He takes a sip. 'Ooh, it's not what I expected,' he says. 'It really warms up your throat as it goes down.'

He gulps a bit more – quite a swig, actually – and splutters into his sleeve. 'Ooh, sorry, it – um – I think there's alcohol in it.'

He passes the cup to me and I take a sniff. Under the strong honey scent is a tang that takes me back to last Christmas – Auntie Kath opening the bottle of Emva Cream she'd nicked from her mother's, then mixing it with orange squash, saying, 'Time you tried a sherry cobbler.' I had two glassfuls, then was sick in the kitchen sink and couldn't eat my pudding.

'You sure it's all right, Roger?' I say, sipping. A bit of heat spreads over my tongue. I swallow quite a lot. 'See what you mean – really warming. You're probably right about the alcohol, but there won't be much, will there, if Mr Thorston's made it at home? I'll just have a bit more to make sure my hiccups go.'

'Pass me the mug,' says Roger, and fills it from the bottle, drinks some more and helps himself to another biscuit. 'Do you know,' he mumbles, 'my head's gone a bit swimmy.'

'That's because you're hungry,' I say, taking the mug back, thinking I'm feeling swimmy too. 'Give us another biscuit.'

After a while I notice the hiccups have gone. For some reason I want to laugh, and have to sit down on the little wooden chair by the table, but the seat seems to move position all by itself and I nearly end up on the floor. I close my eyes for a minute, open them again. Roger is tipping the bottle upside down and shaking it over the empty mug. When only one little drop comes out, he thinks it's really funny. He tries to stand the empty bottle on the draining board but it won't stay up and tips into the sink.

'Wibble wobble, wibble wobble,' he chuckles.

I reach for a biscuit, but there's only the wrapper left. 'Oh, crumbs,' I say, and start to giggle.

I scrunch the paper into a ball and toss it over my shoulder towards the back door behind us.

'Oi!' comes a yell.

I almost fall off the chair.

The door has opened. Someone has walked in. I think I might have hit them.

'What are you ruddy well doing!' a man cries. 'Turn round! If you try anything funny, I'll cut your thieving fingers off!'

I manage to stand, though my knees buckle slightly, and turn, expecting to see Mr Thorston, but to my amazement it's Mr Wragge, snapping at the air with a huge pair of garden shears.

My mouth drops open.

I glance at Roger. He is leaning against the sink with his eyes glazed over, grinning, no flipping use at all.

'Oh, Mr – Mr Wragge,' I mumble. 'We – we came to see Mr Thorston – *hic* – Oh blast – sorry. Hiccups again.'

Mr Wragge creases up his eyes, stares into my face. 'You – you're that girl from Guerdon Hall.' Then he looks at Roger, who is still smiling. 'And you, whoever you are, what are the two of you doing here?' Roger sways a bit. Mr Wragge leans over the sink, takes out the bottle and sniffs the neck. 'And drinking Mr Thorston's mead?'

'What – *hic* – what's mead?' I ask.

'This is, you idiots. How much have you had? Don't tell me it's the entire ruddy bottle—'

'Smelled like honey . . .'

'And where's me blimmin' biscuits?'

I look over to the scrunched-up paper ball on the floor.

Mr Wragge picks it up. 'Flamin' Nora!' he says. 'You've had the whole flippin' lot!'

I should be more ashamed than I am, but actually I feel quite comfy with myself. There's something about Mr Wragge's nose popping in and out of focus that I find quite comical – that and the shears. It's all I can do to stop myself giggling again.

'So, where's Mr Thorston, then?' I say, trying to get myself together.

'Not that it's any of your business, but the poor old chap had a fall, if you must know,' says Mr Wragge. 'The postman found him. He spent a couple of days in Lokswood Hospital, but his daughter, Marjorie – Mrs Harrow, that is – came to take him to live with her on the other side of Ipswich.'

I make a huge effort to steady my thoughts. 'He – he's not coming back here, then, ever – Mr Thorston?'

'Ooh no, this cottage is going to be sold, though no-body'll want it because they like things all modern these days. Since Mrs Thorston died' – Mr Wragge taps his temple with his finger – 'old Hal's gone a bit wandery in the head.' Then he abruptly changes tone. 'But that don't give you *cart blonch* to just walk in off the street and help yourself to his liquor. Serve you right if you're bloomin' well sick. I saw you from the shed, through the window. Thought you was burglars, but you're just a pair of ruddy nincompoops.' He rolls his eyes towards Roger. 'You'd better get him home, stupid idiot.'

As Mr Wragge speaks, my heart drops. My head isn't so cloudy that I don't feel a pang of disappointment at Mr Thorston's absence.

'All right. Sorry, Mr Wragge.'

I steady myself on the table for a moment and pick up Roger's gloves. Roger slumps forward from the sink. I manage to get hold of his coat front and prop him up against the wall instead. He looks a bit green. 'Come on,

Roger, put these back on, er. . . I think that's the left one, and what's happened to your thumbs?'

There's an awful noise – he's retching.

Mr Wragge, quicker on his feet than me, drops the shears, grabs Roger's arm and pulls him out of the back door, just in time.

ROGER

I stagger out of the Patches and up Ottery Lane, all the world hazy, and am sick again outside the post office. Cora pushes my head forward to try and stop it going over my shoes, but I'm not sure if it misses hers.

I am aware of a face peering out at us from a window of one of the new bungalows as I stumble up Fieldpath Road with an arm over Cora's shoulder. Did I put it there or did Cora do it to hold me up? I've no idea.

She leads me up to the front gate and says, 'Are you sure you'll get in all right if I leave you here?' Then I think she may be watching me as I sway gently from side to side across the front garden and climb carefully up the veranda steps.

'Where the ruddy hell have you been?' cries Dad as I reel into the kitchen. 'And shut the blimmin' door.'

I close the door behind me, trip over the old towel

they've stuffed along the gap at the bottom to keep out the draught, and almost knock myself out on the sink.

'Your dinner's gone cold,' snaps Mum without a smidgeon of sympathy as she tosses a bundle of dirty knives and forks into the washing-up. 'Everyone's finished.'

She looks at my boots. 'Just look at the state of you – treading snow all over the floor. For heaven's sake, don't just stand there – go and get the mop.'

I wait for a while as the kitchen moves around me.

Then Mum comes up quite close and peers into my eyes. 'Roger? Have you been drinking?'

She calls Dad, who is out in the hall putting on his coat to go to Grandma's. 'Rex! I think Roger's tipsy.'

He strides in and sniffs my breath. I see his fists clench. 'Who the blazes has given you alcohol?'

'The bees made it.' I yawn and sink down onto one of the kitchen chairs.

'You'd better get off to Mother's, Rex,' Mum says to Dad. 'I'll get to the bottom of this.'

The back door closes with a thud so loud it makes my head pound. Mum throws a plate onto the kitchen table in front of me. I sit there, my head twirling, staring at the bits of lukewarm, fatty meat. Mum runs some tepid water into a bowl, sticks it under the table and tells me to put my frozen feet into it. When I complain that it's too cold, she says if it was any warmer I'd get chilblains.

Looking at the congealed, jellified gravy makes my stomach heave.

Mum whips the plate out from under me. 'Oh, go and lie down, for heavens' sake!' she shouts. 'Take a towel from the bathroom in case you're sick, and if you are, you can jolly well clean it up yourself.'

I fall up the ladder trying to climb up to my bed. When I eventually get there, my head sinks into the pillow and the room goes spinning round and round and round.

CORA

The cold marsh air clears my head a bit, though my feet are a little shaky on the bridge. As I trip over one of the drums of Cerebos salt, I hear, to my relief, laughter coming from inside the house. I pause inside the back door, take a deep breath to steady myself as I walk along the stone passage, then look in at the kitchen door. Ange and Mimi are putting food out on the plates. I am amazed to see Mimi downstairs.

'Haven't you eaten yet?' I ask.

'We got a bit held up, one way and another,' says Ange, turning to fetch the knives and forks from the drawer. Mimi flashes me an odd sideways look, but I don't know what she means by it.

Dad has lit the fire in the dining room. Although the reek of smoke and the oily tang from the paraffin stove in the corner clog together unpleasantly in the air, we still take our dinners in and sit around the table.

Ange makes a huge effort to be cheery; gets us to pretend we're the royal family. Dad seems to have got over his outburst earlier and does a funny turn as Prince Philip, but Ange is even more comical doing the Queen, making Mimi giggle so much I worry she'll get indigestion. Ange dashes out of the room halfway through and comes back wearing around her beehive a crown she's quickly cut out of a page of *The People*, with a picture of President Kennedy right up the front prong.

The giddiness seems to wear off the more I eat, and the food is delicious. Ange has roasted the chicken with a whole lemon up its backside, and the meat is so tender it melts on your tongue – the best dinner I can remember.

Dad tells a whole load of jokes, one of them I haven't even heard before. Ange goes into hysterics laughing, which turns into a burst of coughing so bad I have to fetch her a drink of water and her brown pill bottles.

It feels like it should be Christmas, especially when the snow begins to fall again on the other side of the diamond panes, all soft and light as the evening draws in.

Afterwards Ange makes a pot of tea and we all go into the sitting room, where Dad falls asleep in front of the fire with the newspaper draped over his head, the pages fluttering up every time he snores. Each time it happens, we try not to laugh too loudly so as not to wake him.

Perhaps it's the dreaminess of the alcohol making me go along with this easier way, this attempt to be happy, this need to make things work with Ange. It's better than going back to the uncertainty of where we were before, and there's the sense that if we think ourselves contented for long enough, we might be. Except that I glance at Mimi, poised on the edge of her chair, watching for Dad's newspaper to flicker up again, and wonder if I will ever be really sure what she's thinking.

Ange has brought her big straw bag full of scraps of material. The bag has real cockle shells sewn on the front to look like flower petals, with stems and leaves made of coloured raffia. She shows Mimi and me the things inside her wooden sewing box. Under a tray of cotton reels and embroidery silks is a stuffed felt pincushion like a big ladybird, spiky with needles so it looks more like a hedgehog, a box of long pins with brightly coloured glass heads like jewels, cards of shiny press-studs and hooks and eyes, lengths of black and white elastic, lovely scissors shaped like two entwined silver swans, and a tobacco tin rattling with different sorts of buttons.

'Now, what needs doing?' she asks.

'Your blue cardigan's gone through at the elbow,' I say to Mimi. 'Go and bring it down, and see if you've got anything else needs sewing.'

I notice Ange watching Mimi with a fond smile as she leaves the room.

'She's a lovely little girl, your sister,' she says quietly. 'If I'd had one, I'd have liked her to be like Mimi.'

Dad snores. The fire crackles.

'Have you . . . um, did you ever have a husband?' I ask, seeing as she isn't an especially young woman.

'Yeah, well, did have,' she says, reaching down her legs to smooth her stockings, turning her calves to check that her seams are straight. 'Stan, he was. Died in the war building a railway for the Japanese.'

Ange lights a cigarette. She draws in her first breath of smoke, then a cough explodes out of her, followed by another, then a long, uncontrollable burst. Red in the face, choking, she drops the cigarette, with its waxy ring of red lipstick, into the saucer on the little table. She coughs repeatedly into her fist, her eyes streaming.

After a while the fit subsides. She thumps herself on the chest a couple of times, winces a little, then wipes her eyes with her fingers and picks up the cigarette.

'Think I'm going to go on menthol,' she says. 'These Capstans'll be the death of me.'

'Did you and Stan have any kids?'

'Nah. Well, we did, but it came early, and died. We were living with his mother, God rest her mean little soul, in the East End. I hated it – the city, the noise and dust and everything, coming from the country where it's quiet. Anyway, this big air raid started the baby off. Stan was out on fire watch, and Mrs Russell said the kid would be ages yet and I wasn't to make such a fuss. Then the woman next door came in and saw I was in a bit of a state, and nobody could get hold of the midwife. So when the all clear sounded, the woman came with me on the bus to the hospital, and it took blimmin' ages to get there through the rubble, with me screaming me ruddy head off and scaring all the passengers. When the baby came, the nurse said it wouldn't have lived even if I'd got there before. Didn't even let me see it, said it would upset me. I caught a glimpse of her wrapping it up in some newspaper. Didn't know if it was a boy or a girl.'

Ange drags on her cigarette.

'Not long afterwards Stan went off to the war. Never saw him again. Last I heard he was captured in Singapore. He always wanted a load of kiddies, did Stan. Me an' all.'

Dad shifts in his chair, snuffles, goes back to sleep.

The flames rise in the fireplace.

'Do you have a mum and dad?' I ask.

Ange drops her eyes. 'Died young,' she sighs. 'We

don't make old bones in my family. My sister, Doris, and me ended up in an orphanage, but she's dead now an' all. Oh, look, here's Mimi back with her cardie. Won't do to get maudlin.' Briskly she stubs out her cigarette. 'Did you say you had some other stuff to mend?'

I go into the cold kitchen, look through the washing basket and find a couple of Dad's shirts with missing buttons and some socks for darning.

The telephone rings. I drop the socks and am just through the door when I see that Ange has already picked it up. She listens for a few seconds, then puts it down again briskly, without even speaking.

'Who was it?' I ask; my first thought was Roger – not that he'd be in a fit state to dial anything.

'Wrong number,' she says.

Back in the sitting room, I throw a couple more logs on the fire and it blazes away merrily, while Ange's skinny but nimble fingers darn the worn patch on Mimi's cardigan with a large bodkin and some knitting wool wrapped around a piece of card from the bottom of her box. Then she joins Mimi's gloves with a long piece of elastic to thread through the sleeves of her gabardine mack so they won't get lost, and sews buttons back on Dad's shirts.

I go off to make some more tea, and when I came back with the big tray, Ange is cutting some scraps of fabric from her straw cockle-shell bag into two rag doll-shaped pieces, front and back. Before she sews them together she shows Mimi how to make tiny black French-knot eyes and a little red mouth of running stitches. Mimi smiles and looks up into Ange's face. Ange smiles back, leans forward and plants a kiss on her forehead.

'What colour shall we make her hair? I've got yellow wool or orange,' says Ange.

'Orange, like yours,' says Mimi.

'Orange, indeed!' Ange pouts. 'It's flame, this is, like Rita Hayworth. And what are you going to call your doll when she's finished?'

'Ooh . . .' Mimi thinks for a moment. 'She wants to be Aggie.'

'How do you do, Aggie,' Ange says.

'How do you do, Ange.' Mimi makes a little voice and wiggles Aggie's arm. 'Can you make me some clothes, please? I'm cold.'

'Of course, Aggie,' says Ange. 'What would you like to wear?'

'I like this bit of green,' comes the little voice.

'Ooh yes, I like that too, Aggie.' Ange looks into the little knotted eyes. 'That's from a summer skirt of mine. It used to be long – like with the New Look, you know – but I cut it a bit shorter last year, thought I'd be daring. What do you want – plain skirt or gathered?'

'Gathered please,' says Aggie, 'like a fairy.'

'Wave your magic wand, Aggie,' says Ange, 'and you'll have a dress in two ticks.'

She cuts out a strip of material with her swan-necked scissors, threads her needle with green thread and runs some stitches along the edge, in and out, in and out.

'Ouch!'

'Ooh, what's the matter?' Mimi asks.

'I've pricked my blessed finger,' says Ange, sucking it. 'Oh dear, some blood's got on poor Aggie's face.'

'Doesn't matter.' Mimi smiles. 'Aggie doesn't mind a bit. Look – there's a drop on each side, like red, rosy cheeks.'

Ange takes her finger out of her mouth, puts her arm around Mimi and gives her another little kiss.

I smile to myself.

Mimi used to have a little knitted soldier called Sid; she'd carried him around everywhere with her since she was a toddler. It was the only toy she ever wanted. Then, the day we left Limehouse a couple of weeks ago, the rag-and-bone man came up the street on his horse and cart. We were by the car, waiting for him to go by before we could open the doors to get in, our street was that narrow. When he'd passed us, I just happened to glance up and saw Sid lying there in the cart on top of a dirty old mattress.

'Mimi, look!' I shook her arm. 'Sid's fallen on the cart. I'll run after him.'

But she just turned her back and got into the car, and Sid disappeared with the cart round the corner.

I'm so glad Ange has made a doll for her and that Mimi likes it.

Mimi runs her fingertip along a brooch pinned to Ange's cardigan – three flashy green stones on a bar of small dark gems that sparkle in the firelight.

'Them real diamonds?' she asks.

'Diamonds? Good Lord!' Ange laughs, looking down at it. 'Nah, they're just glass. Cheap as anything.' She strokes Mimi's hair and whispers in her ear, 'Found them in the dustbin outside Buckingham Palace.'

Mimi grins.

I sit and drink my sweet tea, watch the dancing flames, let the unexpected wave of annoyance wash over me – that Mr Thorston has gone and taken away his papers, so I know little more than I did before.

The snow stops falling. Dad wakes up and goes into the hall for his coat, seeing if he can get to the Thin Man on foot. I take Mimi up to bed.

The woman is alone. She tidies away her sewing, sets the dirty cups and saucers on the tray and puffs up the cushions in their places. She is remembering the small cold room in the hospital, the rustle of the midwife's white apron. She is thinking about the dead baby thrown away, seeing it as a little child playing, her arm entwined in her husband's.

An infant gone, a man gone – neither with any resting place in the earth.

I know this wretched hunger for things lost beyond time.

She leans over to turn off the light and notices some crushed paper down the side of the chair, pulls it out, sees it is a letter.

She looks towards the door, glances up at the window, smoothes the page as best she can, then runs her finger along the line of writing at the top, saying softly, 'The Gilead House Institution, Mitre Fields, London, 9th November 1962 . . . Hmm, last Friday week.'

She swivels her head towards the door once more, listens for a moment, then reads under her breath, stumbling over some of the words:

'Dear Mr Drumm,

I thank you for informing us of your new address and take this opportunity to advise you of the present condition of your wife, Susan Drumm. It has been noted that you have not visited since January 1960, and have not contacted us in regard to the last report we sent you. We feel you should be aware that there has been a marked deterioration in her condition of late. As Mrs Drumm was exhibiting symptoms of extreme anxiety prior to her electroconvulsive therapy sessions, Dr Dorritt decided to proceed with a combination of ECT and barbiturate-induced deep sleep treatment, which, in so far as it induces memory loss, has proved successful, but unfortunately has also prompted successive bouts of bronchopneumonia, which we are finding increasingly difficult to treat in Mrs Drumm's weakened state.

I would appreciate it if you would contact me, either by letter or by telephone to my secretary, Miss Thrussell, at the earliest opportunity to make an appointment to discuss your wife's prognosis and treatment.

Yours sincerely,
Dr Hugh Ghent-Plowden
Director'

She has understood enough to whistle gently through her teeth. She looks down the letter once more, mutters, 'Well, who'd have thought it? The mother isn't dead at all . . .'

I did not think of the mother; the other Guerdon still living – that feebly-beating heart.

I must consider this.

The Gilead House Institution, London.

I hide myself deep among the layers of this woman, and bide my time.

Mum pushes me out of the back door, even though I've been telling her since she dragged me out of bed that I'm dying, that my brain's swollen and trying to burst out of my skull, and she needs to get the doctor in.

I slip on the snow. Mum won't open the door, so I knock on the window and groan.

She tweaks the net curtain aside and angrily flaps me away off to school.

'The buses won't be running!' I yell, which makes one eye throb. 'They weren't yesterday!'

'You won't find out till you get to the bus stop!' she shouts back. 'Anyway, the snow's melting!'

Pete and Dennis have already turned into Ottery Lane. I haven't the will or the energy to catch them up, but the bus has had to plough through slush and is late, so unfortunately I don't miss it.

I ache inside and out all day. Over and over again I revisit the horror of actually vomiting in front of Cora, and every time, a ghastly flush surges up my neck and over my cheeks with a horrible, sickly warmth.

Raymond Harty asks me why I keep going red, and I

say the first thing that comes into my head: that Mum's made me wear a woolly vest under my shirt and it's bringing me out in a rash.

CORA

Ange comes into the sitting room.

'Cora? Could you take Mr Wragge this cup of tea?'

'Oh, is he here?'

I jump up from the settee and fetch my coat from the hall.

'He shouldn't be working this late, and in the freezing cold, old bloke like him,' she says.

As I round the house, a bright spread of light from the barn draws me on, the glare of a hurricane lamp blazing away and spilling out of the doorway onto the remnants of the snow. I am so eager to reach him that my feet nearly slip from under me on the bridge, but I manage to hang onto the cup and saucer.

From the barn comes a muffled chinking, followed by the creak of a wheelbarrow.

I tramp across the farmyard and peer round the doorframe. 'Hello, Mr Wragge.'

He jumps nearly a foot in the air. 'Flaming hell!' he says. 'Don't come creeping up on me like that.'

'Sorry. Brought you this cup of tea. It was hot when I left the house.'

'Ta very much.' He takes the cup and saucer and sips it noisily. 'Ooh, that's warming,' he says.

'What are you doing?'

'You can see what I'm doing,' he says, putting down the cup and bending to pick up the base of the bottle with the fused rusty nails and hair, and dropping it into an open sack lying in the barrow. 'Ed's going to try and get the van down here to load up some more of this rubbish.'

He looks at me curiously, his mouth turned up at one corner, almost to a smile. 'I'm surprised you're on your feet today. That was strong liquor yesterday, and it was a big bottle.'

'Roger drank most of it,' I say, moving closer through the straw. I take the piece of pottery from the sack and tease out the hair.

'Mr Wragge, please tell me what these bottles are – why they've got these nails and things in. I know you know.'

'You be careful,' he says. 'Some sharp bits of glass have fallen out of one or two of them.'

'But why – why nails and glass?'

'I told you before, you don't want to be bothering with them,' he says.

'If they're nothing, why don't you want to tell me?

I've nobody else to ask now Mr Thorston's not around. Please, Mr Wragge . . .'

He takes off his hat, scratches his head and puts it back on again. 'It's not for kids,' he says. 'Specially living in that house. What you don't know won't do you no harm.' He starts to throw more pieces into the sack.

'Mr Wragge – did you know about my Auntie Ida – Mrs Eastfield . . . about what happened here four years ago?'

'Might have done,' he mutters without looking up. 'People talk. All over and done with now, over and done. I'm sorry for it if she was family.'

'I – I was here, Mr Wragge.'

There's an awkward silence.

The old man bends to pick up the small bottle with its neck missing. He gives me a quick glance, then lowers his eyes. 'You – you was one of the children, then?' he says. 'I – I heard of some such thing, that there was a couple of kids there.'

'Roger was there too,' I say quickly, then take a breath. 'Mr Wragge . . . um, people died; little children mostly – even my little sister nearly, because people didn't tell people things that might have stopped bad things happening that shouldn't have happened.'

He rubs his nose on his sleeve.

'If you know something about these bottles,' I go on,

'you should tell me. It isn't fair not to say. To be honest, it's a flippin' nuisance.'

Mr Wragge straightens up, sighs, and turns the bottle in one hand, then with the other pushes up the front of his hat and scratches his forehead.

'Please, Mr Wragge,' I plead.

He sighs again. 'Well . . .'

'*Please.*'

He picks up his tea and slurps the last of it through his three teeth. 'I'm not sure you shouldn't leave well alone,' he says, 'but you won't stop with your blimmin' pestering and you've worn me out. These things are – leastways they *were* before they was broken – witch bottles.'

'What?'

'Witch bottles,' he says again, 'and I've never seen so many together in all me life before, and so well-made. Hundreds of years old, they are. Them bits of hair and fingernails, and sometimes blood and piss – 'scuse the French – are put in by scared people who think some witch is like to attack them; come in their house, like. So the witch is drawn in, like, by them human bits and pieces – can't help herself – and then she's trapped inside and gets skewered to death by the iron nails or the bits of glass. Iron's magical, smells like blood. Veins of iron ore run through the earth like the veins in your body. Witches can't abide iron.

'When the witch is caught in the bottle, it's best to throw it on the fire – then it explodes and you can be sure she's well and truly got rid of. I've seen a fair few of these things in me time, in old houses that are being done up or knocked down, but none as old as this lot, and never so many from one place.'

'But I – I didn't see them when I stayed in the house before.'

'Ah, that's because they was hidden, in risky places where a witch could get in easy if you wasn't careful: under doorways, under the hearth. It was really important that they was secret so the witch wouldn't know they were there. Chimneys was always a bit of a worry to people 'cos they're open to the outside and witches could fly down them into the house. They used to shove all sorts of stuff up chimneys in the old days to keep the witches out – dead cats, shoes, all sorts.'

'So why have they been taken out of Guerdon Hall?'

'Well, Ed – Mr Blezzard – just got rid of them when he was clearing out, 'cos your dad wanted it all swish and modern and everything. Even the trees in the garden were special, the sort of trees they planted years ago to keep witches out – you know, rowans, elders, hollies. I told Ed to leave them be. He said he was only doing what he was told to do.'

'And – and you believe all those things?'

Mr Wragge drops the bottle into the wheelbarrow.

'We was raised different when I was a nipper,' he says. 'You can't imagine how dark and quiet it used be at night then; no streetlights nor cars going by nor nothing, and the stories you got told – enough to give you the willies. I ended up scared of every blimmin' thing – nasty little yarthkins in the woods, Black Shuck, the demon dog in the lane, and . . . and the Lankin man down on the marshes, and . . . and why should I not believe any of it? As you say – things happened. Though I was a Hilsea boy, we all knew about the Lankin man and what he would do if he snatched a little kid. We'd never go down to the old church, wouldn't dare. I don't even go there now.'

'But – but there are no witches around now, are there?'

'Well,' he says, knowingly tapping the side of his nose. 'Maybe there's not the sort you would think of, but there are cunning people still about, be sure of it.'

He looks up as we hear the sound of the van chugging carefully along The Chase.

'Ah, here's Ed coming,' he says, dropping the last piece of bottle into the sack and tying up the top; then he buttons up his coat and turns out the lamp. 'Wait while I bring the barrow.'

I take the cup and saucer and walk alongside Mr Wragge as he pushes the barrow in the light from the headlamps, while the van squelches through the muddy wet snow and comes to a halt. We say goodnight and I go over the slippery bridge as Mr Wragge hauls out the sack and throws it into the back of the van.

I am almost at the house when I distinctly hear Mr Blezzard call out from the driver's seat, 'Come on, Gideon, hurry up and I'll get you back to the St Laz. Hope the van'll get back up the hill. It was the devil getting it down.'

The St Laz!

I hurry back to the creek. The van is beginning to move off. I slide over the bridge. Then the engine struggles. The back wheels start to spin. Mr Blezzard pushes his foot hard on the accelerator, but for a few seconds the vehicle stays stuck where it is, splurting out clods of snow and icy water. I blunder across and bang my hand on one of the battered rear doors.

'Wait! Wait!'

Mr Blezzard leans out. 'Oi! Push off! You'll make a dent!'

I hear a mumble from Mr Wragge, weave my way round to the passenger door and thump the window. He winds it down.

'What is it?' he says.

'Mr Wragge – do you live at the St Lazarus Hospital – in Hilsea?'

'I hope you aren't having a go,' he says. 'I know you're supposed to be retired at the St Laz, but I like to keep meself busy and I don't ask much money – just enough to keep me in ale and snout.'

'No, no, it isn't that. You . . .' I fumble in my pocket for the piece of paper, drag it out so quickly it tears along an edge, and push it under his eyes.

'I'm not blind,' he says, batting it away.

'Who are these people?' I say. 'Mrs Lailah Ketch and Miss Iris Jewel – do you know them?'

'Course I flippin' know them. They're the wardens. They look after us at the St Laz. Live in the end house.'

I feel my heart beating faster.

'And what's this – this picture? I tried to explain it before, when you came to the house for the wallpaper – this is what I meant.' I jab at the little drawing with my finger.

'Hold still,' he says. 'You're jiggling it about.' He lifts the front of his fur hat with a dirty thumb, scratches his forehead, looks me in the eye.

'*Please*, Mr Wragge. You obviously know what it is.'

'Might do.'

'Oh, come *on*, Mr Wragge. It can't be any worse than the things you've already told me.'

The old man looks sideways from under his hat at Mr Blezzard, who – amazingly – takes the hint.

'Oh, for heaven's sake where's the blimmin' shovel?' he says, reaching behind his seat for it and opening his door. 'I'll dig out the wheels while you're dithering about.'

Mr Wragge checks in the side mirror that Mr Blezzard is far enough away, waits for the scrape of the shovel, the soft thud of snow.

'It's a witch mark,' he whispers. 'The M is for Mary, like you couldn't ask nobody more holy than the mother of God to stop a witch coming in the house for you. The circle's the moon, the light that keeps away the dark—'

'And what about the twigs I told you about before – a bundle of twigs tied to the door, with red string?'

'Rowan twigs, were they?'

'I've no idea what sort of twigs – and the little white stones?'

He pulls his hat down, purses his lips.

'Mr Wragge?' I plead.

Mr Blezzard gets back in, throws the shovel behind his seat. 'Should be all right now if we hurry up,' he mutters, turning over the engine. 'Finished your flippin' confabulation, have you? I want me dinner.'

I walk beside the van as it starts to move off, hold onto the window rim.

Mr Wragge leans out. 'The same thing,' he hisses. 'To keep out a witch. It's all the same thing . . .'

'Mr Wragge, did you tell those two women, the wardens, about us coming back to Guerdon Hall . . . about the bottles being broken, the trees being cut down?'

He purses his lips. 'Might've done,' he says, then winds up the window so I have to let go, and his breath covers the glass in a misty film.

What did he say . . . ? *There are cunning people still about, be sure of it.* I stand there gazing after the red tail lights as they bob shakily up and down into the distance.

At arm's length Mother Mary Dominic runs her cane along the map, its tip following the curves of the Rhine as it flows from Switzerland, through Germany, to Holland, though I lose track of it somewhere after Cologne, as I can't stop thinking about Mrs Ketch and Miss Jewel, and the name scratched backwards on the leather – *Aphra Rushes*.

I try to recall the little I know of her. She was found in Guerdon Hall with the dead baby, locked up first in Lokswood, then in the tower of All Hallows church, taken to trial, brought back to Bryers Guerdon and burned. That's all I know.

No, not quite all I know – she cursed the Guerdon family.

On the wall the countries of Europe blur into each other, the colours become hazy. I haven't a clue where the Rhine has got to.

I am ridiculously maddened at poor old Mr Thorston – banging his head but having enough sense left to take away his papers. Where did Mr Wragge say he'd gone – Ipswich? How far is it? Ah, I can just see it up there, on the map that is coming back into focus, on that bump that is the edge of England. How on earth would I get there? Are there buses to Ipswich? How else can I find out anything at all about Aphra Rushes?

The girls are opening their exercise books, taking up their pens. I turn a page and look again at the *Good work, Cora* Mother Mary Dominic has written large and red under my homework on the industries of the Ruhr Valley. How did that happen? I suppose Madame Mary St Bernard will be pleased with me at last.

I see her again as she rises to stand behind her desk while her wooden beads click to the vertical – crisply pressed black veil and scapular, stiffly starched white wimple, pale face, unreadable eyes. Behind her the colourless wall, beneath her the hard wooden floor, to one side snow sprinkling the asphalt beyond the window – and to the other the warm brown leather spines of *Sorrel and Brassock's County Records*.

In my mind I stretch out my hand and run it over the gold lettering: *Vol. 21: Daneflete Hundred . . . 1520–1625*.

Four years ago Mr Thorston told us that in England witches were hanged. A burning was very rare indeed, an event worthy of record.

'You don't seem to be writing much, Cora. Are you keeping up?'

'Yes, thank you, Mother Mary Dominic.'

Dad went off London again early this morning, but I don't feel that wave of anxiety about Mimi getting back from school or being left alone. If I'm a bit late home, it won't matter so much now that Ange is there, and things seem to have settled well enough since the blow-up over the two women on Sunday.

After the last bell I take my time in the cloakroom, sit on the hard bench, slowly tightening my shoe laces. Around me is all noisy commotion – soft indoor shoes kicked off stockinged feet, calls, shouts, irritations, hats dropped, retrieved and pulled on, scarves knotted, fingers wiggled into gloves, satchels and bags flung over shoulders, doors banged open, thumped shut.

Two rows of pegs away there is one last coat. Someone is in detention.

I wait.

The wall clock moves time on with its dull tick-ticking.

The bleak strip light whines overhead.

Hurried footsteps from the corridor, the coat is wrenched off its hook, the hat on the peg above squashed down over a forehead, a rush for the door. I sit so still and silent under the overhead racks the girl doesn't even notice me.

A clatter.

Two women in blue-checked overalls clang busily backwards through the door with brooms, mops and buckets.

'What shall we do first, Edie?' says one. 'In here or the toilets?'

'Oh, let's get the worst over with,' says the other,

rattling her way to the green door in the corner. 'Did you remember to put the bleach in your bucket this time?'

As soon as they disappear, I slip out into the corridor.

Some of the lights are out, and a peculiar quiet hangs on the air – a school without pupils, the only sound a vacuum cleaner humming over a distant carpet.

I steal my way along the passage close to the wall. Round the corner and a few yards along is Madame Mary St Bernard's room.

I look furtively behind me, bend my ear to the oak panel, tap gently with my knuckles and listen keenly for the answering voice which doesn't come. I take a breath, glance around, twist the knob, push open the door, and step onto the polished woodblock floor.

The room is in a gloomy half-darkness, the hard edges of the furniture reflecting back the light shining over the netball courts outside the window, where the patchy snow lingers only under the shrub borders and in the deep, unlit angles of the building.

The distorted black shadow of the crucifix sweeps across the wall.

I shut the door behind me, daren't switch on the desklamp, go straight to the bookshelves, peer close and run my finger along the spines.

Vol. 21: Daneflete Hundred inc. South Fairing, North Fairing, Bryers Guerdon & Hilsea, 1520–1625.

I pull the book out. My hands drop under its unexpected weight. I rest it on the desk, screw up my eyes, fan the pages and skim the dense small printing.

Lists. Legal documents. Drainage systems. Land holdings. Sessions. Court cases. Letters. Transfers of deeds and lands.

Dates and headings blur together, my eyes grow sore, but even in the thick concentration of lettering I notice two names that recur again and again, landowning families of influence – *Myldmaye* and *Guerdon*.

Myldmaye – I have heard the name before, but can't summon up more than a speck of memory.

At the very end of the book I land on some collections of letters.

Appendix A: Letters of Bishop Cordwell Vernon in regard to the land pertaining to . . .

Appendix B: Letters of Lady Margaret Winterbourne, of Hove Hall, South Fairing . . .

I stop my thumb.

Appendix C: Letters of Katherine Myldmaye to her sister Mary, Lady Guerdon, 1583–1584. Found in a casket hidden in the wall of the old chapel in Guerdon Hall, Bryers Guerdon, during renovation work April to October 1878. Reproduced by kind permission of the County Archives.

But in 1584 Sir Edmund Guerdon's murdered wife was Ygurne, of the Pleshett family. Who was Lady Mary Guerdon?

I leaf forward, see the name *Kittie Wicken*, turn another page – *Aphra Rushes*.

A noise from behind the door – the clack of a wooden rosary, the rustle of fabric.

I stiffen, dart my eyes from wall to wall.

No other way out.

Heart thumping, I move quickly, duck down behind the desk.

The door opens. The light is switched on.

Barely breathing, I peer out through the kneehole.

Madame Mary St Bernard sweeps across the floor towards the desk, the white hem of her habit swishing over the uppers of her mirror-polished black shoes.

She lifts a sheaf of papers, picks up a bunch of keys.

I cower lower, my lungs straining, drops of sweat collecting on my forehead against the prickly felt of my hat.

Just beside the nun's left heel is the curve of my bag strap. If she were to look down . . .

I gulp down a silent swallow.

The keys jingle gently back onto the desk.

After a few seconds I hear a page turn – then another.

She waits a moment, clearly puzzled, then closes *Sorrel and Brassock's* with a dull thud, picks it up, moves to the wall and pushes it back into its place on the shelf.

Now she will turn, and must see my quivering hat down between the desk and the high-backed chair.

But there is a sound from the corridor.

Madame Mary St Bernard picks up her keys and moves swiftly to the open door. 'Mrs Bunce?' she calls.

I squint out from under the desk, see in the corridor the edge of a blue overall and a hand clutching a duster.

'Yes, Madame?'

'Here are your keys. They were under some papers.'

'Oh, thank you, Madame.' The woman drops a curtsey.

'Try not to be so careless next time.'

'Yes, Madame.'

'By the way, did you remove a book from the shelf?'

Click, and the light goes out. It's darker than before.

'I don't recall doing it,' says the woman.

'Curious,' says the nun.

The door closes. The keys rattle. One of them is selected, turns in the lock.

Footsteps move away down the corridor.

The breath rushes out of my desperate lungs. I get up so quickly my chin scrapes painfully on the edge of the desk.

I run across the room and grab the doorknob. Turn. Pull.

It won't move.

A wave of panic.

I go back to the desk, tug open the drawers one by one, scuffle pens into pencils, ink bottles into paperclips, rulers into erasers, scatter a box of medals and badges.

There must be a key.

I lift files, thumb through papers and holy pictures, account books, reports and index cards . . .

My eyes flit to the window.

I cross the room, try and push up the sash, thump it distractedly with the pads of both palms; then, at eye level, see a metal catch locking the two halves together. I flick it with my thumb, gasp with relief as the upper window slips half an inch, push up the lower one, reach for my bag, strap it over my head, then raise my foot to climb over.

With my hands poised on the sill, I remember the book, slip back in, dart across the room and fumble it off the shelf. Leaning out of the window, I drop the heavy volume and it lands in a bush.

I hike myself out, glance quickly across the netball courts, then stand up in the flowerbed and try to pull the window shut after me. The frames are flatter on the outside. I do my best, but it's difficult to get a purchase, and a gap of a couple of inches remains under the lower sash.

I leave it, pick up the book and begin to move round the courts through the shrubs close to the wall; look up, think I see the dark triangular shape of Madame Mary St Bernard, her cold eyes gazing down at me from the art-room window. There she is again, in the dimly lit archway of the refectory; and there, behind the wrought-iron fence of the nuns' garden, fixing me with her intense stare from beyond the black railing. I know she must be nothing more than an image of my conscience, appalled at what I have just done.

I bolt out of the half-open gates and up the road to the bus stop, the book achingly heavy under my arm.

Sitting in the corner in the emptiness of the upper deck, I wait for my heart to settle, then move my head so the pale globe of the recessed light falls on my knees, where I spread out *Appendix C: Letters of Katherine Myldmaye to her sister Mary, Lady Guerdon, 1583–1584 . . .*

I skim through the first few letters, starting in early October 1583 – Katherine recapturing the quiet nuptials of Mary to Sir Edmund Guerdon at Lokswood; the hint of some debt Lord Myldmaye owes Guerdon; questioning why Mary does not write more often; Katherine missing her sister; the joy that Mary is expecting a baby; the request for more letters. Then, in a letter dated 21st December 1583, the tone changes.

St Thomas Day, 21st December 1583

My dearest Mary,

I think it best that you burn this letter once you have read it. If your lord is disposed to be in this vile temper since the execution of the witch some days past, I advise you not to pester him as to the reason, but let him spend out his bad humour until it abates, as it will in time. Do not seek to vex him further by seeming too prying and curious into his affairs.

I cannot deny that your letter filled me with misgiving and anxiety, although I have, against my own judgement, done my utmost to carry out your request. I have made secret enquiry of one of the more trusted lower servants. You will know her – the same Joan who was most gently attentive to us when Mother died. It seems that the trees your lord has had planted on the inside of the creek at Guerdon Hall are known to form a ring of protection most particularly against the ingress of witches.

As to the men your lord summoned from Fairing at dead of night, Weller Mounce and Ralf Polley, and Polley's boy, Colin, they are, I am informed, cunning men of renown who will ward open chimney shafts and doorways, and bind them with devices, ancient charms and enchantments, expecting to be rewarded handsomely for their trouble. When the physician came to draw both blood and water from you at your lord's behest, do you know what became of the flasks after they left your chamber? Joan wonders if concern for your health might have been a stratagem in order to obtain the elements from your body required for spells. I do not wish to alarm you, dearest sister, but inform you of all I have learned at your insistence. I know you would plague me if I did not tell you all. It seems to me as if your lord is doing all in his power to protect you and the little one you carry from some malignancy.

The little pictures you drew for me are called runes. These most particular ancient and potent symbols of safeguarding against witchcraft are called the Thorn, the Yew and the Day runes.

Joan enquired of me whether this burned witch was properly laid to rest in the manner befitting a handmaid of the Devil. Were her ashes burned again to remove all traces of cunning and magic? Perhaps your lord is afeared lest she rise again like the Phoenix from its fire to cause his family mischief.

This season of Christmas should be one of joy and blessing. It is our first apart from each other, which pains me most sorely. I will pray most fervently that the little Christ Child will shower his graces upon you and your unborn babe.

Your most loving sister,
Kate

Lokswood, 20th January 1584

My dearest Mary,

I have destroyed your letter. If it should have found its way into Father's hands, I cannot imagine how he would deal with any suspicions or gross calumny against his old friend, Sir Edmund. It may be prudent to burn this letter when you have read it. I do not know what communications run between the two of them, or who may be employed to examine or purloin our letters.

I cannot bear to think of you suffering so, but you must shield yourself against malicious gossip and rumour spread abroad by malcontents among the servants. In no wise can you be certain that this infant born to the maidservant, Kittie Wicken, is your husband's child. Unless the babe were birthed before its time, the wench would have had to entice your husband while his innocent lady and her poor murdered boy were yet living. Father would never have married you to a known libertine, but rather to give solace to a man so terribly and recently bereft of the companionship of his wife and little heir.

But if I should be proved wrong, dear sister, and there is some small truth in these wicked rumours, then it is your duty as Sir Edmund's wife and, Deo volente, as a mother in months to come, to bear these ordeals with fortitude and forbearance, as we women must.

Your most loving sister,
Kate

Lokswood, 8th February 1584

My dearest Mary,

I urge you to destroy this letter. Yours I have burned here in the fire in my chamber but a few moments ago, and such a blaze it made that I thought the soot in the chimney would take alight.

I set this out in my hand, but struggle to believe these uncommon things of which you write. You should not place trust in any words issuing from the lips of this wretched creature, Kittie Wicken, even though she came to you privily. You are too much in your own company there, and must not think that any such danger could befall your infant once it has been born. It is not possible for any man, such as this murderous leper, Lankin of the marshes she spoke of, once dead and buried – even mistakenly in hallowed ground – to become in death a hideous great spirit who is impelled to snatch away and consume young flesh where he will find it.

No such creature was ever created. If Kittie Wicken fears for the life of her own son, then she should throw herself and her child upon the mercy of the parish. She means to cause you fright for some reason of her own, and you must not heed her, Mary. You must find your lord when he is in a good humour, and inform him of her ill will towards you, that he may send her off.

These other things she told you of, that the witch Aphra

Rushes, lately burned at Bryers Guerdon, was wet nurse to the very child she killed, and that in life this sinister, corrupted woman gave birth to Lankin's babe, you must put this unwholesome knowledge aside and not mind it, for your own peace. You should be comforted to learn this union was so abhorrent to nature that the infant died even as it entered the world. And Mary, think what agonies Father must have endured in his heart when he was present at the witch's execution, by your lord's very side, and heard her bring down her terrible malediction on the heads of the Guerdons, even unto the very end of the line, knowing that those cursed generations would be of his own flesh and blood as well as Sir Edmund's.

My dearest sister, I am concerned that you do not have enough to occupy you in your new station, and have some anxiety as to the tranquillity of your mind. Could we not bring you home here for your lying-in? Send word and I will come for you. Or I would bring you to Aunt Ankarette's at Missingham, where I am sure you would find some serenity in the quiet and secret beauty of her manor. Please, I beg you to think on this.

Your most loving sister,
Kate

Lokswood, 10th April 1584

My dearest sister,

I cannot tell you how distressed and troubled I am on receipt of your last letter. I am deeply sorry for your anguish at the death of your servant, Kittie Wicken, drowned so miserably in the creek, her wits utterly gone. I cannot believe you still think it possible that Kittie's fears were not groundless after all and that her babe was indeed snatched away by that monstrous creature. We must pray that it is not so, that her talk of this Lankin spirit came from the wandering of her poor moonstruck mind, and that your own infant will thrive heartily and be safe at Guerdon Hall.

You should rather believe what Sir Edmund informed you of – it is much more likely that Kittie, in her madness, killed and buried her own child somewhere on the marshes.

Dearest Mary, please be mindful of your own reason. It will be the shock of Kittie's death, and your present condition, that makes you think you hear her unquiet ghost singing her warning to you in the house. We know that malignant cunning women can be possessed of potent gifts, but it cannot be true what Kittie told you of – that when alive, Aphra Rushes frighted her with the threat that she could creep into Kittie's skin, look out of her eyes and use her hands to do whatever the witch willed with them? This is diabolic work indeed. Surely it cannot be possible under heaven to interfere with another's soul in such a way as this.

Do not concern yourself too much that Sir Edmund is keeping you on your own in your chamber, save for one attendant. I am sure it is for your own welfare and ease at this time. Your lord will not wish you to be subjected to the tittle-tattle of servants, or the discomforts of this unseasonable warm weather.

I harbour a fervent wish that you might still come here to Lokswood Hall, where we would happily feed you up now that the Lenten season has passed, but suspect that in your present condition, it is rather too late in the day for you to travel far. It would cheer your heart to see how delightfully the spring is progressing. We appear to have more lambs in the meadows this March and April than we have had for many a year, and the orchard is quite a wonder with its great burden of white blossom.

Your little Biddy has had a litter of five pups. It is a pity your husband would not allow her to come with you to Guerdon Hall. The pups will be quite grown up when you are able to come and visit us. Please be sure to ask Sir Edmund again if I might have his permission to come to be with you during your confinement.

Your loving sister,
Kate

The bus has stopped. I look up and see to my shock that we are at Bryers Guerdon. I slam the book shut, grab my bag, spring up out of my seat. The bus is about to move off. I reach up and frantically push the bell once, twice, and again, rush down the aisle and thud down the stairs. The conductor touches his cap to me as I leap off the platform.

As I turn into Old Glebe Lane, the sickly yellow light of the streetlamp outside the Thin Man outlines the bare branches of the hedgerows against the blackening fields. I press on past the wrought-iron gates of Glebe House and the gloomy mass of twisting, hissing woods where the sweep of the rectory lawn ends.

My head is so disordered that at first I don't see the small figure hurrying along the road ahead in the darkness.

I stop, puzzled, then quickly move on when I see who it is, but so late home from school – and alone?

'Mimi!'

She spins round.

I run towards her, the heavy book under my elbow, my school bag swinging from side to side.

'Mimi, why are you so late? Where's Ange?'

'She didn't come.'

The darkness has sapped the colour from her face.

'But she said she'd pick you up,' I say.

'I know. I waited and waited. All the other kids had

gone, and when the teachers started coming out, I hid behind the caretaker's shed. I didn't want nobody asking me why I was still there. I could see up the road in case Ange was late, but she never came.'

'Oh, Mimi.' I put my arm round her shoulder and hug her. 'Maybe – maybe she got the time wrong.'

'She was there yesterday – she knows the time.'

With growing unease, I squeeze her shoulder once more.

We turn into The Chase. Above us, stars are already peppering the sky, while to one side the water quietly gurgles along the shadowy ditch under the trees.

As we approach the house, it is plain to see that there is not the smallest glimmer of a light.

'I hope it's not the flippin' electrics again,' I say, trying to sound unconcerned, but my tight grip on Mimi's hand as we cross the bridge is probably giving me away. 'Maybe that's why Ange couldn't come to school. She had to wait for the man to come and fix it.'

We move along the path round the house and into the cobbled yard.

The back door stands wide open, a dark rectangle in the wall.

I whisper to Mimi to stay where she is, then nervously go through the doorway into the stone passage and switch on the light.

'Ange? Are you there?'

I edge my way over the flagstones, hardly breathing.

Footsteps patter behind me.

'Don't leave me on my own,' Mimi whispers.

We turn the corner into the hall and make our way into the kitchen.

I reach round the corner for the switch.

The light blazes on.

Mimi gasps.

A jolt runs through me.

A face is outside, staring through the window.

'Crikey! It's Ange.'

Strands of hair have dropped out of their pins and are hanging down her washed-out cheeks to her shoulders. Her eyes appear not to see us at all.

'Looks . . . looks like she might be ill,' I say to Mimi, trying my best to sound calm, even though my heart is racing. 'You put the kettle on and I'll go and get her in.'

I throw my bag and the book down on the table, hurry back along the stone passage, through the open door and round the corner of the yard. Ange is still at the window, standing motionless on the gravel path, her face and the front of her glowing in the light from the kitchen, her bag dangling from her hand. Her coat hem is dark with dirt, some long blades of pale grass are caught in her untidy hair, and her sheepskin boots are plastered with wet mud.

'Ange?'

She doesn't appear to hear me the first time, but when I call her name again, she turns her head and blinks, as if she has just woken up.

'You all right?' I say, gently taking her by the elbow. 'What's the matter?'

She says nothing, but puts her hand to her head and shivers, then comes with me as I draw her along to the back door.

In the stone passage, she stops for a moment, leans against the wall and rubs her forehead, streaking it with grime from her filthy fingers.

'What are you doing home early?' she says. 'I was just going to get Mimi.'

'Mimi's back.'

'Is she? What's the time?'

'It's dark, Ange. Look.'

'So it is – well, I don't know.' We turn into the hall, and Ange takes a look at herself in the mirror. 'What's happened to me hair? I only just lacquered it before I went out. And look at me coat. Where did all that muck come from?'

'Let's have a cup of tea,' I say, leading her into the kitchen. 'The kettle's on the gas.'

Ange sinks into a chair and puts her handbag on the table.

'Oh, Mimi, I'm sorry,' she says, still in a daze. She reaches into her coat pocket and takes out some small change. 'Look – this was for some sweets at Mrs Wickerby's. I don't know what happened. I feel a bit queer.'

In her hand amongst the change is a little red stone with a hole through the middle.

'Maybe you've forgotten to take your pills,' I say, reaching for the bottle.

'Yeah, maybe – though I thought I did.' Ange shakes a couple out. 'What was I doing for the last couple of hours?'

Far across the marshy wilderness, almost to the river, I found the bubbling freshwater spring where we drank together and, close by, the patch of ground where once his hut stood, where he sheltered me, where I brought forth our wretched child. I sat on the wet earth among the grass tussocks, shut her eyes and thought I might weep, remembering him coming through the doorway with its mat of woven boughs, skinning a coney with his teeth on the narrow bench against the wattle wall and, after the rain, tying fresh reeds onto the roof under the crooked tree.

Once before I had crept back into my past, returning to the house in the woods years after my mothers had been burned inside, and out of the ground, under its coverlet of rotting leaves, the bloodstone had drawn me to it. And so it pulled me again. I knew just where to scratch at the watery soil with her soft nails, dig with her stringy fingers.

And after it came up to me out of the earth, I stood and

looked at the sky through the little hole in its heart, and for a moment became a child again, with my old mother, Zillah, in the woods.

The woman does not know what this is, this little red stone in her pocket, veined black like jasper, the stone that helped to kill a man.

I turn over under my blankets, turn the other way, hear Ange's creaking steps up the stairs on her way to bed. Westminster Chimes strike half past eleven. I steal downstairs in the silent, sleeping, icy house, switch on the cold unwelcoming strip light in the kitchen, and spread out the County Records on the table.

Lokswood, 22nd June 1584

My dearest sister Mary,

Thanks be to God you are safely delivered. The man-servant, Thomas, arrived here with the news at sunrise, trusting your lord would not notice his absence in the excitement of your lying-in. May God bless Thomas for taking all this trouble on our account, knowing how grieved we both are, dear sister, to have been apart so long, most especially at this time. I send him back to you with this letter and my gifts. I hope you like the small garments I have sewn for Carey Edmund Robert Guerdon, and please to note how my stitching has much improved of late. I am particularly proud of the embroidery on the bonnet. The honey comes from the beehives in the clover field. I must close now as Thomas is preparing to depart. I asked him if he might hide me under his cloak and bring me to Guerdon Hall as I long to see you and my new nephew, but he said his lord would not approve of it.

I kiss the paper just here where I have marked it for you to touch. May God send his blessings on you both.

Your most loving and happy sister,
Kate

Dearest Mary,

Please God soon we will embrace and I will hold little Carey in my arms at last. All is prepared at Aunt Ankarette's. I will be there within two hours, and Thomas will bring you so we may both be safely hidden there. He will steal you away in the darkness from that wretched house and you need no longer be afeared that that base, murderous creature who haunts the marshes will snatch away your child. Poor Kittie Wicken, that I did doubt her so, and forgive me, Mary, that I did question my sister's words for so long a time. Do all that Thomas bids you, and soon you will be free from that other polluted, diseased and corrupted creature, your own husband. Please God, it is as the physician has said – that you do not appear to be *suffering from the terrible affliction he has just discovered upon your lord's person.*

Yours in haste,
Kate

There are no more letters.

I don't know how long I sit there, how many times the clock chimes its quarter hours. In the end it is the creeping cold in my bones that sends me up the stairs to my chilly bed. The window on the half-landing is crusted with ice.

WEDNESDAY 21st NOVEMBER

The harsh jangle of the alarm clock jolts me awake from broken, fitful sleep. My eyes ache.

Pulling on my dressing gown and slippers, I step across to the window, draw the curtains aside and look out over the bleak garden. In the half-light, glistening frost crowns the untidy tufts of grass and the sad empty flowerbeds. Even the stunted bushes and misshapen trees are under a light dusting.

Beyond the creek the marshes stretch on into the misty distance. Behind me, the brass alarm clock ticks on, marking out its little divisions of measurable time. Before me, everything is motionless, lifeless as an old faded photograph.

I stand close to the window, my breath clouding the small diamond panes, thinking of Mary Guerdon. Would she have been the same age as me? Did she stand at this window as I do now, looking out over this same pale, unchanged wilderness, frightened, knowing all those things I now know too?

She couldn't bear to destroy her sister's letters – hid them instead.

As I rub the glass clear with my fingers, I am startled to catch through the wet streaks a movement to my left, which begins at the corner of the wall to the edge of the cobbled yard.

A figure moves away from the house, then walks quickly down the garden towards the part of the creek that funnels off towards the river.

The hair is hanging loose, a faded red. It's Ange.

I can hardly believe that on this raw November morning, she is wearing only her nightdress, and absolutely nothing whatsoever on her feet. Oddly, she moves in a straight line, not veering to left or right to avoid the flowerbeds, but walking from the grass, on over the hard, lumpy earth, then back onto the grass on the other side as if it is all one and the same. The only time she swerves is to avoid a tree stump.

For a few dreadful seconds I think she has gone mad and is going to fling herself into the water. My mind races on what's best to do. I am just poised to rush downstairs after her when I realize, even at that distance, that there is hardly any water in the channel and what little there is lies motionless, the tide caught frozen between coming in and going out.

To my amazement, Ange crouches down and disappears behind the stiffened grass on the bank.

For a couple of minutes my heart thuds with anxiety. Once more, I am about to turn for the door when her head comes up again and I see her reach up with one hand. After a struggle, she stands upright, her nightdress, legs and arms streaked and soaking with wet clay that could only have come from under the ice, as the mud on the bank is frosted solid.

Ange looks straight across the garden towards the house and, with the same purposeful stride, marches back in an almost unwavering straight line. Her feet are bloody.

I wait for a while, in a turmoil, not knowing what I should do, then rush downstairs. A freezing draught is sweeping down the hall from the stone passage. The back door must be standing open.

When I look into the kitchen, Ange is sitting staring vacantly at the window, a packet of cigarettes lying untouched on the table in front of her. Our breath is like clouds. I hurry past and along the icy flagstones to close the back door before returning.

Ange's eyes are glassy and red-rimmed. Strands of hair hang down over her feverish-looking face. The room is bitterly cold, but she is still wearing only her dirty nightdress. Her bare feet are mottled blue and red, her hands utterly drained of colour.

I grab a tea towel to wipe her feet, then run into the hall for a coat to put over her shoulders.

'Ange . . . why – why did you go outside? It's perishing.'

Her whole body is quivering. When she turns her head in my direction, the sinews stretch taut and stringy in her neck. She looks but doesn't seem to see me.

She begins to cough, and her hand flies up to shield her mouth. The skin on the back is cut and scratched, her fingernails black and broken.

'You've got to put something warm and dry on,' I urge, 'or you'll catch your death. Do you want me to get you something from your room? Have you had your pills?'

She stands up without speaking, and makes her way stiffly into the hall.

I follow, and watch her slowly climbing the stairs, dream-like, in a trance. Her coat drops from her shoulders and flops down. In only her wet nightdress, she continues upwards, leaving smears of blood from her feet on the stairs.

'I'll bring you a cup of tea,' I call, turning back to the kitchen.

A little later, a hot-water bottle tucked under my arm, I put a tray with cup of tea and a plate of buttered toast down on the carpet outside Ange's room and knock softly on her door.

Hearing nothing, I gently push it open, pick up the tray and move quietly inside.

She is lying in her untidy bed, face to the window, covers pulled up to her chin.

I tiptoe in, elbow the copy of *Woman's Weekly* off the bedside table onto the floor, leaving the tea and toast there.

Turning to lift the covers at her feet, I catch sight of Ange's face and am so startled that I drop the hot-water bottle, sending it slithering off the bed onto the floor.

Her eyes are wide open, her skin covered in a sweaty sheen. She is muttering to herself, 'Too hard . . . too cold . . . frozen . . . too hard . . . too cold . . .'

Unnerved, I can't think what to do. Should I get a doctor?

I tidy the bedcovers as best as I can.

'I – I've made you a cup of tea and some toast,' I say, gently pushing the hair off her forehead. Her eyes begin to droop. She groans.

'Do you need your pills?'

Without answering, she quickly drifts off into a wheezy sleep.

I don't know what to do.

Why isn't Dad here?

I hear light footsteps on the landing. Mimi appears at the door.

'What's the matter with Ange?' she says, peering in.

'I don't know. Maybe it's the 'flu or something. We need to get her warm. She keeps saying she's too cold, too frozen.'

Mimi's eyes fix on Ange with an expression I can't fathom. She doesn't step beyond the threshold.

'I'm going to find some Germolene for her feet – they're all scratched – then leave her in peace for a little while, give her a chance to warm up,' I say, closing the door behind me. 'I'll come back in ten minutes and see if we should get the doctor out.'

I put my hands on Mimi's shoulders and look into her face. 'Are you all right?'

'Think so. What are we going to do about school?'

'We'll have to miss it,' I say. 'Say we were ill.'

I can't go in anyway. Madame Mary St Bernard saw me glance at the book. It will be plain to her that it was me who took it, rummaged through her desk, stole out of the window. I don't know what that will mean, what she will do – expel me? Will another letter arrive, and remain unanswered like the first? What would happen then? I push the thoughts away, my head already too crowded.

Mimi and I drift through the day like ghosts, restlessly moving between rooms, unable to settle. Now and then I spread out the book and re-read Katherine Myldmaye's letters, and every so often go and check on Ange, who sleeps on. Sometimes, her back turned away, Mimi draws in her exercise book, blowing on her icy fingers, then seeing if she can still use a pencil with her gloves on.

In the middle of the afternoon, as the heavy sky begins to press down on the frozen earth, we are startled by a noise from the doorway.

Ange is standing there, in a big, scruffy blue cardigan over a brown woollen dress and zipped sheepskin ankle boots. Her hair is lank and loose, pinned back off her face with a couple of Kirby grips, and her dried-out skin, unevenly powdered and rouged, is drawn tightly over her cheekbones under hollow-rimmed eyes. A smear of lipstick has settled into the lines of her cracked lips.

'Ange! Shouldn't you be in bed?'

'I'm all right,' she says weakly. 'Think I must have missed taking me tablets. I seem to be getting all forgetful.'

'We thought you'd got the 'flu. I was all ready to get the doctor in.'

'I've had a couple of aspirins, done meself up a bit. I'll just sit by the fire, get some mending done.'

'I'll make you a cup of tea.'

She reaches for her sewing box.

The afternoon wears on and the sky grows darker. Mimi and I play Snap and Old Maid with a pack of cards we find in a drawer.

We are running out of logs for the fire. If Roger were here, he could have helped me get some from the barn. The frost hasn't lifted from the ground all day. Maybe it will be warmer tomorrow. I'll get some wood then.

Ange sits with her feet up sideways on the settee, doing a bit of darning, drifting off for a little nap from time to time, then stitching up the frayed edges of cuffs and collars, and patching the odd rip. Her glass-headed pins gleam in the firelight and her fingers deftly push the tip of the needle in and out, then snip the thread with the silver swan-necked scissors.

I go into the kitchen to find something to eat. There isn't much in the cupboard. I mix a tin of baked beans with some scrambled eggs, put three bowls of it on a tray with some spoons and take it into the sitting room.

The Jotmans will be squashed around the table under the airer, its four wooden rails probably draped with socks, having something like shepherd's pie covered in bubbling grated cheese, or a stew in the big pan with the black handles, Pete, Dennis and Roger squabbling over the last bit of meat.

When Mimi has finished eating, she takes her rag doll, Aggie, from behind a cushion.

The lights go out, the radio fades to nothing, and the soft humming of the radiator dies away.

My heart drops.

'Oh no, not again,' says Mimi, propping Aggie up on the small table, against the base of the lamp.

'Must be a power cut,' I say.

In the sudden darkness, the light from the crackling flames in the hearth burns brighter, spreading its golden-reddish glimmer into the corners and outlining the straight edges of the furniture.

'I'll go and fetch some candles.' I half stand, glancing at Ange. When I see her, I sink slowly back into the chair, amazed and disturbed.

She is staring at Aggie sitting on the table top.

Her eyes are like mirrors in the glow of the fire,

alive and glistening with reflected heat. In that strange, distorted half-light of flame and shadow, her lips, which had looked thin and parched only a short while before, seem moist, red and fleshy, and slowly they stretch into a glinting smile.

As if it isn't Ange at all.

The telephone rings out in the hall. We jump.

Is it Wrayness Abbey? My legs go weak. I can't move.

Ange starts to rise but Mimi shoots up.

'No, Mimi, leave it!' I say.

'It might be Dad,' Mimi says, hurrying out.

My heart pounds. Would Madame Mary St Bernard send the police? Can you go to prison for stealing a book?

I hear Mimi speaking, but her voice is muffled, as if she has her hand cupped around her mouth. It can't be the school. They wouldn't bother to discuss my thieving with my sister, but if it's Dad, why is she being so secretive?

All at once Ange gets up and strides out of the room.

'Who is it?' I hear her bark at Mimi.

I can't make out what Mimi says, but the receiver slams down and Mimi runs off. Ange comes back in and sits down heavily in her chair.

'What was that about?' I ask, but Ange says nothing, just stares at the fire.

I get up, go into the hall. 'Mimi?'

No answer.

She isn't in the kitchen.

I go down the stone passage and knock on the toilet door, push it open.

Empty.

I didn't hear her run up the stairs, but I go and look in our bedroom, in the bathroom.

'Mimi? Are you in there?'

Always the old fear, slipping back in so easily.

I press my chest with my fist as my heart starts to thump.

Giddily, I make my way quickly down, go back into the sitting room.

Ange is lying back in the armchair, eyes closed. I shake her by the shoulder.

'Has Mimi come back?'

In my confusion, I don't at first take in the tension in Ange's body, the lack of the natural softness of sleep about her. As I leave the room, I think I hear the rustle of clothes, an outrush of breath, but only fleetingly wonder then if, maybe, she isn't really asleep at all.

In the hall I inch my way along the old panelling under the heavily carved banisters.

The temperature drops as the radiators grow cold. My breath leaves me in a mist.

Which panel below the staircase opened the priest hole all those years ago? I try to remember. Years before,

Mimi disappeared in there. Surely she hasn't done the same again.

I tap lightly, press my ear to the wall. 'Mimi?' I plead. 'Please – please answer me, Mimi. Are you there? Please, Mimi – please.'

Nothing.

I press each panel in turn. Level with my shoulder, one gives a little to my touch. I try again. There's a slight movement, a rough grating sound, a dull ping, but no more. The mechanism seems to have broken. Mimi couldn't have got in.

With growing dread I search until I don't know where else to look.

I come out of the dining room; in despair look both ways along the dim hall.

To the left, at the end of the passage, is the door to Auntie Ida's old kitchen. Just at that moment the lights flicker back on and I see that the key is missing in the lock.

I move down, stand in front of the door, touch it with my fingertips, push it a couple of times.

'Mimi?'

I tap gently with my knuckles.

'Mimi, it's Cora.'

I hear a noise – the grating of a chair leg on the flag-stones.

'Please, *please*, Mimi, let me in.'

Seconds go by. The chair moves again.

More seconds.

The key scrapes in the lock. The door opens inwards a couple of inches. There is Mimi's eye.

'Oh, Mimi!'

I push the door open, fling out my arms and pull her to me, lowering myself to kneeling on the cold hard floor. She is shivering. I stroke her hair and rub her cheeks with the backs of my fingers.

'For heaven's sake, what are you doing here?' I cry. 'I couldn't find you.'

I wrap my arms tightly around her, and for one moment she lets down her guard.

'I miss—' She shudders into my shoulder. 'I want Auntie Ida.'

I can't say a word. Rubbing her back, I gaze over Mimi's head at Auntie Ida's kitchen. In the half-darkness I can make out the hard edge of the old stone sink, the torn curtain still hanging underneath, and the black range with the heavy kettle in its place on top. The huge wooden table stands in the middle of the room, the top crisscrossed with the thread-like trails of woodlice and silver fish; the floorboards beneath are scattered with mouse droppings and crumbs of nibbled paper.

My eyes grow hot.

We drank our tea there, ate boiled eggs from the hens

that once scratched around behind their wire fence in the garden.

There, in deep shadow, is the dresser with its rows of dust-rimmed plates, cups and jugs and, on a shelf, the large Bakelite wireless sits under a film of grey. Draped across the ceiling, spiders' webs loosely droop with the remains of insects.

'Come on, let's get you warm,' I say, stumbling with her into the lighted hall, wiping my wet cheek with my finger.

Still holding her, I manage to pull the door to, and lock it.

I look down at the key in my hand, peer down the hall to see if Ange is awake and watching, then carefully tuck it under a loose corner of the carpet.

'See where I've put it, Mimi?' I whisper.

She nods gravely.

'Would you like to go to bed early? I'll do you a hot-water bottle, and see if I can find a bit of milk to make some cocoa.'

She nods again.

A little while later, in our bedroom, as I pull up her covers, I ask Mimi who was on the telephone.

'Nobody,' she says, and turns over to face the wall.

'Mimi . . .' I put my hand gently on her arm. 'You're not on your own, you know. You can tell me anything. We – we've got each other.'

317

She shrugs me off.

With a sigh, I go downstairs to wash up the cocoa pan, dry it, then crouch down to put it back with the others in the cupboard under the sink. I am about to close the door when I notice a little corner of dull-red card squashed behind a tin of Vim. I yank it out.

It's Mimi's exercise book, the one she's always scribbling in, hiding the drawings inside the crook of her elbow. I open the cover to the first page. Alarmed, I turn to the next page, and the next.

Over and over again it is the same woman, always the same, the body gauzy but the features clear. She is standing on the edge of the creek, sometimes on the far side, on the brink of the marsh, sometimes on the near bank. In other pictures she is on the fringe of the garden itself, on the grass, always looking towards the house. On this page she is half hidden by a corner of the building, on that, she is behind a window, peering in. Mimi has roughly sketched the lines of furniture in the room. Here the woman is in daylight, staring through the sitting-room window, and there she is a pale shape against the darkness. There her face is pressed against the kitchen glass. I turn the page and feel a creeping sensation up my back.

Mimi has drawn her looking into our bedroom.

I lift up our pillow, pull out the crumpled letter.

The Gilead House Institution, Mitre Fields . . .

I now know what has to be done. The woman will take me there. I will use her body, her knowledge, but she will not know why she has come to London.

There is no fresh milk. We need to save the tinned stuff for tea, so Mimi and I are eating our cornflakes dry. Ange comes into the kitchen wearing her hat, coat and sheepskin boots.

'Going out?' I ask needlessly.

She seems a little dreamy, her eyes distant.

'I – I've got to see somebody.'

'Do you think you're well enough? You weren't too good yesterday. Can't it wait?'

'No. I've got to go today.'

'Oh. When will you be back?'

'Not sure – I might be out all day.'

I make no protest whatsoever. When I hear her feet on the gravel path going round the house, I feel almost light-headed.

Mimi looks at me. 'When's Dad coming home?' she says.

'I think he said Monday.'

'I wish he was here,' she says, leaving the room and going upstairs.

Out in the hall, I stare after her for a moment, then pick up the telephone and dial. A gruff voice answers.

''Ello?'

'Hello. Is that the Half Moon? Mr Myers?'

'Alf's down the cellar. It's Bill Gurney 'ere. Who's that then?'

'It's Cora – Cora Drumm, Mr Gurney.'

'Oh, 'ello, love. How are you getting on in the country?'

'All – all right, thank you. Sorry to phone you so early, but is Dad there?'

'Well, nobody's in here yet, are they – we ain't open for ages. Come to think of it, we ain't seen your dad in a while. Shall I tell 'im to ring if he comes in at dinner time?'

'Yes – yes please. Thanks, Mr Gurney.'

'Cheerio, love. Look after yourself.'

I worry as I throw kindling sticks on the fire. How on earth can I get in touch with Dad if he isn't going into the Half Moon? It's the only telephone number we have for him in London. Maybe ... maybe he's at Auntie Kath's. I wonder if her number's lying around somewhere.

I strike a match and light the paper. The little flames turn the edges black.

The sticks begin to crackle. I reach for a log.

Keep to the shadows, be a shadow, in among the noisy people, sitting silently, moving quietly, while the rumble and clatter of iron wheels and the hiss of steam carry us into the city. She takes out the paper, shows it to a woman on the teeming street, who points. We turn a corner between tall buildings, and the din and the rush become nothing more than a low hum behind the high walls.

We wait, tucked against the brickwork, a little way from the arched door with metal words screwed into the wood. She mutters under her breath: 'Gilead House.'

A man comes along the street, pulls on a bell chain. We hear it echo around the spaces inside.

The door opens. A woman in a white apron and cap talks to the man for some time, invites him in through the door.

Keep to the shadows, be a shadow. We slip in, make no sound in our quiet boots as we weave our way round corners deep into the building, searching for a name . . .

Wailing, from somewhere above, passes through walls and down stairwells to reach this noiseless passage, but nobody minds it, or answers it. The people behind these doors are on the other side of weeping, though they must have wept many times. They would not be here otherwise.

Green tiles gleam in the low light. At the end, a glow from an open door and the edge of a white sleeve, an arm resting on a table, barely moving. A green cup askew on a saucer.

Below each glass peephole is a small metal frame around a scrawled name. She whispers them to herself: 'Scribbs Jane . . . Warren Edith . . . Drumm Susan.'

Dying lights seep one by one out of the empty keyholes and through the gaps under the doors – slow, slow deaths behind the green wood.

The distant wailing becomes a cheerless singing:

'There is a balm in Gilead, to make the wounded whole . . .'

I expect the door to be locked, but we turn the knob with our fingers and it moves outwards on its quiet, oiled hinges. We glance down the passage at the doorway but the white sleeve stays unmoving on the table.

'. . . There is a balm in Gilead, to soothe the sin-sick soul.'

We go into the small, hard room, begin to close the door but see there is no handle on the inside. We pull it to, leave a gap. Mustn't be trapped in here with Drumm Susan.

Twelve squares of cold grey sky send a ghostly, slanted reflection of themselves onto the painted wall opposite the metal bed.

She lies there, still and bone-thin in a white shift under a crumpled sheet and rough brown blanket, fair hair matted and knotted around bloodless skin, dark half-moon smudges under the closed eyes, a brownish stain on the pillow near the mouth.

On the small cupboard by the bedhead, a metal spoon stands in a smear of milk at the bottom of an empty glass. An acrid smell comes from it, and the same unpleasant odour hangs on Susan's shallow breath.

In the angle of the shadowed corner is a metal chair with a seat of colourless cloth coming loose on one side. We sink into it and watch the wasted woman on the bed.

A light lifts from the pale body, moves slowly to the sealed window, then crosses the room and disappears into the passage beyond the door. So many lights have left her, little by little over these years, that she has become diluted.

I slip out, leave Ange slumped on the metal chair and move across the narrow space to the bed.

Susan's skin is insubstantial, like a film of water over deeper empty water, memories washed away in almost perpetual sleep, by whatever was in the foul-smelling glass on the cupboard – balm in Gilead. I pass beneath the river bed into the deepness of her, and find a vast blackened place where all recollections have been drowned out. I look for her two daughters, but they no longer exist in this sea of nothingness.

I search and search, and find at last dim, smoky images – the only memories left undestroyed – a door left ajar, the curl of a twisted claw round the frame. I see him as she did, distorted in a mirror – Lankin, almost fleshless, festering, hungry. An empty bed, the barely remembered face of a snatched child, a sister, a name – Annie – a never-ending cry: 'It's all my fault, it's all my fault . . .'

That's all there is.

Two pillows. We could press her face between the two – soft slumber to soft slumber. Maybe a shudder, a slightly raised hand, perhaps not even that, just a gentle slipping away into the night. It would be a mercy, a release for her poor, sunken soul.

But even I know that Ange would not do that for me. She would rise up, struggle, battle to regain herself. I must be cunning, delicate – a twist or a pinprick she would not understand; a little craftiness, use her artfully, not alarm her.

We have the swan-necked scissors in our pocket. I could take a snip of clothing from this woman on the bed, a lock of hair. I have the bloodstone safe. It could all be set quietly in motion before we steal away, then a little bit of sewing in the night.

Or I could leave her to sleep away her wasted life.

Very soon she will be dead. The lights are almost gone, the Guerdon blood thinned in her to a droplet in a vast ocean.

She is no threat to me.

Unlike her forgotten daughters.

I take the box of matches and some newspaper into the sitting room. The hearth is a heap of cold grey ash. There are few logs left in the pile and hardly any kindling, barely enough to get the fire going.

Clutching the rim of the barely warm radiator, I stand at the window, rub away a patch of rime from one of the diamond panes and look out to see if I might get across to fetch some more wood. My breath mists the glass. I wipe it again. It is a bleak grey-cold outside. The frost still clings to the ground, little needles of it stiffening the grass. The black gaping crack of the frozen creek is over-hung by the dark shapes of the stunted trees on the far bank.

With my cheek to the edge of the frame, I can feel the whisper of a light but steady icy draught seeping its way in. No sound comes from beyond the walls, from the hushed world outside.

With a sigh I go back to the fire, prod the ash through the basket with the poker and lay and light the ends of the twisted paper, set a match to some thin twigs, then reach for a piece of wood from the meagre pile.

Something drops down.

I reach behind and tug out the piece of leather I pulled out of the chimney last week.

I run my fingers around the small studded nails, then over the scratched letters – ƎSHSUЯAЯHꟼA – Aphra Rushes. I force my hand into the fold, and although the leather is stiff, I manage to separate one side from the other and open it out. It won't flatten completely – there is a fat lump of a crease – but it opens well enough for me to see what it is: a shoe, plain, slipper-shaped. I am able to wriggle my fingers into the upper.

What did Mr Wragge say? *They used to shove all sorts of stuff up chimneys in the old days to keep the witches out – dead cats, shoes, all sorts.*

'Cora, you said—'

The shoe falls out of my hands and hits the floor with a dull thud. Mimi is in the doorway, her face pale with alarm.

'You said you'd put it back. You *said*, Cora.'

'Mimi – I forgot.'

'*It was the last thing.*'

'What – what do you mean, *the last thing*?'

She turns and rushes out of the room. I run after her.

'Mimi! Come back! What do you mean?'

She stops halfway up the stairs and looks down at me over the rail. 'It was the last thing stopping her! It's your fault, Cora. *You* did it!'

I dash to the bottom of the stairs. 'How do you know all this, Mimi? How do you know?'

She thunders up the rest of the stairs and into our bedroom, slamming the door behind her.

Dazed and confused, I go back into the sitting room, look at the shoe on the floor, pick it up, turn it over. It occurs to me that if what Mr Wragge said was true, then the magic would have gone out of it, the harm done, the moment I pulled it out of the chimney. The place – the chimney – was part of the charm. It would have made no difference whatsoever if I'd put it back.

All my fault.

I hear a rasping cough.

Ange comes in with her sewing box, sits down on the settee and opens the lid, begins to cough again into her hand. She takes out her handkerchief and dabs her mouth.

'What on earth was that about, Cora?' she asks, clearing her throat. 'I've never heard you shout at each other before.'

'Oh, nothing,' I say, slipping the leather into my palm and holding it close to my side, not really knowing why she shouldn't see it.

A small piece of fabric flutters in Ange's hands. I can't think of anything that's left to mend, but she must have found something to keep her fingers busy.

I move towards the door along the back of the settee.

As I pass behind Ange, my hand, with the shoe held stiffly in it, brushes the back of the seat.

Instantly she flinches, sucks in her breath as if she is in pain.

'Ange?'

I put the shoe down on the floor, and hurry back to her.

'Did you hurt yourself? Ange? Do you need your pills?'

She is bent slightly forward. I rub the back of her hand with my fingers.

'Gosh, you're freezing. What's the matter?'

'I – I'm all right.'

Slowly she raises her face to me.

I take a step backwards.

Something isn't right at all. There was a shift in her eyes, a quick movement like a cat's in sudden light; a swift change in the iris, there a moment ago, now gone.

'Why – why don't you move nearer the fire?' I say, swallowing. 'Do you want me to get you a blanket?'

'No, I don't know why you're making such a fuss. I'm warm as toast – look . . .' She holds out her hand. Gingerly I touch it. It *is* warm as toast. 'You go and patch things up with Mimi. I hate to think of you two falling out.'

Behind her I pick up the shoe, look at the letters on the sole, then, with a flicker of unease, at the back of Ange's head, now bowed over some sewing.

A few minutes later, I am knocking gently on our bedroom door.

'Mimi?'

'Go away! It's all your fault.'

Bewildered, I go back downstairs and into the kitchen.

The *County Records* lies beside the sugar bowl. I thumb to Katherine Myldmaye's letters at the back, slowly turn the pages to find the one dated 10th April 1584:

We know that malignant cunning women can be possessed of potent gifts, but can it be true what Kittie Wicken told you of – that when alive, Aphra Rushes frighted her with the threat that she could creep into Kittie's skin, look out of her eyes and use her hands to do whatsoever the witch willed with them? This is diabolic work indeed. Surely it cannot be possible under heaven to interfere with another's soul in such a way as this.

I turn back to the letter written on 21st December 1583.

Joan enquired of me whether this burned witch was properly laid to rest in the manner befitting a handmaid of the Devil. Were her ashes burned again to remove all traces of cunning and magic? Perhaps your lord is afeared lest she rise again like the Phoenix from its fire to cause him mischief.

Forward again, to 8th February 1584.

. . . think what agonies Father must have endured in his heart when he was present at the witch's execution, by your lord's very side, and heard her bring down her terrible malediction on the heads of the Guerdons, even unto the very end of the line . . .

I stare at the page, but the printed words fade and blur under my fingers as all I seem to see is that little shift in Ange's eyes, as if for a fleeting moment someone else was looking out of them.

. . . even unto the very end of the line . . .

That's Mimi and me – the very end of the line.
My hands tremble as I close the book. My mouth goes dry.

In *Julius Caesar* it's hard to decide who is meant to be a goodie and who is a baddie. Some of them start out one way and end up the other. Unfortunately, in this essay I am supposed to work all this out, discuss it and use quotations to back it up. I asked Mum when she was washing up after dinner, but she said she'd only seen the film and she wasn't sure even then, but Marlon Brando doing Mark Antony had been nice to look at.

When she's gone to get Pamela ready for bed, there is a loud rapping at the door.

'Roger?'

It's Cora.

My face goes hot.

She knocks again, almost falls into the kitchen when I open the door and drops a heavy old book onto the table next to my homework.

'I can't stay,' she says breathlessly, 'but please, *please* could you look at something in this book for me. I'll leave it here for when you've got a minute.'

I pick it up, feel its weight. 'Where on earth did you get this old thing from?'

'Please don't tell anyone, but I stole it from school, from the Head's study.'

'Crikey!'

'Ssh. Please, *please* keep it secret.'

'What bit do you want me to look at?'

She spreads it out, and towards the end reaches over for my blotting paper and sticks it between two pages.

'These letters – all right? I've got to go.'

'What? Don't you want a cup of tea?'

'I've got to get back quick as I can. I've left Mimi with Ange.'

And she has gone through the door.

If it wasn't for the book lying there and the icy cold hanging in the air, I would have thought I'd dreamed it.

CORA

I look over my shoulder to where Ange is lying back on the settee cushions, fast asleep in front of the dying fire, some strands of red hair loosened from their grips, a threaded needle still between her fingers. One of Dad's shirts, thin black stripes on white, is draped beside her over the wooden arm, its frayed cuff half repaired on her knee.

I study her face – the little black dots where her eyebrows need replucking, the smudges of blue eyeshadow, the fair lashes edged with caked mascara, lipstick worn off to an outline, the attempts at glamour that never really come together properly. There seems to be nothing threatening about her, nothing out of the ordinary as she lies there, a little whistle escaping from her nose as she lightly snores.

But she is frightening me.

I don't want to think what I am thinking.

And I don't want her in the house any more.

I pull the door almost shut, daren't risk the click of it closing, creep into the hall and lift the telephone receiver, dial, turn my back, half cover the mouthpiece with my hand.

'Mr Gurney?' I hiss hoarsely. 'Is that the Half Moon?'

'What? Why are you whispering? Is this a funny phone call?'

'It's Cora, Mr Gurney – Cora Drumm.'

'What's happened to your voice?'

'Er – terrible sore throat, Mr Gurney. Is – is Dad there today?'

'Funnily enough, he's just on the other side of the counter 'aving a pint of brown ale. I'll get 'im to come round.'

A few seconds later: 'Cora? Are you all right?'

I can't speak for a moment; have to swallow.

'Dad – please come home.'

'What's the matter? Why are you whispering?'

I turn and glance at the sitting-room door, then breathe into the receiver. 'Ange is asleep. I – I don't want her to hear me.'

'Why not? What's wrong?'

I bite my lip. 'There – there's something not right about her.'

'Come on, love, she's only been there a week. You've got to give her a chance to settle in, get used to things. We've all got to learn to give and take a bit. I shouldn't have had a go at her on Sunday. She was only doing her best.'

'No, no it's not that, Dad. Please, *please* could you send her away, find somebody else – *please*, and quickly.

I'll tell you when you come home. Please come back.'

I can hear the irritation in the few seconds of silence, then he laughs.

'Has she been chasing you around the kitchen with the bread knife?'

'Please, Dad. Don't leave us alone with her.'

A few more seconds. I don't know whether he is concerned or cross.

'All right, love,' he sighs. 'I'll get there as soon as I can. Cheerio.'

'Cheerio.'

As I replace the receiver gently in its cradle, I hear the creak of the settee from the sitting room. A wisp of icy air moves across the back of my neck.

We clutch close the scarred man's shirt, stroke one of the sleeves all along its length, lift the cuff and let it fall gracefully down. We feel deep in the pocket of our apron and draw out the bloodstone, rest it on the palm of our thin hand. It glints along one edge as it catches the glow from the red embers of the dying fire.

Mum and Dad are going to the Cricket Dinner and Dance at the Grand Palace Hotel in Wrayness and Dad will bring home the big silver cup for the best bowler, like he does every year.

I sit at the kitchen table with *Sorrel and Brassock's County Records*, trying to read *Appendix C: Letters of Katherine Myldmaye to her sister, Mary* . . .

Auntie Barbara comes round.

'You're in the way there, Roger,' says Mum. 'Can't you go somewhere else with that great big book?'

She makes a pot of tea, then they give each other a shampoo over the kitchen sink, followed by a giggly set at the table, before disappearing into the bedroom, their heads bristling with curlers. I spread the book out again, but when it gets to quarter past six, Dad comes in, a cigarette hanging out of his mouth, to polish his already gleaming shoes. Every thirty seconds or so he either looks up at the clock or checks his watch.

'How long can it take to stick a bit of powder on?' he mutters. 'Don't even know if the car will get to Wrayness in this weather. We can't rush on icy roads.'

Mum and Auntie Barbara emerge, fur stoles draped around their shoulders, all rustling skirts and clicking heels.

'About ruddy time,' cries Dad, rushing into the bedroom and coming out three minutes later in his dinner jacket, doing up his bow tie and trying to smooth back his fringe.

'Who's had my flamin' hair tonic?' he yells. 'The ruddy bottle's empty.'

Uncle Jim parps the horn of his smart Consul Cortina out in the road.

'Don't forget to keep the fire banked up, Roger.' Mum smiles, kissing my cheek. 'And remember I'm relying on you to stop Dennis having a go at Terry.'

They bustle out of the front door. Dad, a stray lock dangling over his forehead, holds out his elbows for Mum and Auntie Barbara. Their new curls lift in the chilly wind as they edge their way across the veranda boards and down the slippery steps in their strappy silver shoes. The cold draught from the briefly opened door pervades every corner, as does the sickly reek of setting lotion, nail varnish, hair lacquer and Old Spice.

I try and go back to the book, but the telephone rings.

For one silly moment I think it might be Cora – hope really, if I'm honest – but it's Phil Chisholm.

'Hello, Jotters,' he shouts down the line. 'Webley, Parker and me are going to the James Bond. Eight o'clock in Daneflete. You coming?'

'Hang on a minute,' I say, putting my hand over the mouthpiece. Dennis and Terry are jostling each other through the kitchen door. 'Where's Pete?' I ask them.

'Doing his hair,' says Dennis. 'You know, for that Gillian Swinburne. Woo-woo!'

'Gillian Swinburne? What are you going on about – Gillian Swinburne?'

'He was waiting for Mum and Dad to go out. He's

meeting her up at the bus stop. They're going to see *Dr No* at the pictures.'

'What? He can't be!'

'He is.'

I take my hand off the mouthpiece. 'You wouldn't flippin' well believe it, Phil. Pete's going to the same showing, so it's muggins here doing the flaming baby-sitting again.'

'Isn't Dennis old enough to do the honours?'

'Oh yes, if he was normal, but Mum doesn't trust him an inch with Terry. She's worried one thump and Terry's new glasses will go west.'

'Really sorry, mate.'

'Not half as sorry as me. Look, if you see Pete at the film, stick your leg out and trip him up the aisle for me – preferably when he's carrying an ice cream so it goes all over Gillian Swinburne and he'll look a right bonce.'

I hear a low whistle.

'Gillian Swinburne? Lucky ruddy sod,' says Phil. 'We've got Webley's skinny sister, Sheila, trolling along. Turn your back for a minute and she'll have disappeared down a drain.'

'See you, mate,' I say quickly, hanging up.

Gillian Swinburne – one of the Young Farmers and Young Conservatives set – lives in a huge house in North Fairing, set back with an in and out drive, a paddock and a sun lounge. When did Pete ever get within a ten-foot range of her? And does she know he's only fourteen?

'How's he got the money to take her to the pictures?' I ask Dennis, still stunned.

'Cleaned the car two weeks running, and Uncle Jim's,' says Dennis. 'He's got nearly ten bob. Her dad's something in the county rugby.'

'Flippin' heck, how the hell do you know all this?'

'I saw them round the back of Ferguson's farm in the snow, all smoochy-coochy. Pete said he'll give me sixpence every week if I don't tell Mum and Dad. I'll take it for two weeks, then make him put it up to a shilling. Here he comes. Woo-woo!'

Pete struts in wearing a button-down collar, his birthday tie from Grandma, Dad's sports jacket, and his hair slicked back with the missing tonic. Even though the jacket's more than a tad gappy around the chest, and the tie's a bit snazzy for my taste, Pete could put on a potato sack and still look like one of those French film stars who have lazy picnics all day in blazing hot cornfields with Brigitte Bardot.

'What a nerve,' I say, irritated. 'Fancy having the cheek to ask Gillian Swinburne to the pictures.'

'You're only jealous, mate,' he says, buffing his fingernails on Dad's lapel. 'Anyway, we might not go to the pictures, I might take her to the Thin Man.'

'What? They won't let you in.'

'Been in before.'

'Crikey, the landlord must be half blind. You're way under age.'

'Tell you, I've been in. He didn't bat an eyelid. Had a shandy.'

He saunters off into the hall for his mac.

'Close your mouth, Roger,' says Dennis.

'Make sure you get back before Mum and Dad,' I call after Pete, 'or you'll be in big trouble, specially wearing his jacket. Don't go spilling lemonade on it!'

'Ha ha with brass knobs on.'

Irritated, I go into the sitting room, spread myself out on the settee with the *Sorrel and Brassock's*.

Pam comes in with *Noddy Gets into Trouble* and pushes it under my nose. 'Read this, Roger?'

'I'm trying to read this one.'

She glances over and is unimpressed. 'It's got no pictures. Read this, *please*.'

As Pete swaggers off down Fieldpath Road for his assignation with Gillian Swinburne, trailing clouds of pointless aftershave, I am on the settee with Pam tucked under my arm, reading *Noddy* and sharing her dolly mixtures. I can't believe I'm actually shuffling through the bag for the jellies. Terry and Dennis lie on the rug in front of the fire, chins resting on hands, gazing up at *Dixon of Dock Green*.

For some reason Pete going off starts me thinking about Cora – again; about us walking back tipsy from

Mr Thorston's. I begin to feel the heat of a blush again. What on earth used to fill up all that empty space in my head before Cora did?

'Roger, you did Mr Plod wrong,' Pam mumbles, her mouth stuffed with sweets. 'You just did Big Ears talking, but it's Mr Plod.'

'Sorry.'

The lights go out. PC Dixon disappears into a small white dot, then a blank screen.

'Awwwwwww!'

'Is it a fuse?'

I get up and pull the curtain aside. The windows of the new bungalows are black.

'Looks like a power cut.'

'Let's put the radio on, then,' says Terry.

'Stupid bonce, there's no flippin' electricity, is there,' says Dennis, thumping him. 'I know – let's play Murder in the Dark.'

'Not a chance,' I say. 'When you were the murderer last time, it very nearly happened. Terry, go and get the candles and matches. They're under the sink.'

'I want to go in the kitchen in the dark,' Pam says, excited.

'Go together, then.'

When Terry and Pam have gone, Dennis says something I would never have expected.

'Why don't you take that Cora to the pictures, Roger?'

'What?'

'She's got nice hair, when it's brushed.'

I shift uncomfortably, glad Dennis can't see much of my face in the firelight.

'It would spoil everything, mate,' I say. 'We – we wouldn't be friends any more.' I sink down into the settee.

'Don't know what you mean,' Dennis says. 'You're not supposed to be *friends* with girls. I'm taking that Maureen in the new bungalows to the bazaar next Saturday.'

'What? The *bazaar*?'

'In the Scout Hut.'

'I know where the flippin' bazaar is.'

'I'll buy her a cake, or something nice from the bric-à-brac. I'm all set. I've already asked Pete about the kissing thing.'

'What!?'

'You know, making sure you don't miss or your nose doesn't get in the way, and I've given up spring onions so I don't taste horrible—'

Thank God, before Dennis can say any more, Terry brings in the candles, and Pam comes through the door holding the lighted torch under her chin so it sends spooky shadows up her face.

'Woooo! We're in Miss Monkey's house in the night,' she says, climbing back up beside me. She shines the fat beam over the book and jabs a page with her finger. 'We were here, Roger,' she says.

It all seems so easy to Dennis, and the truth is, it was a lot easier four years ago. Cora and I are not at the best age to be meeting up again.

'You done it again, Roger,' says Pam. 'That's supposed to be Tessie Bear talking and you just did Mr Wobbly Man.'

SUNDAY 25th NOVEMBER

Dad's gone over to Grandma's. Her pipes are up the spout.

There's a funny atmosphere. I'm at the side table in the sitting room doing my homework and Mum's hardly talking to me. Maybe she's just tired after her night out at the Cricket Dinner and Dance.

Or perhaps it's me.

It was so unsettling, reading Cora's book in bed, by torchlight, and being thrown back into the horrors of the past. I finished Katherine Myldmaye's letters, but they conjured up too many remembered nightmares, and a host of new ones that insisted on breaking into my uneasy sleep.

Pete came back after midnight, clattered noisily around the bedroom in the dark, describing Ursula Andress from every possible angle, then shutting up and leaping into bed when Mum and Dad came back. They were creeping around so as not to wake us, but really, they might just as well have done the hokey-cokey up and down the hall.

The telephone rings. I don't even bother to look up from my Chemistry. It's bound to be Gillian Swinburne, inviting Pete for evening cocktails or croquet on the lawn. He swaggers off into the hall, smoothing his hair. I hear him pick up the receiver, then say, unable to hide his surprise, 'Oh – yes, he's here. Just a minute and I'll get him.'

Not Gillian Swinburne then; probably Maureen in the new bungalows ringing for Dennis – the unkindest cut of all.

'Roger, it's Cora!'

I'm so amazed, the nib of my pen catches in the paper and makes a blot. I try not to get up too quickly, turn a page over, turn it back, saunter through the doorway, all for Pete's benefit. Don't want him thinking I'm too keen or anything.

He holds out the phone, and hovers.

'Hello, er, Cora?' I say.

'Roger, is that you?' she hisses.

'Push off, mate,' I say to Pete.

'What?' says Cora.

'Sorry, not you.'

Terry appears and asks me if I've got a pencil he can lend.

'*Borrow*, not lend,' I say, 'and ask Pete, for heaven's sake – you know, the one standing there with his ears flapping. Can't you see I'm busy?'

'Pardon?' says Cora.

'I'm sorry. It's like Piccadilly Circus in here.'

'Sorry . . .'

There's a click and the burr of an empty line.

'Cora? Are you there?'

Irritated, I shove the phone back down, grab my coat off the peg and get Cora's big book from the foot of my bed. I take it into the kitchen, where Mum and Pam are making jam tarts – at least, Mum's rolling out the pastry and Pam's mouth is ringed with jam – and balance it on the corner of the table while I start to put on my boots by the back door.

'Where are you going, Roger?' says Mum. 'What about your homework?'

'Just out, won't be long.' I do up my coat buttons. 'Have you seen my gloves?'

'Are – are you going down to Guerdon Hall?'

'Does it matter where I'm going?'

'Pam, go and play,' says Mum.

'I *am* playing,' she says.

'In your bedroom.' Mum pushes her through the door.

'What on earth's wrong?' I say, spotting my gloves on the airer and pulling them down.

'You – you can't neglect your studies, Roger. You've got exams in January.'

'Oh, come on, Mum – you know I'll do it when I get back. What's all this about?'

She pushes a drooping wave behind her ear, streaking it with flour, then looks right at me. 'You were with Cora when you got drunk last week, weren't you?'

'What? I was hardly drunk – just a bit tipsy, that's all.'

'Mrs Mount in the new bungalows said at the Cricket Dinner last night, in a voice so loud it stopped everyone talking, that she was shocked to see you and a girl staggering up Fieldpath Road, drunk – in broad daylight. I didn't know where to look. Your dad tried to make a joke of it, but I – I was so embarrassed . . .'

'I was hardly staggering, and Cora definitely wasn't – I don't think so anyway. It was only a bit of mead we'd had by mistake—'

'Mistake!'

I put on a whiny old woman's voice, '*Ooh – drunk, in broad daylight!* Would the nosy old bat have minded so much if we'd been tottering up the road in the dark?'

'Roger! I've never heard you talk like that!'

I pull down my hat, trying to swallow down the bubbling anger.

'And . . .' Mum goes on.

'And *what*?'

'I didn't want to say this' – her voice rises – 'but you know Cora's father has . . . has women living there; women he's not married to, one after the other – brings them down from London—'

'Mum, you don't know anything about it.'

'I do. They were all talking about it last night, at the Cricket Dinner.'

'That's so flippin' unfair. You've always liked Cora – you were so kind letting her and Mimi stay here the other night. I can't believe you're saying all this. Sounds like nobody ate a blimmin' thing at the Cricket Dinner, just sat around gossiping the whole time.'

'Don't be so rude, Roger. And – and I do like Cora, but I don't want you to go down there. God knows what's going on – drink and – and God knows what!'

'We didn't drink down *there*!' I grab Cora's book off the table and pull open the door.

'What?'

I realize how bad that must have sounded, but storm out regardless, slam the door behind me, angrily brush some flour off the book, and tramp across the veranda and down the steps, still frosty from the morning.

As I stride down Fieldpath Road, my heart's going like the clappers. I can't believe I just shouted at Mum.

I'll be in dreadful trouble when I get home; she'll tell Dad all about it when he comes back from fixing Grandma's plumbing. And it's not fair I'm getting all this stick, when it's Pete who should be the one in trouble for sneaking off with Gillian Swinburne in Dad's best sports jacket. Then I think, even if they did find out, they wouldn't give two hoots anyway. After all, Gillian Swinburne's in the Young Farmers, and speaks as if she's swallowed a whole bag of plums.

I bet when the Swinburnes get drunk, it's inside where nobody can see.

And to cap it all, it's so blinking chilly. I pull up my

collar around my scarf, tug down my hat so I can just see out from under it, and plod on.

CORA

Still brooding, Mimi is holed up in our bedroom, and along the landing Ange is fast asleep in hers, so I grab the moment to get some wood to heat the freezing house. Outside, the cold chills the breath in my throat as I crunch across the frozen puddles in the old farmyard and go into the barn.

Opening up the sack, I start tossing in logs from the pile against the back wall. When it's pretty full, I try and lift it. Too heavy. I start to drag it. Too heavy. With an irritated sigh, I begin to take out some of the logs and drop them in the straw. Then, just as I notice Mr Wragge's empty wheelbarrow out of the corner of my eye and think to try it, someone says, 'Want a hand?'

Startled, I turn, and there is Roger in the doorway with the *County Records* under his arm.

'Oh.' I am surprised at how pleased I feel to see him, though his expression is unusually subdued. 'How did you know I was in here?'

'I was coming along The Chase and saw you,' he answers with the bare flicker of a smile and, saying no more, walks across the straw to help me bundle the logs into the barrow. When it's full, we cover the wood with the sack, chuck the book on top and, in an uncommon silence, push it out of the barn and across to the bridge.

'Are you all right?' I ask at last.

He runs his eyes over the crackled grey crust of the frozen creek. 'I've had a bit of a barney with Mum,' he says, 'and I think there's going to be big trouble when I get home.'

'What was it about?'

He doesn't look at me. 'Oh, just . . . um . . . the usual stuff – you know, schoolwork and things – getting good O-Levels so I can go to university.'

'You will, won't you – get good O-Levels?'

'Hope so.'

He rubs his nose with his gloved hand and still won't look at me. Roger was never a good fibber, but I won't press him if he doesn't want to tell me what the row was about, or can't. I look at the book in the wheelbarrow, worry a bit to see that it's dusted with flour.

'I thought perhaps it was those letters I made you read, or – or because I put the phone down on you. It's just, I thought someone was listening.' I say, recalling the creak, the unnatural stillness, as if somebody was waiting, holding their breath, out of sight just beyond the turn of the staircase.

'Everyone listens in our house.' He smiles. 'It's a

flipping nuisance. Sorry – I know it's not the same thing.'

We cross the bridge, Roger still quiet. I try and fill the awkwardness.

'It's just Mimi and me and Ange at home. Dad's coming back as quick as he can. I spoke to him on the telephone yesterday. I've been listening out for the car ever since. And I've got so much to tell you.'

We push the barrow round the corner of the house, stop outside the back door and unload the logs into the stone passage.

'How can you bear it so icy?' he asks, blowing on his fingers through his gloves. 'I'll swear it's colder in the house than it is outside.'

We take bundles of wood in our arms down the passage, our breath streaming white in front of us, and into the sitting room, where the corners are beginning to darken into shadow.

'Do you mind if I just check on Mimi?' I ask.

'I'll start the fire, if you like.'

I hurry up the stairs and push open our bedroom door.

Mimi is alone, sitting on the bed with Aggie, her breath a cloud.

'You all right, sis? Is Ange up?'

She doesn't raise her head. 'Still in bed,' she mutters sourly.

'Roger and me have brought some wood. We'll get

the fire properly roaring in a minute. Do you want a cup of tea – warm you up?'

She says nothing, goes back to the doll.

I tiptoe along the landing to Ange's room. There is no light under the door. I lean in and put my ear to it, hear the faint, regular whistle from her nose.

Downstairs I put the kettle on, fetch the old shoe I've been hiding behind the dining-room curtains, and take it in on the tray with the tea to Roger, who is kneeling in front of the sitting-room fire, blowing softly on the kindling, coaxing it into flame.

'Sorry it's only tinned milk,' I say, putting the cups down beside us, 'and not much sugar. I daren't use any more in case we run out altogether.' Then I show him the piece of leather, unbend it, point out the scratched letters.

'Look – like I said: *Aphra Rushes* backwards.'

'So it is.'

I pull off my gloves and put my hand inside the upper. 'And do you see, it's a shoe; flat like a slipper.'

'Oh yes, it's obvious when you look,' he says, taking it.

I blow on my tea, watch Roger over the rim of the cup as he turns it over and runs a finger around the ring of nail heads. 'How odd.'

'I pestered Mr Wragge to death,' I said. 'In the end he told me people used to put shoes up chimneys to keep witches away.'

'Really?'

'And he told me something else an' all. You know those bits of old pots in the barn I showed you – with nails and hair in? Well, I got him to say what they were.'

He looks up. 'And?'

'Witch bottles.'

'What?'

'Witch bottles. Honestly. The fingernails and hair and blood draw the witch in and trap her if she comes down the chimney, and the iron nails and sharp pieces of glass kill her. It works – specially if the bottle is thrown on the fire and explodes when she's trapped in it. Have your tea, Roger. Don't let it get cold.'

The flames begin to curve over the new logs, coiling in twists of blue-green and yellow, while the wood spits out little specks of fiery bark.

'So in those letters in the book,' Roger says, 'when Katherine Myldmaye talks about the cunning men coming to protect the house, they're the ones who could have put the witch bottles in.'

'Most probably, and buried them under the fireplaces and doorways. But they've been taken out.'

The room darkens behind us. Roger pulls off his hat and scratches his head. 'So, those little white stones and the bundle of twigs on the door . . . ?'

'Well, it turns out Mr Wragge lives at the St Lazarus Hospital,' I say. 'I asked him if he'd told anybody there about Mimi and me coming back here, and that all the charms had gone, and he said he had.' I pull the piece of paper out of my pocket. 'He told Mrs Lailah Ketch and Miss Iris Jewel, the two women we saw – these names here. They're the wardens – look after the old men at the St Lazarus. I bet they put the stones up, and the bundle of twigs. But why did they talk to Mimi and not me? Why did they give her this, with their names and telephone number on? And they must have drawn this funny sign for her – a witch mark, like the other things; a charm to keep witches out of a house. What is it about Mimi?'

I stuff the paper back in my pocket, pick up my cup again. Roger takes the poker and pushes the logs about. The fire roars up in a burst of sparks.

'Mr Wragge said there were cunning people still about,' I continue, sipping my tea, 'and I think that's what those women are. Maybe those drums of salt we saw spilled in the snow last week were part of some spell, but the women weren't able to finish it. You know when Dad was shouting at Ange – it's because she'd yelled at Mrs Ketch and Miss Jewel to go away. I think she recognized what sort of women they were. And they probably saw who *she* was as well.'

Roger looks up. 'What do you mean? What's it to do with Ange?'

'That's why I wanted you to read that book, because

you're the only one who would believe it might be true; that Aphra Rushes has somehow got into Ange – is able to use her because she has no body of her own.'

I reach over for the book, balance it on my knees and turn the pages. 'Here it is. Look.'

I run my finger along the words as I read them: '. . . *Aphra Rushes frighted her with the threat that she could creep into Kittie's skin, look out of her eyes and use her hands to do whatsoever the witch willed with them . . .*'

I slide the book off my lap and back onto the floor and reach for my tea.

'But why would she want to come back?' says Roger. 'And how? She was burned.'

'What do they say – unfinished business? When she was dying, she cursed the Guerdon family for ever, and Long Lankin was part of that curse. He's gone now, but Mimi and me are still here, and we're the end of the line.'

'But you aren't Guerdons.'

'But we are, Roger, we are. We're the last people to have Guerdon blood in us, Mimi and me, except for—'

The words have slipped out. I can't reclaim them.

'Except for what?'

I curve my cold fingers around the cup, struggle to say what I have never spoken aloud to anyone before.

'Except for . . . my mother.'

A piece of damp bark hisses in the fire. An age goes by.

'What happened to her?' Roger says quietly. 'I never liked to ask. I thought maybe she was dead, or – or they'd divorced or something.'

I gulp a mouthful of tea.

'It's all right,' he adds. 'You don't have to tell me.'

I swallow it down. 'She's in an asylum.'

He doesn't move.

My breath comes out oddly.

I glance at him. 'Shall I go on?'

He gives a small nod, but it's a while before I can speak.

'At the beginning of the war,' I say at last, 'Mum – she was about twelve – was sent here from London with her little sister, Annie – who was just a toddler – to stay with Auntie Ida.' The flames snap and sputter. 'And . . . and Long Lankin stole Annie away from the house.' I stare at the rim of my cup. 'You know what will have happened. She was never seen again.' Roger doesn't say a word. I swallow quickly. 'Mum blamed herself for the rest of her life because she'd left a door open when Auntie had told her not to. She's too ill to ever come out. She can't live in the world like other people.'

I dare a glimpse at Roger again, at the line of his face flushed in the firelight.

'Do – do you mind . . . that I've told you?'

'Why should I mind?' he says, turning towards me.

'And you won't tell anyone else, will you?'

Roger's coat rustles as he draws closer. 'Course not.'

I put down my cup. 'So you see,' I breathe, 'if we – if Mimi and me – die before we grow up and have children of our own, then there will never be any more Guerdon blood, ever again. The curse would be done.'

Heads almost touching, we stare into the fire.

The night has drawn in early, but neither moonlight nor starlight can pierce the dark, oppressive clouds. I walk back up the icy hill, digging in my boots to stop myself slipping, recalling every hushed word Cora and I spoke to each other on the bridge a few minutes ago.

'You've got to come and stay with us,' I urged her. 'You and Mimi.'

With the side of her boot she scraped frost off the wooden planks and pushed the white powder off the edge of the bridge onto the frozen water.

'Don't be silly,' she said. 'How on earth would you explain it to your mum – and Pete, for that matter? Anyway, Dad should be back soon, maybe even tonight. I told him on the phone he's got to give Ange the sack. Everything will be all right when Dad gets home. He'll sort it out.'

'Honestly, Cora, apart from all the other things, there's hardly anything to eat in the house. I'll bring you something; we've always got loads.'

'Don't be daft. When Dad comes back with some money, I'll go up to Mrs Aylott's.'

She glanced over her shoulder up to the first-floor windows, every one of them blank and dark.

'What about school?' I asked.

'I haven't been since Tuesday, since I stole that book.' She dropped her eyes. 'I keep thinking a letter's going to come, or the police even. The head's bound to know it was me.'

'Please, *please* be careful, Cora,' I said, and then she did look up and hold my gaze for a moment. 'Let me know what happens with your dad, and telephone, won't you. Even if it rings off, I'll know it was you, that you couldn't talk, and I'll come as quickly as I can.'

She looked back at the house, and at that moment one of the upstairs windows lit up a pale, murky yellow.

'She's woken up,' she said. 'I've got to go.'

'I'll come back in with you.'

'Don't be soppy. I'll be all right. Honestly.' She flapped me away. 'Cheerio.'

'Cheerio,' I said reluctantly, and watched Cora as she hurried off into the darkness, becoming more formless with every step until, ghostlike, she vanished into the shadows around the house.

By the time I cross over the main road, it's so bitterly cold the tension makes my shoulders ache. When I get home, there is no row at all. Mum is in the kitchen making sandwiches. I don't say anything, just pull off my damp hat and gloves and throw them on the table.

'For heaven's sake,' Mum says, pushing them off the cheese, 'how many times have I told you to hang your stuff on the airer?'

As I pick them up, Mum takes me by surprise, reaching over and ruffling my hair.

'You all right?' she asks with a half-smile before turning to put on the kettle.

She hasn't told Dad a thing.

CORA

When I get back in, I find Mimi alone, curled up in a blanket in front of the fire, watching a cowboy film on the television.

'Is – is Ange about?' I ask, a little breathlessly, reaching for a log.

'She ain't come down.'

'Do you want to sleep down here tonight, like we did before?'

'Don't think so. It's all right when the fire's going, but when it goes out, it's freezing.'

I go into the hall and look up the stairs, then climb slowly, listening.

I stop outside Ange's door and knock gently.

There's a slight scuffling noise, then, 'Yes?' she says.

I swallow, then go in.

Ange is sitting up in bed with the contents of her sewing box spread out around her. I can't see what she's working on, but think she must be busy doing something for Dad because there are some little snippets of shirt fabric in the folds of the bedspread.

'It's like the Arctic in here,' I say. 'Shall I put the paraffin heater on for you?'

'Don't worry, I'm all right.'

When Mimi and I go up the stairs to bed, clutching hot-water bottles, I glance along the landing.

Ange's light is still on.

I switch ours off, and for a long time Mimi and I lie there under our blankets in the dark. I can still feel the thread of tension between us.

'Mimi . . . you awake?' I whisper.

'Yes.'

'Are you still cross with me?'

'A bit.'

I wait a little while before saying, 'I know you don't like talking much – you know, about things . . . but can I just ask you why you said to put that leather thing back up the chimney?'

A few seconds go by. I hear the rustle of her sheets.

'And those little stones hanging over the door on Bonfire Night – why didn't you want Auntie Kath to take them down?'

For ages I think she isn't going to say anything, as usual; then her small voice comes out of the darkness.

'I – I'm a sensitive.'

'A *what*?'

'A sensitive. I can see things other people can't – and maybe do things . . .'

My scalp prickles.

For some minutes I lie there, not knowing what to say – then, 'Was it you who chalked that mark on the door?'

'And the front.' I hear a tremor on her breath. 'It was supposed to stop her getting in, that mark, but you washed it off.'

'It would stop *who* getting in?'

'The woman in the garden.'

My chest tightens.

After a while I whisper, 'Do you like Ange?'

'I did when she first came, but now . . .' She shudders. 'She's not right, Cora.'

A mouse scratches behind the wall.

'And it's a shoe,' Mimi says.

'What?'

'That leather thing.'

'I know it's a shoe, but how did you know?'

'I asked Mrs Ketch and Miss Jewel. They said it was an old way of stopping a witch coming down the chimney. She'd go away because her name was spelled wrong, even if she couldn't read. It would muddle her. Your name's a magic thing.'

Some time goes by before I hear Mimi sleeping. I look into the gloomy corners of our bedroom. A red chair with chrome legs stands beside the old fireplace. I get out of bed, sucking in my breath as my bare feet touch the icy lino, lift the chair quietly and take it to the door. The back won't reach as far as the old latch, but I push it as far as it will go against the wood. It might not stop somebody coming in, but if they do, at least I will hear the scraping of the metal legs on the floor and wake up.

I can't believe Mimi has spoken at last. I wish I could say it was because keeping it all to herself became too much to bear, but actually, it was as if she were talking to herself. She would only have said those things in the darkness.

'Repeat after me – *possum, potes, potest, possumus, potestis, possunt.*'

Swish goes the cane up to the blackboard, *swish* goes the sleeve of Mr Sefton's gown. *Click* goes the tip of the cane on each word – *click, click, click . . .*

The wind outside is rattling the tall sash windows.

'*Possum, potes, potest,*' we recite together – *click, click, click . . .* '*possumus, potestis, possunt.*'

And again, '*Possum, potes, potest, possumus . . .*'

Are Cora and Mimi all right? My mind has been churning endlessly – witch bottles, shoes, iron nails and Ange . . . I am so uneasy I can't stop rolling my pencil between my fingers.

Mr Sefton rubs the Present Indicative off the board with the sleeve of his gown and chalks up the Future Simple.

'Repeat after me – *potero, poteris, poterit, poterimus, poteritis, poterunt . . .*'

'*Potero, poteris, poterit—*'

A loud rap at the door.

I drop the pencil, slam it with my palm to stop it rolling down the desk.

'Enter!'

Mr Lennox strides in. 'Excuse me, Mr Sefton. Today I am Mercury to the Jove of Father Carfax. Pay attention, all of you! Gilmore – are you with us? Will somebody wake him up. Webley, flick him on the head, will you.'

Webley obliges, Gilmore flinches, opens his eyes, blinks a few times.

'Now listen carefully, boys. There's a heavy snow warning for this afternoon.'

General air of excitement, shifting of feet, grinning.

'Because they say this is likely to be severe, and may affect trains and buses later on, Father Carfax is allowing boys who live beyond Lokswood, Black Harston, Longcreek, and on Corsey Island, to go home after this lesson. For the remaining boys there may be a change of classes as some of the teaching staff will have to leave as well. Any questions?'

'What about Fecklesham?'

'Didn't you hear me, Parker? I said *beyond* Lokswood. So when did Fecklesham up sticks and move to the other side of Lokswood? Anyone who *non intellego* where his *domus* is can come to the hall after next bell for a Geography test. I expect to see you there, Parker. Thank you, Mr Sefton. Do continue.'

The door shuts behind Mr Lennox. There is a

giddiness in the air. The afternoon off. Maybe longer.

'Repeat after me – *potero, poteris, poterit . . .'*

CORA

As the evening draws in, the snow whirls thickly past the window, catching in the rims of the leaded diamonds. When I clear a misted pane with my fingers, I can barely see a couple of feet beyond the house. Wet soot splatters down the chimney, and although the dining room fills with smoke, the fire is beginning to hiss and snap. In the hall the clock strikes four and the telephone rings.

I dash out of the room and snatch at the receiver.

'Cora?' comes a hissing voice.

'Dad?'

'Can you hear me?'

'Talk louder. The line's all crackly. Where are you?'

'Doesn't matter. Weather's really bad here. The roads are blocked. I'll try and get back on the train. Are you and Mimi warm enough? Is the boiler going?'

'Just about, but it's still freezing. We'll keep the fires lit. I'm doing the dining room right now.'

'There's more wood in the barn if you need it.'

'Don't worry. We've already brought it in.'

'Good girl. How – how are things with Ange?'

'Please come home . . .'

'Sorry – got to go.'

The phone goes dead.

''Bye,' I say.

At the edge of my eye I see a movement – Ange in the sitting-room doorway, listening.

'Was that your father?'

'The roads are bad. He – he's going to try and get back on the train.'

'They've just said on the news that the trains aren't running,' Ange says, turning away.

The smoke from the dining room drifts into the hall and hangs there. For a moment it catches in my throat and stings my eyes. I rub the water away with my hand.

The evening wears on. Miraculously, I find a tin of peaches in syrup tucked away in a dark corner of the cupboard. Ange doesn't want any, so Mimi and I, wrapped together in a blanket in front of the television, eat them slowly one by one while we wait up for Dad, just in case. With each passing chime of the clock, his return seems less and less likely, and I begin to feel heavy with weariness. Ange sits in the armchair with her legs up, twisted around so I can't see her face. Her sewing box is beside her on the floor, its lid closed.

After ten o'clock *Come Dancing* starts, although the

reception is so poor it looks as if the wind has lifted the ballroom roof off and the dancers are moving about in a snowstorm like the one outside. Mimi's head droops against my shoulder.

'I'm going to take Mimi up,' I say to Ange with a sigh. 'You staying down?'

'I'll watch this to the end,' she says, without turning.

The last thing I do before I get into bed is to push the chair against our bedroom door.

The threads begin to weave together. I take my time, but then time has always been my gift.

I choose my glass-headed pins – red, like fresh blood drops – close the box, leave the room.

I run the sharp points of the pins across the panels, two fine scratched lines as I go upwards, stair by stair.

At the top is the door. I lean in close, and listen. They sleep. I hear their gentle breathing. Sleep on – sleep a while longer. This time I will let you wake.

I grip the two pins, move on along the landing and softly push the door.

I pull open the drawer, move aside her silly garments, and there he is. I lift him out, place him on the hard top of the chest, and take a pin in each hand.

Zillah taught me well, but the Bonesmen taught me better still: gave me bone ash to drink in ale and honey, showed me visions, how to gaze along the length of the spirit thread.

I lower my eyelids, and see the scarred man. I see him and all those things in the great city with her eyes, know those things – the buildings, the lights, the hard streets – as she knows them.

He stands with another man, older and stout, under the sign of the Dancing Dog in a pool of cold light from the lamp over the door. The scarred man is ill at ease, and his eyes dart from side to side under the brim of his snow-speckled hat. This is a place he does not know well. To his left the street bends into a road where one or two gas lamps shed their yellow-green gleam a few feet into the darkness; to his right there is the black tunnel of an alley strewn with long-forgotten rubbish poking out of the dirty snow.

'You're in this one up to your neck, 'Arry,' the older man whispers. 'I'm telling yer, yer'll not easy get out of this one.'

'Shut up, Frank, and let me think,' the scarred man hisses.

'Too late to be bloody thinking. You should have bloody thought before. You got two nippers an' all – should have got out before this bloody weather—'

'I said, shut up, Frank. They're none of your flippin' business.'

'And everyone knows your missus is in the funny farm—'

'I said shut your bloody—'

'Charlie knows you want to back out. He ain't pleased, and you're right on 'is manor.'

'I've got to get out of here. Which way's Whitechapel station?'

The older man screws up his eyes and peers into the alley, sees the beam of a torch, hears the thud of boots.

'I'd leg it quick – scarper!'

I raise my hand.

A young, long-legged man leaps into the lamplight, moves easy like a tumbler. A blade flashes.

The older man cries out, runs away into the darkness, slipping in the snow. The scarred man turns one way, then flips his head the other. He begins to run towards the gas lamps – into the path of a heavy man in a long pale coat with a fur collar and leather gloves, who appears out of nowhere and lunges at his stomach.

I plunge the first pin down into the little manikin, twist it as it goes. Ange imagines she is still sewing.

The scarred man is winded, grunts, thinks it is just a blow. He turns, breathless, into the path of the other –

I thrust deep with the second pin.

– who drives his arm forward, pulls away, turns and runs off on his long limbs. The heavy, fur-collared man disappears back into the shadows.

The scarred man drops to one knee, then the other, gasps, sees blood drops in the snow, clutches his stomach. The drops become a trickle, then a stream from under his coat. He crawls back up the step where the lamp shines down on him. Under the sign of the Dancing Dog he reaches up, smearing the door *with a bloody hand, moans, and drops, his head cracking on the stone step.*

His hat rolls off into a heap of slush.

Here they come, the dying lights, floating upwards, first one, then another. More come, then more still, spreading up into the chilly air until they become a glittering throng.

I've come to hate the chiming of the clock in the hall, letting me know in the small, lonely hours of the night how much I'm not sleeping. I won't wind it up when it next runs down.

I can't help thinking that Dad has got himself into some kind of trouble. It was such an odd phone call.

The wind died down shortly after Mimi and I went to bed, and now the early morning is so unusually hushed that I jolt upright when the harsh ring of the telephone reverberates around the wooden panelling.

Dad – I'm thinking of him so intensely, it must be him.

With a glance at Mimi, who sleeps on, but without bothering to throw on my dressing gown, and ignoring the shock of the freezing lino under my feet, I throw up the latch in excitement and hurry down the stairs, anxious in case the telephone stops before I reach it.

I rush to pick up the receiver, fumble with the cord, put it to my ear. 'Dad? Dad – is it you?'

'Who is this, please?'

It's a woman's voice, clipped, efficient.

'Cora – Cora Drumm,' I say.

'I see. Is Mrs Drumm there?'

'No. No, she isn't.'

'Who is there, then? Who is looking after you?'

'Um, Ange – Angela – Mrs Russell.'

'Could you fetch her for me, please?'

'She's asleep. What is it? Who are you?'

'This is the London Hospital. Please could I speak to Mrs Russell?'

'Please tell me, *please*. Is it Dad?'

'I must speak to an adult. Please fetch her.'

'Wait – wait . . .'

I drop the receiver onto the table, dash upstairs two at a time, and thump on Ange's bedroom door. 'Ange! Ange! Wake up! It's the hospital!'

A groan comes from the other side. 'What? What time is it?'

'Don't know. It's the hospital. Please come. I think it's Dad.'

A thump, shuffling, the padding of slippers crossing the room. The door opens. Ange peers round, a little mascara smudged under her eyes.

'The phone. Please come. They won't talk to me.'

Bleary-eyed, Ange shuffles down the stairs, tying up the belt of her quilted maroon dressing gown. She picks up the receiver and yawns before she speaks.

'Who is it? Yes, it's Angela Russell here. What's happened?'

I stand next to her, biting the edge of my thumbnail.

'Oh dear.'

A long pause.

'What sort of operation?'

I move from one foot to another.

'Is he conscious?'

Another pause.

'We're cut off – the snow. Yes, yes. Um, I don't know. What? The police?'

'Ang—?'

'Ssh, Cora. All right. Phone us back when you have more news. Thank you. Goodbye.' She clicks the receiver back.

'What's happened? What is it?'

'There's been an . . . an accident.'

'What – what sort of accident? The car?' I feel dizzy.

'There was a fight,' says Ange, 'outside a pub in Bethnal Green. Flick-knives.'

'Flick-knives? Dad wouldn't have a flick-knife.'

'He's been stabbed in two places – the chest and somewhere in the stomach.'

'Oh, Ange . . . Dad . . . Could – could he die?'

'They didn't say.'

'Have the police caught him – the man who did it?'

'They'll ring us soon as there's any more news.'

'What – what was Dad doing in Bethnal Green?'

I crumple onto the chair by the table. I am aware of Ange reaching for the pegs by the front door, then feel my school coat around my shoulders. Still I can't stop shivering.

How can I get to London? Are any buses running? Trains?

'There's nobody there,' I mumble. 'He'll be all on his own. I've got to see him.'

She rubs my shoulder, just where my coat has slipped down – an odd sensation, as if she's squeezed it just that little bit too hard. I stiffen; almost think I feel sharp fingernails pressing into my skin through my pyjamas.

'I'll just go and get dressed,' she says.

I get up and snatch at her sleeve. 'What was the operation? Is he going to be all right?'

'They had to take out his . . . his spleen or something.'

'What's his spleen?'

'I don't know, Cora. Stop asking questions.' Ange starts to climb the stairs.

'Can't you phone them back?'

'They won't be able to say any more than they've said already.'

I stand there on my numbed feet. 'Don't tell Mimi,' I call after her. 'Please don't tell her.'

ROGER

Pete, Dennis, Terry and I are playing Monopoly on the sitting-room rug. Terry only has the Old Kent Road without so much as a house on it, has spent most of the game in Jail and has used up all his cash to pay rent, mainly to Dennis, and fines to the Bank. On his last go he even had to mortgage the Old Kent Road, and Pete's just declared him bankrupt.

'What's bangrupt?' Terry cries.

'Means you're out, mate,' says Dennis.

Terry's lower lip wobbles, his eyes well up. 'You took all my money,' he wails, pushing Dennis.

'What's going on?' Mum comes in with a plate of biscuits. 'Stop it, you two, or I'm putting these back in the tin. The sooner you're all back at school the better. It's ridiculous – I've never seen this much snow in November in all my life.'

Mum goes back into the kitchen and as we all dive for the only custard cream, we are hit by a blast of cold air as the back door opens. I look up, thinking it must be Dad. He's been out spreading the icy boards of the veranda with ashes from the fire to stop them being so slippery, but it isn't him. It's Cora and Mimi. I can hear them taking off their wellingtons while Mum lays out some clean cardboard to stand them on.

'Those blinking ashes,' Mum is muttering. 'Before you know it they'll be trodden in all over the house.'

Dennis has accumulated huge quantities of cash – some of it, I think, from sitting close to the Bank. To prevent a riot breaking out we agree that Dennis is the winner, then start packing the game away in its box.

'Mimi's here, Pam!' Mum calls.

While Pam skips down the hall to collect Mimi, Pete gets up and, without a word, leaves and goes into our bedroom.

I stand up and make for the kitchen, where I find the door about to be shut in my face.

'Cora wants a word with me,' Mum whispers through the crack. 'Go away.'

'Oh.'

'It's all right, Mrs Jotman,' I hear Cora say. 'I – I don't mind Roger.'

I slip in and Mum closes the door.

Cora looks dreadful – pale, her dark hair damp and messy where she's pulled off her woolly hat.

'Blimey, how did you get up here in this snow?' I whistle.

'Doesn't matter, Roger – they're here, aren't they?' says Mum. 'What is it, dear? Here.' She pulls out a chair and pats it with her hand. Cora sits down.

'It – it's Dad.' Cora twists and pulls the fingers of her gloves. 'He's – he's been hurt.'

'Good gracious,' Mum cries, sitting on the chair next to her. 'What's happened?'

'He's in hospital, the London Hospital on the Mile End Road.' Cora's eyes are brimming, her mouth trembling. 'He – he's been stabbed—'

'Good Lord!'

'Outside this pub in Bethnal Green – last night. There was this fight – with flick-knives . . .'

Mum gasps.

I am so stunned I can't think of a single thing to say or do.

Cora lowers her face and covers it with her hands, still in their gloves. Mum reaches around Cora's shoulders and pulls her towards her.

'Can you – can you ring the hospital' – I hear Cora's muffled voice – 'and find out if he's going to die? They've – they've had to take something out of him. They wouldn't speak to me because I'm not old enough and Ange didn't ask them properly.'

Mum strokes Cora's hair. Her fingers are shaking. 'Of course I will, Cora. What's your dad's first name?'

'Harry – it's Harry.'

'All right. I'll see if I can get the number from the operator. Roger, look after her.'

'Oh, Mrs Jotman' – Cora looks up, eyes all watery – 'I ain't said nothing to Mimi. Don't tell her.'

'No – no, I won't.'

Mum leaves the kitchen, closing the door behind her. I sit down in Mum's chair next to Cora, but am at a complete loss. Words come into my head, but none of them are going to make anything better, so I just sit there uselessly by her side, staring at the same bit of floor she is staring at, the little torn flap in the lino where the crumbs get underneath.

The seconds on the wall clock tick away like heartbeats. I don't know how long we sit there, Cora wiping her eyes with the back of her hand, me sitting there like an idiot with nothing to say to her. I can hear Mum talking to somebody on the phone, but can't make out the words.

All at once the door flies open.

'What's everyone so flippin' miserable about?' cries Dennis, filling up the kitchen with his noise.

'Push off, Dennis,' I say. 'Stop sticking your nose in.'

'Only came in for a bit of bread,' he pouts, going for the bin on the dresser.

'Go away, will you?'

'Got every right to be in here as much as you,' he says, lifting the lid off.

'Dennis! You're not having bread before dinner,' says Mum, coming back in. 'Go away.'

'Woo-woo!' he hoots, looking from Cora to me, before dancing sideways like a crab into the hall.

Mum slams the door behind him. 'Right, I'm not going to beat about the bush,' she says, kneeling down on the cold floor and taking Cora's hand. 'Your dad's on the danger list, but he's in the best possible hands and we must be hopeful. Roger, why on earth didn't you get Cora a handkerchief? From the basket, over there – not that one, the big one – that's better.

'The police are involved, obviously, but the hospital wouldn't tell me anything about that. I got the feeling they were waiting to talk to your dad if . . . *when* he comes round from the operation. His spleen's had to come out.'

'Crikey. What's a spleen?' I ask.

Mum shoots me a look. 'Why don't you do something useful like put the kettle on, Roger, and stir the stew while you're there.' She turns back to Cora. 'There was a wound to the chest and one of his lungs has collapsed, so they've had to draw the air out, or something. The main thing is stop infection.'

'Mrs Jotman, is he going to die?'

I move up the hill through the snow until I come to the part of the fence that is broken. I push my way through and walk in among the skeleton trees, still and silent under the ash-dark sky. There are places which the snow couldn't touch, deep in the spidery thickets. I bend and prod and pry, lift brown, crackling leaves, and leaves like lace, dig and poke and jab the earth.

It has waited to be found, a bloodstone like a crimson almond, and quickly after, in the same scooped hollow, another – a chip of jasper red as a berry.

I push the clogged earth through the little holes with a glass-headed pin, and lick the stones clean with my tongue.

The back door opens. Dad comes in, stamping his feet on the cardboard, clattering the ash pan down onto the floor, clapping his hands together.

'Ruddy perishing out there!' he says. 'Could murder a cup of tea.'

Mum glares at him.

'Kettle's just on,' I say quietly.

'Oh dear,' he says, taking off his boots. 'Can I help at all?'

'You can help by putting more coal on the fire,' Mum says, rolling her eyes at him.

He looks at Cora, gives Mum a little nod and goes off in his socks. Mum gets up and closes the door, peeping around first to make sure nobody is lurking behind it.

'Is Dad going to die?' Cora says again.

'Cora, we – we always have to look on the bright side. When . . . when the weather's better, you'll be able to visit him.'

'All the way up there? How will I get there on my own? And they won't let Mimi in, will they? She's too young.'

'But haven't you got someone looking after you?' says Mum. 'This . . . sorry, what was her name?'

I stir the stew and glance over at Cora through the rising steam. Fleetingly she meets my eyes, then looks down and says, almost under her breath, 'Ange.'

'That's right, Ange. Look, Cora, if there's a problem' – Mum strokes her hand – 'I – I'll take you when the weather's better and your dad's up to seeing you. We could get the train from Daneflete – leave early. Mr Jotman will give us a lift to the station, or we could get the bus when they're running again.'

'Thank you, Mrs Jotman.'

'Look at those dark rings under your eyes,' Mum says. 'You must have some dinner with us, you and Mimi.'

It isn't lost on anyone around the table how Mimi hungrily gulps down her food without any pause between mouthfuls, scraping up the last little bits before Mum has even had a chance to fill her own plate and Dad's.

'Mimi, not so fast,' Cora hisses.

'Cor, she must be starving,' Terry says, wide-eyed behind his glasses.

'Ssh, Terry,' Mum says dismissively. 'It's the cold

weather. Guaranteed to build up a hearty appetite.'

As the girls are putting on their coats to leave before it gets dark, Mum tucks a brown paper bag into Mimi's hand. 'I can't think how I ended up with a load of extra biscuits,' she mutters. 'Here, squash these in your pocket, Mimi – ooh, not too hard – and mind you be a good girl and share them with your sister. No sneaky nibbling on your own.'

'I – I'll see you up the lane,' I say to Cora, 'if – if you fancy a bit of company.'

She gives me a thin smile.

We trek down Fieldpath Road, following the tracks Cora and Mimi made on their way up. The low grey sky has remained the same all day long, with the snow blotting out sound so it seems as if the whole world has gone mute.

Like us really.

Only, when we reach the main road, Mimi looks up at Cora and says, 'When do you think Dad will come back? Tomorrow?'

Cora breathes out with a trembling breath. 'We'll have to wait and see,' she says.

At the top of Old Glebe Lane she turns to me. 'Don't come any further,' she says. 'If you've got to do the hill on your own on the way back and you come a cropper, there'll be nobody with you to get help. At least we're together.'

'Phone, won't you?' I ask, then glance at Mimi, who has already ploughed a bit further on, before lowering my voice. 'And remember, even if you can't talk, let it ring a couple of times. I'll know something's wrong.'

Just a small thing – Cora reaches out and touches my arm – but I feel it warm through my sleeve.

'Cheerio, and thanks,' she says.

I watch them, two forlorn, dark figures getting smaller and smaller, trudging through the lines of their old footprints down the otherwise smooth, white road.

At one point I think Cora turns her head and looks back. I can't be sure in the fading light, but I raise my hand, just in case.

When I get back to Fieldpath Road, I can still feel that little tender place on my arm.

For yet another night I lie between sleeping and waking, unable to tell whether what my sluggish ears pick up is real or conjured up on the edge of a dream.

Do I hear the creak of a door, the scrape of metal legs across the lino? Sounds come to me in waves, near, then distant – a muted *clunk*, the dull *swish* of an opening drawer, the sigh of moving fabric, a muffled *snap, snap, snap*.

Do my drowsy eyes flicker open for a moment – see a shaft of dim light cutting diagonally across the lino, a shadow passing over it and along so the light shifts then goes out altogether? Do I hear the slow, gentle closing of a door?

It's more a feeling than a memory when I waken properly, still tired, fretful and anxious, to a faded pallor spreading a little way over the wall from behind the curtains.

I look over to the door. The chair is a yard across the floor into the room.

It wasn't a dream. Someone came in.

The hands on the alarm are both at twelve. Did it stop

at midnight? I reach across, pick it up, give it a shake, listen. It ticks steadily on. Surely Mimi and I haven't slept until midday? I check my watch. The morning has gone.

Quickly I get out of bed and draw the curtains aside, then blink twice, thinking a film of sleep must still be on my eyes, because everything I see is colourless.

I wipe the freezing glass with my fingertips. Behind the panes, each diamond rimmed with ice, a grey mist hangs over the snow so the garden seems to vanish into a dense, white, featureless haze of nothing, as if the house is suspended in a cloud, as if all the rest of the world has dissolved away, and Guerdon Hall is floating in the emptiness left behind.

I pull on my clothes and look at my washed-out face in the mirror. The watery light from the window high-lights every shadow, every deep hollow. My hair hangs down in tangled strings.

I reach for the hairbrush on top of the chest of draw-ers, but find an empty space. I glance around the room. Mimi is stirring.

'Wake up, Mimi – we've overslept,' I say. 'And what have you done with the hairbrush?'

'On the drawers . . .' she mumbles, still half asleep.

I look again. 'It isn't here,' I say. 'Come on, Mimi, where is it?'

She opens her eyes. 'It was there last night,' she says. 'I left it like normal. Promise.'

'Well, it isn't there now,' I say. 'Please find it, Mimi. I can't go around like this.'

'That's where I put it. Honest.' She turns over. 'You'll have to borrow Ange's.'

I open the top drawer, rummage around, can't find any brush, then pull out the drawer below.

'Flippin' heck, Mimi.' I pick up my blue blouse with the black polka dots, squashed and creased. 'What were you doing with this? If you take something out, fold it up again. I can't wear this now till it's been ironed again.'

'I didn't take it out.'

'*Mimi!*'

'Cora, I'm telling you – what would I want your stupid old blouse for?'

I begin to fold it, but stop, baffled. 'Mimi! What the hell have you done?'

'What do you mean?'

'Look at this – you've cut a piece out of it!'

'No, I haven't.'

'Yes, you have. Right here at the bottom – with scissors!'

Mimi is properly awake now, and gets out of her bed to take a look. 'Cora, I didn't do that. I *didn't.*'

'Don't fib, Mimi. What did you do it for? You've ruined it.'

'Cora, I promise you – *promise*, cross my heart – I didn't cut your flippin' blouse.'

I sigh, push the blouse back in the drawer, too cold and weary to think. I notice when I leave our bedroom that there is light under Ange's door. I hope it means she's up. She seems to do nothing but sleep at the moment.

The poor radiators are on all the time, on the top setting. They are sending out as much heat as they can, but the house is freezing. I shiver all the way down the stairs and into the kitchen.

I try to fill the kettle from the tap. Nothing. Hissing with irritation through my chattering teeth, I swish the kettle around. There's only enough water left in it to make a pot of tea.

'I think the pipes have frozen up,' I say as Mimi comes into the kitchen carrying one of her summer skirts – the pink one with the little flower sprigs.

'Look,' she says, pushing it under my nose. A strip a few inches long has been cut off the bottom, roughly the same size as the missing piece of my blouse. 'I found it in the drawer,' she says. 'I promise it wasn't me, Cora. *Promise.*'

'All right, leave it,' I say as I look in the bin for the two pieces of stale bread I threw out yesterday. I pick off some specks of green mould and stick them under the grill to toast, then when they're ready, cut the slices into small squares.

'Now don't bolt it down like you did yesterday at the Jotmans',' I say to Mimi.

'I was so hungry, Cora,' she says. 'Do you think Ange has got any money so we can get some food?'

'I'll ask her. I saw some light under her door so she must have opened the curtains.'

Mimi sits at the table with her back to the window chewing her toast slowly. Behind her, the blank, formless world seems to be pressing itself into the glass.

'Any more toast?' she asks.

My stomach rumbles. 'I'll find something later,' I say.

The kettle boils. I slurp a few drops of the tinned milk into a cup, pour out the tea and take it upstairs.

I knock gently. No sound comes from behind the door. I knock again, and hear a little cough.

Gently pushing open the door, I go inside. The curtains must have been open all night. The room is bathed in the same cold bleached light as the rest of the house. It's as if nothing else exists. The walls of Guerdon Hall seem to enclose all there is of the world.

The bedcovers rise and fall, but unevenly. Ange's breathing is shallow, with a slight rattle. I tiptoe round the bed, making my way with difficulty over the magazines and clothes strewn across every inch of the lino, anxious not to spill the tea by stumbling over anything. I leave the cup and saucer on the bedside table, and think that while I'm here, I might as well find a hairbrush to borrow and sneak back later.

I glance at Ange. She appears to be sleeping soundly

enough, despite her chestiness. Her face is almost as pale as the mist at the window, the skin of her cheeks stretched over the bones. She looks so thin now. Her left hand is spread out on the pillow by her ear, her fingers like a spray of dried sticks. The pillow must have split along the seam as little curled feathers are scattered over the bed and in the folds of the clothes on the floor.

I move across to the chest of drawers. There's no brush or comb anywhere on top. As quietly as I can, trying to swallow down the feeling that it really isn't something I should be doing, I pull open the top drawer. The sides scrape a little. Holding my breath, I peep back at Ange, but she hasn't changed position.

In the drawer I move some stockings to one side and, to my astonishment, see our hairbrush lying there. The bristles are usually thick with matted hair – my long dark and Mimi's fair wavy mixed together – but the strands seem to have been teased out. It's clean.

I lift it, bewildered; then something else catches my eye in the tangle of nylon and cheap lace – something odd: a little cloth leg poking out, like the leg of a rag doll.

I push back the jumble of underwear.

It *is* a doll, but the strangest I have ever seen.

Sewn onto the head are some strands of dark hair. I touch the hair lightly, then, shocked, jerk my fingers away: it is real, smells faintly, familiarly, of Brylcreem. Wrapped around the doll, crossed over and stitched together in front, is a little scrap of cotton I recognize: thin black stripes on white, a piece cut out of one of Dad's shirts, the one that Ange was mending.

But what makes my heart thump in my chest and my blood flood sickeningly to my head are the two glass-headed pins stuck deep into its body, one in the chest and one in the stomach.

I feel faint, snatch a look at Ange, who still lies sleeping. My head is in such disorder I can't work out what I'm thinking.

The dizzying fear comes back – what if Dad dies?

The pin in the chest is a little to one side, and there, peeping out of the centre, under a jagged slit in the fabric, is the smooth, curved edge of a little red stone – like a heart. It's the stone that lay with the small change in Ange's hand on the evening she didn't collect Mimi from school.

I pinch quivering fingers over the glass head of the pin, bracing myself to pull it out. Then the little face looks up at me – the black knotted eyes, the red stitched line of the mouth.

Will I make it worse if I pull the pins out? Could I kill him?

I don't even know if I should replace the figure in the drawer or take it.

Stifling a sob, confused, reeling, I pull Ange's clothes back over it, then push them aside again and pick it up.

I stand, perplexed and terrified, biting my lip, with our hairbrush in one hand, and the figure in the other.

I look back at Ange, still lying in the same position. Her workbox is on the floor beside the bed, the contents spilled out and messy among all the other rubbish; then I notice something lying there, between the blades of the swan-necked scissors – a tiny snip of fabric – from Mimi's pink skirt.

Has Ange made a doll of Mimi, like she has of Dad? The thought alone makes me so giddy I have to steady myself with my elbow against the chest. If there is a doll, I must find it.

I creep round the bed, look on every surface, not daring to lift anything for fear of making a noise, peep round the open curtains to see if there is anything on the windowsill, move things aside with my foot, trying to contain my rising panic.

Holding the little man out, terrified I might damage him in some way, I bend to lift a corner of the candlewick bedspread. There on the lino is a small frayed square of material from my blue polka-dot blouse.

For a few seconds I can't move, rigid with the enormity of what I have found, the horrific consequence of what Ange seems to have done to Dad – and what she might still do to Mimi and to me.

Maybe the other dolls are in the drawer as well?

I tiptoe back to the chest, go to open the drawer; as I

pull it with one hand, it sticks on the side, and makes a dreadful scraping squeak.

There is a rustle behind me. I look over to the bed.

Ange's eyes flick open. They stare at the ceiling.

Barely able to breathe, heart thudding, I toss the hairbrush back in the drawer, rush out of the room and close the door behind me.

I dash along the landing and down the stairs, my mind a jumble of fearful thoughts. How can Dad be saved – if he isn't already dead? Who can help us?

By the front door, my duffel coat hangs on its hook. A small triangle of white is sticking out of the pocket, a corner of the paper from the St Lazarus Hospital. With my free hand I reach in and pull it out, look at the scrawled names – *Mrs Lailah Ketch* and *Miss Iris Jewel*.

Can we get to Hilsea?

Trying desperately not to disturb the glass-headed pins, I place the doll carefully in one of the deep front pockets, replace the sheet of paper, then snatch down the coat. I thrust my arms into the sleeves, fling my scarf around my neck and pull on my hat.

Mimi comes out of the kitchen.

'Get your coat on! Quick!' I whisper, pulling it off its hook and throwing it into her arms.

'What?'

'Don't ask – just do it! Quick! Quick!'

'Cora—'

'Please – now!'

She begins to push her arms down the sleeves, then pulls her hat out of the pocket.

I think of Roger; don't want to go to Hilsea without him.

Grabbing the telephone receiver, I dial with a shaking finger.

'Who are you phoning?' Mimi breathes.

4 – 1 (almost a 2 by mistake) – 0.

'Ssh,' I hiss. 'I'm trying to get Roger. See if he can come and meet us at the main road.'

It rings once, twice.

There is a noise from upstairs – the door of Ange's room opening.

Clumsily I fumble the receiver back into its cradle. It misses and falls noisily by its cord to the floor.

No time to pick it up. I can hear Ange's footsteps on the stairs beyond the turning.

I head for the stone passage, pushing Mimi in front of me.

'Cora?' Ange is calling.

Our boots won't stay upright. We sway and lurch as we struggle to tug them on.

'Cora, where are we going?' Mimi breathes.

'Ssh. We've got to be quick.'

Our feet in our boots at last, I swing back the door as quietly as I can, and we are out in the freezing mist hanging shroud-like over the snow.

Before I even close the door behind us, my head swarms with sudden fears. What if Ange picks up the dangling telephone and hears Roger at the other end? She was able to hurt Dad even though he was miles away in London. Could she do something awful to Roger too?

I put my finger to my lips. 'Wait here, Mimi. I'll be straight back.'

Mimi stands nervously in the snow in front of the open door. I tiptoe back along the stone passage and, holding my breath, peer round the corner into the hall. Could I sneak in and replace the phone before Ange gets there?

Too late.

With her back to me, Ange has the receiver to her ear, listening. After a few moments she replaces it. I don't know if Roger has spoken or not.

I turn to creep back down the passage when the telephone's shrill ringing sets my nerves jangling and my heart racing in alarm.

Is it Roger ringing back? I stand there, pressed against the wall, biting my lip, willing him not to speak to Ange.

'Yes?' she says. 'This is Mrs Russell speaking.'

A pause.

'What was that? It's a bad line. Infection, did you say? Nothing more at all? Are you sure? How long do you reckon he's got, then? Well, we're snowed in here. There aren't any trains. We couldn't get there in that time, no.'

A few seconds pass.

'No, I'm not the next of kin.' Listening to Ange, I touch my trembling hand to the pocket enclosing the little cloth man. 'Well, his wife has been in an asylum for years. Yes, two girls – fifteen, almost sixteen, and eight. Yes, I'm looking after them for the time being.'

I feel my legs go hollow, lean back against the wall; the round light switch opposite swims fuzzily in and out of focus.

'No, I really don't know nothing the police would be interested in. Yes, thank you. Yes, do that, would you? Bye.' Ange puts the phone down.

Dizzily, I force myself away from the wall, try to move one foot in front of the other, stagger along the passage.

If I can find help, is there still time; any time at all?

I hurry through the back door. Mimi is standing there shivering.

I grab her hand and pull her through the deep snow drifted against the side of the house.

We're already halfway up The Chase when she asks, 'Cora, where are we going?'

'We – we've got to go to Hilsea,' I say.

'There won't be no buses.'

'Then we'll have to go on foot.'

'Can't Roger come?'

'I wish he was here, Mimi, I so wish he was. I tried ringing, but it was too late. We can't waste a second going all the way to his house and back in this deep snow – he might not even be there. We've got to be quicker than we've been in all our lives.'

'Why have we got to go now? It's so cold.'

'I'll tell you later, honest. Give your cheeks a rub. They've gone purple.'

'So have yours.'

While we blunder on as best we can, the ice on the surface of the ditch below the trees makes a cracking sound in the sharp, numbing air. By the turning into Old Glebe Lane the mist has lifted, only to give way to fat, downy snowflakes the size of half-crowns.

'Watch where you're going,' I call. 'There'll be ice on the road under the snow.'

The words have barely passed my lips when Mimi stumbles and falls heavily onto her side. I struggle towards her.

She lets me help her up and brush the white clods off her coat; then she stands and wobbles for a little while, clenching her teeth and rubbing her elbow through her sleeve.

'Are you hurt anywhere?'

'On me arm a bit.'

'Here, take my hand.'

Then all at once the wind picks up and the snowflakes

start to whirl and thicken, spattering our cheeks with flecks of ice. We pull our scarves over our noses and up to our sore, reddened eyes as we climb the hill. The snow begins to sweep blindingly across our path from the fields on one side to the woods on the other, so in only a few minutes we can hardly see where we are going. Wiping our faces every few minutes, we trudge upwards, Mimi having to lift her boots tiringly high to clear the surface. All of a sudden her feet slip again. She shrieks and pulls me with her as she tips backwards into the snow, first onto her bottom, then her back. My instant fear is not to damage the doll in my pocket and I pitch awkwardly, crashing down full length beside her.

I enter the room and pull open the drawer.

The manikin is gone.

The girl has taken it.

I gaze along the spirit thread to the scarred man, unmoving under a starched white linen sheet, colourless face, closed eyes. The bed is cloudy behind thin gauze, the thread still holds, but weakens as the manikin moves away from me. The dying lights rise swarming into the air, glimmering and sparkling even through the thickening mist.

Soon he will die, though whether he lives or dies does not matter to me.

This woman Ange is my means of accomplishing, but there is a wrangle between her spirit and mine. Her flesh is failing her, and resistance to me weakens her still further.

I lift the counterpane. There they lie, two poppets cut and almost stitched, the little one already plump with feathers. The needle is pinned through the face for safekeeping, the lengths of hair laid out for sewing – wavy and fair, long and dark.

Her lack of skill vexes me, the snail's speed at which I am able to work her fingers.

I feel a dull throb in my knee, but manage to raise myself to sitting. 'Mimi?'

I hear a sob.

'Can you get up?'

'Think so.'

I stretch out my arms and help to pull her off her back. She rubs her eyes with her snow-caked gloves and we teeter up together. Mimi almost slides over again, but grabs my arm and steadies herself. Then she turns away, whimpering, 'I can't feel my feet. I'm freezing.'

Gently, I pull her on.

At last we reach the top of the hill. To our left, warm lights glow from the windows of Glebe House. Columns of smoke rise out of the chimneys up to the low grey sky from which the endless snowflakes are blowing.

I try to plough on towards the main road, but Mimi drags further and further behind.

'Come on,' I urge her.

'It's too hard,' she whines, her voice deadened by the

wind. 'The snow's too deep. My knees ache, and my arm. And – and I'm so hungry.'

I trudge back to her and, from the other side of the white, lacy veil drifting between us, Mimi's face crumples.

'Dad should've come home,' she moans. 'He said he would.' She sinks down into the snow, covers her face with her hands and begins to cry.

A lump fills my throat and my eyes start to burn.

I slump down in front of her, my skin stinging as the freezing moisture seeps through the knees of my trousers. I take Mimi's shuddering shoulders in my hands. 'Please, Mimi,' I plead. 'Try and get up.'

'I – I'm so – so cold. And I'm hungry, Cora. Can't we go back?'

Her teeth chatter as she cries, her whole body convulsing as she breathes juddering, shallow breaths. Her tears wash into and melt the speckles of snow that settle on her icy cheeks. Shivering from deep inside my bones, I fold Mimi tightly in my arms and bite back my own tears of frustration. She nestles into me, and for a moment I think how easy it would be just to stay there and let the quiet flakes cover us . . . a soft, feathery eiderdown . . . no one would miss us . . . no more worries . . . nothing at all . . .

An idea floats by on the air: that maybe Ange has done this . . . stepped outside and wrapped our little dolls in a shroud of snow . . .

'For heaven's sake,' someone cries. 'What are you doing down there? You'll freeze to death.'

A firm arm is thrown around my shoulders, another around Mimi.

'Come on, you've got to get moving.'

I turn my head, and gasp. 'Roger!'

He forces us up onto our stiff, numb legs. I am so overjoyed to see him, the tears that threatened to spill a few moments ago begin to seep out and sting my face. I turn away.

In one stride Roger wraps an arm round my head and pulls me into his chest. The snow swirls and eddies around us, and for all the moments he holds me there, tightly pressed against his warm coat, I am dazed by the closeness, the warmth, and the safety of it.

'I thought you were dead,' he breathes.

Mimi tugs on my sleeve, and on Roger's. 'I'm still freezing,' she says.

I pull away, awkwardly wipe my face.

Roger springs into action. 'Stamp your feet, Mimi!' he cries to her. 'Harder! Swing your arms around like this! How about a piggyback?'

He crouches so Mimi can climb up out of the snow. She locks her arms about his neck and tucks in her legs. He gets up, tramps forward a few feet, hoists her up a bit more, then turns in the spiralling snow to wait for me to catch up.

He looks the same, in the black wool coat with the leather buttons, his school scarf knotted around his neck twice in the funny way he does it. But there is something different about him, something purposeful, and serious.

'Where are we going?' he asks.

'Hilsea.'

'The St Laz?'

I nod.

'There's no hope of a bus,' he says. 'Are you up for the walk this time?'

'Of course.'

'Come on, then. Oh, I nearly forgot – I stopped off at Mrs Wickerby's. Hang on a minute, Mimi . . .'

Holding onto her with one hand, Roger reaches into his pocket with the other, pulls out a bar of chocolate and throws it over to me.

'I've just had a sandwich,' he says. 'Couldn't eat another thing. You two have it.'

Greedily, I rip open the paper and break the chocolate into squares, clumsily shoving some all at once into my own mouth before giving the rest to Mimi.

We trudge along the main road. After a while the wind drops and the snow begins to thin to small, sparse flakes. It isn't so deep towards Hilsea. Under the trees there are dark circles of earth and grass that haven't been covered at all. As we pass the entrance gate to a large farm, Mimi at long last wriggles down, deciding she wants to walk.

'Go ahead,' I say to her, 'so we can keep an eye on you.' Once she is out of earshot I ask Roger, 'How did you end up coming to find us?'

'Honestly, I've been so worried I was almost camping out by the phone. When it rang a little while ago, I picked it up, and there was nobody there – at least, nobody said anything, but I could sense someone breathing, and listening.'

'Oh, please don't tell me you spoke to Ange, thinking it was me.'

'No. I knew it wasn't you, and put the receiver back.' He looks at me. 'I told you I'd come.'

When Mimi is at the pillar box on the edge of Hilsea, just far enough in front, I nudge Roger's elbow.

'Could we just stop for a minute,' I say softly, taking off my glove and reaching gingerly into my pocket, shrinking from the touch of the hair on the little man's head. 'I need to show you something. I've been terrified I might have squashed it.'

I glance over at Mimi, see she still has her back to us, and lay the figure on my hand. I hear Roger draw in his breath as he grasps the meaning of it; of the blood-drop pins that stand out red and shiny against the scattered snow.

'I – I found it in Ange's bedroom. This bit of cloth is from one of Dad's shirts, and these pins . . .'

'They're stuck in where he was stabbed, I can see,' he murmurs.

'She was able to do this even though he was way off in London.' I swallow. 'The hospital rang. I overheard Ange talking to them, just before we left. It seems like he . . . he hasn't got long . . .' I try to speak slowly. 'And – and Ange has snipped some little bits out of our clothes as well – Mimi's and mine – and taken hair out of our hairbrush. This isn't the only doll she's made.'

The colour drains out of Roger's face.

Her hands are cold and stiff, her white breath rolls across her fingers, but still she knots the thread, pushes the needle into the head and runs the stitches in and out, in and out, in and out, so all the little fair hairs are fluffy around the face.

Blue for the eyes, loop the yarn, pull it tight, cut with the swan-necked scissors. Loop again, pull it tight, snip.

Red for the little curved mouth . . .

The shops that make up Hilsea High Street stand opposite a long, low wall surrounding the graveyard of St Margaret's, an imposing red-brick church that seems far too grand for such a small village.

'The St Laz is this way.' Roger points and we cross the deserted road.

Skimming the corner of the churchyard and the end of a narrow lane, we pass a large Victorian vicarage covered with the bare winter bones of a creeper, and separated from the vicarage garden by a wicket fence is a row of six ancient houses, standing joined together on a wide, shared expanse of snowy grass. Each one is identical to the next, the walls washed a creamy pink, and the arched doors and carved, pointed gables painted white.

We pause to read the stone plaque on the wall linking the two middle houses:

ST LAZARUS HOSPITAL

FOUNDED 1453 BY WILLIAM WEGG

FOR THE USE AND BENEFIT OF SIX POOR MEN

REBUILT 1714

'Mr Wragge said the women live in the house on the end,' I say, 'but which end?'

The words have barely left me when the door of the house nearest the vicarage garden opens, and a woman in an old brown coat comes out sniffing into a hand-kerchief. She turns to wring the hand of another woman, half hidden by the door frame, then hurries across the grass, head down, passing us without a glance.

Instead of closing the door straight away, the woman in the house lingers for a moment, then moves forward onto the step and, standing perfectly still, turns her face towards us. The reflected sky gleams off her round glasses. She looks curiously old-fashioned, tall and slightly ungainly in her tweed skirt, grey cardigan buttoned to her chin, and heavy brogues, her mouse-brown hair scraped back with two elaborate tortoiseshell combs.

'It's Miss Jewel,' Mimi whispers behind her hand.

After looking all about her, across the grass, over to the fence and the vicarage, Miss Jewel beckons us forward. Roger and I look at each other hesitantly, but Mimi walks on over the snow to the house and we follow.

The lintel is so low Roger has to duck to get under it into the stiflingly hot, narrow hall.

The woman says nothing but leads us into a small sitting room. Roger stands stooped and awkward under the beams as we hover, uncomfortably overheating in our heavy coats, only a few feet across the carpet from the coal fire blazing away in its old cast-iron grate. The air is pungent with an unfamiliar smell, like nettles mixed with aniseed, and as my eyes grow used to the rosy light, I become aware of an array of exotic stuffed birds and animals, bizarre masks and curious ornaments, their contorted shadows quivering up the floral-papered walls.

The woman smiles at Mimi, and Mimi simply nods her head.

Miss Jewel turns in my direction. I feel her magnified eyes lingering on me, and look at the carpet.

'I – I'm Cora Drumm,' I mutter.

'Roger Jotman,' says Roger.

'And I am Mrs Ketch,' comes a voice. 'Lailah Ketch.'

Another woman rises ghost-like out of a wooden chair in a dark corner, its back carved like the wide-open tail of a peacock. Half in shadow, the woman stands impressive and angular, her thick grey hair just skimming the beams. Her eyes, like two chips of black jet, range probingly over Roger and me before settling on Mimi, who returns the gaze.

'Hello, Mimi,' Mrs Ketch says.

'Hello, Mrs Ketch.' Mimi shifts her attention to the objects in the room, her eyes flitting from one thing to another.

'I see you are curious,' says Mrs Ketch. 'There are a lot of treasures, aren't there, Mimi. We were missionaries together, my husband, the Reverend Ketch – God rest his soul – my niece, Iris here, and me, travelling to places you may never even have heard of – Abyssinia, the Congo. We even travelled the Silk Road to Samarkand, but just as war broke out, the good reverend went down with the cholera in Bihar in northern India, and Iris and I returned to England.' She waves a spidery hand around the room. 'As you can see, we brought far too much back with us.'

I notice her eyes flicker up to a clock on the wall emblazoned with large black words: *The Eastern Bengal*

Railway Company. She makes a kind of stirring movement with her hand at Miss Jewel, and rolls her eyes towards the kitchen. The younger woman opens the door and disappears behind it, while the strange smell wafts in and lingers even more strongly than before.

Mrs Ketch lowers herself back into the peacock chair. 'You'd better sit down,' she says.

'No, please don't worry,' I stammer. 'We're in a bit of a hurry.'

Mrs Ketch pats a small stool at her feet. 'Mimi, come and sit near me.'

Mimi gives me a quick glance, then squeezes past the old leather trunk – stuck all over with worn labels from far-off lands – that fills the small space in the middle of the room.

I catch Mrs Ketch's eyes darting from me to Roger, then back to me. I sit impatiently on the very edge of a hard, upright chair, and find myself nervously twisting the woollen fingers of my gloves. Turning my face slightly to avoid the woman's unsettling gaze, I hear the kitchen door open a crack, and catch a movement, reflected flames flickering on a glass circle, and behind it one of Miss Jewel's huge eyes. A second later it's gone and the door creaks shut.

Not knowing what to say to Mrs Ketch with Mimi there, I sneak a glimpse at Roger. His eyes are wandering over the room, from the Zulu spears crossed over the mantelpiece to the stuffed monkey on the wall staring down at us all cock-eyed. Then he turns his attention to a dusty glass case on a small table by his elbow, by the look of it containing some oddly shaped nuts from foreign parts. He seems to fix on something, looks up at me, then makes a little jerk of his head towards a round, red object lying beside the glass case, at the same time furtively pointing at it with his finger.

I squint. It's a ball of red twine.

I peep sideways at Mrs Ketch. Her eyes are on us. All at once she says pointedly, to Mimi on her stool, 'Mimi, why don't you go and help Iris in the kitchen. You might be interested to see what she's cooking.'

Mimi shoots me a look. I lower my eyes and nod.

'Go to Iris, dear, there's a good girl,' says Mrs Ketch.

Mimi gets up, and with a last glance at me, goes into the kitchen, closing the door behind her, the sudden draught sending the flames flaring up in the grate.

'Now, Cora,' says Mrs Ketch. 'What's happened? Why have you come here – in such a hurry?'

'I'm sorry, I'm just not sure—'

After a few moments she looks back up at the clock, then stands abruptly and rests a hand on the crowded sideboard. 'Cora, I'm sorry to be so blunt,' she says, 'but we've just had a visitor – Mrs Bullen from the village, who urgently needs our help – so I'll have to be plainer and quicker with you all than I'd like. I hope you understand.'

'Yes – yes, of course.'

'You need to know where Iris and I come into all this, so I'll start in August 1940, not long after we arrived here from India. The local paper reported that a little girl had gone missing in Bryers Guerdon, and that Mrs Eastfield, who had been looking after the child and her older sister, had briefly been taken in by the police for questioning.'

I look up sharply.

'Of course, being wartime, the paper dropped it soon enough, but Iris and I, as outsiders here, became aware of whispers behind hands, noticed the knowing nods every time Mrs Eastfield was mentioned in the shops or on street corners. Eventually we came to hear about a ghoulish creature who had once been a leper man called Cain Lankin, who apparently roamed the Bryers Guerdon marshes feeding on children, and everyone round about believed that this little girl had most likely been taken by him. We made modest enquiries, and learned more of the story – how this Lankin fellow and a witch, Aphra Rushes, had killed the infant Guerdon heir for his healing blood, and that the witch had been burned and, with her dying breath, cursed the Guerdon family.'

I shift uncomfortably on the hard chair, exchange the flicker of a glance with Roger.

'Things went quiet for a long time, until, four years ago,' Mrs Ketch continues, 'we heard that Mrs Eastfield had suddenly died. Rumours spread, and almost as quickly hushed themselves up, that the monster had at last been killed, and that Mrs Eastfield probably had a hand in it.' She looks hard at the two of us, narrows her eyes. 'And there were murmurs about children being there . . .'

Roger gives an awkward little cough.

'Then, a few months ago,' she goes on, 'the word went round that Guerdon children were coming back to the house. Gideon Wragge, one of our old gentlemen here at the St Lazarus, was asked by Ed Blezzard to help modernize the place. Anyway, Gideon was ill for a few days and couldn't get down, but when he did return to work there, he was horrified to find that Mr Blezzard had taken out and destroyed the witch bottles, painted over the witch marks and hacked down the trees. He told Iris and me about it, because he was worried about you and Mimi – that you, the last of the Guerdons, would be left unprotected.'

'Why you?' I ask. 'What could you do?'

Mrs Ketch sighs, turns towards the fire, bends down and picks up the poker. 'Well, Cora, Iris and I travelled with my husband to some remote and secret places, watched and learned from shamans, magi and conjurers, saw many bizarre and wonderful happenings in the mysterious by-ways of the world. People around here know that; come to us for remedies and healing.' She looks up at the clock again.

'Like Mrs Bullen?' Roger asks.

'Her husband has double pneumonia,' she says. 'He is going into crisis, and the doctor can't get here through the snow from Clevedon.' She glances towards the kitchen door. 'Iris is especially skilled' – she lowers her voice – 'even in her silence, especially in the blending of herbs. She is preparing something to help him. My gift is in the words – I make sure everything is in concord.'

Mrs Ketch prods the coals. Hot ash crumbles down into the hearth.

'Mr Wragge thought we might be able to protect you secretly,' she continues, 'so you wouldn't know and be frightened, but as you found out, it's almost impossible to lay protective charms around a house like Guerdon Hall on the sly, and quietly. Whatever we tried was going to be seen or heard sometime, although we did our best to be discreet.'

She leans the poker back into the fireplace.

'Some things are the same the world over, you know. The remains of a burned witch are believed to be full of lingering spells; they should be burned again so that the witch cannot be reborn, but the north wind took Aphra Rushes' ashes and scattered them before it could be done. Of course, Iris and I had no way of knowing

412

whether she could or would return, but we knew it was unlikely that her spirit could rest while the curse was still to run its course, especially with the last of the Guerdons returning, coming close again.'

'And Mimi?' I ask anxiously. 'Why did you get Mimi to help you – Mimi but not me?'

Mrs Ketch sighs. 'I don't know what happened to Mimi in the past, Cora, but at some moment in her life she must have been touched powerfully by the spirit world, because the child is separate – a sensitive.'

'She told me.' I swallow.

'We sensed it immediately, the first time we saw her,' says Mrs Ketch, 'walking down Old Glebe Lane with the woman who was looking after you—'

'Auntie Kath,' I interrupt.

'Auntie Kath, then,' says Mrs Ketch. 'Well, Mimi recognized it in us too, dawdled behind, then stopped. Most unusual . . . an oddly self-assured thing for a child to do. Of course, as I said, we didn't know whether the witch would return until – until we were in the garden on Bonfire Night. We had hung up the protecting curtain – the little white stones – and afterwards, from the darkness, noticed Mimi looking out across the garden. It was obvious she had glimpsed something in the smoke from the fireworks. Smoke, fog and mist draw spirits in, you see, Cora. That evening we became really worried for you both. We have busy lives looking after the men here, and helping people who seek us out. We thought Mimi could help us, being there . . .'

'But Mrs Ketch, she's only eight years old.'

'We thought it was for the best, Cora; thought her gift could be used for the good . . .'

From somewhere a clock chimes.

'Cora,' Roger says. 'We're all running out of time. You need to show Mrs Ketch what's in your pocket – tell her why we've come.'

'All – all right.' Hesitantly, I stand up. 'It's this, Mrs Ketch.'

Feeling again the sense of revulsion as my fingers close around the head of the cloth figure, I bring it out and lay it in my open hand, the pins pointing upwards.

The woman's eyes widen. 'Oh, Cora, it – it's a poppet,' she breathes. 'You can kill a person with this – without even leaving a mark, or you can direct events to cause them harm, and nobody would know how they died.'

She turns and takes a small, lidless cardboard box from the back of the sideboard, beckons to Roger, and tips the box slightly to show us what's nestled inside.

A shudder passes between us.

'Cunning people have been making poppets since before recorded time,' she says, 'in every dark corner of the world.'

Lying in a bed of shredded newspaper is a small doll

with a crudely carved wooden head and a stuffed cloth body, dressed in scraps of stained, faded fabric, its head stuck all over with tufts of curly human hair. A hand-written brown paper label tied around its neck says: *Vodun (voodoo) fetish doll from the Kingdom of Dahomey, West Africa. Collected GNK 21st March 1932.*

'There is a strong connection – a spirit thread – between the maker and the victim,' Mrs Ketch says darkly.

The kitchen door opens. Mimi is there, Miss Jewel directly behind her. Mimi's eyes go from the doll in the box to the one in my hand. Her mouth drops.

'Daddy . . .' she breathes. 'He's hurt . . .'

The figure trembles in my shaking hand. I look at Mimi, at her crushed face, her round, startled eyes. 'Oh Mimi, Dad – Dad's been stabbed. He's in hospital. I'm sorry. I'm so sorry . . .' My legs seem to fail me. I sink back onto the chair, reach out and circle her waist tightly with my arm. 'Ange must have overheard me saying I wanted him to get rid of her. I – I don't think there's much time – there was a phone call just before we left . . .'

Mrs Ketch puts the box back on the cupboard, then comes to me and says, 'Don't be alarmed, Cora, but could I look at the doll? I'll take great care with the pins. It's best not to disturb them if we can help it.' I place the little man on the woman's outstretched palm.

'This poppet has been artfully made, and to a particularly old pattern,' Mrs Ketch says, examining the stitching, touching the hair with her fingertips. 'Who did it? Was it the woman we saw at Guerdon Hall, the one who shouted at us?'

I nod wretchedly.

'But that wasn't Auntie Kath. She was different,' she says.

'No, she got scared and went back to London. The one who yelled at you was Ange.'

'That's when we knew we were too late,' Mrs Ketch says, glancing at Miss Jewel, her face drawn and anxious. 'The spirit of a returning witch is insubstantial. It needs a body . . . hands to do its work – work like this . . .' She gazes at the poppet. 'It is a difficult thing, a delicate balance, finding the right, vulnerable person to use, knowing how to play their weaknesses, judging how much they will or will not do for you.'

Mimi kneels by my chair and I squeeze her shoulder.

Holding the figure delicately, Mrs Ketch lifts the scrap of shirt to reveal the edge of the small red stone. Her brows knit deep.

'A bloodstone, Iris,' she breathes to Miss Jewel, whose spectacles gleam in golden curves in the light from the fire. 'Makes it much more difficult for a cunning person to undo the harm. This means that only you, Cora' – she inclines her head – 'or you, Mimi – only a blood relative can break the spirit thread that binds Aphra Rushes to your father; then if – if he is still alive, he might be able to fight on his own.'

'But we wouldn't know what to do.' My voice rises. 'And I don't think this is the only one. I'm sure Ange has made more dolls – of Mimi and me.' I hear Mimi swallow. 'She's got our hair and bits of our clothes. She might have stuck pins in them as well. Anything could happen to us – any minute.'

'Now, Cora,' says Mrs Ketch, 'these things take care to make. Ange might not even have finished them yet. We may still have time.'

I pull the stitches tight so the little skirt gathers under the arms, fasten the thread at the back with two more stitches, bite it off with her teeth. I take another piece of rosy pink, wrap it round the shoulders, sew it to the chest and conceal the bloodstone heart, the chip of jasper – one stitch, two, three . . . snip.

Done.

I prop the finished poppet up in a swell of the counterpane, stroke the soft, wavy hair with her fingers, run her nail over the red running-stitch mouth.

Then I pick up the other poppet, its body half sewn.

'Then we've got to find them before she does finish them,' Roger says urgently.

My head swims. Mimi sits glassy-eyed, dazed, on the floor.

The wind whines down the chimney and blows a small cloud of soot into the room.

'Come, Cora.' Mrs Ketch hands me back the poppet. 'Put it away for the moment – carefully now – then up you get, all of you. Get your gloves back on. Oh, and we'll need a good long knife from the kitchen. How much time do we have, Iris? Is Mr Bullen's remedy prepared?'

Iris nods solemnly.

'Then we must be quick,' says Mrs Ketch.

'Where are we going?' I ask, alarmed.

I pull more feathers from her pillow, lay them in a hollow of the blanket, take a small quantity in her fingers and push them up into the head through the slit in the poppet's side. More feathers, more and more, make the head tight. I pad out the little arms. The feathers float across the bed, drift slowly through the air to the ground and seek out all the little dark and dusty corners. Now the poppet is nice and plump, the feathers are leaking from the seam in the side. I pull a length of thread, cut it, hold the end to the eye of the needle . . .

Mrs Ketch, in her long hooded coat and peaked hat, opens the back door at the end of the kitchen. The bitter wind sweeps in, fanning the tea towels folded over the rail on the range, setting the ceiling light bulb swinging on its flex, cooling the green liquid in the saucepan on the gas. 'Shut the door, please!' Mrs Ketch calls as the two women stride down the back steps and over the snowy lawn, their black coats flapping and snapping behind them as they march purposefully on.

Mrs Ketch pulls open a gate in the white fence, and signals us to follow. On the other side a path skirts the back of the vicarage garden. As Roger, Mimi and I hurry after the two women, the overhanging, bustling trees shower us with drops of icy snow.

We hasten towards the lane at the end of the path. Over the road is the low stone wall, crusted white, enclosing the churchyard of St Margaret's, and a few yards along is an old, rusted kissing gate leading inside.

The wind moans and sighs, tossing the dipping branches of the huge yew tree next to the solid bulk of the church, and lifting like dust the snow that powders the stepped bases and arms of the dark crosses and the arches of the gravestones. We move round the building, picking up our feet, by-passing straggling bushes and solitary tombs.

On the boundary furthest from the main road, completely hidden from the shops by the church, stands a small, crooked tree like a bent and withered old body with its shrivelled arms outstretched. The crown, a mass of twisted, thorny boughs, is almost at right angles to the narrow, contorted trunk that leans into the churchyard, forming a web-like roof over two cracked gravestones beneath. The misshapen branches end in knots of spidery twigs like old arthritic hands, bobbing and swaying in the wind.

Miss Jewel is ahead of her aunt, almost at the tree.

'The ground will be frozen, Iris,' calls Mrs Ketch. 'Perhaps you should tackle it first. It'll speed things up a bit.'

Miss Jewel stoops to get under the flattened, spiky crown, then rests both hands, palms outward, on the trunk. She closes her eyes, leans her cheek against the rough bark, and stands there for some time, her mouth moving now and then as if speaking, but otherwise a still and silent figure under the windswept, hissing branches. We stand a few feet away, watching, restless, growing ever colder.

Mrs Ketch's words rise over the wind. 'Even in the winter time the sap flows through a tree like blood through veins,' she says. 'Its roots are deep in earth, its trunk in air; it flows with water which never freezes, and in autumn is crowned with fire in leaf and fruit. It is elemental, and should never be meddled with unless it gives you leave to do so.'

At last Miss Jewel opens her eyes and nods to Mrs Ketch, who passes her the kitchen knife. With a grunt the younger woman kneels on the hard, snowy ground at the foot of the tree, then plunges the blade into the earth. She begins to dig and scrape, both hands clutching the handle, tossing aside the clods, lifting then jabbing again at the frozen soil, the deadened sounds echoing off the church wall behind her. After a few minutes she stops and, with laboured breath, beckons to Mimi.

Mimi looks back at me, her eyebrows knotted, her lip trembling. 'Please, Cora, I don't want to do anything,' she cries miserably. 'What if it doesn't work? What if . . . if Daddy dies? It will be all my fault.'

All my fault . . . I am a child back in Limehouse, listening to my mother howling through the wall . . . *All my fault . . . all my fault.*

If that burden must be borne again, then it must be mine, not Mimi's.

I take a step forward, Roger too, but Mrs Ketch holds us back with a firm hand.

'We must let Mimi do this,' she says. 'Her gift will make the ritual more potent.'

'You said "a blood relative", Mrs Ketch.' I push her arm away. 'Back in the house you said either of us.' I walk on, rub Mimi's head through her hat. 'You go to Roger, Mimi. I can do this as well as you.'

In a moment, Mimi has run to Roger. He gently clasps her shoulder, but looks across at me with an uneasy gaze.

With a sharp glance at Mrs Ketch, Miss Jewel stands aside for me under the crown of the tree and hands me the knife. Deep down the earth is soft, shifts easily. In a short time there is a metallic clunk as the blade jars against the roots.

Miss Jewel lays a soft hand on my arm. I look up. The gas lamp beyond the boundary wall sends a sharp shadow across her face so her eyes become like crescent moons behind the circles of glass. I hesitate. Miss Jewel wipes her moist forehead under her hat, streaking it with soil from her glove, then kneels awkwardly beside me and points at the hole in the ground.

All at once the church-tower clock resounds across the graveyard with a long, slow tolling.

Hurriedly I reach into my pocket for the poppet, lean forward and place the doll deep among the roots.

At the same moment it seems as if a gust of wind catches the bare, knotted branches above. The tree shudders and twists, stretching out then pulling in its finger-like twigs.

Miss Jewel reaches out and lays her hand on the bark, and Mrs Ketch leans forward.

'Cover it up quickly, Cora,' she says, 'but make sure the pins are not pushed deeper in.'

I steady the pins with morsels of soil, adding more, little by little, until only the two gleaming red pinheads are visible at the top of a small mound. Then I begin to cover the rest. The scraps of striped shirt disappear bit by bit, then the arms, the legs, the hair and the stitched-on face vanish into the dark crumble of the earth. When not a speck of the cloth man is to be seen, I gently pat the soil down and reach out for a handful of snow to sprinkle over it.

'We hope the tree will take the poppet,' Mrs Ketch says, her voice low and slightly uneven; 'crush it with its roots and snap the spirit thread.'

'Hope?' I say with dismay. 'Aren't you sure?'

She looks over her shoulder through the net of branches towards the church. 'Nothing is certain in this world, Cora, but the hawthorn mother is very powerful here – her roots are deep in holy ground.'

A sudden jolt of pain.

She winces, drops the needle, presses her fingertips to her head.

Agitated, I seek for the spirit thread, but can see the scarred man no longer. There is no attachment. It is severed.

He is dead, then.

We stretch our lips into a smile.

Now I will hurry her.

Pick up the poppet.

Find the glinting needle.

Pinch the seam together, stop the feathers creeping out. Stitch, stitch, little tiny stitches – one, two, three. Wind the thread around the finger. Loop and tighten. Make fast. Cut. Snip.

Take the workbox, lift the pincushion, put aside the needle-case, lay out the silks – blue, sea-green and ochre. And here, the perfect colour – deep dark brown for the girl's prying eyes . . .

For some time we seem to be held in suspension, motionless – Roger beside Mimi with a hand resting on her shoulder, Mrs Ketch and Miss Jewel, me kneeling under the hawthorn – caught up in a moment that appears to hang shimmering in the air, as if the whole world is stilled and hushed by it.

I struggle up towards Roger and Mimi, see their faces bleached in the gaslight almost like the snow. Miss Jewel sighs and arches her back against her open palms before wearily moving away from the tree. From under Mimi's hat, strands of fair hair blow forward.

Mrs Ketch lifts her head and stands as if listening. 'The wind has changed,' she says.

As we make our way back to the kissing gate, I think at first we are being showered with drops of snow, then realize they are speckles of rain, spotting the white crusts on the crosses and arched gravestones.

Hurrying back along the path under the spitting, wind-twisted trees, I wonder anxiously if Aphra has finished her sewing and is watching us along the spirit thread. Is she standing even now in Ange's bedroom, a glass-headed pin pinched in her fingers? Can she see us crossing the lane beside the vicarage? Is she following us with her gaze through the back door into the St Lazarus Hospital?

We are taken aback to see Mrs Bullen standing by the gas stove, her face gaunt.

'You said you'd come, Mrs Ketch,' she begins to sob, 'and now I've had to leave him with Valerie again – and she's only ten.'

Under the harsh kitchen light Mrs Ketch lowers her hood and places a hand on the woman's shoulder. 'I'm so sorry, Mrs Bullen. Iris, would you take the mixture to Mr Bullen? I'll be along in a few minutes.'

Miss Jewel pours the liquid from the pan into a jug and, glancing in our direction with her night-owl eyes, leads Mrs Bullen out of the back door.

When they have gone, Mrs Ketch's gaze lingers on each of us in turn, her face tense. She grasps my hand. 'Cora,' she says, 'Iris and I have to go to the Bullens' now, but they don't live far. As soon as we've finished, we'll follow you to Bryers Guerdon.'

'Oh, thank you, Mrs Ketch.'

She lifts her hood back over her peaked hat and opens the back door once more. As we round the house into the wind, she says, 'Oh, if only Ed Blezzard hadn't smashed up and cleared away all those witch-bottles – stupid man – maybe we could have done something with them. Iron nails never lose their magic, not even in ten thousand years.'

At the front we walk away across the patchy snow in the opposite direction to Mrs Ketch. I look behind and raise my hand in a wave. She stops there for a while, anxiously watching, and calls out, 'Go on and we'll catch you up!'

We reach the corner of the church wall, and the St Lazarus Hospital disappears behind the vicarage. Where the road turns for Bryers Guerdon the telephone box stands starkly red against the muddy-white fields beyond. An icy dome covers its roof like a beret, but a thread of water is spiralling from a corner, twisting down onto the pavement a few feet from the glass door, turning the snow into a mess of dirty slush.

Black clouds roll above us, turning the sky ash-dark. With every step the wind rises and the rain begins to splatter heavily. We pull down our hats and tighten our scarves. Groaning trees fling drops of water onto the verges, where green tips of grass are beginning to poke out of their icy shell.

On the long road back to Bryers Guerdon, Roger keeps Mimi close, helping her through the gathering water. The unsettled air around us is charged with worry and uncertainty. With every arduous step, as the rain beats down and the wind pummels us from every direction, the sense of dread intensifies.

I imagine Ange waiting for us, the poppets, plump with feathers, ready in her hands.

Ange or Aphra? I can't seem to separate one from the other.

If we find the poppets before she uses them against us, and if by some blessed chance we are able to bury them, what then?

Ange would still be there, and therefore so would Aphra.

The nasty little doll, its stone heart stitched in under a scrap of my father's shirt, is deep among the hawthorn roots, but my mind persists in making terrible pictures: white-tiled walls, a gleaming metal trolley under a bare bulb, a thin sheet, a cold, drooping hand.

The Thin Man comes into sight. The lantern over the door is swinging wildly on its bracket in the wind, tossing a jig-jagging light across the swirl of watery snow. We turn and strain our eyes in the half-darkness, searching back down the road for Mrs Ketch and Miss Jewel.

While we stand there, a massive squall sweeps across the fields from the north-west. Unable to press on for a moment, we huddle together to steady ourselves; then all at once, only a few yards away towards Hilsea, a huge ash tree overhanging a farm gate begins to sway, creaking wildly on its stretching, snapping roots before crashing across the road with a thunderous roar, crushing the timbers of the gate and sending up a swirling gust of splintered twigs and wet brown leaves.

'How on earth are they going to get past that?' Roger cries, shielding his eyes.

'They've got to,' I call. 'We can't do this on our own.'

The road begins streaming as the drains and gutters struggle to draw off the surge of rain and meltwater, and the ditches on either side start to overflow.

Braced, bent forward, our eyes stinging, the wind whipping up strands of soaking hair from under our hats, we turn into Old Glebe Lane.

I'm so frightened, my thoughts whirl unchecked.

How has she chosen to wound us – Mimi and me? Does she intend to pick one of us first, then the other? Will it hurt? Will I be able to bear it for Mimi's sake?

Again I wonder if she is watching us as we battle onwards, our cheeks lashed raw. Is she waiting now because she wants us there so she can see us suffer? And what could she do to Roger? He could have stayed warm at home in Fieldpath Road, but he is here with us, labouring to keep Mimi on the road, constantly looking back to make sure I am still behind them.

The trees of Glebe Woods writhe and hiss and spray as we pause for a moment on the brow of the hill to catch our breath. While liquid mud swirls around our feet, we gaze out over the marshes stretching away before us in the gathering gloom.

The rain is buffeted this way and that, and through it

we can still see, faintly shining in a patch of dying light, the familiar channels shifting into shapeless expanses of water, rippling in the wind, running into each other to form interlinking pools, their loose margins marked only by the tips of the taller clumps of reeds, where large chunks of snow jostle each other as they dam together.

But worryingly, further away, where the river merges into the estuary, a blank darkness surges and spreads. Out there the snaking creeks are no longer visible. From blustering sky to river, to marsh, there is nothing but a mass of heaving, swelling, black water.

Roger shouts over the wind. 'I've never seen anything like that before. Do you know when high tide is?'

'I can't think,' I cry back.

'I hope there's not going to be a flood like there was before,' he yells. 'People died . . .'

With another fruitless look back for the two women, we trudge down the hill and into The Chase through the sodden mud. Small lumps of hard snow ride on the water, which gushes down the sloping fields and across the road before flowing into the swollen ditch.

Roger is straining to keep Mimi upright and moving forward, half lifting her under her arms so the water doesn't slop over the tops of her boots. My freezing feet are so achingly heavy I can hardly drag one in front of the other.

At last we reach Guerdon Hall, a hazy, gloomy hulk

with not one single light glimmering out into the driving rain.

Ange must be fast asleep – or waiting for us in the dark.

My teeth begin to chatter with fear.

Through half-screwed eyes it is just possible to see that much of the creek has already thawed, but flat pieces of ice bob on the surface of the rising water, barely a couple of inches under the bridge. If it swells much more, the planks will be covered. Even now the smallest surge sends shallow waves lapping over the edges, the ice shooting across the wood. In the deepening darkness it is difficult to see a safe place to cross.

'We could do with a light,' Roger calls. 'I should have brought a torch.'

'Mr Wragge had a hurricane lamp in the barn!' I shout. 'Let's go and look!'

We struggle across the swirling mud of the old farmyard. The wind has caught the barn door and is pounding it so violently, the one remaining hinge twists and groans on its single screw.

The shelter is welcome, though the rafters whistle and sigh, and every now and then a slate lifts off and thuds to the ground outside. In several places the water is coming through the roof, here a steady drip, drip, drip, there a thin stream.

Squinting, I see the dim gleam of glass. 'It's here!' I

call, reaching up to unhook the hurricane lamp from its peg on the wall, rocking it gently, relieved to hear the swish of paraffin. A dirty old box of Swan Vestas sits on a rickety shelf nearby. 'How do you light it?'

'I can do that,' says Roger.

He gives his gloves to Mimi, and it takes him no time at all to lever up the glass and strike a match to the wick.

We see each other, soaking, bedraggled and tense, in the quavering light from the yellow flame.

Mimi drops one of Roger's gloves.

I bend to pick it up, dive my hand into the straw.

'Ouch!'

A sharp jag of pain. A warm rush over my palm.

I pull off my woollen glove. There is a ragged cut between my thumb and forefinger and the blood is flowing out in a thick dark stream.

'Crikey, what have you done?' Roger cries. 'Here, hold this, Mimi.'

Cautiously, Mimi takes the lamp from Roger and holds it at arm's length. He reaches into his pocket and pulls out a sodden handkerchief which I press on the throbbing wound. The scarlet blood spreads into the wet cotton. I feel hollow, light-headed, lean against the wall for a moment.

'How did it happen?'

Roger crouches down, warily turns over the straw.

'Hold the lamp a bit lower, Mimi. Ah, look at this.'

He slowly stands and shows us an iron nail, bent at an angle, brown with rust, the point twisted over into a sharp hook. 'It's from one of those witch bottles,' he breathes.

On its tip is a drop of my blood.

A sudden mighty gust of wind bustles through the open doorway, lifts the top layer of straw and sends it spinning around us in a whirl of dust. In the same moment I recall Mrs Ketch's words – *Iron nails never lose their magic, not even in ten thousand years.* I feel a rush in my head, a ripple of excitement.

'Are – are there any more nails?' I ask urgently.

'Why?'

'Just see,' I say, moving some of the straw aside with my foot.

'Mimi, lower the lamp. Look, there's one.'

Again Roger stoops, runs his hands over the earth floor. 'Here, Mimi – now here.'

Another nail comes to light, then one more. He finds some jagged fragments of thick, greenish glass, another bent nail, more broken glass, more nails.

While Roger is searching, I look eagerly around the barn. The shadows of the old cow stalls, wooden beams and hanging chains dance in the nodding light of the hurricane lamp. Then, on the shelf where we found the matches, I see a few dusty, web-threaded old bottles stacked all higgledy-piggledy, some on their sides, most cracked or broken . . . but one of them sets my heart racing.

I fold my cut hand tightly on the handkerchief, and with the other reach for the bottle. My fingers tremble as I lift it off the shelf. Under the thick dust it is half-glazed stoneware, dull cream below and shiny brown at the top. I brush it against my coat and some of the dirt rubs off. Through the remaining grime I read an oval of fancy black letters: *Pepper and Beard's, Lowestoft*, and in its centre, *Traditional Stone Ginger Beer*. Miraculously, still stuck firmly in the neck is a cork and cap stopper, and when I shake it, nothing inside.

'Roger . . .'

I hold out the bottle, roll my eyes towards the glass and iron nails in his hand. At first he seems puzzled, looks down at the nails, back to the bottle, then to my bleeding hand.

In the yellow light I see his cheeks grow pale and a frown appear.

'You seriously think we can make one – a witch bottle?'

I nod quickly. 'See if the cork will come out.'

'Shouldn't we wait for Mrs Ketch and Miss Jewel?' Mimi says. 'They'll know how to do it proper.'

I picture the deep rushing water on the dark Hilsea road, the fallen tree.

433

'I don't think they'll be able to get here, Mimi,' I say. 'Not now. We'll have to try and make one ourselves.'

Roger puts the nails and shards of glass down on an old wooden crate, nervously takes the bottle and pulls at the cap. He twists and tugs and at last the cork squeaks out of the neck.

I swallow and begin to unwrap the wet, bloody handkerchief from my hand. As the hanky loosens, the wound throbs.

Roger's mouth is set in a grim line. 'Are – are you sure?' he whispers.

I stretch out my hand.

'Light, Mimi,' he says, and as she brings it close, he hesitantly takes my fingers and turns my hand thumb downwards so the gash is over the wide neck of the bottle. Then he puts his own hand over mine and squeezes the edges of the torn skin together.

I suck in a sharp breath. The pulsing blood drips in.

Drop by drop.

The lamplight quivers. Mimi's wide glistening eyes are on us, quietly watching.

The top of the bottle smears red and a crimson line travels slowly down the curved side. In a short while the dripping stops, and I press the cut with the handkerchief. Then Mimi sets the lamp down on the wooden crate, pulls off her gloves and lays them down beside the lamp.

Gazing at me all the while, she nibbles one by one at the fingernails of her right hand, she spits out the little slivers into her other hand, reaches across and drops them inside the bottle. Then she pulls off her hat and coils a lock of hair around her hand. She tugs hard, winces, gasps, and holds up the fair curl she has pulled out.

I push back my own hat, wind a length of hair in my fingers near the scalp, shut my eyes and yank once, swallow, try again and, with a grimace, rip out a length. Eyes smarting, I try to persuade both locks of hair into the neck of the bottle, but they stick on the drying blood. Roger twists the hair around a couple of the long rusted nails and pokes them down with the other nails and the jagged fragments of glass, then plugs the top shut with the stopper.

If I was expecting some feeling of enchantment in the air, as I sensed under the hawthorn tree, there is nothing. I feel only the wet chill seeping inside my boots and into my bones. Nothing has changed. The wind continues to thunder and whine through the groaning rafters; the dangling chains sway and chink; water from the leaking roof spatters into the straw; the door thuds back and forth on its loosening hinge.

'What if it doesn't work?' I breathe.

Roger looks at me anxiously. 'What if it does?' he says.

His eyes are mirrors of my own fears, and all the misgivings that beset me on the road from Hilsea come thronging back.

Where does Angela Russell end and Aphra Rushes begin? What if one has become the other, and they are the same? And even if there were two separate people, Aphra Rushes and Angela Russell, in one body, and the bottle drew out and destroyed the witch – Aphra – what would then happen to the shell left behind – Ange?

Can you take one out without hurting the other?

My head aches.

I think of Ange laughing over the fish and chips, wearing her funny crown, snuggling down with Mimi on the settee, sewing . . .

. . . sewing the scraps of fabric to make the little man with the stone heart.

Is Dad alive or dead? I see again the drooping grey hand under the hem of the white sheet, close my eyes for a moment, try and calm myself. But my thoughts turn to the snippets from our clothes, the hair from our hairbrush, the poppets of Mimi and me somewhere in that dark, brooding house over the creek, and Aphra waiting for us with her gleaming glass-headed pins.

We might have stayed there a long time, nervous and uncertain, but a deafening crack and a mighty wrenching sound send all three of us spinning round. The ancient hinge shatters, the door twists, and the wind lifts and pitches it thudding into the mud outside. At the same instant a surge of water gushes inside the open doorway, pushing the straw ahead of it for a couple of feet in a foamy, curving line.

'If we don't go now,' Roger says urgently, 'we might never get over the bridge.'

I take the bottle and push it into one of the deep pockets of my duffel coat, then we make for the doorway and brace ourselves against the gusting, drenching wind.

In Roger's hand the lamp rocks wildly on its metal handle as we battle across the swirling farmyard mud, huddling together in the soaking rain.

At the creek the icy water is washing over the wooden planks.

'I'll go first!' Roger cries, swinging the lamp from one edge of the bridge to the other to find the middle. 'Mimi, you hold onto me. Cora, follow close!'

I steady Mimi under her arms as she clutches Roger's coat. We cross gingerly, one step at a time, wading through the water, pausing for a moment to brace ourselves as a huge gust threatens to blow us off the side. At last we splash one by one onto the submerged gravel on the other bank, and warily approach the house.

The lamp reflects eerily in the diamond panes of the dark, rain-drizzled windows.

We round the corner into a gale that almost knocks us

backwards. It takes a moment to steady our feet in the slopping water.

At the side of the house a reddish light glows out of the sitting room. While Roger and Mimi shelter against the wall, I cautiously peer in. Inside, the fire is burning low, a heap of glowing embers under a powder of grey ash. There is no sign of Ange.

We struggle along the path towards the back of the house, turn the corner, and are almost blown into the wall by the ferocity of the wind as it hurtles the heavy rain against the building, hammering the windows, lifting and whirling the slates and needling our cheeks. The poor maimed shrubs and stunted trees are lashed this way and that. Water sweeps across the garden, ripples across the path in shallow waves, then slaps noisily against the bottom of the wall.

The thunderous, ragged black clouds roll apart here and there to reveal little silvery points of stars and a hazy, sickly half of yellow moon. Under its pale, washed-out light, the world seems to be nothing but water – rising, rising still, in a black, spreading swell across the marshes.

We stumble onto the slippery cobbled yard, with the wind at our backs forcing us on towards the rain-spattered back door. With my split, throbbing hand, still wrapped clumsily in the handkerchief, I fumble in my pocket and under the stoneware bottle for my key, and battle to unlock the door. At last we spill into the cold, greenish light of the passage.

Roger pushes back hard against the door to shut out the wind and the water, but even the ancient wood cannot prevent a trickle fingering its way across the flagstones.

Slowly we move up the passage and turn left. Cold, damp draughts crisscross the hall, sucking any remaining warmth out of our wet clothes. Somewhere from the floor above comes a dripping sound.

'Last time Ange was sewing,' I breathe, 'it was in her bedroom. But she must have come downstairs since, if the fire's lit.'

We creep down the hall towards the sitting room. The curtains at the bend of the stairs waft away from the window and the small glass panes rattle in their leaded diamonds, while the rain seeps in at the bottom edge and runs down the plaster in a long dark line.

Roger moves slowly towards the open doorway. 'Stay there for a minute,' he whispers.

Holding up the lamp, he peers round the frame, inches forward, looks round the back of the door. Dark as a shadow against the flicker of firelight and lamplight, he edges further and further in, cautiously puts the lamp down on the small table, looks all about him.

'There's no one here.' He beckons us in.

'Can you see the poppets?' I hiss, taking a step forward.

'Her sewing things are here on the settee,' he breathes.

We rifle through her box, scattering the cotton reels, the scissors, the cards of hooks and eyes. I tip up the cockle-shell straw bag, and scraps of material and trimmings slip out onto the settee or waft to the floor – among them little bits of Aggie, the green offcut from Ange's skirt that made the rag doll's dress, the reddish wool that made her hair.

'Look, you keep searching in here,' I whisper to Roger. 'Don't miss one cushion or one drawer. Mimi, we'll go and look in the kitchen.'

Roger twists up the wick on the hurricane lamp. 'You'd better take this. I'll stick another log on the fire.'

I pick up the lamp, and Mimi and I steal down the hall to the dark kitchen, with a wary look up the stairs as we go by.

The tap is dripping noisily into the sink and, like a host of spirit voices, the wind moans behind the dresser where the old chimney rises up behind the false wall. The rain beats against the window, and on either side of it, the orange curtains lift and flap.

I set the lamp down on the table next to a couple of discarded packets of Capstan and an overflowing ash-tray. A half-empty cup of scummy tea rests askew on its saucer, which is filled with squashed cigarette butts rimmed with lipstick.

Mimi slips out of my hand, reaches out with a gloved finger, and touches the waxy, crimson ring on one of the stubs.

The tap drips on.

Ange's quilted maroon dressing gown is draped untidily across the back of one of the chairs. I hold it up, reach into one pocket, then the other – nothing inside but balled-up handkerchiefs.

I run my hands through each drawer, open the cupboard doors, but in truth know searching here is useless. Ange will surely have the poppets close to her.

A deafening gust of wind hurls heavy raindrops against the window like a fistful of pebbles.

Would Ange have gone back upstairs to her bed? If she is asleep, there is a chance . . .

'Come on, sis,' I whisper, pulling Mimi gently by the arm.

We move out of the kitchen into the hall and I stop at the staircase and look up.

Alarmingly, water is dripping down from one tread to the next, pooling at the bottom and soaking the carpet.

I step up one stair, lifting the lamp and craning my neck to peer round the bend in the staircase. Through the large window, the black clouds are rolling and pitching, their edges ragged with rain, as they sweep over the crest of the upper field.

'You going up?' Mimi breathes.

'I've got to. You stay down here with Roger, go on.'

She edges towards the sitting room, and I take the stairs one at a time, slowly, slowly, my heart pounding.

As I step up to the landing, the ceiling above me creaks with a long, loud groaning. Holding up the light, I am alarmed to see a gaping black hole. To one side, the ragged ends of splintered beams, laced with clinging wet cobwebs, are poking through the gap. I move towards Ange's room, stumbling over rubble and broken wood, and the pieces of timber chafe together. Fearfully I glance up again, unnerved by the worrying bulge on one side of the hole.

I creep further along the landing and put my ear to Ange's door.

No sound. No light underneath.

I breathe in, put my thumb on the latch, hissing through my teeth at the click, willing it to be quiet as it lifts.

I wait a moment, then push the door open.

The light sweeps across the unmade, empty bed, the tangle of rumpled sheets and blankets. Strewn across the floor is a disorder of clothes, dirty teacups, plates with stale remains of barely picked-at food, cigarette packets, magazines splayed open, everything speckled with small curled feathers.

Leaving the door ajar, I snake my way across the floor, put down the lamp, and rifle through blankets and under pillows. Lifting the corner of the drooping bedspread, I see nestled in the jumble of shoes on the floor two little snippets of pink cotton and a shred of my blue blouse. Sick with fear, I turn to the rest of the room.

With my fingers poised to pull open the top drawer of the chest where I found the little cloth man, I hear a door closing back along the landing.

I know the familiar thud. It is the door to our bedroom.

Has Mimi come upstairs?

I told her to stay with Roger.

I take the lamp, pick my way across the mess and out onto the landing. I can't pass under the yawning hole in the ceiling without a glance upwards. Little by little the huge pieces of blackened wood are edging their way out; small beads of water in loosely connected streams drip onto the floorboards, glistening in the light like strings of pearls.

I inch my way over the pieces of fallen plaster until I reach our bedroom.

Raising my hand to the latch, I lose my nerve and let it fall, then raise it again and press down the thumb-piece.

'Mimi . . . ?' I whisper, pushing the door.

It creaks forward, and the lamplight passes over drawn curtains, over the fireplace, the red chair and the end of my bed, slowly gleaming up the floral eiderdown towards the headboard.

My breath rushes out.

Tucked under my blanket, its head resting on my pillow, is a poppet, locks of my own hair sewn to its scalp, little dark eyes fixed on me, mean mouth grinning.

Trembling, I lift the quavering lamp towards Mimi's bed.

And there is the other – small stuffed arms over the fold of the sheet, its face turned towards me, framed by wisps of Mimi's hair, the red running-stitched lips turned up at the ends in a spiteful smile.

A swish on the lino.

Out of the shadows near the fireplace comes Ange.

Ange – or Aphra?

Who is it looking out from those dark-ringed eyes?

Whose lips are they, stretched back in a sneer?

I don't know. I don't know.

She moves towards me effortlessly, as if gliding across the floor.

I can't reach the dolls. Don't want to touch them.

Can't think.

I turn on my heel, bolt back through the door and launch myself down the slippery stairs. The water splashes under my wellingtons, the lamp swings crazily on its handle as I stumble down, squelching into the sodden carpet at the bottom.

Mimi is waiting for me, her face bloodless.

In the sitting room a drawer slams shut.

Keep quiet, Roger. What will Ange do to you if she knows you are there?

I look behind me.

She is on the stairs.

Mimi glances up, her eyes glazed with fright. She grabs my arm, pulls me, breathless, down the hall to Auntie Ida's old kitchen, stoops and lifts a corner of the wet carpet, picks up the key, drops it, fumbles for it again. Her hand shaking, she pushes it into the lock and puts her shoulder to the old door. Grating on the flagstones, it opens inwards.

Mimi snatches my sleeve and pulls me in, grabs the key out of the lock, then frantically pushes the door shut and locks it with trembling fingers.

We stand there, panting, watching the lamplight spill across the grimy floor, picking out glinting pinpoints of eyes as mice scurry into the shadowy corners, dart into cracks, drop into holes. I lift it higher, and the flare outlines the legs of the chairs, the edges of the cupboards, the pitted rim of the stone sink.

Setting it down on the table, I catch a movement at the window. Terrified for a moment, Mimi and I look across to see our two blurred faces gazing back at us behind the panes, the rainwater on the juddering glass running down our pale reflected cheeks like long, dark tears.

For a few seconds the wind drops, and in that small pause there comes a soft noise from the hall.

Mimi turns her head, tendrils of fair, wavy hair gleaming softly. 'Ange . . .' she breathes.

The strip of light at the bottom of the door is broken by two shadows. Someone is on the other side. The shadows shift slightly, the weight passing from one foot to the other as they sway shakily on the soaking floor.

Mimi and I stand frozen.

The latch rattles, and the door moves slightly, as if Ange is pushing against it. Then, utterly unexpectedly, we hear the low rasp of her voice, close to the wood.

'Cora . . .'

Mimi's fingers twist my sleeve.

'Cora . . . are you there? Cora . . . Mimi?' comes the voice again. 'It won't open . . . help me . . .'

Mimi's grip tightens on my arm. I take a fleeting look at her. Her hand moves to her coat pocket and she pulls out Aggie. For a moment she stares at the red wool hair, the green dress, the round rusty-brown marks of Ange's blood on the little cheeks. A tear slides out of her eye. She pushes the doll into the front of her coat, where the legs stick out of the space between two buttons.

Seconds pass.

'Cora . . . please . . .' breathes the voice. 'There's

something wrong with me . . . help me . . .'

The creak comes again, louder. Ange is leaning against the door.

'Mimi . . . it's me . . . it's Ange . . . please . . .'

There is a loud slithering sound, a thump, a little moan. The line of light is almost completely blocked out.

'She's fallen down,' Mimi whispers. 'What shall we do? What shall we do?'

We wait, trembling, as the wind rises once more and howls around the old chimney.

Then Ange speaks again, weakly, breathlessly, her lips against the gap at the bottom of the door. 'I don't know what's happening . . . Please help me . . .'

My thoughts seem to snag together. Aphra Rushes could hurt us with the poppets whether she could see us or not. Aphra doesn't need us to open the door.

So it must be Ange . . . it must be . . .

ROGER

Ange's back glows in the firelight flickering down the hall from the sitting room. She is quivering along the whole length of her body as she lies on her side across the wet floor, her long cardigan sopping underneath her, her straggling, uncombed hair trailing in the ribbons of glistening water flowing down the stone passage from under the back door.

Moving stealthily, keeping to the shadows, I creep forward as far as the staircase. The wind roars behind the storm-battered window at the bend, and the curtain blows out and flaps back against the plaster. Shiny drops flick off the banisters from the landing above, and a thin stream of water glints down the stairs, tread by tread.

The click of a lock.

A scraping noise.

The old kitchen door is opening, inch by inch. Gloved fingers drag the edge backwards. Part of Cora's face appears, ghostly and guarded. Nervously she looks down at Ange.

The gap widens. Mimi peers round the frame, frowning under her hat. 'What shall we do?' she breathes.

Ange doesn't move.

'I'll try and lift her up,' I hear Cora say. 'Move back, Mimi.'

Just as Cora takes a step forward, the house is rocked by a massive cracking sound from upstairs, echoed and magnified by the wooden panelling. Then comes a mighty thud, and a huge shudder I can feel under my feet, as if the whole building has shifted, and a sudden, icy draught sweeps down from the landing across the back of my neck.

Alarmed, I look up the stairs. The trickle of water

begins to grow and gurgle, bringing scraps of wood down with it. I step away, turn back to Ange, and gasp in horror.

She is on her feet, her profile horribly animated, her eyes gleaming bright.

Something soft, a small rag doll in an oddment of blue, strands of dark hair drooping from its head, dangles in her fingers.

Cora, her face a grimace, lunges at it.

Ange whips it up and, with enormous force, slaps it against the wall.

Instantly, without even a cry, Cora jerks, cracks her head on the edge of the doorframe and drops with a thud to the floor.

'Cora!' Mimi's hands fly to her mouth. She falls to her knees, lifts Cora's head. A stream of dark blood flows from under Cora's hat and into the water.

Sick with terror, my heart beating up into my throat, I try to clear my head, think what to do, struggle in the half-darkness to find some movement in Cora's face.

'Cora . . .' Mimi murmurs, leans over to touch her sister's face. 'Cora . . .'

Ange thrusts the poppet into the pocket of the long, soaking cardigan, then, in a rapid sweep, takes something out of the other. I catch a glimpse of another small cloth figure, fairish hair, pink.

Eyes glinting, half narrowed, Ange tightens one

hand around the doll, squeezing, compressing.

Mimi drops Cora's limp head on the floor, and begins to cough. She pulls off her hat and clutches at her throat with her hands.

The woman's knuckles bulge white. She grits her teeth, squeezes still more, closes her other hand around the doll's neck and, with tendons straining under the raised veins, begins to twist her fingers in opposite directions.

'Ange . . .' Mimi's voice is a gasp, a feeble croak. Pearls of sweat glisten on her forehead. She coughs again. Her face darkens.

I stop thinking, and leap forward.

Ange spins round, sees me, spits out a sound.

I pitch myself headlong towards her and grasp the doll with both hands.

She tries to pull it back, bares her teeth, snarls with effort, tightens her fingers.

'Ange . . . ?' comes Mimi's fading voice again.

Ange twists her head and looks at Mimi, then turns back to me. Something changes, just for a moment – something in her eyes, like a shutter lifting, then falling back – and at the same moment I feel her focus shift, her strength slacken. Her fingers appear now to be nothing more than thin, bluish skin wrapped loosely around scrawny bones.

'Ange?' I breathe.

She looks into my eyes. For a second there is no malice in her expression, just a kind of desperation.

With a grunt I wrench the poppet from her.

Instantly her vigour returns. She snarls, lunges at my arm.

Unbalanced, I lurch over Cora, just miss Mimi, and land unsteadily in the old kitchen, grabbing the edge of the table, jolting the lamp. Immediately I turn.

Mimi, still on her knees, slumps forward, a hand falling on Cora's cheek.

On the other side the woman glares at me, her features glowing yellow in the trembling flame from the hurricane lamp.

She stretches out her hand for the poppet, palm upward, the skinny fingers curving claw-like, drops of water dripping from her sleeve. 'Give it to me,' she hisses in a low, rasping voice. 'Give it to me.'

I swallow. My heart thumps. But I don't move.

'Give it to me,' she says again, moving a step nearer, baring her teeth.

Now the light falls even more fully on her face. Just for a moment I think I see something in the glinting eyes, in the deep, cat-like heart of them – a flicker of hesitation. She is still glaring at me with a burning intensity, but on the margins, her eyes are taking in the barrier of the doorframe, and the threshold where Cora lies in the spreading blood-stained water.

451

Her eyes narrow.

Her hand reaches down and she brings out the Cora doll again, holds it up. The head, with its tangle of long dark hair, falls slightly forward into shadow.

My heart begins to thud.

Her other hand creeps up to the cheap-looking brooch just below the left shoulder of her cardigan – three green stones on a bar of black beads. She fumbles to unclip it, twists it out of the wool. The point of the long, crooked pin gleams in her fingers as she folds it outwards. She lifts the poppet in one hand, the pin in the other, and begins to draw them together, the pin inching its way closer and closer to the little blue dress.

'Give me the poppet,' she hisses.

I swallow, my mind ravelling and unravelling.

I glance at Cora, slumped helpless on the floor.

Ange's eyes begin to gleam. Little by little the sharp point of the pin edges towards the doll.

At that moment a fearful sound thunders through the house – a deafening, grinding, groaning crunch of timber against timber, as if some massive structure in the roof is splitting apart.

I shoot a look to the staircase – see Ange's head spin round.

Mimi seizes the second, springs up, lurches forward.

Ange whirls back, her face distorted, blood-red, the

brooch pin high in one hand, the other hand an open claw – empty.

As Mimi bounds backwards onto the flagstones beside me, clutching the figure, the woman's mouth stretches wide, crimson like a great gaping wound. With a screech she lunges forward, arms outstretched, hands grappling wildly at the air, and heaves herself over Cora towards the poppets . . .

. . . and passes over the bottle inside Cora's coat.

Then it seems as if the wind ceases to roar, the rain to spatter, as if the water swirling through the house becomes motionless, silent and glassy, as if the crystal-like drops falling from the ceiling have suspended themselves quietly in the air. The trickles and rivulets seeping down windows and ragged plaster hold themselves still and glittering, mirroring the points of fire and lamplight.

And in this instant of paused time, Mimi and I freeze too, watching horrified, open-mouthed, as Ange, alone in the hushed moment, moves.

She struggles to crawl on hands and knees across the kitchen floor towards us, but her backbone is juddering crookedly, convulsing all along its length. She tries to stretch out one sinewy arm, then the other, but her elbows twitch outwards and collapse under her. She tries again, but her head drops and her chin cracks on the hard flagstones. Her face contorts, her mouth twists to a grimace through gritted teeth, and between them she

453

grunts and moans and curses, before falling silent.

Her eyes remain open in her still, distorted face.

Behind her, something moves. I hear a quavering voice.

'It's burning . . . burning . . .'

'Cora!'

The wind is howling around the house once more, the water gushing along the floors, streaming out of the cracks in the ceiling. Mimi and I skirt round Ange and rush towards Cora. I sink to the floor, drenching my knees on the soaking carpet, and raise her head out of the water.

'It's burning . . .' she gasps. 'The bottle . . .'

Her eyes flutter open, her hands fumble for her duffel-coat pocket, twisted awkwardly under her where she fell.

'It hurts . . .'

I shove the poppet of Mimi in my pocket, and half lift Cora up. Finding the curve of the witch bottle, I drag it out of her coat. It looks much as it did before, half glazed, *Pepper & Beard's Traditional Stone Ginger Beer*, but it is scorching hot, even through my gloves, and almost pulsating, as if is there is boiling liquid inside, about to blow off the cork. I flip it from one hand to the other.

'The fire . . .' hisses Cora, shaking her head, struggling to push herself up on her hands. 'Get rid of it. Throw – throw it on the fire!'

In seconds I am at the staircase. A fleeting glance upwards shows huge jagged beams, the ripped ends of rafters, trapped in a jostling, watery heap on the bend of the stairs.

Heart in mouth, I hurry past and into the sitting room.

In the fireplace, sooty rain spatters black down the chimney, dotting the powdery grey ash that covers the red embers. Quickly I pick up the poker and push the ash through the iron basket, then blow gently. A few tiny sparks fly up off my breath. At last little yellow flames begin to lick over the back of the blackened logs. I turn them over, frantically stab at them with the poker. All at once, they flare, snapping into life.

I throw in the bottle.

At first it just sits glowing in the wood; then, as the fire rises leaping, swirling and crackling around and over it, there begins a fierce hissing and spitting, and the bottle starts to radiate an intensifying, brilliant jewel-red in the engulfing flames.

Boiling in blood, searing and melting – razor-slicing glass, gripping, pinching and piercing – scarlet-glowing iron nails, throttling hair – bubbling, blistering, purifying fire . . .

I begin to separate – all the tiny, scorching pieces are tearing apart . . . splitting, splitting, tearing . . .

In this sweet burning, the veil rips apart—

I see the half-world . . .

. . . and beyond it, an opening, an enfolding darkness into nothing . . .

I feel an agitated pulling on my sleeve, then become aware of a long, low roaring, like the sound of a monstrous distant engine – from outside, from across the marshes.

'The water's coming, Roger!' It's Mimi. 'We're going to be drowned! We've got to help Cora!'

I turn to see Cora drooping weakly against the doorway at the far end of the hall.

Over the lintel above her head a thin black line is slowly creeping down the plaster and a sputter of water begins to ooze through it.

'Quick, come on!' I whisk Cora's poppet out of Mimi's hand and squash it into my pocket with the other, then pull her into the hall.

On our right, the kitchen door is open. Through the window, beyond the shiny new enamel and gleaming chrome and the drenched orange curtains, there is no garden, no marsh, just a black wall of water.

My heart begins to pound wildly.

I rush over to Cora, who is wiping her blood-smeared face with her sodden gloves. I throw my arm around her shoulders. She leans against me, shivering.

'Can you walk?' I ask urgently.

'Think so . . . Yes, yes.'

'We'll have to go out the front.'

I look up. 'Mimi, we have to— Where are you?'

In the dim light from the hurricane lamp, the last drops of paraffin feeding the tiny, fading flame, I see Mimi kneeling by Ange's head on the old kitchen floor, stroking the tangled hair off her face.

'Mimi,' Ange croaks, raising her shaking hand to touch Mimi's cheek.

Mimi looks up at me, tears welling. 'We – we can't leave her here to drown,' she says. 'It's Ange. The witch has gone in the bottle. It's really Ange.'

She lifts a strand of Ange's dishevelled, wet hair, then looks over at the rattling window and lets out a squeal of alarm. She thrusts her hands under Ange's trembling shoulders and frantically tries to lift her. Ange half rises, then crumples.

'I'm all right,' Cora says, propping herself against the wall. 'Just a bit dizzy. I'll try and open the front door. You help Mimi . . .'

I rush to Ange, lift her in my arms. She feels weightless, like an empty shell. Even through my coat I can feel her bones, brittle like a bird's, sharp against me as I place her arm over my shoulder.

As we hurry back into the hall, a mighty crash rocks the house.

Just behind us in the old kitchen, something heavy

cracks and thuds against the table: a forked branch, ripped, torn and blown from some battered tree, has smashed the diamond panes inwards across the old stone sink. The lamp falls and sputters out. At the same moment a torrent of rain-swept wind blasts across the kitchen, whirling splinters of glass and twisted lead through the air and along the flagstones.

We splash along the hall floor to the huge front door of studded oak.

Cora is there before us. Swaying slightly, she raises a trembling hand to the iron bolt above her head, and manages to push the bar aside.

In every part of the house, wood is splitting and beams groaning. From the top of the staircase above us comes an ominous shifting, creaking and rolling. The crisscross of crunching, tangled timbers on the bend of the stairs is beginning to move slowly forward.

Cora snatches the huge iron key from its hook, pushes it into the lock, grips it hard and turns it with both hands.

The rumbling of the dammed wood becomes a monstrous, thunderous roaring. A torrent begins to gush down the stairs, bubbling, frothing and tumbling.

Cora and Mimi together drag the ancient door open. A surge of liquid mud comes pouring through the gap, rushing in swirling eddies over and around our boots, sprawling its way along the length of the hall and into every room. The freezing, roaring wind blasts us back into the hall, our wet faces lashed by the rush of cold air.

I grasp Ange as tightly as I can, then, pushing Cora and Mimi ahead, plunge forward myself through the flooded porch and out into the churning water. Behind us, the broken wooden beams burst free and hurl themselves headlong down the stairs and lodge across the open doorway.

We splash desperately towards The Chase. A booming sound rises above the gale – the growling, snarling roll of the gigantic incoming wave.

Drenched, heads bent forward against the whipping wind, branches and broken roof tiles flying perilously around us, we hurry on. The floodwater is so high it is almost impossible to make out the curved line of the creek. We must be nearly at the bridge, though can see nothing but an endless wash of dark, gurgling water.

Then the weak moon appears again among the frayed edges of the tumbling black clouds, and the tips of the foaming waves glisten in its feeble light.

Quickly I hoist Ange up and bundle her over my shoulder, grab Cora's hand and pull her stumbling along.

Mimi turns towards me, then freezes, her eyes fixed somewhere over my shoulder.

I twist my neck.

A great foaming surge is gushing round the corners of

both wings of the house. Huge branches, the long brown straps of reeds, bits of fencing posts, tiles, are rushing towards us, tossed and pitched effortlessly on the frothing swell.

'Run, Mimi!'

The dark silhouettes of the two old farm cottages over on The Chase loom up ahead of us out of the darkness.

'Where's the bridge?' Mimi yells.

'Guess!' I shout. 'We can't wait!'

Mimi launches herself into the water. Mercifully it comes just short of the top of her boots. She steadies herself against the flow, then flounders across the submerged planks to the other side.

I brace myself, lock my hand in Cora's and charge forward behind Mimi. Though we are unbalanced for a moment by Ange's dangling body, our feet land on the planks a few inches below the surface. We steel ourselves against the buffeting wind, which nearly blows us into the swollen creek, then stagger across.

A second later, the immense rolling, freezing wave slams into our backs with a howling roar, hurling us forward, slapping out our breath. Cora's hand is wrenched away from mine.

A blundering roar, a thundering hiss.
The flames are quenched in an icy torrent.
The half-world slips away from me.

In my narrow prison I am lifted, tossed and plunged into a whirling swell.

I try and turn towards Cora, struggle to stretch out my hand, but am stunned by the force and weight of the churning water, lifting me off my feet for a few terrifying seconds, threatening to sweep Ange off my shoulder. My clothes, instantly saturated, drag me along with the surge.

The wave washes away from us. I choke filthy water out of my throat, swing Ange, sluggish and drenched, off my back and into my heavy arms, where she splutters and retches. I look around in a panic for Cora, and with a rush of relief see her, panting and coughing, trying to steady herself, a few feet away. I stagger towards her. She clutches at my shoulder, holds on.

'Mimi . . . where's Mimi?' she stammers, a line of fresh blood escaping from under her hat and down her wet cheek.

I squint into the darkness. Mimi is ahead on the other side, wading through the deep, thick mud by the cottages at the bottom of the upper field, which rises steeply up to the edge of Glebe Woods, where the trees curve away from the brow of the hill in a black, wind-tossed mass.

'She's there, Cora – over there!'

Mimi looks up. 'Quick! Quick!' she barks from across The Chase. 'The water's coming back!'

Cora and I lurch forward in our leaden boots and sodden, cumbersome coats, Ange limp and soaking in my arms. Knees and ankles aching, hearts thumping, we stagger up the slope through the sludge of mud and grass, tripping and stumbling, up towards the trees, the wind lashing our wet hair against our cheeks.

Below us, the vast, unstoppable flood crashes once more over the ancient house, then races on over the swollen creek to wash through the two old cottages.

For a time only the roof timbers of Guerdon Hall are visible above the heaving, frothing swell. When the water pulls back for a moment, the house seems to sway in a bubbling, gurgling dance to the groaning of collapsing walls and the crunch of timbers scraping against each other in the submerged rooms and passages.

Over the swirling surface of the water, the foam lifts off the wave crests, arching and feathering into the air like departing ghosts.

And distantly, above the bellowing of the wind, we hear the passing bell of All Hallows church, clanging alone in its empty tower.

Exhausted, my arms straining, I hoist Ange up over my shoulder once more as we stand huddled together gazing down the slope, unable to turn our eyes from the wreckage below.

'I lost Aggie,' Mimi says. 'She floated away.'

THURSDAY 29th NOVEMBER

I am bobbed and buffeted by the gurgling water – for how long I do not know, cannot sense the passing hours, or when night becomes day. It is all the same – Aphra sightless and silent, carried close and confined for whatever passes for time on the foam of the sea.

But the swollen tide turns, lifts me in its hurtling, rushing surge back to the land. I am pounded, struck, shattered into fragments, flung out, scattered among nails and glass, up into dazzling light, down into green-black bubbles, whirled and pulled and twisted. A monstrous, jagged branch rolls past, rocks and swells close by, then drops slowly and comes to rest with me on the soft, drowned earth as the water ebbs away.

But the surface will not hold me. I begin to sink into the soil. I have no hands to feel, no bone or sinew, no skin in which to wrap myself. The woman has gone too far from me, but why do I still sense the iron-smell of her blood? It pulls at me, draws me onward. I gather speed and rush along, formless, through the soaking ground.

The hawthorn stretches out its gnarled, twisted roots to loop and snatch me.

Light, airy voices come to me – Matty the Boy, Little Clim, Dorcas Oates.

'Play with us, stay with us, Aphra . . .'

The ringing, spiteful laughter of Tilly Murrell.

'You are betrayed, Aphra. Your curse has betrayed you . . .
The spell went crooked, Aphra . . .'

They fade into the space between worlds – the little colourless faces, the pale limbs . . .

Still I am hurried on.

Pierced and broken, I peer through the earth for Zillah and Damaris, but in vain, for water did not come and lift them out of the fire that second time, as it did me. The water should not have come, the charm was not in accordance – 'The spell went crooked, Aphra . . .'

I search for him in this place, for Cain Lankin, but know he is nothing more than dust in the heavens.

Then I am sucked up – up out of the sodden ground, between the wet clumps of matted grass, among tangled and broken briars – and come to lie motionless, helpless in the watery mud, under a wash of cold, grey light . . .

Once more I can see the church tower capped by its small spire, and the opening of the belfry window set among the solid stones.

I remember the cutting of the iron anklet, the dragging of the chains, the oozing sores, the gnawing hunger. I looked out from the gap of window there, watched them fetch the wood. I hear again the drummer on his stool, sounding out the heartbeat of my last hour. I see Lord Myldmaye, my judge, and Edmund Guerdon on their high horses, talking together so as not to look upon me, and the priest, Hillyard, muttering his prayers in the bitter cold for my salvation.

And in the high hook of the tree he sits gazing down at me, my own Cain Lankin, disfigured and spoiled.

That day, for his sake I did not want to die, and since then I have suffered the torment of perpetual life.

My curse still holds me here.

But how can I be held by her blood?

The witch bottle shattered in the water. What is this prison that confines me now?

CORA

The stitches pull and prickle. My head throbs.

The wind rattles Roger's bedroom window, thuds and scuds around the house. I hold every muscle taut, hide under the blanket to shut out the noise, lie there shivering, crawling with sweat, trying to unravel the snarled threads.

Ange clammy, ash-grey, breath barely fluttering under the red blanket, the district nurse stroking her forehead, timing her pulse against her watch. The shrill ringing of the bell as the ambulance pushes back through the water swilling over Fieldpath Road, trying to get Ange to hospital by way of North Fairing to avoid the flooded Lokswood road.

Whispering. Frowning.

'Can't have Roger and Pete sleeping in the sitting room indefinitely,' says Mr Jotman. 'Pam had better come in with us, and the boys can go into the loft for the time being.'

Pete storming off to sit by himself in the kitchen.

Telephone calls made and received in hushed voices.

The air hanging heavy with questions.

Mr Jotman battles through the squall to fetch the camp bed from the shed.

'Honestly, Rex, we can't let anyone sleep on that old thing,' says Mrs Jotman. 'It was my father's. It must have seen action in the trenches.'

Pete comes in, his face a frown. 'Well, *I'm* not sleeping on it for a start!'

'You can have Pam's bed, then. Roger won't mind.'

The district nurse's rustling, navy-blue bosom, thermometer, surgical spirit, gleaming scissors. Jerky, spiky stinging, aspirins, iodine, bristling tears, lint and bandage on head and hand.

'Let Mrs Jotman know if you feel sick or dizzy.'

I feel both.

No home. Nothing.

Faded old clothes brought through the wind to the front door by curious, peering neighbours.

Cocoa. The fire blazing, banked high with coal.

Mimi in the armchair, wearing some unknown child's

trousers and cardigan, knees bent under her, staring at the wall, pushing Pam away.

Roger, his face waxy, pulling the army blanket around his shoulders.

The telephone rings yet again.

'Roger?' Mrs Jotman comes in from the hall, strokes Roger's head. 'Do you know a Mrs Ketch – in Hilsea? She says she and her niece couldn't get through to Bryers Guerdon in the flood – was worried about you and the girls, wants to know if you're all safe.'

Roger watches the flames.

'Who is Mrs Ketch?' Mrs Jotman insists.

'Tell her we're all fine. Everything's all right.'

'What happened, Roger? Why on earth were you in Hilsea?'

He looks across at me. Mrs Jotman breathes heavily, goes back to the telephone, mutters something, puts it down.

It's after midnight. The broken clock in the hall whirrs and clunks two o'clock. The bedroom door opens. A swish as Mrs Jotman bends to check on Mimi, then another as she straightens up and leans over me. The faint, sweet smell of Yardley's soap. Her breath is warm on my skin, her fingers light on my forehead. I don't open my eyes.

The door softly closes.

The three lopsided Spitfires dangle on their dusty

strings, and above them, through the joists and battens, newly-laid chipboard and lino, is Roger, in the old khaki camp bed.

I reach up between the little grey aeroplanes, stretch, and touch the ceiling with my fingertips.

That's where he'll be, on the other side of my open hand.

The wind begins to drop, the rain to ease. When the washed-out light of morning starts to pick out the pattern on the curtains, the storm has gone; the air is spent and still.

The telephone rings.

A gentle knocking on the door.

'Cora . . . Cora . . . are you awake?'

Mrs Jotman is wearing a rose-patterned dressing gown, a cup of hot lemon and honey in her hand, a couple of tablets in the saucer. She squints down at Mimi in the lower bunk, then looks at me, our eyes on a level.

'How are you feeling? Did you sleep?'

'I – I'm all right, thank you.'

'I would have left you longer,' she says, 'but – but this is such good news. Your dad's taken a turn for the better. The hospital's just rung. He's had a really good night.'

I can't stop a rush of tears. Mrs Jotman strokes my head gently over the bandage, puts the drink down on the chest of drawers and takes out a handkerchief.

I blow my nose and wince as a jolt of pain shoots across my head.

'Try and drink the lemon and honey,' she says. 'I've cooled it down a bit.'

I dab my eyes.

'Here, have it now.' She brings it over, pats my hand, goes to leave but turns in the doorway. 'By the way,' she adds, 'you're not to worry one little bit about school. Mr Jotman and I are very happy to go to Wrayness Abbey, sort things out for you.'

I hadn't thought about it at all, but thank her.

Taking a little sip of the lemon and honey, I am reminded of Roger and me drinking the mead in Mr Thorston's cottage. In my head, there I am again, looking out over the winter garden with its snowy cabbages and tar-papered beehives, climbing up the narrow staircase behind the cupboard door, peeping into the neat bedrooms.

Nobody'll want it, because they like things all modern these days – that's what Mr Wragge said.

I feel a little stir of excitement.

We could buy it and live there – Dad, Mimi and me. I'll ask the Jotmans about it: how it's all done, how you buy a house.

All morning Mimi is listless, mostly lying on the settee in the sitting room, but a couple of times I catch her in the hall, staring into the corner near the front door, where the boys' school bags are heaped on the floor next to the brown paper parcel for the cleaner's with our filthy wet coats inside.

She says she doesn't want any dinner. I leave everyone eating around the kitchen table and come out to tempt her with a bowl of soup. Startled by a furtive movement near the front door, I spill a bit of it on the lino. She is stuffing something into one of the school bags, sees me, folds down the flap, gets up quickly, looks away.

'What are you doing?'

'Nothing.'

She heads for the bathroom.

'Do you want some soup?'

She goes in and clicks the bolt. I notice the brown paper parcel has been untied and our sodden, muddy coats are spread out on the lino.

Glancing behind me to check that the kitchen door is shut, I put the bowl down on the floor and stoop to wrap the coats again. Once I've reknotted the string, I open the school bag, see by the books that it's Roger's; and there, squashed in, their cloth limbs crushed between his History and Chemistry textbooks, are the two poppets, all soiled and damp, and stinking of dirty water. Mimi must have taken them out of his muddy coat pocket.

My eyes are drawn to their spiteful little faces, lit in the angle of light from the frosted-glass window by the front door, which seems to heighten the crooked lines of their mouths.

In the kitchen, the low murmuring continues around the table while the brown, knotted eyes of the poppet with the long dark hair appear to gaze into mine with a horrible intensity. I think I can almost hear the scratched rasp of a whisper: *We are the same – you and I, Cora.*

I find myself reaching out, touching the familiar blue fabric of its grubby dress and pushing aside a fold. Peeping out from a small frayed hole in its chest is a little red stone.

With a shudder I snatch my hand back, shut the dolls away again into the darkness between the schoolbooks, and clumsily buckle down the straps.

What are we going to do with them?

Roger and I have hardly spoken, barely exchanged a look.

Towards evening the telephone rings yet again. Mrs Jotman pulls the hall door closed behind her. Between the long pauses her muffled, lowered voice sounds grave.

I feel terribly cold. It must be Dad.

After a couple of minutes her head appears round the edge of the sitting-room door. 'Cora . . . ?'

I shuffle across the room in slippers two sizes too big for me.

'Don't worry, it's not your dad.'

My held breath rushes out.

'It's Ange.'

'Oh.'

'She's very poorly, Cora, and – and not just from being caught up in the flood. They've done tests. She – she's been ill for some time, apparently. They're transferring her to London tonight, to specialists, but they're not sure they can do anything for her. She'll probably have to go into a nursing home. They can't trace any family. Did she mention anybody to you, any relatives?'

'Only that she was married years ago, but he didn't come back from the war. There wasn't anybody else. Their baby died.'

Just at that moment the telephone rings yet again.

'When will it ever stop?' With an exasperated sigh Mrs Jotman picks up the receiver. 'Yes!' she says abruptly, then – 'Oh.'

She beckons me across, puts her arm around my shoulder and the phone into my hand. 'It's for you.' Then she disappears into the kitchen and closes the door behind her.

'Y-yes? Who is it?' I ask nervously into the mouthpiece.

'Cora? Cora, is it you?'

The voice is weak, the breath shallow and uneven.

'Oh,' I gasp. 'Oh, Dad . . .'

For a moment I can't make any other words come out.

'Are you still there?' he says faintly down the crackling line.

'Yes, yes. Do you know about – about the flood, the house?'

'Yes, the police said.' He takes a few seconds to draw in some air. 'Are you all right, you and Mimi?'

'Yes, yes, we're all right.'

'Yes . . .' He is barely audible. 'Yes . . . good . . .'

'Mrs Jotman?' A woman's voice comes on the line.

'No, it's Cora. Where's my dad?'

'He can't talk for long,' she says. 'He needs to rest now.'

'Oh. Can – can you please give him a message for me?'

'Yes, of course.'

'Can you tell him I've got us the most lovely place to live – a cottage.'

'Yes, I will, dear.' I can hear her smiling. 'Goodbye.'

'And we'll be able to keep bees,' I say, but she's put the telephone down.

I can't sleep. The old creased canvas feels like it's lined with pencils, the springs need oiling, my feet hang off the end, the angle of the roof makes it impossible to turn over, and Pete's snoring.

The broken clock in the hall coughs out five in the morning.

For two days I've chewed it over and over like a piece of gristle that won't be swallowed. What happened to the witch bottle? Did it explode in the fire or did the floodwater put out the flames?

What became of Aphra Rushes?

And I can't believe I haven't given them a thought until now – the two poppets, still in my coat pocket. Has the parcel gone to the cleaner's yet? I recall Dad saying he wasn't going to get the car out until the muck had been cleared off the roads.

I roll and creak out of the bed, pull over some clothes, get dressed doubled up under the eaves, then steal out of the room and duck down the winding staircase.

The little lamp by the telephone has been left on.

To my relief the parcel is still there, but before I even

get to it I notice that my school bag is separate from the others. I pick it up, see the buckles are done up oddly, and smell something like rotten cabbage.

Screwing up my nose, I open it, and shudder.

A moment later I am outside my bedroom, wondering what's best to do. If I knock, I'll wake Mimi.

I turn the doorknob and go in.

The warm light from the hall falls on Cora's face as she sleeps. Under the bandage her hair makes a dark, tangled fan over the pillow and her fingers lie curved along the line of her cheek.

I watch her, listen to her quiet breathing, uneasy at being there.

I feel I shouldn't touch her, but not knowing what else to do to wake her, I gently pull a fold of her pyjama sleeve.

Her eyelashes flutter for a second, then fall still.

I glance down at Mimi in the lower bunk. She is half in shadow, facing the wall, her back rising and falling in a smooth, steady rhythm.

'Cora . . .' I lean in and hiss close to her ear. 'Cora . . .'

One eye flickers open. 'Roger?'

Startled, she lifts her head, then moans, pressing her hand to the bandage.

'Sorry,' I whisper. 'You all right?'

'Yes, yes,' she mumbles. 'What on earth is it? What's the time?'

'It's just after five.'

'What?'

'Do you think you're well enough to come out?'

'What! Outside?'

'Ssh. You'll wake Mimi.'

I glance down again, lower my voice to barely more than a tremor. 'We've got to get rid of those dolls. Someone put them in my school bag. Was it you?'

She looks intently at me for a moment, then rolls her eyes downwards to the lower bunk.

'Let – let me find some clothes,' she mutters under her breath.

CORA

'Do you think this would fit you?' Roger whispers, holding up a jacket as I come out of the bedroom, yawning. 'It's Dennis's.'

Roger is already wearing his good school coat.

'A bit big, but it'll do.' I push my arms into the long sleeves and fasten the buttons.

We find our hats, gloves and scarves dangling from the kitchen airer and our dried-out wellingtons by the back door. Roger grabs a torch from the cupboard under the sink. We click the kitchen door quietly behind us and hurry down Fieldpath Road, the torchlight gleaming over rough new craters in the wet tarmac clogged with mud and grass, scattered stones and broken twigs. Apart from a few puddles, most of the water has soaked away into the drains and verges.

When we turn right into Ottery Lane, I stop. 'Roger, where are we going? All the way to Hilsea, to that hawthorn tree?'

He breathes out heavily. 'No, well, I've had another idea, but it's up to you – only if you want to. Remember Mrs Ketch said that it was best to find a tree on holy ground?'

'Surely . . . surely you don't mean to go down to All Hallows?'

'It's not as far as Hilsea, but – but not if you'd rather not . . .'

I'm not sure what I would rather do.

'Where are they – the poppets?' I ask.

Roger pats his pocket. 'I've pinched the breadknife to dig with.' He taps the other. 'In here.'

'Don't fall over and stab yourself,' I say, then, 'What was that?'

I glance back over my shoulder to the bottom of Fieldpath Road, and shiver. 'Did you hear something?'

Roger flashes the torch across the bushes on the corner. 'Can't see anything. Perhaps it was a cat, or a fox.'

'Maybe.'

As we trudge on up Ottery Lane, my ears prickle at the slightest sound. Twice more I look back.

Old Glebe Lane is broken up, covered in loose stones, thick brown puddles and clods of mud. Roger shines the torch through the wrought-iron gates to Glebe House. It looks black, wintry and abandoned in the yellow light. The drive is empty of cars. A huge branch lies adrift on the vast, sodden lawn.

We make our way carefully down the slippery hill. Above us in the star-bright sky the moon hangs as a thin sliver of curved light, faintly silvering the vast, whispering washes of flooded pools and beaten, flattened reedbeds stretching away to the far-off river.

'I hope I never have to come here ever again,' I mutter with a shudder as we continue along the pitted road.

We pass the bend of The Chase, but I avoid looking along it; instead I keep my eyes on the torch beam threading its way ahead of us over the brimming ditches and standing water on the track to All Hallows. I notice here and there the light skimming over a piece of diamond-shaped glass, a twisted strip of lead, roof tiles and pieces of jagged wood from Guerdon Hall.

The churchyard slopes gently upwards from the road. Most of the water has already run off, but dribbles are still seeping down through the hedgerow to join the swirl around our boots. I push at the gate, but the bottom is so choked with debris, it won't budge.

I put my foot on the lowest rung to hoist myself over, then think I hear a soft splash from further up the track. Roger sweeps the torchlight from one side of the roadway to the other.

'Can you see anything?'

'Not a thing.'

We wait, listening, but hear only the gentle lapping of the water.

We climb over the gate. The soggy ground in the graveyard is strewn with sand and scattered bricks, broken fencing and crushed vegetation.

As we trudge up the waterlogged path, the zigzagging light beam sends the jagged shadows of crosses and headstones leaping stretched and distorted into the high corners of the church walls, then up across the wooden slats of the belfry window in the black, looming bulk of the tower.

We both start as an unseen hunting owl hoots from somewhere up the hill. It won't find any scurrying creature to catch here, I think to myself. There are only dead things in this place.

We walk round the back of the Guerdon plot, behind the old elder tree arching over Auntie Ida's grave. The storm has uprooted the tree slightly at the back, and it is leaning towards the lychgate, where the force of the floodwater has flattened the briars and brambles between the pillars. Still standing upright among them, directly under the lychgate roof, is the young tree I shook in the snow. It occurs to me that it seems to have chosen that most mysterious of places to set down its roots – the portal between worlds. Auntie Ida's last breath was spent dragging Long Lankin through it, and that is where he fell, exactly there.

Roger sweeps the torchlight across the small tree. 'It's a hawthorn,' he says. 'You can see by the berries.'

Miraculously some still cling to it, gleaming like drops of blood.

He takes the poppets out of his pocket.

As I glance at the doll with the long dark hair, my head begins to throb under the bandage. Again I sense that we are not entirely separate at all. I cannot shake off the feeling that there is something of myself in it, beyond the hair and the dress; something that cannot ever be completely undone.

I look across at the lychgate. In the stillness and the darkness there is that lingering tingle in the air, that sense of some other world, unreachable and unknowable for now, and I don't want that part of the doll that is me, or the part of Mimi's that is her, to be buried there.

I don't want the hawthorn roots to rip us apart in that fearsome place.

I turn my head and gaze at Auntie Ida's grave, then

step over the low railing and walk across the long grass. As I lean forward to run my hand over the arch of the stone, a low, delicate branch of the elder brushes my cheek.

'Here, Roger, under the elder tree.'

'What?'

'With Auntie Ida.'

He looks puzzled. 'Are you sure? Shouldn't it be the hawthorn?'

'Please.'

I move round behind the stone, put my hands flat on the trunk, rest my cheek on the ridged bark, and listen. I fancy I can hear some pulse rising up to me from deep under the ground, imagine the kindly roots curving around Auntie Ida and cradling her in the cold, dark earth. I'm not sure if I put my thoughts into any words as I lean there, but I'm certain I feel a warmth on my skin, and a kind of peace.

I hold out my hand for the breadknife. Roger sighs, 'If you're really sure,' then lays the dolls down in the wet grass. He lights the base of the tree with the torch, and I crouch down and plunge the knife into the ground.

Unlike the hard, frozen earth in the churchyard at Hilsea, here the soil is so wet it takes no more than a few minutes before we see pale roots spreading themselves out like long probing fingers.

'Should be enough,' I say, flicking mud off my gloves with the knife-point.

'Are you ready?' Roger asks, before leaning across for the dolls.

I nod, but am surprised at how unwillingly I take Mimi's poppet from him. I draw in a deep breath, then quickly drop it into the hole.

A cracking sound.

I turn, squint into the darkness.

Roger flashes the torch across the metal gate; then, seeing nothing, shrugs his shoulders. 'Must be another fox, or a rat maybe.' He directs the beam back to the elder roots.

I pick up the poppet in the blue dress, hesitate, look into its eyes, almost believe I can sense a tiny heartbeat throbbing quietly through its body.

'What's the matter?' Roger whispers.

I swallow, force myself to squeeze it into the hole beside the other, crushing them together. I sense a tightening of my throat, a sudden fear. My hand twitches, as if it wants to reach out and snatch them back.

'It's like . . .' I breathe. 'It's like I'm burying us, Mimi and me.'

'Do it quickly,' he says.

I snatch a handful of wet earth, scatter the clods over the pink-sprigged cotton, the blue polka-dot. Mimi's fair hair and my long dark strands begin to disappear under the crumbles of soil. Something catches in my throat. I cough, cough again, reach out for more earth.

The embroidered eyes look out at me, the twisted scarlet mouths smirk one last time.

I shut my eyes and fling more soil into the hole, and another handful, until the little knotted eyes disappear into blackness.

Auntie Ida will look after us, see we come to no harm.

And she will no longer be alone in the dark.

They do not see me as I lie here close to the ground, a muddy rag, misshapen and sodden. I feel the hawthorn at my back, its rough bark and its malice. The branches dip and bend to snatch, but cannot reach me; its roots are unable to break the surface of the soil to snatch me, though they stretch downwards, spreading into the hallowed earth under the lychgate.

Even the air here trembles with power.

The two of them move away, along the path, over the gate and out of the churchyard.

I am alone, wounded and torn.

Perhaps some sick person will stumble by this miserable place, or an ailing animal, barely living, but with enough life remaining to become a casing to hold me, let me move, find the last of the Guerdons once more . . .

A shadowed hand.

I am clasped, lifted up.

There is a change in the light, a small shift in the darkness.

A child's face, close and searching.

Fair, wavy hair.

Hard, narrowed eyes look into mine.

She sees me.

We know each other.

'You're not Aggie,' she whispers. 'You're her.'

She smoothes the green scrap of dress, lifts strands of the flame-coloured woollen hair, now blackened with mud. She touches the face, the rust-brown stains on the rag doll's cheeks.

'Ange's blood . . .' she hisses. 'Pulled you in when it all went wrong.'

Flinging me down into the crushed grass, she starts to tear at the wet soil with her hands, throws it all about her, plunges her fingers in among the roots, wrenching out the earth again and again.

She picks me up, looks into my eyes one last time, then slowly, carefully, presses me deep down into the web of roots.

The clumps of soil thud, pound and spatter as she covers me.

I see her face, the straight, grim line of her mouth, then a heavy, black clod shuts off the light. Closed and squeezed and tight, stamped and stamped down again.

I feel the judder of her footsteps as she moves away.

They will not see her. She is a child of secrets, will keep herself hidden, will wait until they have gone.

A small noise close by. A quiet, vengeful creaking.

It begins then.

A creeping root snakes and twists around a little cloth leg. Another encircles it from underneath. They coil and squirm, and one root pulls against the other. On either side, thin, pale laces curl around my arms, jerk and tug and split them apart from my body, the tearing seams spit out downy feathers. A hand of grasping roots seizes my woollen hair and wrenches the fibres apart, ripping them from the scalp.

I hear Zillah's voice across the years: 'Do not cry out, Aphra! Never cry out!'

I cannot cry out.

The red mouth is stitched shut.

In the dark closeness, the vicious roots grip and shred, and I am pressed into a small black space, smaller and smaller . . . tighter and tighter . . .

And from deep under the ground comes a tremor – growing and spreading outwards and upwards, shivering the stones, the oaken beams and struts of the lychgate. I feel the heat as the ancient magic enfolds me, wraps me into itself.

The veil dissolves, the pain floats away.

I begin to separate, fragment by fragment, into a smoke-like drifting, disconnecting thread.

Here is a spangle of light, tiny like a spark, and another, one more; all around me they loosen themselves from the ripped and twisted pieces, flickering, glimmering, rising up through the crumbling earth and dispersing into the early morning air.

I know them.

They are mine.

My own dying lights.

At last, at last . . . lifting me, detaching themselves one from another, soaring and spreading.

In one last moment of fading consciousness, I dream that a trace of this glittering dust might pass, and know, and touch a mote of his, in some other time, in some far distant place among the stars, somewhere in the high vault of the heavens . . .

As we trudge back up the hill, the light begins to change. Beyond the torchlight a soft, faint grey outlines each twig and stone and mound of crushed grass.

At the top Roger and I turn and look across the marshes again, as we have so many times before. Above us, the long feathery smudge of the Milky Way still glimmers in the deepest darkness, but to the east, the horizon begins to glow in shimmering, rosy bands that shift little by little to yellow-gold, then turquoise, and the small specks of stars in the lower edge of the sky fade one by one into the light of the morning.

He switches off the torch.

We stand there, our coat-sleeves just touching, unable to think of a word to say.

We seem to have broken one spell, yet made another.

I take in the pattern of the mud on Roger's boots, the loose thread on the fringe of his scarf, the silvery glimmer on the rim of one of his coat buttons mirroring the thin crescent of the moon that hangs just on the margin of the fading darkness.

I store all these fleeting things away to remember, because the world takes people away from you, or sends them back damaged, and there may never ever come a moment like this again.

There we stay, Roger and me, saying nothing, as the sun rises gleaming over the marshes.

Acknowledgements

I cannot thank enough my wonderfully supportive and patient editors – Annie Eaton and Natalie Doherty. Thanks also to everyone at RHCP involved in the copy-edit and design, especially Sophie Nelson and James Fraser.

I am grateful to my family – Imogen, Christian and Benjamin, for their comments, and Eleanor, who unselfishly plodded through almost every draft and made many really helpful suggestions.

And at the end, heartfelt thanks to my husband, Richard, who so valiantly held the fort over these last months.

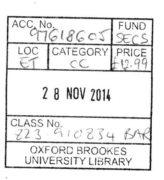